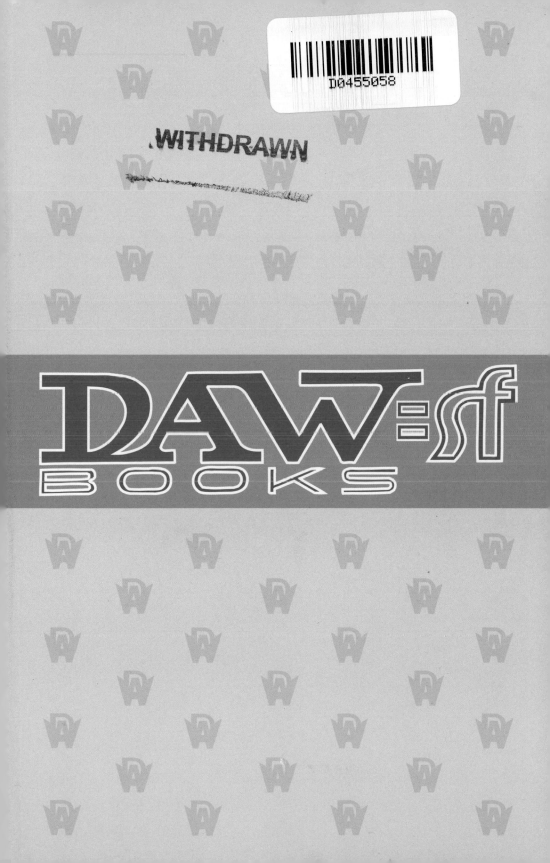

D0455058

DAW=sf
BOOKS

Edited by

ELIZABETH R. WOLLHEIM

and

SHEILA E. GILBERT

DAW BOOKS, INC.

DONALD A. WOLLHEIM, FOUNDER

375 Hudson Street, New York, NY 10014

ELIZABETH R. WOLLHEIM
SHEILA E. GILBERT
PUBLISHERS

http://www.dawbooks.com

Jacket art by G-Force Design.

Text design by Stanley S. Drate / Folio Graphics Co., Inc.

DAW Books Collectors No. 1221.

DAW Books are distributed by Penguin Putnam Inc.

With special thanks to the folks
at Tekno Books for their help in
seeing this project to fruition.

First Printing, May 2002
1 2 3 4 5 6 7 8 9 10

*We dedicate these volumes
in loving memory of our founders,
Donald A. Wollheim
and
Elsie B. Wollheim,
and of our resident curmudgeon,
Mike Gilbert.*

And for all DAW authors, past, present and future

Acknowledgments

THE HOME FRONT ©2002 by Brian Stableford

ABOARD THE *BEATITUDE* ©2002 by Brian W. Aldiss

ODD JOB #213 ©2002 by Ron Goulart

AGAMEMNON'S RUN ©2002 by Robert Sheckley

GRUBBER ©2002 by Neal Barrett, Jr.

THE SANDMAN, THE TINMAN, AND THE BETTY B ©2002 by C. J. Cherryh

THE BIG PICTURE ©2002 by Timothy Zahn

A HOME FOR THE OLD ONES, an excerpt from the forthcoming novel *From Gateway to the Core*, ©2002 by Frederik Pohl. Published by permission of the author.

NOT WITH A WHIMPER, EITHER ©2002 by Tad Williams

THE BLACK WALL OF JERUSALEM ©2002 by Ian Watson

STATION GANYMEDE ©2002 by Charles L. Harness

DOWNTIME ©2002 by C. S. Friedman

BURNING BRIDGES ©2002 by Charles Ingrid

WORDS ©2002 by Cheryl J. Franklin

READ ONLY MEMORY ©2002 by eluki bes shahar

SUNSEEKER ©2002 by Katrina Elliott

THE HEAVENS FALL ©2002 by Steven Swiniarski

PASSAGE TO SHOLA ©2002 by Lisanne Norman

PRISM ©2002 by Julie E. Czerneda

Introduction

MY father never told me that he was planning to leave his job at Ace Books. It was 1971, and I was in college. I can only assume that he didn't want to distract me from my studies—that he wanted to shelter me for as long as he could. So I found out after the fact, with the rest of the science fiction world. It was as much of a shock to me as it was to anyone else. Actually it was *more* of a shock to me than to anyone else—for my dad, the most responsible and loyal man I knew, had just picked up and walked away from his job! It was simply unimaginable but it had happened, and it rattled my world down to its deepest foundations.

Don had been continually employed in editorial positions since 1941 when he had his first (unpaid) job editing pulp magazines. He continued to edit magazines, compiled numerous anthologies, worked in editorial positions at some of the very first paperback book lines ever produced, and in 1952, convinced A. A. Wyn, owner of Ace Publications, to let him initiate a line of paperback books for Ace.

The one thing he *hadn't* been in thirty years was unemployed.

My dad took his responsibility to our family very seriously. He also took his work very seriously. But something monumental had begun to happen to the publishing industry. Publishing was becoming "big business" and was no longer the intimate, eccentric, personality-driven industry it had once been. Don, who had been present during the birth of the paperback book, didn't like what was happening. He was Editor-in-Chief of Ace Books for nineteen and a half years and eventually became the Vice President as well. He considered Ace *his* list, *his* creation, and for most of our field at the time, the name Donald A. Wollheim was synonymous with Ace Books. But Ace wasn't really Don's company, and with the death of A. A. Wyn in 1968 that became glaringly obvious.

As Ace became more and more "corporate," passing from the hands of one owner to another, the situation became less and less tolerable for Don. By 1971, he had come to the end of his rope—so he did the unthinkable. With no concrete prospects for the future, and no warning to his employers, he left his office at Ace Books, never to return.

It was a very tense time for our family, for although Elsie, my mom, had been a professional woman before my birth, my father had been the sole support of our household since 1951. Don wasn't entirely sure what to do. What he *was* sure of was this: he would never again work for years building an editorial list only to lose it. There was only one way to avoid that: by founding his own publishing company. But how could he? As a long-term employee of a notoriously frugal publisher, he had never been able to amass the money necessary for such an enterprise. All Don had was his reputation.

Luckily, it proved to be enough.

In the fall of 1971, Don met with Herb Schnall, one of the chief executives of New American Library. After several brief meetings, Herb made a statement which would change publishing history: he told Don that New American Library would take him "any way [he wanted] to come." Don could write his own ticket.

It was an offer Don couldn't refuse.

Elated, Don came home to think about his options. My dad, my mom, and I sat at the table in our narrow galley kitchen in Queens, and tried to define Don's dream. He wanted the strong national distribution which only a big company could offer—hence his meeting with NAL—but unlike most independently distributed lines, he also wanted the professional production and promotion facilities of a big publishing company. He wanted his company's list to be sold aggressively with the strength of a big corporate imprint, yet he wanted total artistic freedom, not only inside his books but in relation to the cover art and design as well, and he did not want to share the ownership of his company. Basically, he wanted to form a private corporation and enter into a contractual arrangement with New American Library to provide the services that he needed.

But corporate parameters were not Don's only concern.

For thirty years Don had edited all types of fiction. He had edited not only literary books but most of the genres—from westerns to crime to thrillers to mysteries to detective and horror novels. He had put the light into the window of the ever present mansion on the cover of the Gothic romance, had published William Burroughs' first work, and had introduced J.R.R. Tolkien's *The Lord of the Rings* to the American paperback audience. He even edited nurse novels and cookbooks. But since the age of eleven he had had only one real love—science fiction. He had waited a lifetime for this opportunity, and he decided to dedicate his new company to the books he loved the most. He wanted to found the first publishing company devoted exclusively to science fiction and fantasy.

In November of 1971, NAL agreed to Don's proposal, and DAW Books, Inc. was born.

My father had signed a contract, but he was still a long way from fulfilling his dream. As we sat in the kitchen—our traditional spot for family discussions— and Don thought aloud about possible employees to help him in his new venture, I noticed my mom, Elsie, becoming more and more agitated. Finally, she exploded: "Don, what about ME?" My dad looked quite stupefied. It was clear that he had never even considered that his wife would join him in this enterprise, but Elsie was the logical choice: she had legal experience, and had run her father's company. The obvious solution was staring him straight in the face.

Bringing Elsie into the company may very well have been Don's shrewdest business decision. Elsie embraced her new position as Corporate Secretary-Treasurer of DAW with all the fervor of a mother grizzly defending her young. Every aspect of DAW and all DAW authors were sheltered under her huge protective wing. And for a petite woman, she had enormous wings indeed! Marion Zimmer Bradley once said, "Elsie has the spirit of a lion in the body of a sparrow." And it was never more true than when she took up her position as Champion-Of-All-Things-DAW.

The next six months were a nightmare.

With liftoff scheduled for April 1972, Don was under the gun to purchase, edit, and package six months' worth of titles in thirty days to catch up with NAL's production schedule. Elsie had to set up accounts payable, accounts receivable, royalty reports, book-keeping, and an entire subsidiary rights department. Together, they wrote the first DAW boilerplate contract. For my father, himself a published author with eighteen books and numerous short stories to his credit, it was important to formulate a writer-friendly contract.

My parents were nervous wrecks. Don couldn't sleep or eat—I remember more than one occasion when Elsie or I had to run to the kitchen to get Don something sweet because he was feeling light-headed. Don and Elsie were exhausted, but it was with the excited exhaustion of new parents. It was a frightening and exhilarating time.

The following spring, the first DAW books were due to debut at the 1972 Lunacon, but the night before the convention started, they still hadn't left the warehouse in New Jersey. Elsie and Don were up the entire night collecting their very first DAW books and hand delivering them to the dealers at New York's local convention. Lunacon was thereafter a very special time for my folks.

As for me, I went back to college and graduated with a degree in English Lit, while serving a simultaneous four-year stint in art school. My parents had kept me apprised of the goings-on at DAW, and sent me occasional manuscripts to read and comment on, particularly when Don had discovered someone he felt was noteworthy. I especially remember Don's excitement in 1974 when he sent me *Gate of Ivrel*, C. J. Cherryh's first novel, and *The Birthgrave*, Tanith Lee's first full-length fantasy novel.

Although I was Corporate Vice President of DAW from the get go, and had always been involved on a certain level, Don never pressured me to come home to New York right after graduation. He thought it would be healthier for me to find my own sea legs in the business world. With my experience working as a free-lance copyeditor for Ace Books (under my father's stern tutelage) during high school, I landed a job in one of the last hot-type printing houses in Cambridge, Massachusetts as a proofreader, then later, a dual position as proofreader and darkroom technician for one of the very first computerized printing houses in the industry. What a disaster! For every mistake corrected, the printing computer (which took up most of a good-sized wall) would generate numerous new ones. Whole chapters would suddenly become italicized. Thankfully, computers have improved enormously since those days. My two years working for printers have proved invaluable to me as a publisher.

Finally, in 1975, I came home and took up a position as Don's general assistant and Associate Editor. By this time DAW was an established, successful line, and Don and Elsie were a recognized corporate couple. However, it is never easy working with your parents, and Don and Elsie were no exception. One of the saving graces of my situation was the presence of my old friend Sheila Gilbert, who was working as a copywriter for NAL. Sheila and I had known each other since we were thirteen and eleven, respectively, and had bonded through various embarrassing fan activities, such as the Galaxy of Fashion Show at the 1967 NYcon, where I was the "Bride of the Future," and Sheila and her oldest sister Marsha were "The Gemini Twins." Numerous were the times I sought refuge in my old friend's office, and as the years passed, Sheila was promoted to head up the Signet science fiction list, and I wrested more and more editorial and art direction control from the unyielding hands of my father. Sheila and I became close friends.

Neither of us realized just how important that friendship would prove to be.

In April 1985, when I had been working with my parents for ten years, catastrophe struck. Don went into the hospital with a complicated critical illness, and remained there on the brink of death for seven brutal months. We were just about to launch the fledgling DAW hardcover list, which was my exclusive domain, with a novel from our most important writer, C. J. Cherryh, as well as a first novel from a very promising newcomer, Tad Williams. Elsie bravely insisted that I attend the American Booksellers Association Convention in San Francisco, where the DAW hardcover list was being debuted with special bound galleys, and where I was planning to meet Tad for the first time. I left New York not knowing if I would ever see my father alive again.

Well, Don survived, but it didn't take me long to discover what had made him so sick. At fourteen years of age, the health of DAW Books had begun to flag. The science fiction and fantasy industry had gone through some fundamental changes, and our company was desperately in need of renovation. During those terrible months, Elsie and I fought not only to keep Don alive, but to save the life of DAW as well.

Meanwhile, Sheila had been considering leaving her job at Signet. Elsie and I realized that she would be the perfect person to join us: she had editorial experience, knew our list, and was practically part of the family already. With no guarantee that we would be able to pull the company out of its slump, she agreed.

1985 was a difficult year, but Don survived and so did DAW. During Don's long illness and recovery—it was a year before he would return to the office—Sheila and I, with the loving support of Elsie, took over the company.

Don would never again be well enough to lead DAW.

Now, thirty years and more than twelve hundred titles since its founding, Don and Elsie are gone, but the essence of DAW remains the same: a small, personal business owned exclusively by me and Sheila. Sheila and I were startled to realize, as we were writing these introductions, that we have now been running the company longer than Don did. Like Don and Elsie before us, we are committed to keeping a "family" spirit at DAW—something we feel (as Don did) is all too rare in today's world of international conglomerate publishing. If anything, DAW is even more family-oriented now than it was in the beginning. Sheila and I brought our husbands, Mike Gilbert and Peter Stampfel, into the business. Our Business Manager Amy Fodera introduced us to her husband, Sean Fodera, who is now our Director of Subsidiary Rights, Contracts, and Electronic Publishing. Our Managing Editor Debra Euler is single, but we've told her that when she does marry, her husband will have a job waiting for him at DAW! (Or conversely, she has first right of refusal if we hire another employee.) Even our wonderful free-lance cover designer has been with us for nearly a dozen years.

With just six hardy employees (sadly, we lost Mike in August 2000), DAW Books manages to stay afloat in a sea of ocean liners. But our true family extends far beyond the DAW corporate offices. This real family includes the many wonderful authors who publish with us, the artists who grace the covers of our books with their beautiful paintings, and you, the readers who have loyally supported our little company for thirty years. We couldn't have done it without you—and we plan to keep giving you the finest in science fiction and fantasy for decades to come.

BETSY WOLLHEIM

I REMEMBER the day DAW was born. I remember it because the events which led up to DAW's birth had a definite impact on my own life, and though I didn't know it at the time, the creation of DAW Books, Inc. in the fall of 1971 would eventually affect my future both personally and professionally.

Of course, my relationship with the Wollheim family began long before DAW was even the glimmering of an idea in Don Wollheim's imagination. I first met Don, Elsie, and Betsy at a Lunacon in Manhattan in the spring of 1963. I was thirteen years old and it was my first science fiction convention. And among the many interesting people I had a chance to meet (some of whose works filled the bookcases of my own science fiction and fantasy reading family) were the Wollheims. My memory is that they were quite patient with and welcoming to an enthusiastic teen at her first convention. Perhaps the fact that Betsy was eleven at the time had something to do with it. Perhaps it merely foreshadowed the days when we would begin referring to Elsie as our "corporate Mom," a title any DAW author who was fortunate enough to become part of our DAW family while Elsie was still alive would certainly understand.

Over the following seven years, I continued to run into the Wollheims at conventions and parties, and when I graduated college and started looking for a job in publishing I sent Don, who at the time was the Editor-in-Chief at Ace Books, a letter of inquiry about a job. Fortune smiled upon me, because the day after I had accepted—but not yet started—a job at another publishing company, I received a phone call from Don. He had a junior editorial position to fill, and he wanted me to come in for an interview. The idea of being paid to read and work on the books I would have been reading anyway seemed like a dream come true.

I started working for Don at Ace Thanksgiving week of 1970, and life was good. Then, one day in the fall of 1971, Don walked into my office to say good-bye. He was leaving the company that very day. I was totally stunned by the news.

Later, I heard that Don was starting his own company, DAW Books, Inc., which would be distributed by New American Library. Perhaps a month after that, I had a phone call from Ruth Haberstroh, a friend who had once shared an office with me at Ace and who was working at New American Library. She told me that before calling me she had asked Don if he was going to hire me. He responded that he wasn't going to be hiring anyone for a while, and so Ruth offered me a job at NAL. So in January 1972, I left Ace and joined NAL. One of the benefits of this move was that I could now frequently see Don and Elsie—and Betsy, as well, once she joined her parents in the family business.

In 1978, I took over the Signet science fiction line, which, in theory, might have put me in competition with DAW, but in reality it did nothing of the kind. Our lists were extremely compatible.

In 1985, Don became critically ill and Betsy had to take on the full responsibility for running DAW. She and Elsie asked me to join them, and after the July Fourth weekend, that was exactly what I did. And, of course, I've been here ever since. In the ensuing years, various members of my family—my husband Mike, and my sisters Marsha and Paula—began working with us in a freelance capacity, with Mike eventually becoming our resident curmudgeon until his untimely death in August of 2000.

We've always said that we consider DAW and everyone associated with it as one big extended family. And that is truly the way we feel about our own terrific staff and all the people we work closely with at Penguin Putnam, Inc., about our stalwart freelancers who never let us down, the artists who create such eye-catching images for us, and, of course, our authors, who, over the years we've worked with them, have become our close friends as well as our valued colleagues.

As thirty is a fairly momentous birthday in human terms (rest assured, however, that you will still be able to trust DAW to provide you with the kind of reading experiences you've come to expect), we wanted to celebrate this coming of age in a special way. And, we reasoned, what could be more appropriate than a book of stories written by the authors who have been such an important part of DAW over the last three decades. As we looked down our impressively large list of names, though, we realized that the only way this project could be accomplished without becoming completely unwieldy would be to divide the stories into two volumes by category. Thus, the books you now see before you: *DAW 30th Anniversary: Science Fiction* and *DAW 30th Anniversary: Fantasy*.

Of course, thirty years is a long time, and as we went through our list we were saddened by the knowledge that a number of the authors we would have loved to have stories from were no longer around to provide them. Despite that, we are very pleased with the number of authors who were kind enough to join us in our thirtieth birthday celebration by creating the wonderful tales you'll find included here. Some of the contributors wrote stories which take place in the universes in which their popular DAW series are set, others have chosen to explore entirely new territory, and yet others have given us a glimpse of the worlds and characters from novels which will see publication in the upcoming years.

When DAW Books was founded, the original logo used on all our books read: DAW = sf, a corporate emblem designed by well-known science fiction artist Jack Gaughan. At that time the logo was extremely appropriate. We were the first company devoted exclusively to the publication of science fiction and fantasy, and as far more science fiction was being published (certainly this was true for DAW in those days) the genre hadn't been broken down into two distinct categories. But over the course of the 1970s, '80s, and '90s, as more writers came into the field from the social sciences and humanities rather than the hard sciences, both styles and subject matter began to change. And as technological leaps began to transform science fiction into science fact, creating believable yet innovative science-based fiction became far more difficult. At the same time, the ever-increasing changes wrought by technology in both the working place and our own homes led more people to read fantasy, probably as a means to escape the stresses and demands of the "real" world.

In recognition of these changes, the very look of DAW Books, as well as the contents, began its own evolutionary process, one that continues to this very day. Our logo went from DAW = sf to a design which incorporated the three letters in our name, and also labeled the particular book it appeared on as either science fiction or fantasy. Of course, this led to a bit of a dilemma when a novel or series didn't fall fully into one category or the other but actually melded elements of both.

What you now hold in your hands is your invitation to join our 30ᵗʰ anniversary celebration. The stories in each volume appear in chronological order, based on the first time the author was published by DAW. Thus our fantasy volume begins with Andre Norton, whose *Spell of the Witchworld* was the very first DAW book to see print in April 1972. The first story in the science fiction volume is by Brian Stableford, whose *To Challenge Chaos* was published in May 1972.

We hope that you will find these anthologies as enjoyable as we have, and that it will offer you a chance to read some new work by old favorites, or perhaps afford you the pleasure of discovering some of our authors for the very first time. Thank you for helping to make our first thirty years as memorable as they have been, and we look forward to sharing many more years of good books with all of you.

SHEILA GILBERT

Contents

CONTENTS

SCIENCE FICTION DAW

Brian Stableford

The science fiction field has been tremendously fortunate in attracting editors who care deeply and passionately about the genre and its potential, among which the two most important were John W. Campbell, Jr. and Don Wollheim. If it were not for Don's efforts, first as a magazine editor, then as a paperback editor and finally as a publisher the field would not have proliferated or progressed as quickly as it did, and many fine writers might have been lost to it.

Don gave crucial publishing opportunities to dozens of writers, some of whom went on to become important figures in modern American literature (including Philip K. Dick and Ursula le Guin) while others were enabled by him to produce work of striking and defiant originality treasured by the few (including Barrington J. Bayley and Michael Shea). He was far more useful to writers like the latter stripe than any small press publisher because he never lost sight of the need to attract readers to his lines by publishing solid commercial fiction in economically effective packages.

Don was by far the most eclectic editor ever to work in the SF field, sustaining the careers of a dozen British writers whose domestic market was too tiny to offer adequate commercial support, and also introducing numerous foreign-language writers into the American market. I am one of the least of many writers who would not have been able to follow their vocation without his interest and help; he was a crucial element in shaping my life as a reader and writer and the hindsight I have gained since his death has allowed me to see ever more clearly how extraordinarily valuable his input was. I am very pleased and proud to be able to make a memorial contribution to this anthology.

—BS

THE HOME FRONT
Brian Stableford

NOW that we have lived in the security of peace for more than thirty years a generation has grown up to whom the Plague Wars are a matter of myth and legend. Survivors of my age are often approached by the wondering young and asked what it was like to live through those frightful years, but few of them can answer as fully or as accurately as I.

In my time I have met many doctors, genetic engineers, and statesmen who lay claim to having been in "the front line" during the First Plague War, but the originality of that conflict was precisely the fact that its real combatants were invading microbes and defensive antibodies. All its entrenchments were internal to the human body and mind. It is true that there were battle-grounds of a sort in the hospitals, the laboratories, and even in the House of Commons, but this was a war whose entire strategy was to strike at the most intimate locations of all. For that reason, the only authentic front was the home front: the nucleus of family life.

Many an octogenarian is prepared to wax lyrical now on the feelings of dread associated with obligatory confinement. They will assure you that no one would risk exposure to a crowd if it could possibly be avoided, and that every step out of doors was a terror-laden trek through a minefield. They exaggerate. Life was not so rapidly transformed in an era when a substantial majority of the population still worked outside the home or attended school, and only a minority had the means or the inclination to make all their purchases electronically. Even if electronic shopping had been universal, that would have brought about a very dramatic increase in the number of people employed in the delivery business, all of whom would have had to go abroad and interact with considerable numbers of their fellows.

For these reasons, total confinement was rare during the First

Plague War, and rarely voluntary. Even I, who had little choice in the matter after both my legs were amputated above the knee following the Paddington Railway Disaster of 2119, occasionally sallied forth in my electrically-powered wheelchair in spite of the protestations of my wife Martha. Martha was almost as firmly anchored as I was, by virtue of the care she had to devote to me and to our younger daughter Frances, but it would have taken more than rumors of war to force Frances' teenage sister Petra to remain indoors for long.

The certainty of hindsight sometimes leads us to forget that the First Plague War was, throughout its duration, essentially a matter of rumor, but such was the case. The absence of any formal declaration of war, combined with the highly dubious status of many of the terrorist organizations which competed to claim responsibility for its worst atrocities, sustained an atmosphere of uncertainty that complicated our fears. To some extent, the effect was to exaggerate our anxieties, but it allowed braver souls a margin of doubt to which they could dismiss all inconvenient alarms.

I suppose I was fortunate that the Paddington Disaster had not disrupted my career completely, because I had the education and training necessary to set myself up as an independent share-trader operating via my domestic unit. I had established a reputation that allowed me to build a satisfactory register of corporate and individual clients, so I was able to negotiate the movement of several million euros on a daily basis. I had always been a specialist in the biotech sector, which was highly volatile even before the war started—and it was that accident of happenstance more than any other which placed my minuscule fraction of the home front at the center of the fiercest action the war produced.

Doctors, as is only natural, think that the hottest action of the plague wars was experienced on the wards which filled up week by week between 2129 and 2133 with victims of hyperflu, assertive MSRA, neurotoxic Human Mosaic Virus and plethoral hemorrhagic fever. Laboratory engineers, equally understandably, think that the crucial battles were fought within the bodies of the mouse models housed in their triple-X biocontainment facilities. In fact, the most hectic action of all was seen on the London Stock Exchange, and the only hand-to-hand fighting involved the sneakthieves and armed robbers who continually raided the nation's greenhouses during the six months from September 2129 to March 2130: the cruel winter of the great plantigen panic.

I never laid a finger on a single genetically modified potato or carrot, but I was in the thick of it nevertheless. So, perforce, were my wife and children; their lives, like mine, hung in the balance throughout. That is why my story is one of the most pertinent records of the First Plague War, as well as one of the most poignant.

Although my work required fierce concentration and a readiness to react to market moves at a moment's notice, I was occasionally forced by necessity to let Frances play in my study while I worked. It was not safe to leave her alone, even in the adjacent ground-floor room where she attended school online. She suffered from an environmentally induced syndrome which made her unusually prone to form allergies to any and all novel organic compounds.

In the twentieth century such a condition would have proved swiftly fatal, but, by the time Francis was born in 2121, medical science had begun to catch up with the problem. There were efficient palliatives to apply to her occasional rashes, and effective ways of ensuring that she received adequate nutrition in spite of her perennial tendency to gastric distress and diarrhea. The only aspects of her allergic attacks which seriously threatened her life were general anaphylactic shock and the disruption of her breathing by massive histamine reactions in the throat. It was these possibilities that compelled us to keep very careful control over the contents of our home and the importation of exotic organic molecules. By way of completing our precautions, Martha, Petra and I had all been carefully trained to administer various injections, to operate breathing apparatus, and—should the worst ever come to the worst—to perform an emergency tracheotomy.

Frances was very patient on the rare occasions when she had to be left in my sole care, and seemed to know instinctively when to maintain silence, even though she was a talkative child by nature. When business was slack, however, she would make heroic attempts to understand what I was doing.

As chance would have it, she was present when I first set up my position in plantigens in July 2129, and it was only natural that she should ask me to explain what I was doing and why.

"I'm buying lots of potatoes and a few carrots," I told her, oversimplifying recklessly.

"Isn't Mummy doing that?" she asked. Martha was at the supermarket.

"She's buying the ones we'll be cooking and eating. I'm buying ones that haven't even been planted yet. They're the kind that have to be eaten raw if they're to do any good."

"You can't eat raw potatoes," she said, skeptically.

"They're not very nice," I agreed, "but cooking would destroy the vital ingredients of these kinds, because they're so delicate."

I explained to her, as best I could, that a host of genetic engineers was busy transplanting new genes into all kinds of root vegetables, so that they would incorporate large quantities of special proteins or protein fragments into their edible parts. I told her that the recent arrival in various parts of the world—including Britain—of new disease-causing viruses had forced scientists to work especially hard on new ways of combating those viruses. "The most popular methods, at the moment," I concluded, "are making plantibodies and plantigens."

"What's the difference?" she wanted to know.

"Antibodies are what our own immune systems produce whenever our bodies are invaded by viruses. Unfortunately, they're often produced too slowly to save us from the worst effects of the diseases, so doctors often try to immunize people in advance, by giving them an injection of something harmless to which the body reacts the same way. Anything that stimulates the production of antibodies is called an antigen. Some scientists are producing plants that produce harmless antigens that can be used to make people's immune systems produce antibodies against the new diseases. Others are trying to cut out the middle by producing the antibodies directly, so that people who've already caught the diseases can be treated before they become seriously ill."

"Are antigens like allergens?" Frances asked. She knew a good deal about allergens, because we'd had to explain to her why she could never go out, and why she always had to be so careful even in the house.

"Sort of," I said, "but there isn't any way, as yet, of immunizing people against the kind of reaction you have when your throat closes up and you can't breathe."

She didn't like to go there, so she said: "Are you buying plantigens or plantibodies, Daddy?"

"I'm buying shares in companies that are spending the most money on producing new plantigens," I told her, feeling that I owed her a slightly fuller explanation.

"Why?"

"Plantigens are easier to produce than plantibodies because they're much simpler," I said. "The protection they provide is sometimes limited, but they're often effective against a whole range of closely related viruses, so they're a better defense against new mutants. The main reason I'm buying plantigens rather than plantibodies, though, has to do with psychological factors."

She'd heard me use that phrase before, but she'd never quite gotten to grips with it. I tried hard to explain that although plantibodies were more useful in hospitals when sick people actually arrived there, ordinary people were far more interested in things that might keep them out of hospitals altogether. As the fear of the new diseases became more widespread and more urgent, people would become increasingly willing—perhaps even desperate—to buy large quantities of plantigen-containing potatoes and carrots to eat "just in case." For that reason, I told Frances, the sales of plantigen-producing carrots and potatoes would increase more rapidly than the actual level of threat, and that meant that it made sense to buy shares in the companies that were investing most heavily in plantigen development.

"I understand," she said, only a little dubiously. She wanted me to be proud of her. She wanted me to think that she was clever.

I *was* proud of her. I did think she was clever. If she didn't quite understand the origins of the great plantigen panic, that was because nobody *really* understood it, because nobody really understood what makes some psychological factors so much more powerful than others that they become obsessions.

No sooner had I taken the position than it began to put on value. Throughout August and early September I gradually transferred more and more funds from all my accounts into the relevant holdings—and then felt extremely proud of myself when the prices really took off. From the end of September on, the only question anyone in the market was asking was how long the bull run could possibly last—or, more specifically, exactly when would be the best moment to cash the paper profits and get out.

From the very beginning, Martha was skeptical about the trend. "It's going to be tulipomania all over again," she said, at the beginning of November.

"No, it's not," I told her. "The value of tulips was purely a matter of aesthetic and commercial perception, with no utilitarian component at all. At least some plantigens are genuinely useful, and some of the ones that aren't useful yet will become useful in the future. As each new disease reaches Britain—whether terrorists really are importing them in test tubes or whether the viruses are simply taking advantage of modern population densities to spread from points of natural origin—possession of the right plantigens might well be a matter of life or death for some people."

"Well, maybe," she conceded. "But people aren't actually buying them as a matter of rational choice. It's not just shares, is it? There are plantigen *collectors* out there, for Heaven's sake, and potato theft is becoming as common as car crime."

I'd noticed that the items I'd seen on the TV news had begun to lose their initial jokey tone, but I was still inclined to laugh off the lunatic fringe.

"It's not funny," Martha insisted. "It was okay when there was still a semblance of medical supervision, but now that it's becoming a hobby fit for idiots the trade is entirely driven by hype and fraud. Every stallholder on the market is trying to talk up his perfectly ordinary carrots and every white van that used to be smuggling cigarettes through the tunnel is busy humping sackloads of King Edwards around. You never get out, so you don't know what it's like on the streets. All you ever see are figures on the screen."

"Share prices are just as real as anything else in the world," I said, defensively.

"Sure they are—and when they go crazy, everything else goes crazy, too. Soon there won't be a seed potato available that isn't allegedly loaded with antidotes to everything from the common cold to the black death. Have you seen what's happening to the price of the stock on the supermarket shelves, since the local wide boys started selling people do-it-yourself transformation kits? It's ridiculous! I wouldn't care, but ever since the gulf stream was aborted, the ground's as hard as iron from October to April. No one who buys a magic potato now can possibly cash in on his investment until next summer, so it's open season for con men."

"That's one of the factors driving the spiral upward," I observed. "The fact that nobody can start planting for another four or five months is making people all the more anxious to have the right stock ready when the moment comes."

"But the hyperflu won't wait," she pointed out. "It'll peak in February just like the old flu used to do, and if the rumors are right about human mosaic viruses, *they* won't mind the cold either, because they can crystallize out. If neurotoxic HMV does break out in London, the most useful weapons we'll have to use against it are imported plantibodies from the places where it's already endemic. Why aren't you buying those by the cartload?"

I had to explain to her that putting money into foreign concerns isn't a good idea in a time of war, especially when you don't know who your enemies are.

"But we know who our *friends* are," she objected. "Spain and Portugal, the southern USA, Australia . . . they're all on our side."

"Perhaps they are," I said, "but it's precisely the fact that we're still semiattached to the old Commonwealth and the European Federation while maintaining our supposedly special relationship with America that puts us in the firing line for practically every terrorist in the world. Then again, anxiety breeds paranoia, which breeds universal suspicion—how can we be sure that our friends really are our friends? Trust me, love—I know what I'm doing. Whether it's wise money or not, the big money is flooding into the companies that are trying to develop plantigens against the entire spectrum of HMVs, especially the ones that don't exist yet although their gene-maps are allegedly pinned to every terrorist's drawing board. This bubble still has a lot of inflation to do."

There's a world of difference, of course, between wives and clients. Martha was worried that I was pumping too much money into a panic that couldn't last forever, but the people whose money I was handling were worried that I wasn't committing enough. Most of my individual clients were the kind of people who didn't even bother to check the closing prices after they finished work in normal times, but the prevailing circumstances changed nine out of every ten of them into the kind of neurotic who programs his cell phone to sing the hallelujah chorus every time a key stock puts on five percent.

There is something essentially perverse in human nature that makes people who can see themselves growing richer by the hour worry far more about whether they ought to be growing even richer even faster than they do about the possibility of the trend turning turtle. I'd never been pestered by my clients half as much as I was in January and February of 2130, when every day brought news of hundreds more hyperflu victims and dozens more rumors about the killing potential of so-called HMVs and plethoral hemorrhagic fever. The steadily increasing kill-rate of iatrogenic infections didn't help at all, although there was little evidence as yet of assertive MRSA migrating out of the wards.

I weathered the storm patiently, at least until Petra decided that it was time to start a potato collection of her own.

"Everyone's doing it," she said, when the true extent of her credit card bills was revealed by a routine consent check. "Not just at the tech, either. The playground at the secondary school's a real shark's nest."

"Sharks don't build nests," I said, unable to restrain my natural pedantry. "And that's not the point. You don't know that any of those potatoes has any therapeutic value whatsoever. Even though you've been paying through the nose for them, the overwhelming probability is that they haven't. You're a bright girl—you *must* know that."

"Well, whether they have or they haven't, I could sell them all for half as much again as I paid for them," she said.

"So do it!" I told her. "Now!" Even that seemed moderate, given that the profits she was contemplating were entirely the produce of misrepresentation. But there were limits to the extent of any holier-than-thou stance I could convincingly maintain, as she knew very well.

"But you of all people," she complained, "should appreciate that if I wait until next week I'll get *even more.*"

"You can't guarantee that," I told her. "If you hang on to them for one day—one *hour*—longer than the bubble takes to burst, all you're left with is debts. Debts that you still have to pay off, even if it takes you years."

"I know what I'm doing," she insisted. "I can judge the mood. *I thought you'd be proud of me.*"

If it had been tulips, perhaps I would have been, but I'd meant what I'd said to Martha. Come the evil day, some plantigens would make a life-or-death difference to some people. On the other hand, it was surely safe to assume that none of them would come from potatoes traded in a schoolyard, or even in the corridors of a technical college.

"If everybody in your class knows you've got them," Martha pointed out, "that makes us a target for burglary. You know now how dangerous that could be, with Frances in the house. You know we have to be extra careful." That was a good tactic. Petra loved her sister, and was remarkably patient about all the precautions she had to take every time she came into the house. The idea of burglars breaking in, dragging who knew what in their wake, wasn't one she could easily tolerate.

"Get rid of them, Petra," I told her, seizing the initiative while I could. "If they aren't out of the house by dinnertime, we'll be eating them."

"Hypocrite!" she said—but she knew when she was beaten.

When Petra had calmed down a little, Martha joined forces with me as we tried to explain that what *I* was buying and selling were shares in wholly reputable companies with well-staffed research labs, where every single vegetable on site really had had its genes well and truly tweaked, but Petra refused to be impressed. The only thing that stopped her from carrying on the fight was that Frances had an attack, as she often did when family quarrels were getting out of hand. Ventolin and antihistamines stopped it short of a dash to the hospital but it was a salutary reminder to us all that if hyperflu ever crossed our threshold, we'd have at least one fatal casualty.

As hyperflu's kill-rate increased, so did the rumors. It's never easy to tell "natural" rumors from the ones that are deliberately let loose to ramp prices upward, and there's little point in trying. As soon as they appear on the bulletin boards rumors take on a life of their own, and their progress thereafter is essentially demand-led. No rumor can be effective if people aren't ready to believe it, and if people are hungry to believe something no amount of common sense or authoritative denial will be adequate to kill it.

Given that the war itself was a matter of rumor, there was a certain propriety in the fact that rumors of defensive armory were driving the whole economy.

Looking back from the safe vantage point of today's peace, it's easy to dismiss the great plantigen panic as a folly of no real significance: a mere matter of fools rushing to be fleeced. But bubbles, however absurd they may seem in retrospect, really do affect the whole economy, as Charles Mackay observed in respect of tulipomania in his classic work on *Extraordinary Popular Delusions and the Madness of Crowds*, published in 1841. "Many persons grow insensibly attached to that which gives them a great deal of trouble, as a mother often loves her sick and ever-ailing child better than her more healthy offspring," says Mackay. "Upon the same principle we must account for the unmerited encomia lavished upon these fragile blossoms. In 1634, the rage among the Dutch to possess them was so great that the ordinary industry of the country was neglected, and the population, even to its lowest dregs, embarked in the tulip trade."

So it was in February and March of 2130.

It was, I suppose, only natural that the mere hint that a company had developed a plantigen giving infallible protection against hyperflu was adequate to multiply its already inflated share price three- or four-fold. It is less easy to explain why companies that were rumored to have perfected potato-borne immunizations against diseases that were themselves mere rumors should have benefited to an even greater extent. The money to feed these momentary fads had to come from somewhere, and it wasn't only the buyers who risked impoverishment. All kinds of other enterprises vital to the economic health of the nation and continental Europe found themselves starved of capital, and all kinds of biotechnological enterprises with a far greater hope of producing something useful were denuded even of labor, as the salaries available to plantigen engineers soared to unmatchable heights.

The advent of the spring thaw was eagerly awaited by everyone, because that was when planting would become possible again and all the potential stored in the nation's potatoes and carrots would be actualized. The process of actualization would, of course, take an entire growing season, but in agriculture as in the stock market anticipation is all; the initiation of movement is more significant, psychologically speaking, than any ultimate result.

I knew, therefore, that prices would continue to rise at least until the end of March and probably well into April, but I also knew that I had to be increasingly wary once the vernal equinox was past, lest the mood began to change. Collapses are far more abrupt than escalations; they can happen in minutes.

Martha continued to urge me to play safe and get out "now." She had said as much in December, January, and February, and her pleas increased their urgency at exactly the same rate as the value of my holdings.

"At least take *our* money out," she begged me, on the first official day of spring "Your clients have far more money than we have, and fewer responsibilities; they can afford to gamble. They don't have Frances' home schooling fees or your mobility expenses to deal with, let alone the prospect of huge medical bills if more effective treatments are ever developed for either or both of you."

"I can't do that," I told her. "I can't do one thing on behalf of my clients and another on my own behalf. It would be professional suicide to admit that I daren't follow my own advice."

"So pull it all out," she said.

"I can't do that either," I lamented. "Even if my timing is spot on, I'll still miss the published peak prices. The clients never understand why it's impossible to sell out at the absolute top, and every percentage point below the published peak increases their dissatisfaction. If any of my competitors gets closer than I do, my clients are likely to jump ship. Loyalty counts for something when everything's just bumping along, but it counts for nothing in times as crazy as these. I have to get this right, Martha, or I'll lose at least half my business."

I had to compromise in the end, by cashing just enough of everyone's holdings to make certain that nobody could actually lose, but I knew that if I didn't manage to hang on to the rest until the day before the crash, if not the hour before, then those sales records would come back to haunt me. The clients would see every one as an unnecessary loss rather than a prudent protective move.

As the last day of March arrived I could see no sign of the boom ending. Every day brought new tales of horrid devices being cooked up in the labs of terrorist-friendly governments and clever countermeasures developed in our own. The pattern established in January was still in place, and the drying of the ground following the big thaw was proceeding on schedule, increasing the anticipatory enthusiasm of professional and amateur planters alike.

Everybody knew that prices could not continue to rise indefinitely, but no one had any reason yet to suppose that they would not do so for another month, or a fortnight at least. There was even talk of a "soft landing," or a "leveling off," instead of a collapse.

To increase optimism even further, the plantigen manufacturers were beginning to increase the rate at which they released actual *products.* Forty new strains of potatoes and six new strains of carrots had been released in the month of March, and there was hardly a household in the country that did not place each and every one of them on the menu, even though the great majority of the diseases against which they offered protection had not registered a single case in Europe.

I understood that this kind of news was not entirely good, because few of the new strains would generate much in the way of repeat business, and people would realize that when they actually used them. But the short-term psychological effect of the new releases seemed wholly positive.

There was no reason at all to expect trouble, and April Fool's Day passed without any substantial incident in spite of the usual crop of preposterous postings. April the second went the same way, but the fact that spring was so abundantly in the air had other consequences for a family like ours.

Even now, people think of spring as a time when "nature" begins to bloom, but that's because we like to forget the extent to which nature has been overtaken by artifice—a process which began with the dawn of civilization and has accelerated ever since. The exotic organic compounds to which Frances was so prone to form allergies were not confined to household goods; they were used with even greater profligacy in the fields of the countryside, and with blithe abandon in the gardens of suburbia.

I had hoped that 2130 might be one of Frances' better years, on the grounds that few people with land available would be planting ornamental flowers while they still had their pathetic potato collections. Alas, the possession of alleged plantigens actually made more people anxious to prepare their ground as fully as possible, and much of the preparation they did involved the new season's crop of exotic organic compounds.

We kept the windows tightly shut, and we controlled Petra's excursions as best we could, but it was all to no avail. On the third of April, at approximately 11:30 a.m., Frances' breathing became severely restricted.

Frances was in her own room when the attack began, in attendance at her web based school. She did nothing wrong. She logged off immediately and called for Martha. Martha responded instantly, and followed the standard procedure to the letter.

When it became obvious, at 11:50 or thereabouts, that the ventolin and the antihistamines were not inhibiting the closure of her windpipe, and that insufficient oxygen was getting through from the cylinder to our little girl's lungs, Martha dialed 999 and called for an ambulance. She was in constant touch thereafter with the ambulance station, which told her exactly where the ambulance was.

The traffic was not unusually heavy, but it was bad, and by noon Martha knew that it would not arrive in time for the last few emergency medical procedures to be carried out by the paramedics.

She had already told me what was happening, and I had told her to call me if the situation became critical. She would, of course, have called me anyway, and I would have responded.

Strictly speaking, I had no need to leave my computer. Martha had undergone exactly the same training as I had, and the fact that she had legs and I did not made her the person capable of carrying out the procedure with the least difficulty. To say that, however, is to neglect the psychological factors that govern such situations.

If I had hesitated, Martha would have carried out the emergency tracheotomy immediately, but I did not hesitate. I *could* not hestitate in a situation of that kind. I had always taken it for granted that if anyone had to cut my daughter's throat in order to give her a chance to live, it ought to be me. I maneuvered my wheelchair to the side of Frances' bed, took the necessary equipment out of the emergency medical kit that lay open on her bedside table, and proceeded with what needed to be done. Martha could and would have done it, but the psychological factors said that it was my job, if it were humanly possible for me to do it.

It was, and I did.

The ambulance arrived at 12:37 precisely. The paramedics took over, and Martha accompanied Frances to the hospital. I could not go, because the ambulance was not a model that could take wheelchairs as bulky as mine. I returned to my computer instead, arriving at 12:40.

I had been away for no more than forty-five minutes, but I had missed the collapse. Shares in plantigen producers were already in free fall.

I had missed the last realistic selling opportunity by sixteen minutes.

Would I have been able to grasp that opportunity had I been at my station? I am almost certain that I would have been able to bail out at least part of my holdings, but I cannot know for sure. The only thing of which I can be certain is that I missed the chance. I missed the vital twenty minutes before the bubble burst, when all kinds of signs must have become evident that the end was nigh.

With the aid of hindsight, it is easy to understand how the collapse happened so quickly, on the basis of a mere rumor. When a rumor's time is ripe, it is unstoppable, even if it is absurd. The rumor that killed off the great plantigen panic was quite absurd, but it had a psychological timeliness that made it irresistible.

One of the most widely touted—but as yet undeployed—weapons of the imaginary war was what everyone had grown used to calling "human mosaic virus." There is, in fact, no such thing as a human mosaic virus and there never was. The real and hypothetical entities to which the name had been attached bore only the slightest analogy to the tobacco mosaic virus after which they had been named. Tobacco mosaic virus was not merely a disease but a favorite tool of experimental genetic engineers. Strictly speaking, that had no relevance to neurotoxic HMV or any of its imagined cousins, but the language of rumor is utterly devoid of strictness, and extremely prone to confusion.

There is and was such a thing as potato mosaic virus, which also doubled as a disease and a tool of genetic engineering. The rumor which swept the world on the third of April 2130 was that terrorists had developed and deployed a new weapon of plague war, aimed in the first instance not at humans but at potatoes: a virus that would transform benign plantigens into real diseases: HMVs that could and would infect any human beings who ate plantigen-rich potatoes in the hope of protecting themselves.

Scientifically, technologically, and epidemiologically speaking it was complete nonsense, but all the psychological factors were in place to make it *plausible* nonsense—plausible enough, at any rate, to knock the bottom right out of the market in plantigen shares.

I wasn't ruined. None of my clients were ruined. Compared to the base from which the bubble had begun six months earlier, we had all made a small profit—considerably more than one could have made in interest had the money been on deposit in a bank. But no one—not even me—was disposed to compare the value of his holdings with their value on last October the first, let alone July the first. Every eye was firmly fixed on the published peak, weeping for lost opportunity.

And *that*, my dear young friends, is what it was really like to be on the home front during the First Plague War.

Frances recovered from the allergy attack. She recovered again the following year, and again the year after that. Then new treatments became available, and the necessity of administering emergency tracheotomies evaporated. They were expensive, but we managed in spite of everything to meet the expense. By 2136 she was able to leave the house again, and she went on to attend a real university rather than a virtual one. She was never completely cured of her tendency to form violent allergies to every new organic molecule that made its debut on the stage of domestic technology, but her reactions ceased to be life-threatening. They became an ordinary discomfort, a relatively mild inconvenience.

By then, alas, Petra was dead. She was an early casualty, in July 2134, of one of the diseases that the ill-informed still insist on calling HMVs. She died because she was too much a part of the world, far too open to social contacts and influences. Of the four of us, she had always been the most likely casualty of a plague war, because she was the only one of us who thought of her home as a place of confinement. Petra always thought of herself as a free agent, a free spirit, an everyday entrepreneur.

We were grief-stricken, of course, because we had always loved her. We miss her still, even after all this time. But if I am honest, I must confess that we would have suffered more had it been Frances that we lost—not because we loved Petra any less, but because Frances always seemed more tightly bound to the nucleus of our little atom of community.

Unlike Petra, Frances was never free.

Nor am I.

Thanks to the march of biotechnology, I have a new pair of legs to replace the ones I lost in 2119. They were costly, but we managed to meet the cost. I still have a loving wife, and a lovely daughter. I have everything I need, and I can go anywhere I want, but I feel less free today than I did on April the second, 2130, because that was the day before the day on which a prison of circumstances formed around me that I have never been able to escape. Although neither my family nor my business was completely ruined by my failure to get out of plantigens in time to avoid the crash, that was the last opportunity I ever had to become seriously rich or seriously successful. The slightly-constrained circumstances in which we three survivors of the First Plague War have lived the rest of our lives always seemed, albeit in a purely theoretical sense, to be both unnecessary and blameworthy. If they were not quite the traditional wages of sin—with the exception of the price paid by poor Petra—they were surely the commission fees of sin.

The prison in question is, of course, purely psychological; I have not yet given up the hope of release. In much the same way, I continue stubbornly to hope that we poor and pitiful humans will one day contrive a world in which psychological factors will no longer create cruel chaos where there ought to be moral order.

Brian W. Aldiss

It's odd to recall that I first flew to the States from England in a turbo-prop plane. That would be in 1965. I was newly married to Margaret, and the first thing we did, even before checking into our hotel, was go for a lunch appointment with Don Wollheim. Memory suggests he had Terry Carr with him.

Don was then at Ace. He published some of my early novels as Ace Doubles: *Vanguard from Alpha* and *Bow Down to Nul* had appeared in 1959 and 1960. He was a generous man, chipping in with a contribution to my airfare over. In later years, we used to meet at various conventions.

When I heard that Don had left Ace, without knowing anything of the politics involved, I did not realize how DAW Books suddenly prospered, and sent Don a collection of short stories to show support. He published it as DAW Book No. 29—*The Book of Brian Aldiss*—thus turning a favor I hoped to do Don into one he did me. Good old Don, I say . . .

—BWA

ABOARD THE *BEATITUDE*
Brian W. Aldiss

"It is axiomatic that we who are genetically improved will seek out the Unknown. We will make it Known or we will destroy it. On occasions, we must also destroy the newly Known. This is the Military Morality."
—Commander Philosopher Hijenk Skaramonter in *Beatitudes for Conquest*

THE great brute projectile accelerated along its invisible pathway. The universe through which it sped was itself in rapid movement. Starlight flashed along the flank of the ship. It moved at such a velocity it could scarcely be detected by the civilizations past which it blasted its course—until those civilizations were disintegrated and destroyed by the ship's weaponry.

It built on the destruction. It was now over two thousand miles long, traveling way above the crawl of light, about to enter eotemporality.

Looking down the main corridor running the length of the structure you could see dull red lurking at the far end of it. The Doppler effect was by now inbuilt. Aboard the *Beatitude*, the bows were traveling faster than the stern. . . .

«Much of the ship is now satisfactorily restored. The hardened hydrogen resembles glass. The renovated living quarters of the ship shine with brilliance. The fretting makes it look like an Oriental palace.

«In the great space on C Deck, four thousand troops parade every day. Their discipline is excellent in every way. Their marching order round the great extent of the Marchway is flawless. These men retain their fighting fitness. They are ready for any eventuality.»

It paused here, then continued.

«The automatic cleaners maintain the ship in sparkling order. The great side ports of the ship, stretching from Captain's Deck to D Deck, remain brilliant, constantly repolished on the exterior against scratches from microdust. It is a continual joy to see the orange blossom falling outside, falling through space, orange and white, with green leaves intertwined.

«All hand-weapons have been well-maintained. Target practice takes place on the range every seventh day, with live ammunition. The silencing systems work perfectly. Our armory systems are held in operational readiness.

«Also, the engines are working again at one hundred-plus percent. We computers control everything. The atmosphere is breathed over and over again. It could not be better. We enjoy our tasks.

«Messing arrangements remain sound, with menus ever changing, as they had been over the first two hundred years of our journey. Men and women enjoy their food; their redesigned anatomies see to that. Athletics in the free-fall area ensure that they have good appetites. No one ever complains. All looked splendidly well. Those dying are later revived.

«We are now proceeding at FTL 2.144. Many suffer hallucinations at this velocity. The *Beatitude* is constantly catching up with the retreating enemy galaxy. The weapons destined to overwhelm that enemy are kept primed and ready. If we pass within a thousand light-years of a sun, we routinely destroy it, whether or not it has planets. The sun's elements are then utilized for fuel. This arrangement has proved highly satisfactory.

«In ten watches we shall be moving past system X377 at a proximate distance of 210 light-years. Particular caution needed. *Computer SJC1*»

Ship's Captain Hungaman stood rigid, according to Military Morality, while he waited for his four upper echelon personnel to assemble before him. Crew Commander Mabel-Mo Hole was first, followed closely by Chief Technician Ida Precious. The thin figure of Provost-Marshal of Reps and Revs Dido Shappi entered alone. A minute later, Army Commander General Barakuta entered, to stand rigidly to attention before the ship's captain.

"Be easy, people," said Hungaman. As a rep served all parties a formal drink, he said, "We will discuss the latest summary of the month's progress from Space Journey Control One. You have all scanned the communication?"

The four nodded in agreement. Chief Technician Precious, clad tightly from neck to feet in dark green plastic, spoke. "You observe the power node now produces our maximum power yet, Captain? We progress toward the enemy at 2.144. More acceleration is needed."

Hungaman asked, "Latest estimate of when we come within destruction range of enemy galaxy?"

"Fifteen c's approximately. Possibly fourteen point six niner." She handed Hungaman a slip of paper. "Here is the relevant computation."

They stood silent, contemplating the prospect of fifteen more centuries of pursuit. Everything spoken was recorded by SJC2. The constant atmosphere control was like a whispered conversation overheard.

Provost-Marshal Shappi spoke. His resemblance to a rat was increased by his small bristling mustache. "Reps and revs numbers reduced again since last mensis, due to power node replacement."

"Figures?"

"Replicants, 799. Revenants, 625."

The figures were instantly rewired at SJC1 for counter-checking.

Hungaman eyed Crew Commander Hole. She responded instantly. "Sixteen deaths, para-osteoporosi-pneu. Fifteen undergoing revenant operations. One destroyed, as unfit for further retread treatment."

A nod from Hungaman, who turned his paranoid-type gaze on the member of the quartet who had yet to speak, General Barakuta. Barakuta's stiff figure stood like a memorial to himself.

"Morale continuing to decline," the general reported. "We require urgently more challenges for the men. We have no mountains or even hills on the *Beatitude*. I strongly suggest the ship again be enlarged to contain at least five fair-sized hills, in order that army operations be conducted with renewed energy."

Precious spoke. "Such a project would require an intake of 10^6 mettons new material aboard ship."

Barakuta answered. "There is this black hole 8875, only three thousand LY away. Dismantle that, bring constituent elements on board. No problem."

"I'll think about it," said Hungaman. "We have to meet the challenges of the centuries ahead."

"You are not pleased by my suggestion?" Barakuta again.

"Military Morality must always come first. Thank you."

They raised ceremonial flasks. All drank in one gulp.

The audience was ended.

Barakuta went away and consulted his private comp, unaligned with the ship's computers. He drew up some psycho-parameters on Ship's Captain Hungaman's state of mind. The parameters showed ego levels still in decline over several menses. Indications were that Hungaman would not initiate required intake of black hole material for construction of Barakuta's proposed five hills.

Something else would need to be done to energize the armies.

Once the audience was concluded, Hungaman took a walk to his private quarters to shower himself. As the walkway carried him down his private corridor, lights overhead preceded him like faithful hounds, to die behind him like extinguished civilizations. He clutched a slip of paper without even glancing at it. That had to wait until he was blush-dried and garbed in a clean robe.

In his relaxation room, Barnell, Hungaman's revenant servant, was busy doing the cleaning. Here was someone with whom he could be friendly and informal. He greeted the man with what warmth he could muster.

Barnell's skin was gray and mottled. In his pale face, his mouth hung loosely; yet his eyes burned as if lit by an internal fire. He was one of the twice-dead.

He said, "I see from your bunk you have slept well. That's good, my captain. Last night, I believe I had a dream. Revs are supposed not to dream, but I believe I dreamed that I was not dreaming. It is curious and unscientific. I like a thing to be scientific."

"We live scientific lives here, Barnell." Hungaman was not attending to the conversation. He was glancing at his standalone, on the screen of which floated the symbols *miqoesiy.* That was a puzzle he had yet to solve—together with many others.

With a sigh, he turned his attention back to the rev.

"Scientific? Yes, of course, my captain. But in this dream I was very uncomfortable because I dreamed I was not dreaming. There was nothing. Only me, hanging on a hook. How can you dream of nothing? it's funny, isn't it?"

"Yes, it's very funny," agreed Hungaman. Barnell told him the same story once a mensis. Memories of revs were notoriously short.

He patted Barnell's shoulder, feeling compassion for him, before returning down the private corridor to the great public compartment still referred to as "the bridge."

Hungaman turned his back to the nearest scanner and reread the words on the slip of paper Ida Precious had given him. His eye contact summoned whispered words: "The SJC1 is in malfunction mode. Why does its report say it is seeing orange blossom drifting in space? Why is no one else remarking on it? Urgent investigation needed."

He stared down at the slip. It trembled in his hand, a silver fish trying to escape back into its native ocean.

"Swim away!" He released his grasp on the fish. It swam across to the port, swam through it, swam away into space. Hungaman hurried to the port; it filled the curved wall. He looked out at the glorious orange blossom, falling slowly past, falling down forever, trying to figure out what was strange about it.

But those letters, *miqoesiy*—they might be numbers . . . *q* might be 9, *y* might be 7. Suppose *e* was = . . . Forget it. He was going mad.

He spread wide his arms to press the palms of his hands against the parency. It was warm to the touch. He glared out at the untouchable.

Among the orange blossom were little blue birds, flitting back and forth. He heard their chirruping, or thought he did. One of the birds flew out and through the impermeable parency. It fluttered about in the distant reaches of the control room. Its cry suggested it was saying "Attend!" over and over.

"Attend! Attend! Attend!"

They were traveling in the direction of an undiscovered solar system, coded as X377. It was only 210 LYs distant. A main sequence sun was orbited by five planets, of which spectroscopic evidence indicated highpop life on two of its planets. Hungaman set obliteration time for when the next watch's game of Bullball was being played. Protesters had been active previously, demonstrating against the obliteration of suns and planets in the *Beatitude*'s path. Despite the arrests then made, there remained a possibility that more trouble might break out: but not when Bullball championships were playing.

This watch, Fugitives were playing the champions of F League, Flying Flagellants. Before 27 and the start of play, Hungaman took his place in the Upper Echelon tier. He nodded remotely to other Uppers, otherwise keeping himself to himself. The dizziness was afflicting him again. General Barakuta was sitting only a few seats away, accompanied by an all-bronze woman, whether rep or real Hungaman could not tell at this distance.

The horn blew, the game started, although the general continued to pay more attention to his lady than to the field.

In F League, each side consisted of forty players. Numbers increased as leagues climbed toward J. Gravdims under the field enabled players to make astonishing leaps. They played with two large heavy balls. What made the game really exciting—what gave Bullball its popular name of Scoring 'n' Goring—was the presence of four wild bulls, which charged randomly round the field of play, attacking any player who got in their way. The great terrifying pitiable bulls, long of horn, destined never to evolve beyond their bovine fury.

Because of this element of danger, by which dying players were regularly dragged off the field, the participants comprised, in the main, revs and reps. Occasionally, however, livers took part. One such current hero of Bullball was fair-haired Surtees Slick, a brute of a man who had never as yet lost a life, who played half-naked for the FlyFlajs, spurning the customary body armor.

With a massive leap into the air, Slick had one of the balls now—the blue high-scorer—and was away down the field in gi-

gantic hops. His mane of yellow hair fluttered behind his mighty
shoulders. The crowd roared his name.

"Surtees . . . Surtees . . ."

Two Fugs were about to batter him in midair when Slick took
a dip and legged it across the green plastic. A gigantic black bull
known as Bronco charged at him. Without hesitation, Slick flung
the heavy ball straight at the bull. The ball struck the animal full
on the skull. Crunch of impact echoed through the great arena
(amplified admittedly by the mitters fixed between the brute's
horns).

Scooping up the ball, which rebounded, Slick was away, leaping
across the bull's back toward the distant enemy goal. He swiped
away two Fug revs who flung themselves at him and plunged on.
The goalkeeper was ahead, rushing out like a spider from its lair.
Goalkeepers alone were allowed to be armed on the field. He drew
his dazer and fired at the yellow-haired hero. But Slick knew the
trick. That was what the crowd was shouting: "Slick knows the
trick!" He dodged the stun and lobbed the great ball overarm.
The ball flew shrieking toward the goal.

It vanished. The two teams, the Fugitives and the Flagellants,
also vanished. The bulls vanished. The entire field became instantly empty.

The echo of the great roar died away.

"Surtees . . . Surtees . . . Sur . . ."

Then silence. Deep dead durable silence.

Nothing.

Only the eternal whispered conversation of air vents overhead.

Hungaman stood up in his astonishment. He could not comprehend what had happened. Looking about him, he found the
vast company of onlookers motionless. By some uncanny feat of
time, all were frozen; without movement they remained, not
dead, not alive.

Only Hungaman was there, conscious, and isolated by his consciousness. His jaw hung open. Saliva dripped down his chin.

He was frightened. He felt the blood leave his face, felt tremors
seize his entire frame.

Something had broken down. Was it reality or was it purely a
glitch, a seizure of his perception?

Gathering his wits, he attempted to address the crew through
his bodicom. The air was dead.

He made his way unsteadily from the Upper Echelon. He had reached the ground floor when he heard a voice calling hugely, "Hungaman! Hungaman!"

"Yes, I'm here."

He ran through the tunnel to the fringes of the playing field.

The air was filled with a strange whirring. A gigantic bird of prey was descending on him, its claws outstretched. Its aposematic wings were spread wide, as wide as the field itself. Looking up in shock, Hungaman saw how fanciful the wings were, fretted at the edges, iridescent, bright as a butterfly's wings and as gentle.

His emotions seemed themselves almost iridescent, as they faded from fear to joy. He lifted his arms to welcome the creature. It floated down slowly, shrinking as it came.

"A decently iridescent descent!" babbled Hungaman, he thought.

He felt his life changing, even as the bird changed, even as he perceived it was nothing but an old tattered man in a brightly colored cloak. This tattered man looked flustered, as he well might have done. He brushed his lank hair from his eyes to reveal a little solemn brown face like a nut, in which were two deeply implanted blue eyes. The eyes seemed to have a glint of humor about them.

"No, I said that," he said, with a hint of chuckle. "Not you."

He put his hands on his hips and surveyed Hungaman, just as Hungaman surveyed him. The man was a perfect imitation of human—in all but conviction.

"Other life-forms, gone forever," he said. "Don't you feel bad about that? Guilty? You and this criminal ship? Isn't something lost forever—and little gained?"

Hungaman found his voice.

"Are you responsible for the clearing of the Bullball game?"

"Are you responsible for the destruction of an ancient culture, established on two planets for close on a million years?"

He did not say the word "years," but that was how Hungaman understood it. All he could manage by way of return was a kind of gurgle. "Two planets?"

"The Slipsoid system? They were 210 LYs distant from this ship—offering no threat to your passage. Our two planets were connected by quantaspace. It forms a bridge. You destructive people know nothing of quantaspace. You are tied to the material world. It is by quantaspace that I have arrived here." He threw off his cloak. It faded and was gone like an old leaf.

Hungaman tried to sneer. "Across 210 LYs?"

"We would have said ten meters."

Again, it was not the word "meters" he said, but that was how Hungaman understood it.

"The cultures of our two Slipsoid planets were like the two hemispheres of your brain, I perceive, thinking in harmony but differently. Much like yours, as I suppose, but on a magnificently grander scale. . . .

"Believe me, the human brain is, universally speaking, as obsolete as silicon-based semiconductors . . ."

"So . . . you . . . came . . . here . . ."

"Hungaman, there is nothing but thinking makes it so. The solid universe in which you believe you live is generated by your perceptions. That is why you are so troubled. You see through the deception, yet you refuse to see through the deception."

Hungaman was recovering from his astonishment. Although disconcerted at the sudden appearance of this pretense of humanity, he was reassured by a low rumbling throughout the ship: particles from the destroyed worlds were being loaded on board, into the cavernous holds.

"I am not troubled. I am in command here. I ordered the extinction of your Slipsoid system, and we have extinguished it, have we not? Leave me alone."

"But you are troubled. What about the orange blossom and the little blue bird? Are they a part of your reality?"

"I don't know what you mean. What orange blossom?"

"There is some hope for you. Spiritually, I mean. Because you are troubled."

"I'm not troubled." He squared his shoulders to show he meant what he said.

"You have just destroyed a myriad lives and yet you are not troubled?" Inhuman contempt sounded. "Not a little bit?"

Hungaman clicked his fingers and began to walk back the way he had come. "Let's discuss these matters, shall we? I am always prepared to listen."

The little man followed meekly into the tunnel. At a certain point, Hungaman moved fast and pressed a button in the tiled wall. Metal bars came flashing down. The little man found himself trapped in a cage. It was the way Barakuta's police dealt with troublemakers on the Bullball ground.

"Excellent," said Hungaman, turning to face the intruder. "Now, I want no more conjuring tricks from you. Tell me your name first of all."

Meekly, the little man said, "You can call me Manifold."

Manifold was standing behind a leather-bound armchair in a black gown. Hungaman was on the other side of a desk, the top of which held nothing but an inset screen. He found he was sitting down on a hard chair. A ginger-and-white cat jumped onto his lap. How the scene had changed so suddenly was beyond his comprehension.

"But—but how—"

The little man ignored Hungaman's stutter.

"Are you happy aboard your ship?" Manifold asked.

Hungaman answered up frankly and easily, to his own surprise: it was as if he was glad to find that metal bars were of no account. "I am not entirely happy with the personnel. Let me give you an example. You realize, of course, that we have been making this journey for some centuries. It would be impossible, of course, without AL—aided longevity. Nevertheless, it has been a long while. The enemy galaxy is retreating through the expanding universe. The ship is deteriorating rapidly. At our velocities, it is subject to strain. It has constantly to be rebuilt. Fortunately, we have invented XHX, hardened hydrogen, with which to refurbish our interiors. The hull is wearing thin. I think that accounts for the blue bird which got in."

As he spoke, he was absentmindedly stroking the cat. The cat lay still but did not purr.

"I was consulting with Provost-Marshal Shappi about which revs and reps to use in this Bullball match, which I take it you interupted, when a rating entered my office unannounced. I ordered him to wait in the passage. 'Ah,' he said, 'the passage of time.' It was impertinent to answer back like that. It would not have happened a decade ago."

The little man leaned forward, resting his elbows on his thighs and clasping his hands together. Smiling, he said, "You're an uneasy man, I can see. Not a happy man. The cat does not purr for you. This voyage is just a misery to you."

"Listen to me," said Hungaman, leaning forward, unconsciously copying the older man's attitude. "You may be the figment of a great civilization, now happily defunct, but what you have to say about me means nothing."

He went on to inform his antagonist that even now tractor beams were hauling stuff into one of the insulated holds, raw hot stuff at a few thousand degrees, mesons, protons, corpuscles, wave particles—a great trail of material smaller than dust, all of which the *Beatitude* would use for fuel or building material. And those whirling particles were all that was left of Manifold's million-year-old civilization.

"So much for your million-year-old civilization. Time it was scrapped."

"You're proud of this?" shrieked Manifold.

"In our wake, we have destroyed a hundred so-called civilizations. They died, those civilizations, to power our passage, to drive us ever onward. We shall not be defeated. No, I don't regret a damned thing. We are what humanity is made of." Oratory had hold of him. "This very ship, this worldlet, is—what was that term in use in the old Christian Era?—yes, it's a *cathedral* to the human spirit. We are still young, but we are going to succeed, and the less opposition to us there is, the better."

His violent gesture disturbed the cat, which sprang from his lap and disappeared. Its image remained suspended in midair, growing fainter until it was gone.

"Mankind is as big as the universe. Sure, I'm not too happy with the way things are aboard this ship, but I don't give a tinker's cuss for anything outside our hull."

He gave an illustrative glance through the port as he spoke. Strangely, the Bullball game was continuing. A gored body was being elevated from the trampled field, trailing blood. The crowd loved it.

"As for your Slipsoid powers—what do I care for them? I can have you disintegrated any minute I feel like it. That's the plain truth. Do you have the power to read my mind?"

"You don't have that kind of mind. You're an alien life-form. It's a blank piece of paper to me."

"If you could read it, you would see how I feel about you. Now. What are you going to do?"

For response, the little man began to disintegrate, shedding his pretense of humanity. As soon as the transformation began, Hungaman pressed a stud under the flange of the desk. It would summon General Barakuta with firepower.

Manifold almost instantaneously ceased to exist. In his place a mouth, a tunnel, formed, from which poured—well, maybe it was a tunnel mouth for this strange concept, *quantaspace*—from which poured, *poured*—Hungaman could not grasp it . . . poured what?—solid music? . . . wave particles? . . . pellets of zero substance? . . . Whatever the invasive phenomenon was, it was filling up the compartment, burying Hungaman, terrified and struggling, and bursting on, on, into the rest of the giant vessel, choking its arteries, rushing like poison through a vein. Alarms were sounding, fire doors closing, conflagration crews running. And people screaming—screaming in sheer disgusted horror at this terrible irresistible unknown overcoming them. Nothing stopped it, nothing impeded it.

Within a hundred heartbeats, the entire speeding *Beatitude* worldlet was filled completely with the consuming dust. Blackness. Brownness. Repletion. Nonexistence.

Hungaman sat at his desk in his comfortable office. From his windows—such was his status, his office had two windows—he looked out on the neat artificial lawns of academia, surrounded by tall everlasting trees. He had become accustomed to the feeling of being alive.

He was talking to his brainfinger, a medium-sized rep covered in a fuzzy golden fur, through which two large doggy eyes peered sympathetically at his patient.

Hungaman was totally relaxed as he talked. He had his feet up on the desk, his hands behind his neck, fingers locked together: the picture of a man at his ease, perfect if old-fashioned. He knew all about reps.

"My researches were getting nowhere. Maybe I was on the verge of an NB—you know, a nervous breakdown. Who cares?

That's maybe why I imagined I saw the orange blossom falling by the ports. On reflection, they were not oranges but planets.''

"You are now saying it was not blossom but the actual fruits, the oranges?'' asked the brainfinger.

"They were what I say they were. The oranges were bursting—exploding. They weren't oranges so much as worlds, whole planets, dropping down into oblivion, maybe meeting themselves coming up.'' He laughed. "The universe as orchard. I was excited because I knew that for once I had seen through reality. I remembered what that old Greek man, Socrates, had said, that once we were cured of reality we could ourselves become real. It's a way of saying that life is a lie.''

"You know it is absurd to say that, darling. Only a madman would claim that there is something unreal about reality. Nobody would believe such sophistry.''

"Yes, but remember—the majority is always wrong!''

"Who said that?''

"Tom Lehrer? Adolf Hitler? Mark Twain? Einstein McBeil? Socrates?''

"You've got Socrates on the brain, Hungaman, darling. Forget Socrates! We live in a well-organized military society, where such slogans as 'The majority is always wrong' are branded subversive. If I reported you, all this—'' he gestured about him, ''—would disappear.''

"But I have always felt I understood reality-perception better than other people. As you know, I studied it for almost a century, got a degree in it. Even the most solid objects, chairs, walls, rooms, lives—they are merely outward forms. It is a disconcerting concept, but behind it lies truth and beauty.

"That is what faster-than-light means, incidentally. It has nothing to do with that other old Greek philosopher, Einstein: it's to do with people seeing through appearances. We nowadays interpret speeding simply as an invariant of stationary, with acceleration as a moderator. You just need a captain with vision.

"I was getting nowhere until I realized that an oil painting of my father, for instance, was not really an oil painting of my father but just a piece of stretched canvas with a veneer of variously colored oils. Father himself—again, problematic. I was born unilaterally.''

The brainfinger asked, "Is that why you have become, at least in your imagination, the father of the crew of the *Beatitude*?"

Hungaman removed his feet from the desk and sat up rigidly. "The crew have disappeared. You imagine I'm happy about that? No, it's a pain, a real pain."

The brainfinger began to look extra fuzzy.

"Your hypothesis does not allow for pain being real. Or else you are talking nonsense. For the captain of a great weapon-vessel such as the *Beatitude* you are emotionally unstable."

Hungaman leaned forward and pointed a finger, with indications of shrewdness, and a conceivable pun, at the brainfinger.

"Are you ordering me to return to Earth, to call off our entire mission, to let the enemy galaxy get away? Are you trying to relieve me of my command?"

The brainfinger said, comfortingly, "You realize that at the extra-normal velocities at which you are traveling, you have basically quit the quote real world unquote, and hallucinations are the natural result. We brainfingers have a label for it: TPD, tachyon perception displacement. Ordinary human senses are not equipped for such transcendental speeds, is all . . ."

Hungaman thought before speaking. "There's always this problem with experience. It does not entirely coincide with consciousness. Of course you are right about extra-normal velocities and hallucination. . . . Would you say wordplay is a mark of madness—or near-madness?"

"Why ask me that?"

"I have to speak to my clonther shortly. I need to check something with him. His name's Twohunga. I'm fond of him, but since he has been in Heliopause HQ, his diction has become strange. It makes me nervous."

The brainfinger emitted something like a sigh. He felt that Hungaman had changed the subject for hidden motives.

He spoke gently, almost on tiptoe. "I shall leave you alone to conquer your insecurity. Bad consciences are always troublesome. Get back on the bridge. Good evening. I will see you again tomorrow. Have a nice night." It rose and walked toward the door, narrowly missed, readjusted, and disappeared.

"*Bad conscience!* What an idiot!" Hungaman said to himself. "I'm afraid of something, that's the trouble. And I can't figure out what I'm afraid of." He laughed. He twiddled his thumbs at great speed.

The *Beatitude* had attained a velocity at which it broke free from spatial dimensions. It was now traveling through a realm of latent temporalities. Computer SJC1 alone could scan spatial derivatives, as the ship-projectile it governed headed after the enemy galaxy. The *Beatitude* had to contend with racing tachyons and other particles of frantic mobility. The tachyons were distinct from light. Light did not enter the region of latent temporalities. Here were only eotemporal processes, the beginnings and endings of which could not be distinguished one from another.

The SJC1 maintained ship velocities, irrespective of the eotemporal world outside, or the sufferings of the biotemporal world within.

Later, after a snort, Hungaman went to the top of the academy building and peered through the telescope. There in the cloudless sky, hanging to the northwest, was the hated enigmatic word—if indeed it was a word—**hiseobiw** . . . *Hiseobiw*, smudgily written in space fires. Perhaps it was a formula of some kind. Read upside down, it spelt **miqoesiy.** This dirty mark in space had puzzled and infuriated military intelligentsia for centuries. Hungaman was still working on the problem, on and off.

This was what the enemy galaxy had created, why it had become the enemy. How had it managed this bizarre stellar inscription? And why? Was **miqoesiy** aimed at the Solar system? What did it spell? What could it mean? Was it intended to help or to deter? Was it a message from some dyslexic galactic god? Or was it, as a joker had suggested, a commercial for a pair of socks?

No one had yet determined the nature of this affront to cosmology. It was for this reason that, long ago, the *Beatitude* had been launched to chastise the enemy galaxy and, if possible, decipher the meaning of **hiseobiw** or **miqoesiy.**

A clenched human fist was raised from the roof of the academic building to the damned thing. Then its owner went inside again.

Hungaman spoke into his voxputer. "Beauty of mental illness. Entanglements of words and appearances, a maze through which we try to swim. I believe I'm getting through to the meaning of this enigmatic sign. . . .

"Yep, that does frighten me. Like being on a foreign planet. A journey into the astounded Self, where truth lies and lies are truth. Thank god the hull of our spacevessel is not impermeable. It represents the ego, the eggnog. These bluebirds are messengers, bringing in hope from the world outside. TPD—must remember that!"

Hungaman, as he had told the brainfinger to little effect, had a clonther, a clone-brother by the name of Twohunga. Twohunga had done well, ascending the military ranks, until—as Steel-Major Twohunga—he was appointed to the WWW, the World Weaponry Watch on Charon, coplanet of Pluto.

So Hungaman put through a call to the Heliopause HQ.

"Steel-Major here . . . haven't heard from you for thirty-two years, Hungaman. Yes, mmm, thirty-two. Maybe only thirty-one. How's your promotion?"

"The same. You still living with that Plutottie?"

"I disposed of her." The face in the globe was dark and stormy, the plastic mitter banded across its forehead. "I have a rep—a womanroid—for my satisfactions now. What you might call satisfactions. Where are you, precisely? Still on the *Beatitude*, I guess? Not that that's precise in any way . . ." He spoke jerkily and remotely, as if his voice had been prerecorded by a machine afflicted by hiccups.

"I'm none too sure. Or if I am sure, I am dead. Maybe I am a rev," said Hungaman, without giving his answer a great deal of thought. "It seems I am having an episode. It's to do with the extreme velocity, a velocillusion . . . We're traversing the eotemporal, you know." He clutched his head as he spoke, while a part of him said tauntingly to himself, You're hamming it up. . . .

"Brainfinger. Speak to a brainfinger, Hungaman," Twohunga advised.

"I did. They are no help."

"They never are. Never."

"It may have been part of my episode. Listen, Twohunga, Helipause HQ still maintains contact with the *Beatitude*. Can you tell

me if the ship is still on course, or has it been subjugated by life-
forms from the Slipsoid system which have invaded the ship?"

"System? What system? The Slipsoid system?"

"Yes. X377. We disintegrated it for fuel as we passed."

"So you did. Mm, so you did. So you did, indeed. Yes, you
surely disintegrated it."

"Will you stop talking like that!"

Twohunga stood up, to walk back and forth, three paces one
way, swivel on heel, three paces the other way, swivel on heel, in
imitation of a man with an important announcement in mind.

He said, "I know you keep ship's time on the *Beatitude*, as if
the ship has a time amid eotemporality, but here in Sol system
we are coming up for Year One Million, think of it, with all the
attendant celebrations. Yep, Year One Million, count them. Got
to celebrate. We're planning to nuclearize Neptune, nuclearize it,
to let a little light into the circumference of the system. Things
have changed. One Million . . . Yes, things have changed. They
certainly have. They certainly *are* . . ."

"I asked you if we on shipboard have been subjugated by the
aliens."

"Well, that's where you are wrong, you see. The wrong question. Entirely up the spout. Technology has improved out of all
recognition since your launch date. All recognition . . . Look at
this."

The globe exploded into a family of lines, some running
straight, some slightly crooked, just like a human family. As they
went, they spawned mathematical symbols, not all of them familiar to Hungaman. They originated at one point in the bowl and
ricocheted to another.

Twohunga said, voice-over, "We used to call them 'black
holes,' remember? That was before we domesticated them. Black
holes, huh! They are densers now. *Densers,* okay? We can propel
them through hyperspace. They go like spit on a hot stove. Propelled. They serve as weaponry, these densers, okay? Within
about the next decade, the next decade, we shall be able to hurl
them at the enemy galaxy and destroy it. Destroy the whole
thing . . ." He gave something that passed for a chuckle. "Then
we shall see about their confounded *hiseobiw,* or whatever it is."

Hungaman was horrified. He saw at once that this technological advance, with densers used as weapons, rendered the extended voyage of the *Beatitude* obsolete. Long before the ship could reach the enemy galaxy—always supposing that command of the ship was regained from the Slipsoid invader—the densers would have destroyed their target.

"This is very bad news," he said, almost to himself. "Very bad news indeed."

"Bad news? Bad news? Not for humanity," said Twohunga sharply. "Oh, no! We shall do away with this curse in the sky for good and all."

"It's all very well for you to say that, safe at Heliopause HQ. What about those of us on the *Beatitude*—if any of us are there anymore . . . ?"

Twohunga began to pace again, this time taking four paces to the left, swivel on heel, four paces to the right, swivel on heel.

He explained, not without a certain malice, that it was not technology alone which had advanced. Ethics had also taken a step forward. Quite a large step, he said. He emitted a yelp of laughter. A considerably large step. He paused, looking over his shoulder at his clonther far away. It was now considered, he stated, not at all correct to destroy an entire cultured planet without any questions asked.

In fact, to be honest, and frankness undoubtedly was the best policy, destroying any planet on which there was sentient life was now ruled to be a criminal act. Such as destroying the ancient Slipsoid dual-planet culture, for instance. . . .

As Captain of the *Beatitude*, therefore, Hungaman was a wanted criminal and, if he were caught, would be up for trial before the TDC, the Transplanetary Destruction Crimes tribunal.

"What nonsense is this you are telling—" Hungaman began.

"Nonsense you may call it, but that's the law. No nonsense, no! Oh, no. Cold fact! Culture destruction, criminal act. It's you, Hungaman, you!"

In a chill voice, Hungaman asked, "And what of Military Morality?"

"What of Military—'What of Military Morality?' he asks. Military Morality! It's a thing of the past, the long long past! Pah! A criminal creed, *criminal* . . . We're living in a new—In fact, I should not be talking to a known genocidal maniac at all, no, not a word, in case it makes me an accessory after the fact."

He broke the connection.

Hungaman fell to the floor and chewed the leg of his chair.

It was tough but not unpalatable.

"It's bound to be good for him," said a voice.

"They were an omnivorous species," said a second voice in agreement—though not speaking in speech exactly.

Seeing was difficult. Although it was light, the light was of an uncomfortable wavelength. Hungaman seemed to be lying down, with his torso propped up, enabling him to eat.

Whatever it was he was eating, it gave him strength. Now he could see, although what he could see was hard to make out. By what he took to be his bedside two rubbery cylinders were standing, or perhaps floating. He was in a room with no corners or windows. The illumination came from a globular object which drifted about the room, although the light it projected remained steady.

"Where am I?" he asked.

The two cylinders wobbled and parts of them changed color. "There you are, you see. Typical question, 'Where am I?' Always the emphasis on the Self. I, I, I. Very typical of a human species. Probably to be blamed on the way in which they reproduce. It's a bisexual species, you know."

"Yes, I know. Fatherhood, motherhood . . . I shall never understand it. Reproduction by fission is so much more efficient—the key to immortality indeed."

They exchanged warm colors.

"Quite. And the intense pleasure, the joy, of fission itself . . ."

"Look, you two, would you mind telling me where I am. I have other questions I can ask, but that one first." He felt the nutrients flowing through his body, altering his constitution.

"You're on the *Beatitude*, of course."

Despite his anxiety, he found he was enjoying their color changes. The colors were so various. After a while he discovered he was *listening to the colors*. It must, he thought, be something he ate.

Over the days that followed, Hungaman came slowly to understand his situation. The aliens answered his questions readily enough, although he realized there was one question in his mind he was unable to ask or even locate.

They escorted him about the ship. He was becoming more cylindrical, although he had yet to learn to float. The ship was empty with one exception: a Bullball game was in progress. He stood amazed to see the players still running, the big black bulls still charging among them. To his astonishment, he saw Surtees Slick again, running like fury with the heavy blue ball, his yellow hair flowing.

The view was less clear than it had been. Hungaman fastened his attention on the bulls. With their head-down shortsighted stupidity, they rushed at individual players as if, flustered by their erratic movements, the bulls believed a death, a stillness, would resolve some vast mystery of life they could never formulate.

Astonished, Hungaman turned to his companions.

"It's for you," they said, coloring in a smile. "Don't worry, it's not real, just a simulation. That sort of thing is over and done with now, as obsolete as a silicon-based semiconductor."

"To be honest, I'm not sure yet if *you* are real and not simulations. You are Slipsoids, aren't you? I imagined we had destroyed you. Or did I only imagine I imagined we had destroyed you?"

But no. After their mitochondria had filled the ship, they assured him, they were able to reestablish themselves, since their material was contained aboard the *Beatitude*. They had cannibalized the living human protoplasm, sparing only Hungaman, the captain.

It was then a comparatively simple matter to redesign quantaspace and rebuild their sun and the two linked planets. They had long ago mastered all that technology had to offer. And so here they were, and all was right with the world, they said, in flickering tones of purple and a kind of mauve.

"But we are preserving you on the ship," they said.

He asked a new variant of his old question. "And where exactly are we and the *Beatitude* now?"

"Velocity killed. Out of the eotemporal."

They told him, in their colors, that the great ship was in orbit about the twin planets of Slipsoid, "forming a new satellite."

He was silent for a long while, digesting this information, glad but sorry, sorry but glad. Finally, he said—and now he was rapidly learning to talk in color—"I have suffered much. My brain has been under great pressure. But I have also learned much. I thank you for your help, and for preserving me. Since I cannot return to Earth, I hope to be of service to you."

Their dazzling bursts of color told Hungaman they were gazing affectionately at him. They said there was one question they longed to ask him, regarding a matter which had worried them for many centuries.

"What's the question? You know I will help if I can."

There was some hesitation before they colored their question.

"What is the meaning of this *hiseobiw* we see in our night sky?"

"Oh, yes, that! Let me explain," said Hungaman.

He explained that the so-called letters of *hiseobiw*, or preferably *miqoesiy*, were not letters but symbols of an arcane mathematics. It was an equation, more clearly written—for the space fires had drifted—as

$$M\pi7\varpi \ni (=)X!_9,$$

They colored, "Meaning?"

"We'll have to work it out between us," Hungaman colored back. "But I'm pretty sure it contains a formula that will clear brains of phylogenetically archaic functions. Thereby, it will, when applied, change all life in the universe."

"Then maybe we should leave it alone."

"No," he said. "We must solve it. That's human nature."

SCIENCE
FICTION
DAW

Ron Goulart

Since Don Wollheim was one of the people who got me hooked on science fiction in the first place, it seemed only fair that he eventually bought some twenty of my books in the genre, the majority of them for DAW.

Back in 1947, by way of a junior high book club, I acquired a copy of *The Pocket Book of Science-Fiction,* edited by Donald A. Wollheim. This was the first time I'd encountered the work of such writers as Heinlein, Sturgeon, John Collier, and Stanley Weinbaum. Weinbaum's *A Martian Odyssey* helped plant the idea that there was a place for humorists in science fiction. About a year later, I discovered Wollheim's *Avon Fantasy Reader* and I bought every issue from then on.

I first met Don Wollheim in the middle Sixties, when he was visiting San Francisco and addressed a group I belonged to. Later in the decade, when my wife and I had relocated in the East, I encountered him again at Ace. I'd gone up there to pitch something to Terry Carr and he reintroduced me to Don. In a fairly short time I sold a book to Don *(The Fire Eater)* and one to Terry *(After Things Fell Apart).* That sale to Don Wollheim caused me to part company with my then agents. A sedate and conservative outfit, they didn't want me to taint my reputation by writing directly for paperbacks.

When Don left Ace to start DAW, I sent him pitches there. Between 1972 and 1983, I sold him sixteen novels and a short story collection. Like my father, Don Wollheim never turned my head with enthusiastic praise. I'd send him a proposal—usually three chapters and an outline—and in a few weeks he'd send a note. Usually he'd say something like, "This is okay. Contract follows." For a freelancer that was better than effusive words of encouragement. The only thing Wollheim ever changed was some of my titles—*Naps* became *When The Waker Sleeps* and *Slow Virus* was converted to *Upside Downside,* etc. But he seldom changed a word of any of the novels and he allowed me to be as funny as I wanted. He even mentioned in the cover blurbs that the novels were humorous. Outside of larger advances, who could ask for anything more?

—RG

ODD JOB #213
Ron Goulart

THEIR new client arrived in a small neometal carrying case.

Jake Pace had been in the large kitchen of their Redding Sector, Connecticut estate dictating a recipe for vegan curry to the database of the botstove. His wife Hildy was loafing in the solarium, idly playing new Goldberg Variations on the banjo.

The voxbox of the secsystem said, "Visitors."

"Be right back," Jake told the stove.

"I can carry on without you, sir," offered the stove.

"Not unless you wish to cease to be." A long, lanky man in his middle thirties, Jake went hurrying into the main living room.

Hildy, long-legged and auburn-haired, was already at one of the high, wide viewwindows. Her electronic banjo dangled from her left hand. "It's merely John J. Pilgrim," she informed her approaching husband.

Out on the realgrass back acre a venerable skycar was in the process of executing a wobbly landing. "That souse," muttered Jake.

"John J. quit drinking over a year ago," Hildy reminded, leaning her banjo against a plazchair. "In the spring of 2032. He hasn't had a drink since."

"His previous lifetime of boozing has permanently affected him," observed Jake. "His sense of balance is shot for good and his sense of decorum is worse than it—"

"He's a brilliant attorney." Hildy watched the small rumpled lawyer come scrambling out of the landed blue skycar. "And, keep in mind, Jake, that he's brought Odd Jobs, Inc. some very lucrative cases."

"We are, and I say this with all modesty and humility, one of the best private investigating outfits in the land," her husband mentioned. "Therefore, in point of fact, we really don't need a rumdum—an erstwhile rumdum shyster to hustle up jobs for us."

"What's that John J. brought along?"

Pilgrim had tugged a small silvery carrying case out of the rear of the battered skycar. He was squatting now on the grass, seemingly arguing with the neometal box.

"In the old days it would've been a suitcase full of plazflasks of Chateau Discount fortified wine," said Jake.

The silvery case did a backflip, somersaulting on the sward.

"You'd best go out and escort him in," suggested Hildy. "He appears to be having a squabble with his carrying case."

". . . and won the plaudits of all fourteen judges of the Supreme Court, including the two androids, I'll have you know," the rumpled little attorney was hollering as Jake came loping up. "So, buster, I can sure as hell sum up your case so an overrated gumshoe like Jake Pace can comprehend it. You're, in my opinion, an extremely arrogant tin-plated piece of—"

"Special alloy, dopey, not tin," corrected a high-pitched little voice from within the carrying case. "And, keep in mind, that it is *I* who hired *you* to represent me. Therefore, I retain the privilege of instructing you, dimbulb, and—"

"You taking up ventriloquism, John?" inquired Jake, halting nearby.

"You're looking extremely gaunt, Jake," observed the attorney, standing up. "Something fatal eating away at you, perhaps?"

"No such luck." Jake grinned one of his bleaker grins. "What's in the carrying case?"

"A fiendish device." Very gingerly, Pilgrim reached out and, after hesitating for a few seconds, grabbed the handle of the neometal case. "Were I better able to avoid the temptation of substantial fees, I'd never have hired out to the enclosed gadget nor agreed to ferry it here to consult you and the fair Hildy."

"Hey, halfwit," complained the voice in the case, "I'm not an it. I'm a male, so refer to me as 'he' henceforth."

Frowning, Jake took a look through the grilled side of the carrying case in Pilgrim's freckled hand. "Some sort of toy?"

"Toy, my ass," said the contents of the case. "I just happen to be, dumbbell, the most sophisticated robot cat in the world. I'm the latest, most advanced version of TomCat™."

"And also, at the present time, a fugitive," added the attorney. "From out on the Coast, in SoCal."

"Why, exactly, have you brought him here?"

"Tom wants to hire you," replied the lawyer.

"I wish to employ Odd Jobs, Inc.," Tom corrected. "Not just you, Pace. I understand that it's Hildy who's the brains of the setup."

After giving a brief sigh, Jake invited, somewhat reluctantly, "Come on in, both of you."

Slouched in a yellow hip-hugger chair, Jake urged, "Give us some details of the damn case."

The chrome-plated robot cat was reared up on the piano bench, whapping out *Pinetop's Boogie Woogie* on the white upright living room piano. "You were expressing doubts as to my versatility, dimwit," reminded Tom. "Therefore, this demo."

Hildy, sitting on the rubberoid sofa, said, "You have to admit he's got a great left paw, Jake."

"For a cat," he conceded. "Now explain what you want to hire us for—and how you intend to pay our fee."

From his orange hip-hugger chair Pilgrim said, "He's got the dough."

"How can a robot cat, and a runaway at that, have money?"

The attorney, his face taking on an even more sour look, answered, "He's done very well on the stock market. And he wins the National Numbers Game with suspicious frequency."

Smacking out a final chord, the cat ceased playing and settled into a comfortable sprawl on the tufted piano bench. "I didn't rig anything, peckerwood. It's simply that I'm a bit psychic and the winning numbers come to me in dreams."

"Robots don't have dreams," said Jake.

"Sez you," said Tom, glancing over at Hildy. "How'd you come to hook up with such a nebbish?"

"I was just out of the convent school at the time and didn't know any better," she replied, crossing her long legs.

"Geeze," remarked the cat, "living with this goof has turned you into a wiseass."

After coughing into his hand, Pilgrim said, "What it . . . what he wants to consult you about is a missing dame who—"

"I'm capable of giving a coherent account of the situation," cut in the robot cat.

"Do so," suggested Jake.

Tom's silver tail switched back and forth twice. "As you probably know, the TomCat™ brand of robot felines is designed and created by BotPets International. Run by Ward McKey, a fughead if there ever was one, and based in the Laguna Sector of Greater Los Angeles in the state of SoCal, BotPets grosses just shy of a billion smackers per year. The majority of this impressive sum comes from the sale of the incredibly popular TomCat™ house pets for the well off and a few—"

"The Fido™ dogbots net over $400,000,000," put in the attorney.

"Dogs. Fooey," observed the cat. "Okay, we're getting close to the nub of the problem. The head of Research & Development/ Cat Division is a lovely, intelligent young woman named Marijane Kraft. She—"

"The little dickens has got a terrific crush on this dame," supplied the attorney.

"Hush, John," advised Hildy, frowning at him and shaking her head. "Let Tom talk."

Rising up on his hind legs, the cat bowed toward her. "You are a rose among thorns, dear lady," he said, settling down again. "For over a year the most expensive model cat has been able to talk. That was an innovation that Marijane came up with and—"

"I thought," said Jake, "you mentioned that she was intelligent."

Looking over at Hildy, the robot cat inquired, "How long have you been married to this gink?"

"Eleven years."

"Oy, such fortitude," said Tom. "I happen to be the working model of the latest and most advanced robot cat. Marijane finished me just three months ago and has been refining my—"

"You became independently wealthy in just three months?" asked Jake.

"Listen, bozo, I did that in three weeks," answered the cat. "The point is, I look upon Marijane with considerable fondness."

Hildy said, "Something's happened to her?"

"Exactly. Six days ago she disappeared."

Pilgrim added, "It's his *belief* that she disappeared. BotPets maintains that she sent in her resignation while visiting friends."

"Friends?" Tom arched his metallic back. "Who in the heck would have friends in the People's Republic of Ohio?"

Hildy said, "Ohio seceded from the Union back in 2027 and elected that fat guy Dictator."

Nodding, Jake said, "Vincent Eagleman, yeah, founder of the Homegrown Fascist Party. Why'd your friend Marijane journey to the People's Republic of Ohio?"

Tom gave a shake of his silvery head. "All she told me before she took off was that something seriously wrong was going on and she wanted to investigate."

Hildy asked, "Something wrong in Ohio? Something wrong at BotPets?"

"I suspect a conspiracy twixt the two, a conspiracy that involves both Vincent Eagleman and Ward McKey. They're quite probably in cahoots and up to no good."

"What are they conspiring about?" Jake sat up.

"I don't know for sure," answered the cat. "I'm assuming, though, it involves one of the BotPets products."

"Whereabouts in Ohio did she go?"

"Youngstown, the capital of the republic."

"Did she contact you at all after she got there?"

"The first two days, yep."

"How?"

The robot cat scratched his silvery side with a hind paw. "Marijane installed a voxphone in my interior. That's not standard equipment, but she and I were pals, and she used to phone most nights after she got home and—"

"She stopped communicating with you from Youngstown?" asked Hildy.

"Exactly, ma'am. She ceased calling after the second day, and the Ritz Mussolini Hotel in Youngstown claims she checked out."

"Going where?"

"No forwarding address. She never came back to Greater Los Angeles, though," said Tom forlornly. "Two days after she disappeared, McKey voxed all the BotPets staff to announce that

Marijane had resigned for personal reasons. He knew everyone would join with him in wishing her well wherever she decided to go."

"Which was where?"

"He didn't mention that."

Jake rose up out of his chair. "And she hasn't called you or contacted you since?"

"If she had would I have furtively arranged my escape from the R&D facility in GLA, given this bedraggled ambulance chaser an outrageous retainer and hired him to convey me to Odd Jobs, Inc. as secretively as possible?"

"Probably not," conceded Jake, starting to pace on the thermal rug. "What do you think, Hildy?"

"She found out something, they shut her down."

"She's not dead," insisted the cat.

"You can't be positive. And you have to be prepared for—"

"I told you, Marijane designed me to be a bit psychic. So I know she's alive."

"Be nice," said Jake, "if you were psychic enough to tell us where."

Hildy asked him, "Want to take the case? Sounds interesting."

Stopping near the piano bench, he frowned down at the robot cat. "Did Pilgrim explain our fee structure?"

"Sure. $100,000 in front—nonrefundable. Another hundred thou if you find her, no matter in what shape," answered Tom. "Plus a bonus of $100,000 should you also clear up whatever mess Marijane was looking into."

"Can you afford that?"

The cat made a brief metallic purring sound. "There's $100,000 in your Banx account as of now, Sherlock. So do we have a deal?" He held up his right forepaw.

Jake shook it. "Indeed we do."

As his skycar sped westward, the day ceased to wane and the sky outside commenced growing lighter. Pushing the Automatic Flight button on the dash panel, Jake leaned back in his seat and rubbed the palm of his hand across his forehead a few times.

The pixphone buzzed.

"Okay, yeah," he said.

The slightly chubby bald man who appeared on the rectangular screen was wearing a two-piece plaid bizsuit and sitting on an under-inflated neoprene airchair. He was surrounded by modified computer screens, databoxes, and a jumbled assortment of electronic tapping equipment. "Did I outline my new billing system thoroughly when you hired me a couple hours ago?"

"You did, Steranko."

Steranko the Siphoner said, "So my initial bill of $1,000 won't shock or stun—"

"$850 was the aforementioned quotation."

"Naw, it couldn't have been, Jacob, my boy, since my new fee list has been in effect since last Xmas."

"$850 is all that Odd Jobs, Inc. is going to pay, be that as it may."

The small informant sighed, and at the same time an exhalation of air came wheezing out of his inflated chair. "Were it not for the fact that I've been doing business with you and that scrawny missus of yours for untold aeons, Jake, I would never put up with your high-handed—"

"Before any more aeons untold, Steranko, tell me what you've found out so far. Assuming you have found out anything."

"Hey, I happen to be, as you well know, chum, the best tapper on Earth," he said. "Or on the Moon for that matter. How about $900?"

"$850."

Sighing again, Steranko reluctantly said, "All right. Here's a one-minute animated ID pic of Ethan Greenway, the lad your client claims was the missing Marijane's dearest friend at BotPets."

A tanned, just barely handsome man of forty appeared on the screen. Smiling amiably, he displayed his full face and then his left and right profiles. "My name is Ethan Greenway. I'm the Associate Copychief in the Fido™ Division of BotPets International."

"You emphasized the word *claims*. You think this guy wasn't her beau?"

"Far be it from me to contradict a robot kitty gifted with speech," said the Siphoner. "Marijane and this boob did date now and then . . . However."

"However what?"

"I have to dig into this a bit further, Jake, but I'm already getting strong hints that friend Greenway was actually an Internal Affairs Agent for BotPets. A fellow who checked on employees who weren't trusted completely."

"Meaning he might have had something to do with her vanishing?"

The hairless Steranko shrugged one shoulder. "I'd seriously consider that possibility, yes."

"Where can I find him?"

"At the moment he's attending the West Coast Robotic Pets Trade Show in the Malibu Sector of Greater Los Angeles. It's being held at the Malibu Stilt Ritz Hotel now through Friday."

Jake nodded. "What about Marsha Roebeck?"

"You now see her before you."

A heavyset woman of about fifty, with short-cropped gray hair, appeared on the screen and went through a ritual similar to Greenway's. "I'm Marsha Roebeck, a Director Second Class of the TomCat™ Division R&D Department at BotPets International."

"Okay, she's the one Tom says helped smuggle him out of the joint," said Jake. "If I can talk to her, I can maybe—"

"That, old buddy, is going to be tough," cut in the plaid-suited informant. "Apparently the lady came down with a rare Moon Base virus and is in the Isolation Ward at the Thorpe Private Hospital in the Santa Monica Sector of Greater LA."

"No visitors, huh?"

"Only medics."

"I can impersonate one if need be."

"Be careful, since the lady is being very closely and belligerently guarded."

"All the more reason to have a talk with her," said Jake. "Did you come up with anything else?"

"You've already had more than $850 worth of pertinent information."

"Okay, dig us up another $850 batch, and I'll get in touch with you once I get to SoCal."

"How much is that pussycat paying you folks?"

"Sufficient."

Steranko said, "It's a pity you don't pass along a bit more of the outrageous fees you bilk out of gullible customers. Were this an equable society, my share would automatically—"

"Talk to you again in a few hours." Jake ended the call.

The robot security guard gave a long, low appreciative whistle. "Gosh all hemlock," he exclaimed out of his coppery voxgrid, "you surely are right pretty, Miss Beemis."

"I am that," agreed Hildy, holding out a packet of expertly forged IDs to the mechanical man at the entrance to the Bingo Heaven Multidome in the heart of Youngstown. She was a silvery blonde now, deeply tanned, wearing a short one-piece sinsilk skirtsuit. "I have an appointment with Mr. Leon Bismarck."

After ogling her again, the robot said, "I hope you'll forgive my overtly masculine reaction, Miss Beemis, but I used to be a doorman up in Orbiting Vegas II, and I was programmed to react positively to chorines."

"One wouldn't think such behavior would be considered acceptable in the more conservative Republic of Ohio."

The big coppery bot nodded in agreement. "I was rushed down here to fill in after some malcontents blew up my predecessor," he explained. "I haven't had my outlook modified." He held her fabricated credentials up to the scanner panel built into his wide coppery chest. "Ah, Miss Theresa Beemis, Contributing Editor of *Militant Chic*. Isn't that the multimedia mag with nearly 6,000,000 subscribers per week in fascist dictatorships worldwide?"

"Nearly 7,000,000," Hildy corrected as he returned her IDs.

"My statistics base hasn't been upgraded since they dumped me here either," the robot told her. "Well, you'll find Mr. Bismarck's office in Dome Three of Bingo Heaven. On the second level right above the Virtual Bingo pavilion."

"Thanks, and good luck on your eventual overhaul."

"You sure are some looker," said the robot, standing aside to let her pass into the building.

"Orderly, get over here at once!" cried Jake.

He now had shaggy blond hair, spurious retinal patterns,

altered fingerprints, and a small fuzzy mustache. He was wearing a two-piece off-white medsuit and standing at the reception desk of the Isolation Ward on the Second Below-Ground Floor of the Thorpe Private Hospital.

The middle-sized human orderly came trotting over. "May I be of service, Doctor . . . " He leaned closer to read the name on Jake's counterfeit digital name tag. "Doctor Bushwanger."

Jake, a bit disdainfully, pointed at the android nurse sitting behind the aluminum reception counter. "This mechanism is obviously malfunctioning, which I must say does not speak highly of your facility."

Blankly staring, the white-clad android said, "Gulp gulp gulp," paused and then said it again.

Two minutes earlier Jake had felt compelled to use a disabler on the andy because she was asking questions he wasn't prepared to answer. That sometimes happened on rush impersonations.

"What the heck's wrong, Irma?" the curly-haired young man asked, going up on tiptoe and staring across the counter at her.

"Gulp gulp gulp."

"This is all very vexing," observed Jake in an annoyingly nasal voice. "I didn't fly in from the Tijuana Sector of Greater LA to be delayed by a mechanism that's obviously gone flooey."

"Why *are* you here, Dr. Bushwanger?"

"Hasn't your Chief of Staff, Dr. Erringer, notified the entire crew that he was brining me in to consult on the Marsha Roebeck case?"

"I thought Dr. Erringer was on a second honeymoon in the Safe Zone of Argentina."

"Be that as it may, he sent for me." Jake impatiently jiggled the medical bag he was carrying. "I happen to be the leading expert on lunar viruses in this hemisphere."

"Patient Roebeck is in an Extreme Isolation room, Doctor, and you can't—"

"I'd hate to have to file a Negative Performance Report on you, Gribble."

"My name is Gibbons."

"Have your ID tag refonted then, Gibbons," suggested Jake, even more impatiently. "But first, take me to my patient immediately."

Gibbons glanced at the still gulping android nurse. "Very well, Doctor," he said resignedly. "I can't afford to have another black mark on my record. Come along."

Using the compact needle gun on the plump woman's upper arm, Jake said, "This stuff ought to counteract the control drugs they've been shooting into you, Miss Roebeck."

"I am completely happy here. I will make no trouble for anyone," she droned. Wearing a polka dot hospital gown, she was sitting up in a gray floating bed at the center of the small gray room. "I will forget all that . . . What the hell is this?" Marsha blinked, scowled at Jake. "Are you one of those bastards who want to hurt Marijane?"

"On the contrary," Jake assured her. "I've disabled the monitoring gear in your room, but they'll tumble to that fairly soon. So tell me what you know about—"

"And who the Billy Jesus might you be, jocko?"

"Jake Pace from Odd Jobs, Inc.," he told her. "What we—"

"So Tom did get to you."

"That he did. Now what do *you* know about what's happened to Marijane?"

"After I smuggled that little dingus out of there, I did some nosing around on my own," she said. "That wasn't, as it turned out, so very smart. They grabbed me, dumped me in this hole, and diddled with my coco so that I was about three steps away from being a vegetable."

"Who put you here?"

She answered, "It was that prissy Ethan Greenway. I tried to tell poor Marijane that he wasn't on the up and up, but she sort of felt sorry for the gink. I found out, too late, that Greenway's a company spy. He reports directly to McKey, and he found out that Marijane was on to something. When she took off for Ohio to dig further, they alerted them back there to detain her."

"What was she on to?"

Marsha shook her head. "All I know is that it has something to do with a shipment of 1,500 TomCat™ bots that were sent to Eagleman, the dictator of the Republic of Ohio," she answered.

"I'm pretty sure, too, that they have a clandestine R&D department, one they never told Marijane or me about."

"Anything different about that shipment?"

"I suspect they'd been modified some, but I don't know how."

Jake stood. "Can you pretend you're still in a stupor?"

"Easy."

"Soon as I talk to Greenway, I'll send a crew of local troubleshooters in to spring you from this joint," he promised. "The guy leading them will probably be a mercenary name of Oskar Tortuga, just back from New Guatemala."

"Is he cute?"

"Not to me, but you may react differently." He eased out of the gray room.

"This is neat," observed Leon Bismarck, a rotund man of fifty clad in a three-piece yellow bizsuit with sinfur trim. "*Our* truth disks are much bulkier." He was gazing with admiration at the tiny silver oval she'd just slapped onto his fat left wrist.

Hildy, sitting with long legs crossed on the edge of his wide tin desk, said, "You're supposed to answer my queries, Bismarck, not comment on the equipment."

"Fire away, sister. You sure are cute, and that's the truth."

"Where's Marijane Kraft?"

Bismarck's official title was Press Secretary to Dictator Eagleman, but some information Hildy had obtained from an informant of her own while flying out here to the Republic of Ohio had alerted her to the fact that he was also in charge of intelligence operations. Posing as a reporter with *Militant Chic* eager to interview him about the new paramilitary uniforms he'd helped design for all the republic's schoolchildren had, as she'd anticipated, enabled her to get an immediate interview.

After, very skillfully, incapacitating the Press Secretary in his private office, Hildy had slapped a truth disk on him.

"She ain't here," he said now, his buttery voice taking on a slight drone.

"Where then?"

"We shipped her back to Greater Los Angeles for a mindwipe."

"Shipped her where?"

"To the Thorpe Private Hospital in the Santa Monica Sector of GLA. They do very good work, and we often send political dissidents out there. Eventually I hope to build our own—"

"What did Marijane find out?"

Bismarck chuckled. "Well, now, ma'am, that's an interesting story."

"Tell me," she suggested.

Jake was heading toward the Malibu Sector in his rented landcar when the skyvan full of Ethel Mermans crashed a few dozen yards ahead of him on the yellow stretch of reconstituted beach.

The big blue-and-gold van had come wobbling down out of the blurred yellow afternoon sky, producing raspy wailing noises. It hit the sand on its belly, sliding and bouncing and sending up swirls of beach grit mingled with sooty smoke, and rattled to a halt. When the twin doors at the rear of the beached skyvan flapped open, at least a dozen android replicas of the twentieth century Broadway singer Ethel Merman came spilling out.

Jake had, by this time, pulled his vehicle to the side of the highway, parked, disembarked and gone running toward the crashed van.

As the Ethel Merman andies hit the sand, some of them were activated and, staggering to their feet, began singing. The majority were belting out Cole Porter's *Anything Goes*, but at least two were rendering Irving Berlin's *Doin' What Comes Naturally*.

When Jake was a few feet from the pilot compartment, he head a faint cry, all but drowned out by the chorus of Ethel Mermans. "Help, please," requested a female voice.

Jake approached the compartment door, carefully opened it. "Anything broken?"

There was a slim blonde young woman of no more than nineteen slumped in the pilot's seat. She was wearing a two-piece, short-skirted flysuit. "I don't think so, except my ankle . . . that one . . . feels funny."

"Unhook your safety gear. I'll lift you out."

"That's awfully kind of you. I feel like such an enormous whipjack crashing this way." She unbound and unzipped.

He hefted her out. "Want to try to stand?"

She grimaced. "Okay, if you hold me up." Very gingerly she planted both booted feet on the stirred up sand. "That doesn't hurt much. I'm guess I'm all right. My name's Bermuda Polonsky, by the way,"

"Jake Pace." He stepped free of her.

"Not Jake Pace the internationally renowned private investigator and musical great?"

"I'm a pretty good detective, yeah," he admitted. "Music, however, is simply a hobby."

"You played at the Moonport Jazz Festival last autumn, didn't you? A marvelous bebop medley, consisting of wonderful renditions of jazz tunes in the style of Thelonious Monk, Bud Powell, Horace Silver, and Elmo Hope."

"That was me. How'd you hear about it?"

"I was going with the fellow who played oboe in the Julliard Neobop Ensemble and I was up there," explained Bermuda. "It's a wonder you didn't notice me, the way I was jumping up and down and applauding wildly after you'd . . . Oh, shit."

"Something?"

"I just now noticed that my vanload of Ethel Mermans is scattered all to hither and yon and bunged up."

"They can be repaired and—"

"Oh, I'm certain they can," agreed Bermuda. "But, you see, I was supposed to deliver them to the Malibu Sector Bop & Jazz Festival by three this afternoon."

"It's nearly three now."

The young woman gave a forlorn sigh. "These androids make up the Ethel Merman Choir, and they're scheduled to perform a medley of jazz standards at 3:15," she told him. "Whatever am I to do since . . . Hey, wait a sec. Can I prevail upon you to substitute?"

"I can't sing like even one Ethel Merman."

"No, I meant could you do your bebop piano medley," she asked hopefully. "Unless, of course, you were en route to some important rendezvous."

Jake considered. "I suppose I can spare you an hour," he decided. "Be a shame to have a gap in the program."

"Oh, that's marvelous," Bermuda said, smiling up at him. "I'll just pop into the cab and phone the . . . damn." Her left leg gave out suddenly, and she dropped to her knees on the yellow sand.

Jake lunged to help her up.

Bermuda, smiling again, put an arm around his neck to steady herself.

There was something sharp in her hand. It jabbed into Jake's neck.

Before he could express his chagrin at once again allowing his vanity about his music to lead him astray, he passed out.

Hildy tried to contact Jake again. She was less than an hour away from SoCal and this was her third attempt since leaving the Republic of Ohio. Her skycar was carrying her toward Greater Los Angeles, where she was assuming she and her husband could work out a plan for rescuing Marijane Kraft from the Thorpe Private Hospital.

But he was answering neither his skycar phone nor his portable communicator.

Hunching slightly in the pilot seat, she tapped out a call to John J. Pilgrim's GLA offices.

TomCat™ answered the call. "Ah, the competent side of the Odd Jobs team," he said, his silvery tail switching. "Well, sister, have you found my pal Marijane?"

"We know where she is."

"Where, pray tell?"

"At the Thorpe Private Hospital. They're planning, if they haven't already, to use a mindwipe on—"

"There's a coincidence for you," said the robot cat. "That happens to be where your halfwit hubby is locked up even as we speak."

"What are you—"

"Scram, get away from the damn phone." The rumpled attorney had appeared in the background to scoop Tom off the phone chair. "If you're hiding out here, you shouldn't be answering calls."

"Hey, I've got built-in caller ID, so I knew—"

"What's happened to Jake?" Hildy asked John J. Pilgrim.

The lawyer made one of his sour faces. "It appears he walked into some kind of trap, Hildy."

"I bet somebody asked him to play trombone in a Dixieland band or piano in—"

"Don't have the details on that," said the lawyer. "Steranko called me about an hour ago. While he was digging up some information for Jake, he came across the fact that Jake himself was being held at Thorpe now."

"Steranko's not all that reliable."

"The Siphoner doesn't much like you either, kid, which is why he passed the information on to me," said Pilgrim. "I was just about to call you."

"I'll be arriving out there in less than an hour, John," she told him. "Get floor plans of the hospital and send them to me. I'll work out a—"

"I already printed out the Thorpe floor plans, sis," put in the robot cat, jumping up onto Pilgrim's rumpled lap. "And I've got a pretty neat plan figured out. The two of us can—"

"That's not wise. Tom. Somebody's liable to recognize you."

"Didn't I get around to telling you I was an expert at disguise? When next you see me, you'll think I'm an everyday alley cat," he assured her. "Plus which, I've got all sorts of built-in weapons. And although I'm not all that enthusiastic about your mate, I really have to be in on rescuing Marijane."

After a few seconds, Hildy said, "All right, we'll work together. But I'll cook up the plan."

Jake awakened in an uncomfortable gray restraining chair. "This is not the Malibu Sector Bop & Jazz Festival," he realized.

"A fine champion you turned out to be." Marsha Roebeck was strapped into another chair across the small gray room from him. "Tell me to expect some thug named Tortuga to come rescue me and then get tossed in here yourself."

"I apologize," said Jake.

"I'm sure Mr. Pace meant well," said Marijane Kraft, who was restrained in the third chair a few feet to Jake's right. "And he hasn't been any stupider than I was by barging into—"

"You're an amateur, dear, and this clunk is a pro who—"

"Let's not give up hope," advised Jake, glancing around the

gray room. "And let's not discuss escape plans, since our cell is no doubt monitored."

"Escape plans? Hooey," observed Marsha. "They're going to mindwipe the lot of us sometime later today."

"Who are they exactly?"

"Since I was only pretending to be stupefied, I got a look at some of them," said Marsha. "Several hospital staffers are involved, obviously, but I also saw McKey himself once."

"The head of BotPets, yeah," said Jake.

"These goons are also going to give us a dose of truth spray," added Marsha. "McKey is eager to know where TomCat™ has got to."

"Is Tom okay?" asked Marijane, a slender dark-haired woman of about thirty.

"Far as I know," Jake told her. "Now, before we all start suffering from forgetfulness, exactly what did you find out about those 1,500 robot cats that were shipped to the Republic of Ohio?"

"It's very distressing," she replied and began to explain.

Whispering, Hildy mentioned, "You're not a very convincing cat."

"I *am* a cat," reminded Tom, whom she was carrying under her arm.

"What I was referring to was your feline disguise," she amplified. "The sinfur is a little tacky and I really wish we'd had time to do a better job of—"

"Don't blame me if your halfwit hubby got himself abducted to this dump and you had to rush over here to rescue the poor goof," said the robot cat. "I think you're still miffed because the info as to his plight came to you by way of that skinhead Steranko, whom you loathe and—"

"I'm also still a bit miffed that you insisted on tagging along."

"Listen, cookie, I'm essential to this daring rescue scheme. The plan we've contrived to rescue your hapless spouse and, more importantly, Marijane, calls upon me to play a crucial role," reminded TomCat™. "And look at the thanks I get for risking my—"

"Hush now, we're at the hospital entrance."

The plaz doors at the top of the winding ramp slid aside and Hildy, who was wearing a conservative three-piece gray neowool bizsuit, entered the main lobby of the three-tier Thorpe Private Hospital.

"Rowr," said Tom.

"Not a very convincing meow."

"A lot you know, sister. I was playing a caz of an authentic field recording of a real damn cat."

"Even so." She went striding up to the boomerang-shaped tin reception desk.

"How may I help you, ma'am?" inquired Gibbons.

"Ah, this is most impressive, a live receptionist," she said in a vaguely French accent. She smiled and brushed a strand of dark hair from her forehead. "Usually the receptionists are androids or robots."

The curly-haired young man pointed a thumb at the ceiling. "Usually ours are, too, but they had to transfer Ida up to the Extreme Isolation wing to take Irma's place," he explained. "Some loon named Dr. Bushwanger went berserk yesterday and used some kind of fritzer on her."

Hildy gave a surprised gasp. "But *I'm* Dr. Bushwanger."

Gibbons sat up. "One Dr. Bushwanger is enough. I'm afraid I'll—"

"I assure you I am the authentic Dr. Frances Bushwanger. If some slattern has been impersonating me, I'll see that she—"

"This was a gent. Tall, lanky bloke with—"

"Rowr rowr," said Tom.

"Oh, and we don't allow pets."

"This isn't a pet, this is my companion. His name is Mutton."

"Rising from his chair, the orderly asked, "Muffin?"

"Mutton."

"Odd name for a cat."

"Don't blame me, he picked it out."

"The cat named himself?"

"No, actually I was alluding to my husband," she said, smiling again. "Now might I see Dr. Thorpe?"

"Afraid she's away on a second honeymoon with Dr. Erringer."

"How disappointing. She and I are old chums, and I was hoping—"

"Rowr. Meow." Twisting, Tom jumped free of Hildy's grasp, hit the multicolored plaztile floor and, as planned, went speeding off down a corridor.

"We can't allow cats to run loose in here, Dr. Bushwanger." Gibbon hopped out from behind the counter, taking off in pursuit of the disguised robot cat. "And judging by that fur of his, he's also suffering from a bad case of mange."

"It's actually stress-related." She kept pace with him.

According to the floor plans of the hospital, the Security Control Center was around the bend and at the end of the corridor Tom had gone streaking down.

When Gibbons and Hildy rounded the bend, they saw that the wide plazdoor marked *SecCon* was standing half open.

"That's not supposed to be unlocked." Gibbons slowed and approached the doorway with caution.

"Be careful, there's no telling what we're liable to find."

"Good gravy!" exclaimed the orderly from inside the room. "All of the security staff plus the secbot are sprawled at their workstations and apparently comatose."

"What about my Mutton?" Hildy crossed the threshold.

"I don't see him, but that's the least of our worries."

"Nope, dimbulb, it should be your top worry." Rearing up atop a rubberoid desk, Tom pointed a shaggy paw at him.

"How come you can talk?"

Instead of an answer, Gibbons got a yellowish beam from the cat's built-in stungun.

Jake, who'd done a dissertation on Houdini while earning one of his earliest PhDs, succeeded in unobtrusively deactivating his restraints in a little over two hours after he'd awakened in the bowels of the private hospital.

For the past several minutes, giving the impression that he was still trussed up, he remained sitting, watchfully, in his gray chair. He'd done the rearranging of his bonds so deftly and subtly that he was almost certain nobody monitoring their cell would've noticed. He planned to remain in the chair until somebody came into the room, then he'd move and improvise a way out.

"Whatever's the matter with you, Pace?" inquired Marsha. "You've been twitching and twisting for hours."

"It's an unfortunate neurological condition," he answered quietly.

"How's that again? Speak up."

"I'm suffering from Reisberson's Syndrome," he said in a somewhat louder voice. "It causes uncontrollable hyperactivity now and then. I'm fine now."

"Good, then maybe you can cease thrashing about and come up with some way to get us out of this dump."

"Marsha, don't heckle Mr. Pace," said Marijane. "After all, he wouldn't be in this pickle if he hadn't attempted to find me."

"Good intentions don't cancel colossal screwups, honey."

The metal cell door started to quiver, then began rattling.

Jake straightened up in his chair, alert. Producing an odd keening noise, the door slid open. Shedding the straps, Jake dived forward.

"Sit and meditate," advised Tom on the threshold. "We don't need any derring-do from you, buster."

Smiling, Hildy stepped carefully into the room, stun gun in hand. "It's us, Jake. You can relax."

Taking a slow deep breath, he straightened up out of his crouch. "You heard about my plight, huh?" He commenced releasing the two women from their chairs.

"Steranko found out you were here, and I found out that Marijane Kraft was here," she answered. "Marsha Roebeck is a bonus."

"I take it you're the sensible half of Odd Jobs, Inc.," said the plump woman as she stood up, shedding her bonds.

"We're a team," answered Hildy. "Sometimes I save him, sometimes he saves me. It makes for an interesting marriage—so far anyway."

From out in the corridor a gruff voice ordered, "Nobody move. A wall of weapons is waiting out here."

Jake called, "Oskar, you're on our side."

A large, wide, tanned man with a shaggy blond beard appeared in the doorway. He lowered his stun gun to his side. "We're just getting around to rescuing the lady you mentioned, Jake, old man."

"I appreciate that, Oskar," he said. "But we've taken care of that. However, you and your boys can help us get out of here safely."

"A piece of cake," said the mercenary, grinning.

"You're right," Marsha told Jake. "He's not cute."

Jake grinned, clicking off the vidwall in the media room of their Redding Sector estate. "The Newz account of BotPet's collaboration with Dictator Eagleman was fairly accurate," he observed. "And they gave a handsome plug to Odd Jobs, Inc."

"Best of all," said Hildy, "they didn't mention how you walked right into Greenway's trap, nor how you had to be bailed out by me and a robot cat."

"Sometimes my altruism gets the best of my judgment," he admitted, settling into a rubberoid armchair facing the one his wife was sitting in. "But keep in mind, that when you arrived, I'd freed myself and was about to—"

"Altruism isn't the word I'd pick," she said. "Hubris would be high on my list, followed by vanity, egomania or—"

"Hey, they seemingly wanted a gifted jazz pianist, which I happen to be," he pointed out. "Admittedly I could have been a mite less trusting."

"Letting a frail teenager knock you out and dump you in—"

"She was nearly twenty."

"Then ending up in the same hospital with Marijane Kraft and that Roebeck woman, all of you candidates for mindwipes."

"Made the rescue operation much easier." He stood up and started to pace the neowood floor. "I appreciate you and Tom helping get me out of there. Also keep in mind that Oskar Tortuga and the crew of former commandos I hired to spring Marsha Roebeck busted into the place shortly after you arrived. So it's quite possible they could've rescued us without your having to—"

"Some rescue team you hired. They almost used a stungun on me."

Jake made a let's-stop gesture with both hands. "Be that as it may, Odd Jobs, Inc. did what it was hired for," he reminded her. "We located Marijane, rescued her, and found out what was going on. As a result, several high-placed BotPets execs—including Greenway and the CEO himself, McKey, are being held for kidnapping and aiding a foreign government—namely Ohio."

"You think what Eagleman, McKey, and Greenway had in mind would've worked?"

"Well, the 1,500 specially modified TomCat™ bots were designed to work as spies, saboteurs, and occasional assassins," answered Jake. "If Eagleman had succeeded in planting most of them in the homes of key political figures and businessmen in Indiana, Kentucky, and Michigan, it could've helped him in his plan to expand the territory of his republic." He shrugged. "Maybe it would've worked, maybe not."

"When Marijane found out what they were planning and tried to track the doctored robot cats, they grabbed her," said Hildy. "She wasn't too smart, trusting Greenway and confiding in him and then investigating this on her own. Of course, BotPets weren't too bright in the way they went about trying to silence her."

"They didn't know we'd be brought into the case."

"Had they known a formidable bebopper would be unleashed, they might have called the whole thing off."

"What say we call a truce?"

Hildy said, "Okay by me."

He moved closer to her chair, leaned to kiss her.

"Visitors," announced a dangling voxbox.

Jake kissed his wife, then moved to a viewindow and unblanked it.

A sleek crimson skycar was landing outside.

When it settled on the grass and the cabin door popped open, Hildy said, "It's Marijane Kraft, and she's got Tom with her. I'll go out and escort them in."

"Does that robot cat have to come in?"

"Certainly. He helped save you."

"Okay," conceded Jake, "But tell him to stay away from the piano."

Robert Sheckley

Many years ago I wrote a story called "Zirn Left Unguarded, the Jenzhik Palace in Flames, Jon Westerly Dead." Don Wollheim called me. He was interested in acquiring rights to the story. He wanted to hire someone to expand it into a novel. We discussed the possibility of me writing it. I remember Don's voice over the phone—an incisive New York voice. Trouble was, I was tied up with other assignments at that time, and didn't want to commit myself too far ahead. We decided to talk about it again further down the line—maybe in a year. I guess we both forgot about the project—until now, when you asked me for an anecdote about Don. This is the best one I can remember—maybe the only one. I still regret never having written that novel for Don.

I was born in New York in 1928. Raised in New Jersey, I settled in New York again after my tour of duty in the Army. I've done a lot of traveling over the years, and a lot of writing. I'm still going strong, and hope to continue indefinitely.

—RS

AGAMEMNON'S RUN
Robert Sheckley

A GAMEMNON was desperate. Aegisthus and his men had trapped him in Clytemnestra's bedroom. He could hear them stamping through the hallways. He had climbed out a window and made his way down the wall clinging by his fingernails to the tiny chiseled marks the stonecutters had left in the stone. Once in the street, he thought he'd be all right, steal a horse, get the hell out of Mycenae. It was late afternoon when he made his descent from the bedroom window. The sun was low in the west, and the narrow streets were half in shadow.

He thought he had got away free and clear. But no: Aegisthus had posted a man in the street, and he called out as soon as Agamemnon was on the pavement.

"He's here! Agamemnon's here! Bring help!"

The man was a beefy Spartan, clad in armor and helmet, with a sword and shield. Agamemnon had no armor, nothing but his sword and knife. But he was ready to tackle the man anyhow, because his rage was up, and although Homer hadn't mentioned it, Agamemnon was a fighter to beware of when his rage was up.

The soldier must have thought so. He retreated, darting into a doorway, still crying the alarm. Agamemnon decided to get out of there.

A little disoriented, he looked up and down the street. Mycenae was his own city, but he'd been away in Troy for ten years. If he turned to his left, would the street take him to the Lion Gate? And would Aegisthus have guards there?

Just that morning he had ridden into the city in triumph. It was hateful, how quickly things could fall apart.

He had entered Mycenae with Cassandra beside him in the chariot. Her hands were bound for form's sake, since she was technically a captive. But they had been bedmates for some weeks, ever since he had bought her from Ajax after they sacked Troy. Agamemnon thought she liked him, even though Greek soldiers had killed her parents and family. But that had been while their blood rage was still high; their rage at so many of their companions killed, and for the ten long wasted years camped outside Troy's walls, until Odysseus and his big wooden horse had done the trick. Then they'd opened the city gates from the inside and given the place over to rage, rape, and ruin.

None of them were very proud of what they'd done. But Agamemnon thought Cassandra understood it hadn't been personal. It wasn't that he was expecting forgiveness from her. But he thought she understood that the important ones—Agamemnon himself, Achilles, Hector, Odysseus—were not bound by the rules of common men.

They were special people, and it was easy to forget that he was not the original Agamemnon, not the first. The lottery had put them into this position, the damnable lottery which the aliens had set over them, with its crazed purpose of replaying events of the ancient world, only this time with the possibility of changing the outcomes.

He was Chris Johnson, but he had been Agamemnon for so long that he had nearly forgotten his life before the lottery chose him for this role.

And then there had been all the trouble of getting to Troy, the unfortunate matter of Iphigenia, the ten years waiting in front of the city, the quarrel with Achilles, and finally, Odysseus' wooden horse and the capture and destruction of Troy and nearly all its inhabitants, and then the long journey home over the wine-dark sea; his return to Mycenae, and now this.

And before that? He remembered a dusty, small town not far from the Mexican border. Amos' water tower had been the tallest building on the prairie for 200 miles in any direction. Ma's Pancake House had been the only restaurant. When he made his lucky draw in the lottery, he remembered thinking it would be worth life itself just to get out of here, just to live a little.

It had never been easy to get out of Mycenae. The city's heart was a maze of narrow streets and alleys. The district he was in, close to the palace, had an Oriental look—tiny shops on twisting streets. Many of the shopkeepers wore turbans. Agamemnon had never researched the life of the ancient Greeks, but he supposed this was accurate. The creators of the lottery did what they did for a reason.

The street Agamemnon was on came out on a broad boulevard lined with marble statues. Among them, Agamemnon recognized Perseus and Achilles, Athena and Artemis. The statues had been painted in bright colors. He was surprised to see a statue to himself. It didn't look much like him, but it had his name on it. In English letters, not Greek. It was a concession the lottery had made to modern times: everyone in this Greece spoke English. He wondered if the statue represented the first Agamemnon. He knew that the lottery was always repeating the classical roles. Had there ever been a first Agamemnon? With myths and legends, you could never be quite sure.

He saw that a procession was coming down the boulevard. There were musicians playing clarinet and trumpet. Timpani players. Even a piano, on a little cart, drawn by a donkey.

That was obviously not legitimate. But he reminded himself that the lottery was staging this, and they could make it any way they wanted it. He didn't even know where their Greece was. Behind the musicians there were dancing girls, in scanty tunics, with wreaths around their heads and flowers in their hair. They looked drunk. He realized that these must be maenads, the crazed followers of Dionysus, and behind them came Dionysus himself. As he came closer, Agamemnon recognized him. It was Ed Carter from Centerville, Illinois. They had met in one of the lottery staging rooms, where they had gone for their first assignments.

"Dionysus!" Agamemnon called out.

"Hello, Agamemnon, long time no see. You're looking good." Dionysus was obviously drunk. There were wine stains on his mouth and his tunic. He didn't seem able to pause in his dancing march, so Agamemnon walked along beside him.

"Going to join me?" Dionysus asked. "We're having a feast later, and then we're going to tear apart King Pentheus."

"Is that strictly necessary?"

Dionysus nodded. "I was given specific orders. Pentheus gets it. Unless he can figure something out. But I doubt this one's up to it."

Agamemnon asked, a bit formally, "How is it going with you, Dionysus?"

Dionysus said, "Pretty well, Agamemnon. I'm getting into this. Though it was no fun being killed last week. A real bummer."

"I didn't hear about that."

"I didn't anticipate it myself," Dionysus said. "But they jump you around in time, you know, to make sure you cover all the salient points of your character's life. No sooner had I been married to Ariadne—did you ever meet her? Lovely girl. Abandoned by Theseus on the isle of Naxos, you know—and then I came along and married her. A bit sudden on both our parts, but what a time we had! Naxos is a lovely place—I recommend it for a holiday—anyhow, immediately after that, I found myself newborn in the Dictean cave. I think it was the Dictean. And these guys, these Titans with white faces were coming at me, obviously intending murder. I put up a hell of a struggle. I changed into a bird, a fish, a tree. I could have pulled it off, but the contest was rigged against me. I had to die in order to be reborn. They seized me at last and tore me apart, as my maenads will do for Pentheus. But Apollo gathered my bits, and Zeus took me into himself, and in due course I was reborn. And here I am, leading my procession of crazy ladies down the main street of Mycenae. Not bad for a kid from Centerville, Illinois, huh? And what about you, Agamemnon?"

"I've got some trouble," Agamemnon said. "Remember my wife, Clytemnestra? Well, she's sore as hell at me because she thinks I sacrificed our daughter Iphigenia."

"Why did you do that?"

"To call up a wind so the fleet could get to Troy. But I didn't really do it! I made it look like a sacrifice, but then I arranged for Artemis to carry Iphigenia away to Aulis, where she has a nice job as high priestess."

"Everyone thinks you had your daughter killed," Dionysus said.

"They're wrong! There's that version of the story that says I didn't. That's the one I'm going with. But that bitch Clytemnestra and her sleazy boyfriend Aegisthus won't buy it. They've got guards out all over the city with orders to kill me on sight."

"So what are you going to do?"

"I need a way out of this! Can you help me? Isn't there some way I can get out of this whole mess?"

"Maybe there is," Dionysus said. "But you'd have to ask Tiresias for specifics."

"Tiresias? He's dead, isn't he?"

"What does that matter? He was the supreme magician of the ancient world. He'd be glad to talk to you. He likes talking to live ones."

"But how do I get to the underworld?"

"You must kill someone, then intercept the Charon-function when it comes to carry off the shade, and accompany them across the Styx."

"I don't want to kill anyone. I've had enough of that."

"Then find someone on the point of death and it'll still work."

"But who?"

"What about Cassandra?"

"No, not Cassandra."

"She's doomed anyway."

"We think we've figured an out for her. Anyhow, I won't kill her."

"Suit yourself. Actually, anybody will do."

"I'm not going to just grab some person off the street and kill him!"

"Agamemnon, it's really not a time to be finicky. . . . What about a plague victim? One not quite dead, but on the way?"

"Where would I find a plague victim?"

"Follow a plague doctor."

"How will I know Charon when he comes? His appearance is always invisible to any but the dead."

Dionysus frowned for a moment, then his brow cleared. He reached inside his tunic and took out a purple stone on a chain.

"They gave me this in Egypt. It's an Egyptian psychopomp stone. Some kind of amethyst, I believe. Take it. There's a doctor over there! Good luck, Agamemnon! I really must go now."

And with a wave of his hand, Dionysus danced off after his maenads.

Agamemnon saw the person Dionysus had been referring to: a tall, middle-aged man in a long black cloak, carrying an ivory cane, and wearing a conical felt cap on which was the symbol of Asclepius.

Agamemnon hurried over to him. "Are you a doctor?"

"I am. Strepsiades of Cos. But I can't stop and chat with you. I am on my way to a call."

"To a plague victim?"

"Yes, as it happens. A terminal case, I fear. The family waited too long to send for me. Still, I'll do what I can."

"I want to go with you!"

"Are you a doctor? Or a relative?"

"Neither. I am—a reporter!" Agamemnon said in a burst of inspiration.

"How can that be? You have no newspapers here in Mycenae. I've heard that Argive Press managed to run for a while, but the price of copper went through the ceiling, and Egypt stopped exporting papyrus . . ."

"It's a new venture!"

The doctor made no comment when Agamemnon fell into step beside him. Agammmemnon could tell the man wasn't pleased. But there was nothing he could do about it. He might even have been furious; but Agamemnon wore a sword, and the doctor appeared to be unarmed.

After several blocks, Agamemnon saw they were going into one of the slum areas of the city. *Great*, he thought. *What am I getting myself into?*

They went down a narrow alley, to a small hut at the end of it. Strepsiades pushed open the door and they entered. Within, visible by the gray light from a narrow overhead window and a single flickering oil lamp on the floor, a man lay on a tattered blanket on the ground. He appeared to be very old, and very wasted. Strepsiades knelt to examine him, then shook his head and stood up again.

"How long does he have?" Agamemnon asked.

"Not long, poor fellow. He's approaching the final crisis. You can tell by the skin color. Sometimes these cases linger on for a few hours more, half a day, even a day. But no longer."

"Let me look at him," Agamemnon said and knelt down beside

the sick man. The man's skin was bluish gray. His lips were
parched and cracked. Thin lines of blood oozed from his nostrils
and the corners of his eyes. The turgid blood was the only sign of
life in the man.

Agamemnon was acutely aware that he had little time in which
to make his escape from Mycenae. But the man was still alive.
How long did he have to wait until he died? A minute? An hour?
How long before Aegisthus' soldiers found him? He had to get it
over with. He tried to make up his mind whether to smother or
strangle the man.

He started to reach toward the man's throat. The man opened
his eyes. With the man suddenly staring at him with bloodshot
blue eyes, Agamemnon hesitated—

"King Agamemnon!" the sick man whispered. "Can it be you?
I am Pyliades. I was a hoplite in the first rank of the Argolis Pha-
lanx. I served under you in the Trojan War. What are you doing
here, sir?"

Agamemnon heard himself say, "I heard of your plight, Pyliades, and came to wish you well."

"Very good of you, sire. But then, you always were a good
man and a benevolent commander. I'm surprised you remember
me. I was only a common soldier. My parents had to sell the farm
in order to purchase my panoply, so I could march with the others
and avenge Greece for the unfair abduction of our Helen."

"I remembered you, Pyliades, and came to say farewell. Our
war is won. The might of Greece has prevailed. Of course, we had
Achilles. But what good would Achilles have been if it weren't for
men in the ranks like you?"

"I remember Prince Achilles well, and the burial fires we lit for
him when he was killed. I hope to see him again, in Hades. They
say—"

The sick man's meandering discourse was broken as the door
to his room was suddenly slammed open. Two armed soldiers
pushed their way in. They hesitated, seeing the doctor in his long
robe. Then they spotted Agamemnon.

The leading soldier, a burly red-bearded man, said, "Kill them
all. Aegisthus wants no witnesses. I'll take care of Agamemnon
myself."

The second soldier was the one who had spotted Agamemnon

coming out of the palace window, and had run from him. He advanced now on the doctor, who raised his ivory cane to protect himself, saying, "There's no need for this. I am a neutral, a physician from Cos, here only to treat the sick and injured. Let me go, I'll never say a word about what's going on here."

The soldier glanced at the red-bearded man, evidently his officer, who muttered, "No witnesses!" Then he turned back to Agamemnon.

Agamemnon saw the doctor suddenly lift his staff and bring it down on the soldier's head. The rod broke. Growling, sword poised, the soldier advanced on the doctor.

Agamemnon could see no more, because the red-bearded man was coming at him. Agamemnon had his sword out, but without armor, he knew he stood little chance against an experienced hoplite. He circled around the sick man on his blanket, and the red-bearded soldier pursued, cautiously but relentlessly.

Agamemnon heard a scream. The doctor had been wounded, but was still fighting, trying to stab his assailant with the stub of his ivory cane. Agamemnon continued circling, winding his cloak around his left arm, but he knew it was hopeless, utterly hopeless. . . .

And then, in an instant, everything changed.

Pyliades, with the last vestige of his strength, reached out and clutched the red-bearded soldier around the legs. The soldier staggered and cut viciously at the sick man. That moment offered Agamemnon's only chance, and he took it. With a hoarse cry he threw himself against the soldier, overbalancing him. The weight of the man's armor did the rest. He fell heavily over Pyliades' body, his sword caught in the sick man's chest, trapped between two ribs.

Agamemnon was on top of him. Releasing his own sword, Agamemnon pulled the knife from his belt and tried to stab the man in the face. The knife bounced off the metal nose guard, breaking at the tip. Agamemnon took better aim and pushed the knife through an opening in the helmet, past a missing cheek guard, into the man's cheek, up into his eye socket, and then, with a twist, into his brain.

Pyliades was croaking, "Good for you, Commander. We'll show these Trojan swine a thing or two . . ."

Agamemnon was already rolling to his feet, just in time to see the other soldier thrust his sword deep into the doctor's belly. The soldier's helmet had come off in the fight. Agamemnon seized him from behind, bent back his head, and cut his throat. There was silence in the house of the sick man.

There were four corpses on the floor. The doctor had just passed away. Pyliades was dead, but with a grin on his face. Agamemnon hoped it was a grin of triumph rather than the sardonic grin of the plague victim.

The soldier whose throat he'd cut lay in a pool of his own blood. Steam was rising from it. The red-bearded soldier, with the knife in his brain, wasn't bleeding much. But he was as dead as the others. Agamemnon himself was uninjured. He could scarcely believe it. He shook himself to make sure.

He was fine. Now, to find Charon.

He reached inside his tunic, pulled out the amethyst that Dionysus had given him. He looked around the room through it.

The room was a dark violet. The proportions weren't as he remembered them. The amethyst seemed to have disturbing properties. Agamemnon experienced a wave of dizziness. He sat down on the floor. Taking a deep breath, he calmed himself with an effort of will and looked around the room again.

He saw what looked like a wisp of smoke taking shape. Was it from the oil lamp? No, that had been broken during the fight—a wonder it hadn't set the place on fire.

At the same time he felt the walls of the hovel changing, expanding, dissolving.

Agamemnon blinked. The room was transforming fast. He was disoriented. He could no longer see the walls. He was outside. He lowered the amethyst to reorient himself.

He was indeed outside. Not even in Mycenae. He was sitting on a boulder on a low, marshy shore. There was a river in front of him. Its waters were black, sleek, oily. It appeared to be twilight or early evening. The sun was nowhere in sight, although it had been afternoon when all this began. There were no stars in the darkness, no light anywhere. Yet he could see. Some distance ahead of him, on a low ridge of rock poking out of the mud, there were four figures. Agamemnon thought he knew who they were. In the gloom he could also make out a sort of dock on the shore beyond the four figures. A long, low boat was tied to one of its pillars, and a man was standing in it.

The man was gesturing, and his voice came through clearly. "Come on, you guys! You know the drill. Come to the boat. The boat's not going to come to you."

The four rose and began walking to the dock. Their steps were the slow, unhurried footsteps of the dead. Agamemnon got up and hurried to join them.

He reached the dock at the same time they did. He recognized the doctor, Pyliades, and the two soldiers.

The man in the boat was urging them to move along, get aboard, get on with it.

"Come on," he said, "I have no time to waste. Do you think you're the only dead awaiting transportation? Move along now, get aboard . . . You there," he said to Agamemnon, "you've got no business here. You're still living."

Agamemnon held up the amethyst. "I need to come aboard. You're Charon, aren't you?"

"His son," the man said. "One of his sons. We're all called Charon. Too much work for the old man alone. Too much for us now, too! But we do what we can. You've got the psychopomp stone, so I guess you can come aboard." He turned to the others. Did you bring any money for the passage?"

They shook their heads. "It was all too sudden," the doctor said.

"I will stand surety for them," Agamemnon said. "And for myself as well. I'll deposit the money wherever you want upon my return. You have the word of Agamemnon, king of kings."

"Make sure you don't forget, or when your time comes, your shade will be left here on the shore."

"How much do you want?" Agamemnon asked.

"The fee is one obol per dead man, but five obols for you because you're alive and weigh more. Go to any Thomas Cook, have them convert your currency into the obol, and deposit it in the Infernal Account."

"Thomas Cook has an infernal account."

"Didn't know that, did you?"

Agamemnon and the others got on Charon's boat. It was narrow, with two rows of built-in benches facing each other. Agamemnon and Pyliades sat on one side, the two soldiers on the other, and the doctor, after a moment's hesitation, sat on a little bench in front of a shelter cabin, at right angles to the benches. Charon untied the mooring line and pushed the boat away from the dock. Once free, he set a steering oar in place, and stood on the decked stern and began to gently scull the boat.

They sat in silence for a while as the boat glided over the dark waters.

At last Agamemnon said, "Is this going to take long?"

"It'll take as long as it takes," Charon said. "Why? You in a rush?"

"Not exactly," Agamemnon said. "Just curious. And interested in getting to the bottom of these mysteries."

"Give your curiosity a rest," Charon said. "Here in the land of the dead, just as in the land of the living, no sooner do you understand one mystery than another comes up to replace it. There's no satisfying curiosity. I remember when Heracles came through here. He was in a tearing hurry, couldn't wait to wrestle with Cerberus and bring him up to the world of the living."

"They say he succeeded," Agamemnon said.

"Sure. But what good did it do him? When he got back, King Eurystheus just had another job for him. There's no end of things to do when you're alive."

The red-bearded soldier abruptly said, "I just want you to know, Agamemnon, that I bear you no ill will for having killed me."

"That's good of you," Agamemnon said. "After you tried so hard to kill me."

"There was nothing personal about it," the red-beard said. "I am Sallices, commander of Aegithus' bodyguard in Mycenae. I was ordered to kill you. I follow orders."

"And look where they have brought you!" Agamemnon said.

"Where else would I be going but here? If not this year, then the next, or the one after that."

"I didn't expect to be killed," the other soldier said. "I am Creonides. My time in Aegisthus' service was over at the end of the week. I was going back to my little farm outside Argos. Returning to my wife and baby daughter."

"I can't believe this self-pitying nonsense," the doctor said. "My name is Strepsiades. I am a respected doctor of Cos, an island famous for its healers. I came to Mycenae for purely humanitarian reasons, to give what help I could to victims of the plague that you fellows carried back from Asia. And how am I rewarded? A villainous soldier kills me so there should be no witnesses to the illegal and immoral execution of his lord."

"But I was just following orders," Creonides said. "My immediate commander, Sallices here, ordered me to do it." "And I," Sallices said, "was following the orders of my commander, the noble Aegisthus."

"But those were immoral orders!" Pyliades said, sitting up and speaking now for the first time in a firm deep voice, with no signs of plague on him. "Any man can see that!"

"Do you really think so?" Sallices asked. "And what if the orders were immoral? What is a soldier supposed to do, question and decide on each order given to him by his superiors? I've heard that you fellows did a few things you weren't so proud of during the Trojan War. Killing the whole population of Troy, and burning the city."

"We were avenging ourselve for the theft of Helen!" Plyiades declared hotly.

"And what was Helen to you?" Sallices asked. "Your wife or daughter? Not a bit of it! The wife of a king not even of your own country, since you are Argives, not Spartans. And anyhow, according to all accounts, the lady left Menelaus and went away with Paris willingly. So what were you avenging?"

"Our slain companions," Pyliades said. "Achilles, our beloved leader."

"Now that is really a laugh," Sallices said. "Your companions were there for the booty, and Achilles was there for the glory. Furthermore, he made his choice. It was prophesied he'd die gloriously at Troy, or lead a long inglorious life if he stayed home.

No one had to die for poor Achilles! He made his choice to die for himself."

There was silence for a while. Then Doctor Strepsiades said, "It must all have seemed different at the time. Men's choices are not presented to them in a reflective space. They come in the clamor and fury of the moment, when a choice must be made at once, for better or worse."

"Is it the same with you, Doctor?" Agamemnon asked. "Or are you alone blameless among us?"

Dr. Strepsiades was silent for a long while. At last he said, "My motives were not entirely humanitarian. I might as well confess this to you, since I will have to tell it to the Judges of the Dead. Queen Clytemnestra sent a herald to our school of physicians on Cos, imploring us for help with the plague, and offering a recompense. I was able to buy a nice little house in the city for my wife and children before I embarked."

"Clytemnestra!" Agamemnon said. "That murderous bitch!"

"She was trying to look out for her people," Strepsiades said. "And besides, she had her reasons. We have it on good authority that you sacrificed your daughter Iphigenia to call up a breeze to carry you and your men to Troy."

"Now wait a minute," Agamemnon said. "There's another version of the story in which the goddess Artemis took Iphigenia to Aulis, to be high priestess to the Taurians."

"I don't care about your face-saving version," Strepsiades said. "It was probably inspired by political reasons. In your heart you know you sacrificed your daughter."

Agamemnon sighed and did not answer.

"And not only did you do that, but you also involved your son, Orestes, in matricide, from which came his agony and his madness."

"None of that could be predicted at the time," Agamemnon said. "Charon, what do you think?"

Charon said, "We have been doing this ferrying for a long time, my father, my brothers, and I, and we share all the information we pick up. We have some questions, too, first and foremost about ourselves."

Charon took a drink of wine from a leather flask lying in the bottom of the boat, and continued.

"What are we here for? Why is there a Charon, or a Charon-function? Are we anything apart from our function? Just as you might ask, Agamemnon, whether you are anything apart from the morally ambiguous story of your life? A story which, for all intents and purposes, has no end and no beginning, and which in one guise or another is always contemporaneous, always happening. Do you ever get any time off from being the Agamemnon-function, do you ever have a chance for some good meaningless fun? Or do you always have to operate your character? Can you do anything without your act proposing a moral question, a dilemma for the ages, ethically unanswerable by its very nature?"

"What about the rest of us?" Strepsiades asked. "Are our lives negligible just because they don't pose a great moral question like Agamemnon's?"

"You and Agamemnon alike are equally negligible," Charon said. "You are merely the actors of old stories, which have more or less significance as the fashions of the times dictate. You are human beings, and you cannot be said to be with or without significance. But one like you, Agamemnon is a symbol and a question mark to the human race, just as the human race is to all intelligent life in the Kosmos."

A chilling thought crossed Agamemnon's mind. "And you, Charon? What are you? Are you human? Are you one of those who brought us the lottery?"

"We are living beings of some sort," Charon said. "There are more questions than answers in this matter of living. And now, gentlemen, I hope this conversation has diverted you, because we are at our destination."

Looking over the side of the boat, Agamemnon could see a dark shoreline coming up. It was low, like the one they had left, but this one had a bright fringe of sandy beach.

The boat made a soft grating sound as Charon ran it onto the sand.

"You are here," Charon said, and then to Agamemnon: "Don't forget you owe me payment."

"Farewell, Commander," said Pyliades. "I hope for a favorable judgment, and to see you again in the palace of Achilles, where they say he lives with Helen, the most beautiful woman who ever was or ever will be. They say the two of them feast the heroes of the Trojan War, and declaim the verses of Homer in pure Greek. I was not a hero, nor do I even speak Greek; but Achilles and Helen may welcome people like me—I have a cheery face now that death has removed the plague from me—and can be counted upon to applaud the great heroes of our Trojan enterprise."

"I hope it turns out so," Agamemnon said. It may be a while before I come there myself, since I am still alive."

The others said their farewells to Agamemnon, and assured him they bore him no ill will for their deaths. Then the four walked in the direction of the Judges' seats, which were visible on a rise of land. But Agamemnon followed a sign that read, "This way to the Orchards of Elysium and the Islands of the Blest." For these were the regions where he expected to find Tiresias.

He walked through pleasant meadowlands, with cattle grazing in the distance. These, he had been told, were part of Helios' herd, which were always straying into this part of Hades, where the grass was greener.

After a while he came to a valley. In the middle of the valley was a small lake. A man stood in the middle of the lake with water up to his mouth. There were trees growing along the lakeshore, fruit trees, and their branches hung over the man in the water, and ripe fruit drooped low over his head. But when he reached up to pick a banana or an apple—both grew on the same tree—the fruit shrank back out of his reach.

Agamemnon thought he knew who this was, so he walked to the shore of the lake and called out, "Hello, Tantalus!" The man in the water said, "Why, if it isn't Agamemnon, ruler of men! Have you come to rule here in hell, Agamemnon?"

"Certainly not," Agamemnon said. "I'm just here for a visit. I've come to talk with Tiresias. Would you happen to know where I might find him?"

"Tirisias keeps a suite in Hades' palace. It's just to your left, over that rise. You can't miss it."

"Thanks very much, Tantalus. Is it very onerous, this punishment the gods have decreed for you? Is there anything I can do?"

"Good of you to ask," Tantalus said. "But there's nothing you could do for me. Besides, this punishment is not as terrible as it might seem. The gods are relentless in decreeing punishment, but they don't much care who actually does it. So a couple of us swap punishments, and thus get some relief from the same thing over and over."

"Who do you trade with, if you don't mind my asking?"

"By no means. A bit of conversation is a welcome diversion. Sisyphus, Prometheus, and I from time to time take over one another's punishments. The exercise of pushing Sisyphus' boulder does me good—otherwise I might get fat—I tend to gorge when I get the chance."

"But to have your liver torn out by a vulture when you take over for Prometheus—that can't be much fun."

"You'd be surprised. The vulture often misses the liver, chews at a kidney instead, much less hurtful. Especially when you consider that here in hell, sensation is difficult to come by. Even King Achilles and Queen Helen, each blessed with the unsurpassed beauty of the other, have a bit of trouble feeling desire without bodies. Pain is a welcome change to feeling nothing."

Agamemnon set out again in the direction Tantalus had indicated. He went across a high upland path, and saw below a pleasant grove of pine trees. There were a dozen or so men and women in white robes, strolling around and engaging in animated conversation.

Agamemnon walked over to them and announced who he was. A woman said, "We know who you are. We were expecting you, since your trip here was mentioned in several of the books that were lost when the great library at Alexandria burned. In honor of your arrival, several of us have written philosophical speeches entitled 'Agamemnon's Lament.' These speeches are about the sort of things we thought we would hear from you."

"Since you knew I was coming, why didn't you wait and hear what I actually did say?"

"Because, Agamemnon, what we did is the philosophical way, and the way of action. We wrote your speech ourselves, instead of passively waiting for you to write it, if you ever would. And, since you are not a philosopher yourself, we thought you were unlikely to cast your thoughts into a presentation sufficiently rigorous for an intelligent and disinterested observer. Nor were you a dramatist, so your thoughts were unlikely to have either the rigor or beauty of a philosophical dramatist such as Aeschylus or Sophocles. Since words once said cannot be unsaid, as conversation permits no time for reflection and revision, we took the liberty of putting what we thought you would be likely to say into proper grammatical form, carefully revised, and with a plethora of footnotes to make the meaning of your life and opinions clear to even the meanest understanding."

"Very good of you, I'm sure," said Agamemnon, who, although deficient in philosophy, had a small but useful talent for irony.

"We don't expect our work will represent you, Agamemnon, the man," another philosopher said. "But we hope we've done justly by you, Agamemnon the position."

"This is all very interesting," Agamemnon said. "But could you tell me now how I might find Tiresias?"

The philosophers conferred briefly. Then one of them said, "We do not recognize Tiresias as a philosopher. He is a mere shaman."

"Is that bad?" Agamemnon asked.

"Shamans may know some true things, but they are not to be relied upon because they do not know why or how they know. Lacking this—"

"Hey," Agamemnon said, "The critique of shamanism is unnecessary. I just want to talk to the guy."

"He's usually in the little grove behind Achilles' palace. Come back if you want a copy of our book of your opinions."

"I'll do that," Agamemnon said, and walked away in the direction indicated.

Agamemnon passed through a little wood. He noticed it was brighter here than in the other parts of Hades he had visited. Although no sun was visible, there was a brightness and sparkle to the air. He figured he was in one of the better parts of the underworld. He was not entirely surprised when he saw, ahead of him, a table loaded with food and drink, and a masked man in a long cloak sitting at it, with an empty chair beside him.

The man waved. "Agamemnon? I heard you were looking for me, so I've made it easy by setting myself in your path. Come have a chair, and let me give you some refreshment."

Agamemnon walked over and sat down. "You are Tiresias?

"I am. Would you like some wine?"

"A glass of wine would be nice." He waited while Tiresias poured, then said, "May I ask why you are masked?"

"A whim," Tiresias said. "And something more. I am a magician, or shaman, to use a term popular in your time. Upon occasion I go traveling, not just here in ancient Greece, but elsewhere in space and time."

"And you don't want to be recognized?"

"It can be convenient, to be not too well known. But that's not the real reason. You see, Agamemnon, knowing someone's face can give you a measure of power over him. So Merlin discovered when he consorted with the witch Nimue, and she was able to enchant him. I do not give anyone power over me if I can help it."

"I can't imagine anyone having power over you."

"I could have said the same for Merlin, and one or two others. Caution is never out of place. Now tell me why you seek me out. I know, of course. But I want to hear it from your own lips."

"It's no secret," Agamemnon said. "My wife, Clytemnestra, and her lover, Aegisthus, have sworn to kill me. I come to you to ask if there is some way out of this Greek trap I am in."

"You are supposed to be slain for having sacrificed your daughter Iphigenia, so your fleet could sail to Troy."

"Now wait a minute!" Agamemnon said. "There's another version in which I did not kill Iphigenia. She's alive now in Aulis!"

"Don't try to deceive me with tricky words," Tiresias said. "Both versions of your story are true. You both killed and did not kill your daughter. But you are guilty in either version, or both. Have you ever heard of Schrödinger's cat? It was a scientific fable popular in your day and age."

"I've heard of it," Agamemnon said. "I can't pretend I ever really understood it."

"The man who concocted the fable is condemned, though no cat was ever slain. And this is true in the two worlds."

Agamemnon was silent for a while. He had been watching Tiresias' mask, which at times seemed made of beaten gold, at other times of golden cloth that billowed when he spoke.

After a while, Agamemnon asked, "What two worlds are you speaking of?"

"The world of Earth with its various time lines, and the world of the lottery."

"So there's no escape?"

"My dear fellow, I never said that. I only wanted to point out that you're in a far more complicated and devious game than you had imagined."

"Why have the people of the lottery done this to us?"

"For the simplest and most obvious of reasons. Because it seemed a good idea to them at the time. Here was Earth, a perfect test case for those who could manipulate the time lines. Here were the stories of the Greeks, which the human world is not finished with yet. It seemed to the makers of the lottery that here was a perfect test case. They decided to live it through again, and again, to see if the moral equations would come out the same."

"And have they?"

The tall figure of Tiresias shrugged, and Agamemnon had the momentary impression that it was not a man's form beneath the cloak

"As I said, it seemed a good idea at the time. But that was then, and yesterday's good idea doesn't look so good today."

"Can you tell me how to get out of here?"

Tiresias nodded. "You'll have to travel on the River of Time."

"I never heard of it."

"It's a metaphor. But the underworld is a place where metaphors become realities."

"Metaphor or not, I don't see any river around here," Agamemnon said.

"I'll show you how to get to it. There's a direct connection, a tunnel from here to Scylla and Charybdis, both of which border the ocean. You'll go through the tunnel which will lead you there."

"Isn't there some other way to get there?"

Tiresias continued, "This is the only way. Once past Scylla and Charybdis, you'll see a line of white breakers. Cross them. You will be crossing the river in the ocean that goes into the past. You don't want that one. You'll see another line of breakers. Cross these and you will be in the river that will carry you from the past into the future."

"The past . . . but where in the future?"

"To a place you will know, Agamemnon. Wait no longer. Do this now."

Agamemnon got up and walked in the direction Tiresias had indicated. When he looked back, the magician was gone. Had he been there in the first place? Agamemnon wasn't sure. The indirections of the lottery were bad enough. But when you added magic . . .

He saw something light-colored, almost hidden beneath shrubbery. It was the entrance to a tube burrowing down into the earth. Wide enough so he could get into it. A tube of some light-colored metal, aluminum, perhaps, and probably built by the lottery people, since aluminum hadn't been used in the ancient world.

Was he really supposed to climb through it? He hesitated, and then saw that there was a woman standing close to the tube. From the look of her, he knew it could only be one woman.

"Helen!"

"Hello, Agamemnon. I don't believe we ever got to meet properly before. I have come to thank you for sending me home to Menelaus. And to offer you my hospitality here in the Elysian Fields."

"You are too kind, Queen Helen. But I must go home now."

"Must you?"

Agamemnon hesitated. Never had he been so sorely tempted. The woman was the epitome of all his dreams. There could be nothing as wonderful as to be loved by Helen.

"But your new husband, Achilles—"

"Achilles has a great reputation, but he is dead, Agamemnon, just as I am. A dead hero does not even compare to a live dog. You are alive. Alive and in hell! Such a wonderful circumstance is rare. When Heracles and Theseus were here, they were only passing through. Besides, I was not here then. Things might have been different if I had been!"

"I am alive, yes," Agamemnon said. "But I will not be allowed to stay here."

"I'll talk Hades into it. He likes me—especially with his wife Persephone gone for half a year at a time."

Agamemnon could glimpse the future. It thrilled him and frightened him. But he knew what he wanted. To stay here with Helen—as much of Helen as he could get. . . .

She held out her hand. He reached toward her—

And heard voices in the distance.

And then he saw shapes in the sky. One was a tall, handsome, thickset middle-aged woman, with long loose dark hair. The other was young, tall, slim, with fair hair piled up on her head and bound with silver ornaments.

The women seemed to be walking down the sky toward him, and they were in vehement discussion.

"You must tell him to his face what he did!" the older woman was saying.

"Mummy, there's no reason to make a scene."

"But he had you killed, can't you understand that? Your throat cut on the altar! You must tell him so to his face."

"Mummy, I don't want to accuse Daddy of so gross a crime. Anyhow, there's another version that says that Artemis rescued me and carried me to the Taurians, where I served as high priestess."

"Agamemnon killed you! If not literally, then figuratively, no matter which version of the story you're following. He's guilty in either version."

"Mummy, calm down, I don't want to accuse him."

"You little idiot, you'll do as I tell you. Look, we're here. There he is, the great killer. Ho, Agamemnon!"

Agamemnon could listen no longer. Letting go of Helen's hand, aware that he was forsaking the good things of death for the pain and uncertainty of life, he plunged into the underbrush and hurled himself into the white metal tube.

Agamemnon had been prepared for a precipitous passage down-ward, but not for the circling movement he underwent as the tube spiraled in its descent. It was dark, and he could see no light from either end. He was moving rapidly, and there seemed nothing he could do to hasten or slow his progress. He was carried along by gravity, and his fear was that his wife and daughter would enter the tube in pursuit of him. He thought that would be more than he could bear.

He continued to fall through the darkness, scraping against the sides of the tube. The ride came to an abrupt end when he sud-denly fell through the end of it. He had a heart-stopping moment in the air, then he was in the water.

The shock of that cold water was so great that he found himself paralyzed, unable to make a move.

And he came out on a corner of a small south Texas town. There was José, standing beside the pickup parked in front of the general store. José gasped when he saw Chris. For a moment he was fro-zen. Then he hurried over to him. "Senor Chrees! Is it you?" There were hugs, embraces. When he'd left for the lottery and distant places, he'd left them to run the ranch. Make what they could out of it. But it was still his ranch, and he was home. Maria said, "I make your favorite, turkey mole tonight!" And then she talked about their cousins in Mexico, some of whom he'd known as a boy.

There was more shopping, and then they were driving down the familiar dirt road with its cardboard stretches, to the ranch. José drove them to the ranch in his old pickup. The ranch looked a little rundown, but very good. Chris lounged around in the kitchen. Chris dozed on the big old sofa, and dreamed of Greece and Troy. And then dinner was served.

After dinner, Chris went into the front room and lay down on the old horsehair sofa. It was deliciously comfortable, and the smells were familiar and soothing. He drifted into sleep, and knew that he was sleeping. He also knew when the dream began: it was when he saw the tall, robed figure of Tiresias.

Tiresias nodded to him and sat down on the end of the couch. It crossed Chris' mind that he might be in danger from a dream-figure, but there was nothing he could do about it.

"I came here to make sure you got home all right. When you enter the River of Time, you can never be too sure."

"**Y**es, I am back where I ought to be. Tell me, Tiresias, is there a danger of Clytemnestra finding me here?"

"She will not find you here. But punishment will. It is inescapable."

"What am I to be punished for? I didn't do anything!"

"When you were Agamemnon, you killed your daughter. For that deed, you owe Necessity a death."

"But the version I'm going by—"

"Forget such puerile nonsense. A young woman has been killed. In Homer, whose rules we're going by, there is no guilt. But there is punishment. Punishment is symbolic of the need for guilt, which still hadn't been invented in Homer's time. We learn through guilt. Thus we return to innocence."

"I thought, if I came home, I'd be free of all that. And anyhow, Artemis—"

"Forget such specious nonsense. It shows why Plato hated sophists. No one learns anything by making the worse case the better. The Agamemnon situation is a curse, and it goes on and on, gathering energy through expiation and repetition. The Greeks had a predilection for creating these situations—Oedipus, Tantalus, Sisyphus, Prometheus, the list is endless. One character after another falls into a situation that must be solved unfairly. The case is never clear, but punishment always follows."

"Does it end here?"

"The expiation for mythic conditions never ends. Opening into the unknowable is the essence of humanity."

Then Chris dreamed that he sat up on his couch, opened his shirt, and said, "Very well, then—strike!"

"A truly Agamemnon-like gesture, Chris. But I am not going to kill you."

"You're not? Why are you here then?"

"At these times, a magician is always present to draw the moral."

"Which is?"

"It is an exciting thing to be a human being."

"You're here to tell me that? So Clytemnestra gets her revenge!"

"And is killed in turn by Orestes. Nobody wins in these dreams, Chris."

"So that's what you came here to tell me."

"That, and to take care of some loose ends. Good-bye, Chris. See you in hell."

And with that, Tiresias was gone.

Chris woke up with a start. The dream of Tiresias had been very real. But it was over now, and he was back at his Texas ranch. He sat up. It was evening. It had turned cold after the sun went down. He got up. Hearing his footsteps, Maria came running in from the kitchen. She was carrying his old suede jacket.

"You put this on, Mr. Chris," she said, and threw the jacket around his shoulders.

The jacket was curiously constricting. Chris couldn't move his arms. And then José was there, and somehow they were bending his head back.

"What are you doing?" Chris asked, but he really didn't have to be told when he caught the flash of steel in José's hand.

"How could you?" he asked.

"Hey, Mr. Chris, we join the lottery, me and Maria!" José said. "I'm going to be the new Agamemnon, she's Clytemnestra, but we take care of the trouble before it begins. We kill the old Agamemnon, so it doesn't have to happen again!"

Chris thought it was just like José to get things mixed up, to try to solve a myth before it began. He wondered if Cassandra had hinted at this outcome, and if he had ignored her, since that was her curse. He sank to the floor. The pain was sharp and brief, and he had the feeling that there was something he had left undone, though he couldn't remember what it was. . . .

He couldn't know it, not at that time, that a man in a yellow buffalo-hide coat had gone to the local branch of Thomas Cook and put in a payment. He had it directed to the Infernal Account. The clerk had never heard of that account, but when he checked with the manager, there it was.

The payment ensured that Chris wouldn't be left for eternity on the wrong shore of Styx, and that the other four were paid for, too.

It was a little nicety on the part of Tiresias. He hadn't had to do it, but he did it anyhow. Those old magicians had class. And anyhow, that's what a good magician does—he ties up loose ends.

SCIENCE
FICTION
DAW

Neal Barrett, Jr.

I wrote six books for Don between 1976 and 1982—four in the *Aldair* series, one called *Stress Pattern* (one of my own favorites), and finally, *The Karma Corps.* I had published three books before that—two in 1970 and one in 1971—and a number of short stories beginning in 1960.

Still, I will always feel that the work I did for Don during that period gave me the right push, and brought in a lot of readers. I'm still getting comments on the *Aldair* series, after all these years, and more than once I've used the themes from those books in my work—most recently in *The Prophecy Machine* and *The Treachery of Kings.* I seem to have this thing about animals getting back at Man for all the dirty tricks he's played on them.

Of course, after *Aldair*, friends and fans would come up, stare at me, and say "Hey, man, PIGS IN SPACE!"

I only had the pleasure of meeting Don once, in New York City, somewhere around 1980. We had corresponded so often, I felt I knew him well, but I discovered he was even more charming and affable in person. And, more than that, a guy who knew writers, and what writing was all about. Science fiction would not have been the same without him.

—NB

GRUBBER
Neal Barrett, Jr.

1

KHIRI remembered a round piece of cold. Far, far away, then chill-bone close. He shrank into the warmdark, back into the never, back into the no, but it was too late to run, too late to hide and he was thrust, rushed, into the born, into the terrible be . . .

He sensed the bigger warms, sensed they were Mothers though they didn't have a name. They kept away the hunger, kept away the cold. There were others like himself nearby, but they were small and useless, too.

It was easy to tell when the Fathers came near. The Mothers became very still, their colors so low he could scarcely sense them at all. They would shiver, they would quiver, they would not-quite-be, they were somewhere Khiri couldn't see.

It was an awesome, wonderful thing to feel the Fathers about. They were big, rumbly, grumbly, their colors were black, vermilion, and blood. He couldn't understand why the Mothers tried hard to get away, tried hard not to be.

The first time a thought like this blinked into his mind, another came to chase it away. The new thought said it was not good to *be* when the Fathers were around. And, in an instant, he found out why. They saw him, knew he was there. Their colors screamed with anger, burned, seared, with a fierce and terrible heat. One, the biggest of them all, came so close he could feel its heavy sniff, feel its shuffle, feel its nuzzle-muzzle-breath.

Khiri didn't move, didn't think, didn't blink. Then, at once, he wasn't anywhere at all. He was *there*, in the not-place, though no one showed him where, no one showed him how.

He dared not show his fear. Now he knew what fear was for. Fear was to show the Fathers you were there. . . .

When the Fathers went away, he knew something else he

hadn't known before. He knew about death. Death was not the same as the not-place, death was even farther off than that. The death hadn't happened to a Mother. It happened to one of the others like himself. It was torn, ragged, thick with a vile and fetid smell. He was curious about it, but the Mothers quickly nosed it away.

Sometimes Khiri would touch the others. The feathery brush of another was a new thing to do. Touching the others, he learned about himself. He learned he was hard with a softness underneath. He learned he could move from one place to the next. There were things in his soft that moved him this way or that. Some of the others were learning, too, and they darted all about until the Mothers made them stop, warned them they had to be still.

During the still, the Mothers would touch him with the slenders they kept beneath their soft. One of the touches meant danger. Others meant stop-come-go. Wake-sleep-bad. Food-wet-dry. And, as he grew, he learned you could string these touches together like a line of pebbles on the ground. When you strung them together, they meant much more than they ever meant alone.

Just as he was getting used to one set of slenders, another sprang from nowhere—and another, and another after that. Whenever something new broke through, he was certain he would die. The larger and thicker the new things became, the greater was the pain.

When it was done, and the new things were there, he learned how useful they could be. He could pick something up, hold it, carry it about. All he could find were pebbles and stones, but it was something new to do.

He began to know others like himself. One of the others was Ghiir. They learned how to fight. They learned how to play. The best thing they learned was they didn't even have to rub slenders to give each other words. They could *think* about the words, and the words were simply there.

They learned they were not all the same. Phaen helped them learn about that. They would have learned more if the Mothers hadn't lashed them soundly and sent Phaen quickly away.

Going was Khiri's favorite thing to do. He had to go alone. Ghiir would go with him to the nears, but Ghiir would never venture to the fars. Khiri saw a number of strange and fearsome things. Colors he'd never seen. Places he could scarcely describe.

The things he would never go near were the *lines*. Whenever they appeared, he would choke up his food and get sick inside his head. The lines were too terrible to see.

2

For a while, he hardly knew the Mothers were gone. He could find his own food now and didn't really care. There seemed no end to the passageways and holes that led everywhere. Sometimes things were high, sometimes they were deep with no bottom at all. Nothing bothered Khiri. His slenders would take him wherever he wished to go.

The strangest thing he found was the thing. It wasn't a Mother, it wasn't a Father, it wasn't like anything he'd ever seen before. He ran his slenders across its dusty shell. To his great surprise, he found it was hard all over, with no soft at all.

"What kind of thing are you?" he asked it. "Soft is for inside, hard is for out. And you have no slenders to touch or feel or know."

"Foolish Khiri. Why do you speak to a thing that cannot speak to you?"

Khiri started. He was so intent on the creature he had not sensed the Mother at all.

"I know I am not supposed to be here," he said. "You don't have to tell me that."

"No. But you are. You are often where you are not supposed to be."

"I cannot understand what I have found. It is not like a Mother or a Father. It is not like me."

"It is dead, Khiri. It has no bloodsmell about it, for it died a long time ago."

"What was it, then? What was it called?"

"It was what you are," the Mother said. "It was just the same as you. It wandered off to a place it shouldn't be."

3

He was larger, now. Nearly as large as the Fathers. He feared them when they came, but knew how take himself where the Fathers couldn't see.

He was learning a great deal. Most of the things he learned were how to hide and stay alive.

Lately, he was learning to understand the lines. He could get much closer to them now. They seldom made him sick, seldom gave him dizzies in the head. He didn't know what the lines could be, but they didn't look at all like they had when he was small.

4

He couldn't remember when he stopped seeing Ghiir. He didn't miss him, didn't want to see him, didn't really want to see anyone at all.

He caught the scent of a Mother once, as he roamed through the endless passages and halls. She sensed his presence as well— tried to hide her colors, tried not to be. But Khiri knew she was there. He could sense the dark odor of her fear.

Why? What was she afraid of, why was she acting this way? For a moment, a new, peculiar kind of rage stirred within him. A picture of Phaen flicked through his head. Only this wasn't Phaen, this was a Mother down the hall.

The smell of the Fathers was heavy on the air. It had been like that all day. Their almost-presence made him tense, irritated, filled him with a hate he had seldom felt before.

When the Fathers finally came, he was so hot with anger he nearly forgot about the not-place, nearly forgot to get away. A

great, rumbly Father nearly had him, a Father hungry for his
bloodsmell, hungry for his life.

Khiri shook with rage, ashamed that he had run, that he had
not stayed to fight. He knew he would have died, but how could
that be worse than the way he felt now?

And, when the Father was out of sight, he looked around for
something to make this feeling go away.

He found the Mother later in the day. He was nearly upon her
before she knew he was there.

"Phaen. I remember you."

"I do not know you. I am Traea, not Phaen."

"You are Phaen," he said.

5

His encounter with the Father had changed him. He was no
longer angry or afraid. Sometimes, he wished he could find that
anger again. Anger was better than feeling nothing at all. He did
not even try to find the Phaen who said it was a Traea.

There were others of his kind around. He did not want to see
them. He waited, now, until the foodplace was clear, a thing he
had never done before.

When the ache was too sharp in his belly, he scuttled to the
foodplace, choking down his meal so he could quickly go away.

He heard the other coming up behind. The intruder was silent,
but Khiri knew who it was.

"Ghiir. Go away. I am at the foodplace now."

"I am here as well," Ghiir said.

"Then you must wait until I am done."

"I do not have to wait for you."

"You will wait, Ghiir."

"No, I will not—"

Ghiir came at him. Without even thinking, Khiri sucked in his
slenders and rolled away. Something whipped him sharply about
the head. Khiri backed off, keeping the thick part of his shell very
low to the ground, and always facing Ghiir. He and Ghiir had

played at fighting, but this was not the same. This was bloodsmell fighting, and Ghiir knew it, too.

Ghiir began a slow half circle to Khiri's right. He watched Ghiir's thick, bony slenders stab the air. They curved in a sharp, wicked arc, like his own. He knew what Ghiir meant to do. He wanted to back Khiri in a corner. Khiri decided that was the thing to let him do.

Ghiir sprang, slashing in quick, vicious thrusts. Khiri blocked every blow, making no effort to strike back. There was a pattern to his foe's attack—the more Ghiir came at him, the better Khiri understood. When the time came, when Ghiir grew weary . . .

Only, Ghiir showed no sign of slowing down. He flailed at Khiri with one blow after the next. Khiri decided the defender's role was not as easy as he'd thought. Ghiir hadn't hurt him, but his fierce assaults were taking their toll. A dull ache had begun at the back of Khiri's head. Each time he countered Ghiir's thrust, he moved a little slower than before.

Ghiir sensed this at once and came in for the kill. He was certain he had Khiri now, and Khiri was not at all sure that he was wrong. He might not stop the next blow, or the one after that. If he made one mistake—

Suddenly, there it was again, Ghiir's familiar pattern. In an instant, Khiri knew what to do next. He moved, caught Ghiir's slenders against his own. Pressed himself against the wall and shoved with all the strength at his command.

Ghiir stumbled, caught off guard. Khiri slashed up at his enemy's soft underbelly. Ghiir jerked back, tried to right himself, but he was helpless now. Khiri found his mark again. Ghiir rolled on his back, quivered once, and lay still.

Khiri was too tired to move. Almost too tired to take himself to the not-place, but he knew he had to do that. Soon, the Fathers would come to see what the bloodsmell was about.

6

In the not-place, Khiri didn't think about Ghiir. He didn't think about anything at all. This was a place for *being*—it was not a place to do.

All he had to do was wait for the Fathers to go away. He knew they were there, for there was something, a shadow-part of himself, that always stayed behind. He didn't understand the shadow-part. He only knew it was there. It would tell him when the Fathers were gone.

He had never, ever stayed so long in the not-place. The longer he stayed, the more he sensed things he had never sensed before. Silent waves of color washed around him. Deep chords of silence hummed and thrummed about, quivered and shivered, whispered and sang.

It was something he had often sensed before, but never in the not-place, always in the real. Now, with a sudden, awesome burst of understanding, he knew what the hum and the thrum was all about. It was the *lines*. There was no mistake about that. But what were they doing in the not place, what were they doing there?

The question had scarcely taken shape before the answer came: *The lines and the not-place were one and the same. That's what the not-place was about—if you knew how to use it, it was the door, the pathway into the lines. . . .*

Khiri was startled by this amazing new knowledge—so vibrant, so clear to him now, he wondered why he hadn't understood it all before.

And there was more, so much more—all the maybes, all the heres and theres, all the somewhens and the wheres.

He knew, too, that now he could not be Khiri-here and Khiri-there. If he followed the lines, he would have to let the Khiri-shadow go. And how could he dare to do that? The Khiri-shadow was the only thing that could take him back to real.

He remembered, then, the real was not all that safe just now. The Fathers were there. They were there for Ghiir's bloodsmell. If he went back now, there would be a Khiri bloodsmell, too.

He knew, with a fear that made him tremble within his shell, that he was slipping back, that he had stayed in the not-place much too long, that the shadow-self was desperately pulling him back.

And, if he could not go to the real, there was only one place to go. He would have to take that step from the not-place, into the lines, into a place that was nowhere at all. . . .

7

It was real, in a way, but not the real he knew. If he looked back at the not-place it was wavy and indistinct—a pale tracery that winked in and out. The world he saw before him was a thing he had never imagined before. High above him was a ball of every color, squeezed into a hotness so strong it seemed to burn through his shell.

There were other things to see. Prickly-colored things beneath his feet. Stone things, immense and unbelievably high. Things that were near. Things that were farther than anything could be.

"You are Khiri. I know who you are."

Khiri was so absorbed in the new things around him he didn't see the Father. He jerked up, nearly frightened out of his wits. He had never really *seen* a Father. Not like this!

The Father seemed unconcerned with his fear. "If you have found your way here, you are ready to go to work. You are not a child anymore. You cannot stand around and stare at the sky. I am busy, and have no time to show you what to do."

"You do not have to show me," Khiri heard himself say. "I know what to do."

The Father didn't answer. As suddenly as he had come, he was gone.

Khiri *did* know.

He was not a child anymore. He knew what he was, and he knew what to do. And, for the first time in his life, he was not afraid of the Fathers anymore. He was not afraid, for he was one of them too.

8

He worked with the others who were new. No one told him what the lines were for, or where they had to go. He knew, though, what was right and what was wrong. He knew if the no-colors felt the way they should. He knew if the silence, if the hum, if the song was the way it ought to be. If it wasn't, he told a Father who was always nearby, a Father who knew what to do.

That was his job. He was a Listener, because he was new. Later, if he learned his job well, he would be a Toner, working in the lines, working in the great, wondrous Pattern itself. The Pattern was what the lines were called, when they all came together exactly as they should.

Khiri came to know other Fathers, those who were new like himself. The older Fathers seldom spoke to him at all. He knew, now, only those who found their way out of the dark down below ever made it to the lines. He remembered Jhiril and Dhiss. He remembered Ghaan. He learned that very few from a single birthing found their way up to the lines.

He worked, and he learned. He learned what his kind were called. They were S'ai, and a S'ai was a grand thing to be, for only the S'ai could do what they could do.

He learned—to his surprise—there were other beings who were not like the S'ai. There were Sacar, great, heavy creatures built close to the earth. Their skin was on the outside, hard, mottled and the color of stone.

He didn't like the Sacar. He liked the Dri even less. Dri looked like brittle bundles of sticks. Sometimes, Khiri could catch the edge of their thoughts. When he did, he drew quickly away. The minds of the Dri were cold, colder than cold could ever be. The Sacar were often about, but the Dri kept to themselves.

Neither the Sacar nor the Dri worked on the Pattern. They knew it was there, but it was something they could only imagine, a thing they could never see. That was something only the S'ai could do.

Khiri learned about the stars. They were hot, fierce points of light, much farther than the one that warmed the world beneath him now. He learned there were other worlds, too, that one of those worlds was his own.

Finally, one of the older Fathers put pictures of that world inside his head. Khiri was stunned. He had never imagined such a place before. He longed to go there himself some day. Could that ever be? The Father couldn't answer, the Father didn't know.

One day, a horde of strange creatures swarmed out of the high, rocky places and tried to kill the Fathers. Khiri, like the others, simply winked into the Pattern and disappeared.

The creatures were two-legs like the Sacar, only not really like them at all. The Sacar fell upon the intruders, and few of them got away.

"Why do they do that," Khiri asked a Father, who would sometimes speak to those who were new. "Why do they want to kill the S'ai?"

"This is their world," said the Father, whose name was Bhir. "It's theirs and they don't want us here."

"Why?" Khiri wanted to know "All the S'ai are doing is building a Pattern. A Pattern is not a thing to fear."

The Father made a noise, the kind of noise an elder makes to show what he thinks of the young.

9

Sometimes, Khiri went with the other Fathers back down in the dark. The Mothers tried to hide, to not-be when they came. When they found a Mother who could not hide her color, she would shut down her senses, and pretend they weren't there. This was the way it had always been among the S'ai.

Often, he would search the dark for younglings, probing and snuffing for the scent of their fear. When he found one, he would rip it, shred it, tear it apart, until only the bloodsmell was there.

Khiri knew this had to be. Those who could not get away would never learn to leave the dark. They would never get past the not-place, never find the lines. They would never truly be S'ai.

10

Khiri knew he had been a Listener long enough. No one had to tell him, Khiri simply knew. He even knew what he would be. He would not be a Toner, even though that was the next thing to be.

He was ready to be a Former now. He could *feel* the Pattern. He knew where it was going, knew how it should be. He could hear it quiver and sing. He could sense it folding in upon itself in endless wheres and whens. He could help it become the very best Pattern the S'ai had ever made.

Khiri found Thil. Thil was a Former. He had been a Former long before Khiri was born.

"Thil," Khiri said, "I am ready to take your place now. I must ask you to leave."

"Why would I want to do that?" Thil said. "You are only a Listener. Even if you were ready to be a Former, there are many ahead of you."

"I am better than they are now. I am better than you—"

Thil winked out of sight. Khiri followed. The place Thil had chosen was a place Khiri had never been before, a place wild and shattered, a fearsome place to be. This was where the Formers came to gather the uncreated power for the Pattern. It was raw, unborn. No-where and no-when.

This was not a fight like Khiri's fight with Ghiir. There would be no bloodsmell here. Khiri fought to lose, not to win. To win was to fade into the chaos of the uncreated void. To lose was to skirt the edge of being, to find that point, and leave Thil forever in what would never be.

Thil was good. But Khiri was right. He was better, and he alone returned to the real again.

11

Khiri learned quickly. Soon, he was setting the pace for many of the older, more experienced S'ai. They didn't like Khiri, but they knew what he could do.

Finally, only Dhin was above him in his skills. Dhin was Master Former. He knew even better than Khiri how good Khiri could be. He showed Khiri everything he knew.

Khiri didn't dream of challenging Dhin's position. You did not fight to become a Master Former. That was a thing for lesser S'ai.

When the time came, Dhin knew it. He had worked long and hard. He had gained great honor and respect among the S'ai. He did not even think about staying to finish his final Pattern. He had done what he could. Khiri would add richness to the firm foundation Dhin had begun. The S'ai would remember it was Dhin's Pattern.

When the next worktime began, Dhin was not there. Khiri knew he was not coming. He knew he was Master Former of the S'ai.

12

When the Pattern was nearly complete, Vhid himself came to see Khiri. Khiri was honored and showed his respect. Vhid was a Planner. There were less than half a hundred Planners among the S'ai, on all the worlds where the S'ai had built a Pattern. More than that, Vhid was a Grand Planner, one of the Eight.

Vhid glanced at the vast tracery of the Pattern, then studied Khiri with some amusement, an emotion rare among the S'ai.

"You are a good Former, Khiri. This is a fine Pattern. You do honor to the S'ai. However, in case it had crossed your mind— and I see that it likely has—you are not yet ready to take my place. You are a good Master Former, but you are not yet a Planner."

Khiri was horrified, and frightened as well. It was a thought he had kept very far back in his mind.

"Master Vhid, I hope you don't imagine—"

"Why not? You have clearly dreamed of becoming everything *else* a S'ai can be. You had best keep dreaming for a while. I will not remind you again. You may well be a Planner. Though not as quickly as you'd like."

Khiri was much too busy to think about being more than what he was. The Pattern was nearing completion, and there was more to be done than there were hours in the day. There were a thousand questions to be answered, a thousand more to be asked. And, in the end, it was up to the Master Former to be sure they were all answered right.

He was in the midst of a dozen tasks when word came that Vhid wished to see him again. *Now?* Khiri wanted to say, but of course he said nothing at all.

Instead, he followed a guide past the long, deep valley directly beneath the Pattern, a path that took him past a high stone place where the two-legs lived—past another to a broad and empty plain.

Khiri was astonished, frightened at the sight, for there lay the starship of the Dri. He knew the ship was there, but only the oldest of the S'ai had ever seen it before.

Khiri did not like the Dri, and wanted nothing to do with anything that was theirs. Still, he could not keep Vhid waiting. He could not tell a member of the Eight he was frightened of a starship of the Dri.

13

Vhid met him under the high, dull portal of the ship. Past Vhid, Khiri could see shadowy forms of both the Sacar and the Dri. This close, the Sacar looked enormous. Even the fragile Dri stood heads above the S'ai, but the Sacar were fearsome giants. How could they live that way, teetering above the ground like uprooted stones? How could they stand to be what they were? They could never imagine the not-place. They could never see the Pattern. They could do nothing the S'ai could do.

Yet, for all the things they were and were not, Khiri was frightened in their presence. And, because he feared them, he hated them all the more.

Khiri understood nothing that had been said at the meeting with the Sacar and the Dri. The Sacar croaked like mud-things. The Dri merely rattled like leaves. If Vhid wished to speak, he touched a shiny thing with his slenders. When he did, a sound came out, but it was not the voice of Vhid.

"I see you are in no great haste to become a Planner now," Vhid said later. "I see you understand it is not the same as working on the Pattern, or any of the things a S'ai was born to do."

"No," said Khiri, "it is not. It is truly like nothing I imagined. I do not see how I can ever become a Planner, for I can scarcely stand to deal with such strange, disgusting forms of life—if, indeed, those things are creatures at all."

"Oh, they are, Khiri. It is difficult to imagine, but they are."

Khiri was dismayed. Even though Vhid had told him much of what was said in the meeting, he understood very little at all.

Maybe there was nothing wrong with being a Master Former. Certainly, it was an honorable thing to be. Not everyone could hope to be a Planner. Why should he try to be something he was not?

While Khiri walked back across the plain with Vhid, two of the giant Sacar came out of the ship. Behind them came a train of the two-legs. They were gaunt and pitiful creatures. Some wore rags of cloth. Some wore nothing at all. Each of the two-legs carried a box upon its shoulders. The boxes were clearly heavy, and, as Khiri watched, one of the creatures staggered and fell.

The box dropped to the ground. The Sacar became very angry. They yelled in their mud-tongue, and beat the two-legs until it lay still. Then they made another of the beings pick up the box and move along.

"Why do they do that?" Khiri wanted to know. "The Sacar have devices that could carry much more. Using the two-legs is not the best way to get things from one place to the next."

"The Sacar use the creatures in this manner because they like to," Vhid said. "Because it shows they are stronger than the two-legs."

Khiri was puzzled. "Everyone knows the Sacar are stronger. If they were not, they would not have conquered this world. We would not be building a Pattern here."

"You are thinking like a S'ai, Khiri. This is why I took you to the meeting, so you would begin to see the things a Planner must understand. The S'ai fight among themselves, for only the best among us must survive.

"We show we are strong, but only to better the S'ai. The Sacar show their strength, because they imagine one day they could find some creature that is stronger than themselves. This has never happened, but it is something they will always fear. Do you understand what I say?"

"I must tell you I do not," Khiri said. "Perhaps I will never be a Planner, Master Vhid."

"You will. But you are not a Planner now."

14

He could not stop thinking about the great starship on the plain—about the strange worlds where the starship had been. He wondered what these worlds were like, and how many he himself might see.

More than anything, though, he thought about the two-legs. He could not forget how the Sacar had beaten it until it was ground into the dirt. Could Vhid be right in what he said? How could a fearsome creature like the Sacar be afraid of anything at all?

As work neared completion, he spent more and more time with Vhid. To Khiri's great relief, the Master Planner did not take him to any more meetings with the Sacar and the Dri. Instead, he set to work teaching Khiri a great many things he had no desire to learn. He learned about the scratches, marks, and see-things the Sacar and the Dri used to remember what they said. He tried to understand the noises they made with their faces when they spoke. He knew, now—though it was almost impossible to believe—that noises were the *only* way they could communicate at all.

"You will learn," Vhid told him more than once. "It simply takes time. You cannot understand other beings simply because you know what they are saying. That, I must tell you, is the easiest part. What they *mean* is something else.

"The Sacar do not like the Dri, and the Dri do not like them. One is stronger. One knows how to build machines. The S'ai do neither of these. Yet, we do something the others cannot. The S'ai can make a Pattern. That is why they need us. And that is why, young Khiri, they fear us and hate us more than they fear and hate each other, or any of the other creatures among the stars."

Vhid paused to let Khiri consider this. "Now you see why it is vital to learn their ways. Why it is so important to become a good Planner. It is the highest calling among the S'ai, the greatest thing you can ever hope to do. . . ."

15

In the days that followed, he had many talks with Vhid. One of the things a Planner had to do was learn to think like the Sacar and the Dri. Of course, this was impossible to do, but a Planner had to try.

The most dreadful, appalling thing he learned was how the Sacar and the Dri looked upon the S'ai. Each in their way, scorned the S'ai, and laughed at their manner and appearance. Each, in the tongue they used to speak to one another, called them The Grubbers, a name they had for ugly creatures that scurried about beneath the ground.

"They have no right to demean us like that," Khiri said, outraged at Vhid's words. "If we stopped building their Patterns, they would regret this attitude. They would value what the S'ai do then!"

For a moment, Vhid said nothing at all. Instead, he looked up into the dark night sky.

"As you know, Khiri, the S'ai have a world of their own. Though you have never seen it, you have been given the pictures in your head."

Yes, Vhid, I have."

"And you know what a starship can do to a world. You are aware of that as well."

"They would never do that. They cannot build a Pattern without the S'ai."

"This is so. And this is why the S'ai are free, and yet not free at all. The Sacar are a savage, thoughtless race. If they had their way, they would treat us no better than they do the creatures here.

"The Dri, though, are cunning and wise. They do not know us well—they can never be certain what these *grubber* things might do if we were faced with a terrible choice some day.

"And that is what a Planner is for, Khiri. Now you understand what I am—and what you, too, must be."

16

When the task was done, when there was nothing more to do, he stood with the others in the night and looked at the Pattern against the sky. Its perfection laced the stars from one horizon to the next. It bound this world in its delicate web of power. It sang a song that only the S'ai could ever hear. It glowed with a color that only the S'ai could see.

In the morning, the starship would rise above the plain and give itself to the Pattern. For a moment that never was, a time that could never be, it would touch the pale breath of forever. Then, it would wink along the Patterns of a thousand other worlds, trailing a wisp of nowhere in its wake.

Khiri wondered where this journey would take him, and what he might see. He knew, only, there would be another world, and another Pattern to build.

He thought about the two-legs, huddled in fear in their rocky hollows above the plain. For a moment, he imagined he could hear them, see the faint whisper of their minds. It was scarcely a sound, scarcely an image at all, for the two-legs were not the S'ai. They could never know the Pattern, never know the beauty he could see, for they were as blind to that great wonder as the Sacar and the Dri. . . .

C. J. Cherryh

In 1975, something rather incredible happened at DAW Books. My father received two unsolicited manuscripts from an unpublished writer whom he knew, almost at once, was destined to become one of the great voices in science fiction. The writer was a young Oklahoma teacher of classics, and her name was Carolyn Janice Cherry.

Carolyn Janice Cherry.

In 1975, science fiction was still a male-dominated genre. Would a buy buy a science fiction book by a writer with such a feminine name? Would a man, for that matter? This young writer's name was really more suited to an author of romances (perish the thought!) Even the veteran author Alice Norton had had to use the androgynous pen name Andre throughout her career. But how would Ms. Cherry react if a publisher called her from out of the blue and said, "We like your books, but your name—it just won't work!" Don thought it over. What if, rather than asking her to completely change her name, he just proposed a slight alteration. Many female authors had dropped their given names in favor of their initials, so proposing that the author use C.J. rather than Carolyn, would be obvious. But what about Cherry? It was really a very nice name, bringing to mind not only images of sweet fruit, but of lovely blossoms as well, but it just wouldn't sell in SF—no way. What if one were to put a silent 'h' on the end, making it Cherryh? C.J. Cherryh—it would still be pronounced the same way, was still essentially the same name—*her* name—but now it looked rather exotic, almost alien. How perfect!

Luckily, Carolyn liked the idea.

And so C. J. Cherryh was born. . . .

And she went on to become, just as Don had predicted, one of the greatest voices our field has ever heard. An author with more than fifty books to her credit, who has won three Hugo Awards (so far), and been the inspiration for numerous hard science fiction writers of both genders. Her vision of the far future, of life in space, her depiction of humans living among alien races is unparalleled because it is so *real.* When I read her books, I can truly believe *that's how it could be.*

Her fans call her C.J., her family calls her Janice, but to me she'll always be Carolyn.

—BW

THE SANDMAN, THE TINMAN, AND THE BETTYB
C. J. Cherryh

CRAZYCHARLIE: *Got your message, Unicorn. Meet for lunch?*

DUTCHMAN: *Charlie, what year?*

CRAZYCHARLIE: *Not you, Dutchman. Talking to the pretty lady.*

T_REX: *Unicorn's not a lady.*

CRAZYCHARLIE: *Shut up. Pay no attention to them, Unicorn. They're all jealous.*

T_REX: *Unicorn's not answering. Must be alseep.*

CRAZYCHARLIE: *Beauty sleep.*

UNICORN: *Just watching you guys. Having lunch.*

LOVER 18: *What's for lunch, pretty baby?*

UNICORN: *Chocolate. Loads of chocolate.*

T_REX: *Don't do that to us. You haven't got chocolate.*

UNICORN: *I'm eating it now. Dark chocolate. Mmmm.*

T_REX: *Cruel.*

CRAZYCHARLIE: *Told you she'd show for lunch. Fudge icing, Unicorn . . .*

CRAZYCHARLIE: *. . . With ice cream.*

DUTCHMAN: *I remember ice cream.*

T_REX: *Chocolate ice cream.*

FROGPRINCE: *Stuff like they've got on B-dock. There's this little shop . . .*

T_REX: *With poofy white stuff.*

DUTCHMAN: *Strawberry ice cream.*

FROGPRINCE: *. . . that serves five different flavors.*

CRAZYCHARLIE: *Unicorn in chocolate syrup.*

UNICORN: *You wish.*

HAWK29: *With poofy white stuff.*

UNICORN: *Shut up, you guys.*

LOVER18: *Yeah, shut up, you guys. Unicorn and I are going to go off somewhere.*

CRAZYCHARLIE: *In a thousand years, guy.*

Ping. Ping-ping. Ping.

Sandwich was done. Sandman snagged it out of the cooker, everted the bag, and put it in for a clean. Tuna san and a coffee fizz, ersatz. He couldn't afford the true stuff, which, by the time the freight ran clear out here, ran a guy clean out of profit—which Sandman still hoped to make but it wasn't the be-all and end-all. Being out here was.

He had a name. It was on the records of his little two-man op, which was down to one, since Alfie'd had enough and gone in for food. Which was the first time little *BettyB* had ever made a profit. No mining. Just running the buoy. Took a damn long time running in, a damn long time running out, alternate with *Penny-Girl*. Which was how the unmanned buoys that told everybody in the solar system where they were kept themselves going. Dozens of buoys, dozens of little tenders making lonely runs out and back, endless cycle. The buoy was a robot. For all practical purposes *BettyB* was a robot, too, but the tenders needed a human eye, a human brain, and Sandman was that. Half a year running out and back, half a year in the robot-tended, drop-a-credit pleasures of Beta Station, half the guys promising themselves they'd quit the job in a couple more runs, occasionally somebody doing the deed and going in. But most didn't. Most grew old doing it. Sandman wasn't old yet, but he wasn't young. He'd done all there was to do at Beta, and did his favorites and didn't think about going in permanently, because when he was going in and had Beta in *BettyB's* sights, he'd always swear he was going to stay, and by the time six months rolled around and he'd seen every vid and drunk himself stupid and broke, hell, he was ready to go back to the solitude and the quiet.

He was up on three months now, two days out from Buoy 17, and the sound of a human voice—his own—had gotten odder and more welcome to him. He'd memorized all the verses to *Matty Groves* and sang them to himself at odd moments. He was working on St. Mark and the complete works of Jeffrey Farnol. He'd downloaded Tennyson and Kipling and decided to learn French on the return trip—not that any of the Outsiders ever did a damn thing with what they learned and he didn't know why French and not Italian, except he thought his last name, Ives, was French, and that was reason enough in a spacescape void of reasons and a spacetime hours remote from actual civilization.

He settled in with his sandwich and his coffee fizz and watched the screen go.

He lurked, today. He usually lurked. The cyber-voices came and went. He hadn't heard a thing from BigAl or Tinman, who'd been in the local neighborhood the last several years. He'd asked around, but nobody knew, and nobody'd seen them at Beta. Which was depressing. He supposed BigAl might have gone off to another route. He'd been a hauler, and sometimes they got switched without notice, but there'd been nothing on the boards. Tinman might've changed handles. He was a spooky sort, and some guys did, or had three or four. He wasn't sure Tinman was sane—some weren't, that plied the system fringes. And some ran afoul of the law, and weren't anxious to be tracked. Debts, maybe. You could get new ID on Beta, if you knew where to look, and the old hands knew better than the young ones, who sometimes fell into bodacious difficulties. Station hounds had broken up a big ring a few months back, forging bank creds as well as ID—just never trust an operation without bald old guys in it, that was what Sandman said, and the Lenny Wick ring hadn't, just all young blood and big promises.

Which meant coffee fizz was now pricey and scarce, since the Lenny Wick bunch had padded the imports and siphoned off the credits, which was how they got caught.

Sandman took personal exception to that situation: anything that got between an Outsider and his caffeine ought to get the long, cold walk in the big dark, so far as that went. So Lenny Wick hadn't got a bit of sympathy, but meanwhile Sandman wasn't too surprised if a few handles out in the deep dark changed for good and all.

Nasty trick, though, if Tinman was Unicorn. No notion why anybody ever assumed Unicorn was a she. They just always had.

FROGPRINCE: *So what are you doing today, Sandman? I see you . . .*

Sandman ate a bite of sandwich. Input:

SANDMAN: *Just thinking about Tinman. Miss him.*
FROGPRINCE: *. . . lurking out there.*
SANDMAN: *Wonder if he got hot ID. If he's lurking, he can leave me word.*

T_REX: *Haven't heard, Sandman, sorry.*
UNICORN: *Won't I do, Sandman?*
SANDMAN: *Sorry, Unicorn. Your voice is too high.*
UNICORN: *You female, Sandman?*
T_REX: *LMAO.*
FROGPRINCE: *LL&L.*
SANDMAN: *No.*
DUTCHMAN: *Sandman is a guy.*
UNICORN: *You don't like women, Sandman?*
T_REX: *Shut up, Unicorn.*
SANDMAN: *Going back to my sandwich now.*
UNICORN: *What are you having, Sandman?*
SANDMAN: *Steak and eggs with coffee. Byebye.*

He ate his tuna san and lurked, sipped the over-budget coffee fizz. They were mostly young. Well, FrogPrince wasn't. But mostly young and on the hots for money. They were all going to get rich out here at the far side of the useful planets and go back to the easy life at Pell. The cyberchat mostly bored him, obsessive food and sex. Occasionally he and FrogPrince got on and talked mechanics or, well-coded, what the news was out of Beta, what miners had made a find, what contracts were going ahead or falling through.

Tame, nowadays. Way tame. Unicorn played her games. Dutchman laid his big plans on the stock market. They were all going to eat steak and eggs every meal, in the fanciest restaurant on Pell.

Same as when the war ended, the War to end all wars, well, ended at least for the next year or so, before the peace heated up. Everybody was going to live high and wide and business was just going to take off like the proverbial bat out of the hot place.

Well, it might take off for some, and it had, but Dutchman's guesses were dependably wrong, and what mattered to them out here was the politics that occasionally flared through Beta, this or that company deciding to private-enterprise the old guys out of business. They'd privatized mining. That was no big surprise.

But—Sandman finished the coffee fizz and cycled the container—they didn't privatize the buoys. Every time they tried, the big haulers threatened no-show at Pell, because they knew the rates would go sky-high. More, the privatizers also knew they'd come under work-and-safety rules, which meant they'd actually have to provide quality services to the tenders, and bring a tender-ship like *BettyB* up to standard—or replace her with a robot, which hadn't worked the last time they'd tried it, and which, to do the job a human could, cost way more than the privatizers wanted to hear about.

So Sandman and *BettyB* had their job, hell and away more secure than, say, Unicorn, who was probably a kid, probably signed on with one of the private companies, probably going to lose her shirt and her job the next time a sector didn't pan out as rich with floating junk as the company hoped.

But the Unicorns of the great deep were replaceable. There were always more. They'd assign them out where the pickings were supposed to be rich and the kids, after doing the mapping, would get out of the job with just about enough to keep them fed and bunked until the next big shiny deal . . . the next time the companies found themselves a field of war junk.

Just last year the companies had had a damn shooting war, for God's sake, over the back end of a wrecked warship. They'd had Allied and Paris Metals hiring on young fools who'd go in there armed and stupid, each with a district court order that had somehow, between Beta and Gamma sectors, ended up in the Supreme Court way back on Pell—but not before several young fools had shot each other. Then Hazards had ruled the whole thing was too hot to work.

Another bubble burst. Another of Dutchman's hot stock tips gone to hell.

And a raft of young idiots got themselves stranded at Beta willing to work cheap, no safety questions asked.

So the system rolled on.

T_REX: *Gotta go now. Hot date.*
FROGPRINCE: *Yeah. In your dreams, T_Rex.*

You made the long run out from Beta, you passed through several cyberworlds—well, transited. Blended through them. You traveled, and the cyberflow from various members of the net just got slower and slower in certain threads of the converse. He could key up the full list of participants and get some conversations that would play out over hours. He'd rather not. Murphy's law said the really vital, really interesting conversations were always on the edges, and they mutated faster than your input could reach them. It just made you crazy, wishing you could say something timely and knowing you'd be preempted by some dim-brain smartass a little closer. So you held cyberchats of the mind, imagining all the clever things you could have said to all the threads you could have maintained, and then you got to thinking how far out and lonely you really were.

He'd rather not. Even if the local chat all swirled about silly Unicorn. Even if he didn't know most of them: space was bigger, out here. Like dots on an inflated balloon, the available number of people was just stretched thin, and the ones willing to do survey and mine out here weren't necessarily the sanest.

Like buoy-tenders, who played chess with ghost-threads out of the dark and read antique books.

Last of the coffee fizz. He keyed up the French lessons. *Comment allez-vous, mademoiselle?* And listened and sketched, a Teach Yourself Art course, correspondence school, that wanted him to draw eggs and put faces on them: he multitasked. He filled his screen with eggs and turned them into people he knew, some he liked, some he didn't, while he muttered French. It was the way to stay sane and happy out here, while *BettyB* danced her way along the prescribed—

Alarm blipped. Usually the racket was the buoy noting an arrival, but this being an ecliptic buoy, it didn't get action itself, just relayed from the network, time-bound, just part of the fabric of knowledge—a freighter arrived at zenith. Somebody left at nadir.

Arrival, it said. Arrival within its range and coming—

God, coming fast. He scrambled to bring systems up and listen to Number 17. Number 17, so far as a robot could be, was in a state of panic, sending out a warning. *Collision, collision, collision.*

There was an object out there. Something Number 17 had heard, as it waited to hear—but Number 17 didn't *expect* trouble anymore. Peacetime ships didn't switch off their squeal. Long-range scan on the remote buoys didn't operate, wasn't switched on these days—power-saving measure, saving the corporations maintenance and upkeep. Whatever it picked up was close. Damned close.

Maintenance keys. Maintenance could test it. He keyed, a long, long way from it receiving: turn on, wake up longscan, Number 17, Number 17.

He relayed Number 17's warning on, system-wide, hear and relay, hear and relay.

He sent into the cyberstream:

SANDMAN: *Collision alert from Number 17. Heads up.*

But it was a web of time-stretch. A long time for the nearest authority to hear his warning. Double that to answer.

Number 17 sent an image, at least part of one. Then stopped sending.

Wasn't talking now. Wasn't talking, wasn't talking.

Hours until Beta Station even noticed. Until Pell noticed. Until the whole buoy network accounted that Number 17 wasn't transmitting, and that that section of the system chart had frozen. Stopped.

The image was shadowy. Near-black on black.

"Damn." An Outsider didn't talk much, didn't use voice, just the key-taps that filled the digital edges of the vast communications web. And he keyed.

SANDMAN: *Number 17 stopped transmitting. Nature of object* . .
SANDMAN. . . . *unknown. Vectors from impact unknown . . .*
SANDMAN: *. . . Impact one hour fifteen minutes before my location.*

The informational wavefront, that was. The instant of spacetime with 17's warning had rolled past him and headed past Frog-Prince and Unicorn and the rest, before it could possibly reach Beta. They lived in a spacetime of subsequent events that widened like ripples in a tank, until scatter randomized the information into a universal noise.

And *BettyB* was hurtling toward Number 17, and suddenly wasn't going anywhere useful. She might get the order to go look-see, in which case braking wasn't a good idea. She might get the order to return, but he doubted it would come for hours. Decision-making took time in boardrooms. Decision-making had to happen hell and away faster out here, with what might be pieces loose.

He shifted colors on the image, near-black for green. Nearer black for blue. Black stayed black.

Ball with an inward or outward dimple and a whole bunch of planar surfaces. He didn't like what he saw. He transmitted his raw effort as he built it. Cigar-shape. Gray scale down one side of the image, magnification in the top line. Scan showed a flock of tiny blips in the same location. Scan was foxed. Totally.

"God."

SANDMAN: *Transmitting image. Big mother.*

A keystroke switched modes. A button-click rotated the colorized image. Not a ball. Cigar-shape head-on. Cigar-shape with deflecting planes all over it.

SANDMAN: *It's an inert. An old inert missile, inbound. It's blown Buoy 17 . . .*
SANDMAN: *. . . Trying to determine v. Don't know class or mass. Cylindrical.*
SANDMAN: *. . . Buoy gone silent. May have lost antenna. May have lost orientation . . .*
SANDMAN: *. . . May have been destroyed. Warn traffic of possible buoy fragments . . .*
SANDMAN: *. . . originating at buoy at 1924h, fragments including . . .*
SANDMAN: *. . . high-mass power plant and fuel.*

Best he could do. The wavefront hadn't near reached Beta. And the buoy that could have given him longscan wasn't talking—or no longer existed. The visual out here in the dark, where the sun was a star among other stars, gave him a few scattered flashes of gray that might be buoy fragments. He went on capturing images.

BettyB went hurtling on toward the impact-point. Whatever was out there might have clipped the buoy, or might have plowed through the low-mass girder-structures like a bullet through a snowball, sending solid pieces of the buoy flying in all directions, themselves dangerous to small craft. The inert, the bullet coming their way, was high-v and high-mass, a solid chunk of metal that might have been traveling for fifty years and more, an iron slug fired by a long-lost warship in a decades-ago war. Didn't need a warhead. Inerts tended to be far longer than wide because the fire mechanism in the old carriers stored them in bundles and fired them in swarms, but no matter how it was oriented when it hit, it was a killer—and if it tumbled, it was that much harder to predict, cutting that much wider a path of destruction. Mass and velocity were its destructive power. An arrow out of a crossbow that, at starship speeds, could take out another ship, wreck a space station, cheap and sure, nothing fragile about it.

After the war, they'd swept the lanes—Pell system had been a battle zone. Ordnance had flown every which way. They'd worked for years. And the last decade—they'd thought they had the lanes clear.

Clearly not. He had a small scattering of flashes. He thought they might be debris out of the buoy, maybe the power plant, or one of the several big dishes. He ran calculations, trying to figure what was coming, where the pieces were going, and he could use help—God, he could use help. He transmitted what he had. He kept transmitting.

FROGPRINCE: *Sandman, I copy. Are you all right?*
SANDMAN: *FrogPrince, spread it out. I need some help here . . .*
UNICORN: *Is this a joke, Sandman?*
SANDMAN: *I'm sending raw feed, all the data I've got. Help. Mayday.*
LOVER18: *Sandman, what's up?*
SANDMAN: *Unicorn, this is serious.*
DUTCHMAN: *I copy, Sandman. My numbers man is on it.*

Didn't even know Dutchman had a partner. A miner's numbers man was damned welcome on the case. Desperately welcome.

Meanwhile Sandman had his onboard encyclopedia. He had his histories. He hunted, paged, ferreted, trying to find a concrete answer on the mass of the antique inerts—which was only part of the equation. Velocity and vector depended on the ship that, somewhere out there, fifty and more years ago, had fired what might be one, or a dozen inerts. There could be a whole swarm inbound, a decades-old broadside that wouldn't decay, or slow, or stop, forever, until it found a rock to hit or a ship full of people, or a space station, or a planet.

Pell usually had one or another of the big merchanters in.

Sandman searched his news files, trying to figure. The big ships had guns. Guns could deal with an inert, at least deflecting it— *if* they had an armed ship in the system. A big ship could chase it down, even grab it and decelerate it. He fed numbers into what was becoming a jumbled thread of inputs, speculations, calculations.

Hell of it was—there was one thing that would shift an inert's course. One thing that lay at the heart of a star system, one thing that anchored planets, that anchored moons and stations: that gravity well that led straight to the system's nuclear heart— the sun itself. A star collected the thickest population of planets, and people, and vulnerable real estate to the same place as it collected stray missiles. And no question, the old inert was infalling toward the sun, increasing in v as it went, a man-made comet with a comet-sized punch, that could crack planetary crust, once it gathered all the v the sun's pull could give it.

T_Rex: *Sandman, possible that thing's even knocked about the Oort Cloud.*
T_Rex: *Perturbed out of orbit.*
Unicorn: *Perturbing us.*
Lover18: *I've got a trajectory on that buoy debris chunk . . .*
Lover18: *. . . no danger to us.*

Alarm went off. *BettyB* fired her automated avoidance system. Sandman hooked a foot and both arms and clung to the counter, stylus punching a hole in his hand as his spare styluses hit the bulkhead. The bedding bunched up in the end of the hammock. It was usually a short burst. It wasn't. Sandman clung and watched the camera display, as something occluded the stars for a long few seconds.

"Hell!" he said aloud, alone in the dark. Desperately, watching a juggernaut go by him. "Hell!" One human mote like a grain of dust.

Then he saw stars. It was past him. What had hit the buoy was past him and now—now, damn, he and the buoy were two points on a straight line: he had the vector; and he had the camera and with that, God, yes, he could calculate the velocity.

He calculated. He transmitted both, drawing a simple straight line in the universe, calamity or deliverance reduced to its simplest form.

He extended the line toward the sun.

Calamity. Plane of the ecliptic, with Pell Station and its heavy traffic on the same side of the sun as Beta. The straight line extended, bending at the last, velocity accelerating, faster, faster, faster onto the slope of a star's deep well.

DUTCHMAN: *That doesn't look good, Sandman.*
UNICORN: *:(*
DUTCHMAN: *Missing Pell. Maybe not missing me . . .*
DUTCHMAN: *. . . Braking. Stand by.*
UNICORN: *Dutchman, take care.*
LOVER18: *Letting those damn things loose in the first place . . .*
T_REX: *Not liking your calculations, Sandman.*
LOVER18: *. . . what were they thinking?*
FROGPRINCE: *I'm awake. Sandman, Dutchman, you all right out there?*
DUTCHMAN: *I can see it . . .*
UNICORN: *Dutchman, be all right.*
DUTCHMAN: *I'm all right . . .*
DUTCHMAN: *. . . it's going past now. It's huge.*
HAWK29: *What's going on?*
LOVER18: *Read your damn transcript, Hawkboy.*
CRAZYCHARLIE: *Lurking and running numbers.*
DUTCHMAN: *It's clear. It's not that fast.*
SANDMAN: *Not that fast *yet.**
DUTCHMAN: *We're running numbers, too. Not good.*
SANDMAN: *Everybody crosscheck calculations. Not sure . . .*
SANDMAN: *. . . about gravity slope . . .*
CRAZYCHARLIE: *Could infall the sun.*
UNICORN: *We're glad you're alright, Dutchman.*
SANDMAN: *If it infalls, not sure how close to Pell.*
WILLWISP: *Lurking and listening. Relaying to my local net.*
T_REX: *That baby's going to come close.*

Sandman reached, punched a button for the fragile long-range dish. On *BettyB*'s hull, the arm made a racket, extending, working the metal tendons, pulling the silver fan into a metal flower, already aimed at Beta.

"Warning, warning, warning. This is tender *BettyB* calling all craft in line between Pell and Buoy 17. A rogue inert has taken out Buoy 17 and passed my location, 08185 on system schematic. Looks like it's infalling the sun. Calculations incomplete. Buoy 17 destroyed, trajectory of fragments including power plant all uncertain, generally toward Beta. Mass and velocity sufficient to damage. Relay, relay, relay and repeat to all craft in system. Transmission of raw data follows."

He uploaded the images and data he had. He repeated it three times. He tried to figure the power plant's course. It came up headed through empty space.

CRAZYCHARLIE: *It's going to come damn close to Pell . . .*

CRAZYCHARLIE: *. . . at least within shipping lanes and insystem hazard.*

DUTCHMAN: *I figure same. Sandman?*

UNICORN: *I'm transmitting to Beta.*

WILLWISP: *Still relaying your flow.*

HAWK29: *Warn everybody.*

UNICORN: *It's months out for them.*

DUTCHMAN: *Those things have a stealth coating. Dark . . .*

DUTCHMAN: *. . . Hard to find. Easy to lose.*

UNICORN: *Lot of metal. Pity we can't grab it . . .*

FROGPRINCE: *Don't try it, Unicorn. You and your engines . . .*

UNICORN: *. . . But it's bigger than I am.*

FROGPRINCE: *. . . couldn't mass big enough.*

UNICORN: *I copy that, Froggy . . .*

DUTCHMAN: *It's going to be beyond us. All well and good if it goes . . .*

UNICORN: *. . . Thanks for caring.*

DUTCHMAN: *. . . without hitting anything. Little course change here . . .*

DUTCHMAN: *. . . and Pell's going to have real trouble tracking it.*

HAWK29: *I feel a real need for a sandwich and a nap . . .*

UNICORN: *Hawk, that doesn't make sense.*

HAWK29: *. . . We've sent our warning. Months down, Pell will fix it . . .*

HAWK29: *. . . All we can do. It's relayed. Passing out of our chat soon.*

T_REX: *Sandman, how sure your decimals?*

FROGPRINCE: *We can keep transmitting, Hawk. We can tell Sandman . . .*

FROGPRINCE: *. . . we're sorry he's off his run. His buoy's destroyed . . .*

FROGPRINCE: *. . . He's got to find a new job . . .*

UNICORN: *They'll be running construction and supply out. I'll apply, too.*

FROGPRINCE: *Use a little damn compassion.*

SANDMAN: *T_Rex, I'm sure. I was damned careful.*

T_REX: *You braked.*

DUTCHMAN: *We both braked.*

SANDMAN: *I've got those figures in. Even braking, I'm sure of the numbers.*

T_REX: *That's real interesting from where I sit.*

FROGPRINCE: *T_Rex, where are you?*

T_REX: *About an hour from impact.*

UNICORN: *Brake, T_Rex!*

SANDMAN: *T_Rex, it's 5 meters wide, no tumble.*

T_REX: *Sandman, did I ever pay you that 52 credits?*

Tinman?

Damn. *Damn!* Fifty-two cred in a Beta downside bar. Fifty-two cred on a tab for dinner and drinks, the last time they'd met. Tinman had said, at the end, that things had gone bad. Crazy Tinman. Big wide grin hadn't been with them that supper. He'd known something was wrong.

He'd paid the tab when Tinman's bank account turned up not answering.

The Lenny Wick business. The big crunch that took down no few that had thought Beta was a place to get rich, and it wasn't, and never would be.

SANDMAN: *Dutchman, you copy that? T_Rex owes me 52c.*

DUTCHMAN: *Sandman, we meet on dockside, I owe you a drink . . .*

DUTCHMAN: *. . . for the warning.*

Dutchman didn't pick up on it. Or didn't want to, having fingers anywhere on the Lenny Wick account not being popular with the cops. Easy for Pell to say it was all illegal. Pell residents didn't have a clue how it was on Beta Station payroll. Didn't know how rare jobs were, that weren't.

The big score. The way out. Unicorns by the shipload fell into that well. And a few canny Tinmen got caught trying to skirt it just close enough to catch a few of the bennies before it all imploded.

SANDMAN: *I copy that, T_Rex. If you owe me money . . .*
SANDMAN: *. . . get out of there.*
T_REX: *Going to be busy for a few minutes.*
UNICORN: *T_Rex, we love you.*
T_REX: *Flattery, flattery, Unicorn. I know your heart's . . .*
DUTCHMAN: *You take care, T_Rex.*
T_REX: *. . . for FrogPrince. (((Poof.)))*
UNICORN: *He's vanished.*
LOVER18: *This isn't a damn sim, Unicorn.*
UNICORN: *:(*
FROGPRINCE: *T_Rex, can we help you?*
UNICORN: *Don't distract him, Froggy. He's figuring.*

Good guess, that was. Sandman called up the system chart—the buoys produced it, together, constantly talking, over a time lag of hours; but theirs wasn't accurate anymore. The whole Pell System chart was out of date now, because their buoy wasn't talking anymore. The other buoys hadn't missed it yet, and Pell wouldn't know it for hours, but the information wasn't updating, and the source he had right now wasn't Buoy 17 anymore.

They all had numbers on that chart. But the cyberchat never admitted who was Sandman and who was Unicorn. It never had mattered.

They all knew who Sandman was, now. He'd transmitted his chart number. He could look down the line and figure that Dutchman, most recently near that juggernaut's path, was 80018.

He drew his line on the flat-chart and knew where T-Rex was, and saw what his azimuth was, and saw the arrow that was his flatchart heading and rate.

He made the chart advance.

Tick.

Tick.

Tick.

SANDMAN: *I've run the chart, T_Rex. Brake to nadir . . .*
SANDMAN: *. . . Best bet.*

The cyberflow had stopped for a moment. Utterly stopped. Then:

UNICORN: *I've run the chart, too, T_Rex. If you can brake now, please do it.*
SANDMAN: *I second Unicorn.*

What the hell size operations had Tinman signed on to? A little light miner that could skitter to a new heading?

Some fat company supply ship, like *BettyB*, that would slog its *v* lower only over half a critical hour?

SANDMAN: *T_Rex, Dutchman, I'm dumping my cargo . . .*
SANDMAN: *. . . I'm going after him.*
HAWK29: *BetaControl's going to have a cat.*
UNICORN: *Shut up, Hawk. I'm going, too.*
SANDMAN: *T_Rex, if you can't brake in time, have you got a pod? . . .*
SANDMAN: *. . . I'm coming after you. Go to the pod if you've got one . . .*
SANDMAN: *. . . Use a suit if not. Never mind the ETA . . .*
SANDMAN: *. . . I'll get there in time.*
FROGPRINCE: *Sandman, go.*
SANDMAN: *I'm going to full burn, hard as I can . . .*
SANDMAN: *. . . Right down that line.*

Button pushes. One after the other. Hatches open, all down BettyB's side. Shove to starboard. Shove to port. Shove to nadir. Sandman held to the counter, then buckled in fast as the scope erupted with little blips.

T_REX: *It's coming. I've got it on the scope. Going to full burn . . .*
T_REX: *. . . It's not getting past me.*
FROGPRINCE: *T_Rex, that thing's a ship-killer. You can't . . .*
FROGPRINCE: *. . . deflect it. Get away from the console.*
FROGPRINCE: *T_Rex, time to ditch! Listen to Sandman.*
T_REX: *Accelerating to 2.3. Intercept.*
UNICORN: *T_Rex, you're crazy.*
T_REX: *I'm not crazy, lady. I'm a friggin ore-hauler . . .*
T_REX: *. . . with a full bay.*
FROGPRINCE: *You'll scatter like a can of marbles.*

T_REX: *Nope. She's coming too close and she's cloaked . . .*
T_REX: *. . . If station can't spot her, she can take out a freighter . . .*
T_REX: *. . . Going to burn that surface off so they can see . . .*
T_REX: *. . . that mother coming.*
T_REX: *((Poof))*
UNICORN: *Not funny, T_Rex.*

Sandman pushed the button. *BettyB* shoved hard, hard, hard.

SANDMAN: *I'm on my way, T_Rex. Get out of there.*
WILLWISP: *I'm still here. Relaying.*
CRAZYCHARLIE: *I'm coming after you, Sandman, you and him.*
SANDMAN: *By the time I get there, I'll be much less mass . . .*
SANDMAN: *. . . T_Rex, you better get yourself to a pod.*
SANDMAN: *. . . I'm going to be damn mad if I come out there . . .*
SANDMAN: *. . . and you didn't.*

Faster and faster. Faster than *BettyB* ever had gone. Calculations changed. Sandman kept figuring, kept putting it into nav.

The cyberflow kept going, talk in the dark. Eyes and ears that took in a vast, vast tract of space.

UNICORN: *I know you're busy, Sandman. But we're here.*
LOVER18: *I've run the numbers. Angle of impact . . .*
LOVER18: *. . . will shove the main mass outsystem to nadir.*
FROGPRINCE: *Fireball will strip stealth coat . . .*
FROGPRINCE: *T_Rex, you're right.*
HAWK29: *T_Rex, Sandman and Charlie are coming . . .*
HAWK29: *. . . fast as they can.*

Nothing to do but sit and figure, sit and figure, with an eye to the cameras. Forward now. Forward as they bore.

"APIS19 *BettyB*, this is Beta Control. We copy re damage to Buoy 17. Can you provide more details?"

The wavefront had gotten to Beta. They were way behind the times.

"Beta Control, this is APIS19 *BettyB*, on rescue. Orehauler on chart as 80912 imminent for impact. Inert stealth coating prevents easy intercept if it clears our district. Local neighborhood has a real good fix on it right now. May be our last chance to grab it, so the orehauler's trying, BetaControl. We're hoping he's going to survive impact. Right now I'm running calculations. Don't want to lose track of it. *BettyB* will go silent now. Ending send."

FROGPRINCE: *I'll talk to them for you, Sandman . . .*
FROGPRINCE: *I'll keep them posted.*

Numbers came closer. Closer. Sandman punched buttons, folded and retracted the big dish.

Numbers . . . numbers . . . coincided.

Fireball. New, brief star in the deep dark.

Only the camera caught it. Streaks, incandescent, visible light shooting off from that star, most to nadir, red-hot slag.

The wavefront of that explosion was coming. *BettyB* was a shell, a structure of girders without her containers. Girders and one small cabin. Everything that could tuck down, she'd tucked. Life within her was a small kernel in a web of girders.

Wavefront hit, static noise. Light. Heat.

BettyB waited. Plowed ahead on inertia. Lost a little, disoriented.

Her hull whined. Groaned.

Sandman looked at his readouts, holding his breath.

The whine stopped. Sandman checked his orientation, trimmed up on gentle, precise puffs, kicked the throttle up.

Bang! Something hit, rattled down the frame. Bang! Another.

Then a time of quiet. Sandman braked, braked hard, harder.

Then touched switches, brought the whip antennae up. Uncapped lenses and sensors.

In all that dark, he heard a faint, high-pitched ping-ping-ping.

"Tinman?" Sandman transmitted on low output, strictly local. Search and rescue band. "Tinman, this is *BettyB*. This is Sandman. You hear me? I'm coming after that fifty-two credits."

"*Bastard*," came back to him, not time-lagged. "*I'll pay, I'll pay. Get your ass out here. And don't use that name.*"

Took a while. Took a considerable while, tracking down that blip, maneuvering close, shielding the pickup from any stray bits and pieces that might be in the area.

Hatch opened, however. Sandman had his clipline attached,

sole lifesaving precaution. He flung out a line and a wrench that served as a miniature missile, a visible guide that flashed in the searchlight.

Tinman flashed, too, white on one side, sooted non-reflective black on the other, like half a man.

Sandman was ever so relieved when a white glove reached out and snagged that line. They were three hours down on Tinman's life-support. And Sandman was oh, so tired.

He hauled at the line. Hauled Tinman in. Grabbed Tinman in his arms and hugged him suit and all into the safety of the little air lock.

Then he shut the hatch. Cycled it.

Tinman fumbled after the polarizing switch on the faceplate shield. It cleared, and Tinman looked at him, a graying, much thinner Tinman.

Lips moved. "Hey, man," came through static. "Hate to tell you. My funds were all on my ship."

"The hell," Sandman said. "The hell." Then: "I owe you, man. Some freighter next month or so—owes you their necks."

"Tell that to Beta Ore," the Tinman said. "It was their hauler I put in its path."

CRAZYCHARLIE: *I've got you spotted, Sandman.*
SANDMAN: *Charlie, thanks. Got a real chancy reading . . .*
SANDMAN: *. . . on the number three pipe . . .*
SANDMAN: *. . . think it got dinged. I really don't want . . .*
SANDMAN: *. . . to fire that engine again . . .*
SANDMAN: *. . . I think we're going to need a tow.*
CRAZYCHARLIE: *Sandman, I'll tow you from here to hell and back . . .*
CRAZYCHARLIE: *. . . How's T_Rex?*
SANDMAN: *This is T_Rex, on Sandman's board.*
UNICORN: *Yay! T_Rex is talking.*
FROGPRINCE: *Tracking that stuff . . .*
FROGPRINCE: *. . . nadir right now. Clear as clear, T_Rex . . .*
FROGPRINCE: *. . . You know you *bent* that bastard?*
SANDMAN: *T_Rex here. Can you see it, FrogPrince?*
FROGPRINCE: *T_Rex, I can see it clear.*
WILLWISP: *Word's going out. Pell should know soon what they missed.*

UNICORN: *Or what missed *them*. :)*

SANDMAN: *This is Sandman. Thanks, guys . . .*

SANDMAN: *. . . You tell Pell the story, WillWisp, Unicorn. Gotta go . . .*

SANDMAN: *. . . I'm hooking up with Charlie . . .*

SANDMAN: *. . . Talk tomorrow.*

UNICORN: *You're the best, Sandman. T_Rex, you are so beautiful.*

SANDMAN: *. . . going to get a tow.*

CRAZYCHARLIE: *You can come aboard my cabin, Sandman.*

CRAZYCHARLIE: *. . . Got a bottle waiting for you.*

CRAZYCHARLIE: *. . . A warm nook by the heater.*

SANDMAN: *Deal, Charlie. Me and my partner . . .*

SANDMAN: *. . . somewhere warm.*

FROGPRINCE: *Didn't know you had a partner, Sandman . . .*

FROGPRINCE: *. . . Thought you were all alone out here.*

SANDMAN: *I'm not, now, am I?*

SANDMAN: *T_Rex speaking again. T_Rex says . . .*

SANDMAN: *. . . This is one tired T_Rex. ((Bowing.)) Thanks, all . . .*

SANDMAN: *. . . Thanks, Sandman. Thanks, Charlie.*

SANDMAN: *. . . ((Poof))*

Timothy Zahn

Timothy Zahn was born in 1951 in Chicago and spent his first forty years in the Midwest. Somewhere along the way toward a Ph.D. in physics, he got sidetracked into writing science fiction and has been at it ever since. He is the author of over seventy short stories and twenty novels, of which his most well-known are his five *Star Wars* books: *The Thrawn Trilogy* and *Hand of Thrawn* duology. His most recent book is the stand-alone novel *Angelmass,* published in 2001. Though most of his time is now spent writing novels, he still enjoys tackling the occasional short story. This is one of them. The Zahn family lives on the Oregon coast.

THE BIG PICTURE
Timothy Zahn

THE southwest corner of the black fortress wavered in the scope image, its clean lines obscured by distance, a rapid-moving line of wispy clouds, and the distortion that came from the natural turbulence of Minkta's planetary atmosphere. From *Defender Fifty-Five's* synchronous orbit twenty-two thousand miles above the surface, Jims Harking reflected, there was a lot of distance and atmosphere to look through.

But the clouds, at least, he could do something about. He watched the image on his monitor, finger poised over the "shoot" button; and as the trailing edge of the cloud patch swept past, he gave the key a light tap.

And that was it for his shift. Four hundred and thirty high-magnification photos, covering the entire Sjonntae outpost and much of the surrounding terrain, all painstakingly set up and shot over the past eight hours.

As he'd done during his previous eight-hour shift. And the one before that, and the one before that.

Leaning tiredly back in his seat, Harking tapped the scrub key. The last photo, still displayed on his monitor, quickly sharpened as the sophisticated computer programs cleaned as much of the distance and atmosphere from the image as they could.

And with the scrubbing Harking now could see that there were also two figures in the photo, standing just outside the door at that corner of the fortress. Sjonntae, undoubtedly; the aliens never let the indigenous population get that close to their outpost.

Possibly looking up in the direction of the human space station high overhead.

Probably laughing at it.

Harking glared at the photo, trying to work up at least a stirring of hatred for the Sjonntae. But there was nothing there. He'd already expended all the emotion he had on the aliens, all the anger and hatred and fear that a single human psyche could generate. All that was left now was the cold, bitter logic of survival.

Perhaps that was all humanity itself had left. With a sigh, he touched the key that would send the scrubbed photo into the hopper with the rest of the shift's work. The analysts would spend *their* next shift poring over all of it, trying yet again to find a way through the damper field that protected the fortress from attack. A subtle pattern in Sjonntae personnel movements, perhaps, or some clue in animal activity that might indicate where the vulnerable whorl in the field might be located. Something that would help break the desperate war of attrition Earth found itself in.

Behind him, the door slid open. "Shift change, Ensign Harking," Jorm Tsu gave the official greeting as he stepped into the room. "I relieve you from your station."

"Shift change, aye," Harking gave the official response, pushing back his chair and standing up. "I give you my station."

Tsu stepped past him and sat down. "So," he said, the formalities concluded. "Anything new?"

"Is there ever?" Harking countered. "I saw what looked like a confrontation between an overseer and a group of slaves, and I saw a couple of Sjonntae outside the fortress who were probably giving us a one-finger salute. Otherwise, it was pretty quiet."

"Mm," Tsu said. "What happened with the slaves?"

Harking shrugged. "I don't know. By the time I finished the pattern and got back to that area, they were all gone."

"At least they weren't all lying there dead."

"Unless the survivors took the bodies away with them," Harking pointed out.

"Maybe," Tsu agreed. "But that would at least indicate the Sjonntae hadn't killed more than a third of them. It takes two live bodies to carry one dead one, right?"

Harking grimaced. The logic of survival. "Right," he conceded. "I didn't notice any drag marks either."

"Must not have been a really serious confrontation, then," Tsu concluded. "Either that, or the overseer was feeling generous today."

Harking shook his head, this time trying to work up some emotion for the hapless native beings down there who had been enslaved by the Sjonntae. But he didn't have anything left for them either. "There must be *something* we can send down to help them," he ground out. "*Some* kind of weapon that'll work in the middle of the Shadow field."

Tsu snorted. "Hey, you invent one and the war will be over in a week," he pointed out. "But what are you going to use? Technology's what draws the Shadows; and any weapon worth a damn against the Sjonntae will have to have *some* technology to it."

"I know, I know," Harking said, an edge of impatience stirring within him. Like everyone else in the Expansion, he'd gone over this whole thing a thousand times. Any weapon more advanced than a crossbow gathered the inexplicable, insubstantial Shadows around it. And in the presence of enough Shadow, sentient beings became desperately ill.

In the presence of more than enough Shadow, they died.

"What about explosives?" he suggested. "I seem to remember hearing a news report a while back about them using explosive crossbow bolts on Heimdal and Canis Seven. I never heard how it came out, though."

Tsu shrugged. "It worked fine for a time, only then the Sjonntae got explosives sniffers set up. They're probably still using them, at least off and on. Problem is, that kind of weapon only works against individual Sjonntae soldiers."

"Right," Harking said, the brief twinge of hope fading away. "And we don't care all that much about killing single Sjonntae soldiers."

"*They* care about it," Tsu said dryly. "But as far as breaking the stalemant goes, we need to find a way to take out the heavier stuff."

Harking nodded. The frustrating thing was that the Shadows didn't bother the technology itself. They could send a self-guided nuclear missile down to the surface, and even though every Minkter within miles of the thing would die from the concentration of Shadow it would quickly gather around itself, the missile itself would function just fine.

Only there would be nothing useful for the missile to do. The damper field went all the way to the ground, with only living beings able to pass through it.

So they couldn't send weapons or useful equipment to the Minkters. They couldn't break the Sjonntae damper field, either from orbit or from the surface, unless they could find the whorl, the one spot where the field was weak enough for human weaponry to destroy it. And they couldn't find the whorl.

And so the fortress sat there, filled to the brim with intact Sjonntae technology they would never be able to pull apart and examine and find a defense against.

The logic of defeat.

"By the way," Tsu added as Harking turned toward the door, "the commander said for you to drop by after your shift."

Harking frowned. "Did she say why?"

"Not to me," Tsu said. "She seemed a little on the grumpy side, though."

"Probably a bad photo or something," Harking said sourly. "Thanks."

Commander Chakhaza was in her office near the station's battle command center. "Ensign," she nodded a greeting as he knocked on the open door. "Come in."

"Thank you," Harking said, tucking his folded cap under his arm and coming to attention exactly two paces from her desk. Humanity might be doomed to destruction, but there was no reason to be sloppy while it was happening.

"At ease," Chakhaza said. "Sit down."

"Thank you," Harking said, pulling down the visitor's jump seat and easing into it. Chakhaza never let anyone sit while she was chewing them out, which implied this wasn't about some screwup on his part.

She also never went out of her way to be this courteous to the lower ranks either. That implied this might be good news. Either that, or very, very bad news.

"How'd the session go?" she asked.

"Pretty routine," Harking said. Apparently, she'd decided to ease into the main topic through a side door. "The weather was mostly clear. I got some good shots, I think."

"Anything of interest going on?"

Harking shrugged. "Not really. I spotted a slave confrontation, but I didn't see any bodies when I got back to the spot, so I presume the overseer didn't kill anyone. Oh, and I caught a couple of patrols, too. Three Skyhawks each, flying standard formation. Again, it looked pretty routine."

"Good," Chakhaza said absently. "Tell me, have you ever heard of a woman named Laura Isis?"

Harking searched his memory. The name definitely seemed familiar. "Someone from Maintenance?" he hazarded.

Chakhaza shook her head. "News reporter."

"Oh, of course," Harking said, nodding as it suddenly clicked. He'd read her name or seen her face on a hundred different stories coming from the front lines of the war. The woman really got around. "What about her?"

"She's on her way."

Harking blinked. Minkta was about as far from the fighting as you could get and still be in theoretically disputed territory. "On her way *here?*"

"Yes," Chakhaza said, her expression suddenly unreadable. "She's found out about Lieutenant Ferrier."

An old knife Harking had thought long gone twisted itself gently into his gut. "Oh," he said, very quietly.

Something that almost looked like sympathy creased through the lines and scars on Chakhaza's face. "I'm sorry," she said. "I know what he meant to you. But Supreme Command has issued orders that we're to give her the whole story." She paused. "I thought you might prefer to be the one to handle the job."

Harking's first impulse was to turn it down flat. To have to go through all those bitter memories again . . .

But if he didn't do it, someone else would. Someone who didn't know or understand the big picture, who might paint Abe Ferrier as an ambitious glory-grabber or a delusional lunatic. "Thank you, Commander," he said. "I'd be honored to speak with Ms. Isis."

Chakhaza gave a crisp nod. "Good. Her transport's due in thirty hours. Try to work her around your regular duty shift if you can; if she insists on setting her own timetable, let me know and I'll try to shuffle people around to accommodate you. Any questions?"

"No, ma'am," Harking said.

"Very well, then," Chakhaza said. Just as happy, Harking guessed, that she wouldn't be the one sweating it out in front of Ms. Isis' recorder.

Especially since she was the one who'd bought into Abe's plan in the first place. Had bought into it hook, line, and cautiously enthusiastic sinker. "Dismissed," she said.

And had then sent him to his death.

Laura Isis was pretty much as Harking expected: mid-thirties, dark blonde, still petite but with a figure that time and gravity were starting to pull at. The quick smile and probing eyes were as he remembered from her various news appearances.

But there were also differences. Her hair wasn't as professionally coifed as it inevitably was on TV, her cheekbones not nearly as sharp, and her clothing far more casual. She was shorter than he would have guessed, too, barely coming up to the shoulder boards of his dress uniform, and that quick smile seemed somehow to have a hard edge to it.

And there was something oddly wrong with the left side of her face. Something he couldn't quite put his finger on. . . .

"Welcome to *Defender Fifty-five*, Ms. Isis," he greeted her as she passed her bag to one of the hatchway guards for inspection and came toward him. "I'm Ensign Jims Harking. Commander Chakhaza asked me to act as your liaison and assistant while you're on the station."

"Thank you," she said. "It's nice to be here on *Elvie*."

There must have been something in his face, because she smiled again. "Or do you use a different private name for your station?"

"No, *Elvie* is it," Harking said. "I was just surprised you knew it."

She shrugged slightly. "I've been hanging around the military since the war started," she reminded him. "And not just the upper brass. I know a lot about how the common soldiers and starmen think and behave. Did Commander Chakhaza tell you why I'm here?"

The abrupt change in topic didn't catch him by surprise; it was a technique he'd seen her use on camera many times. "Yes, ma'am, she did," he confirmed.

"And did she assign you to me because you know a lot about the Ferrier operation?" she went on. "Or because you know very little about it?"

He looked her straight in the eye. "She assigned me because Abe Ferrier was my friend."

"Ah." If she was taken aback by his response, it didn't show. "Good. I presume you have quarters set up for me?"

Harking had hoped to get the interview over with as quickly as possible, which would have let him start the process of putting the ghosts back to sleep that much earlier. Perversely, Isis decided she wanted a tour of the station first.

". . . and this," he said as he gestured her into his usual duty station room, "is the Number One Photo Room. This is where we take all the high-mag telephotos of the Sjonntae outpost and vicinity for analysis. The telescopes themselves are through that door over there."

"Ah," Isis said, stepping in and looking around. "So this is the real nerve center of *Elvie*'s mission, is it?"

Tsu, had he been on duty, would undoubtedly have made some unfortunate comment in response to that one. Fortunately, it was Cheryl Schmucker's shift, and all she did was lift a silent eyebrow in Harking's direction and then return to her work. "Hardly," Harking told Isis stiffly. "All we do here is take the photos. It's the analysis group's job to find a hole in the Sjonntae defenses."

"Of course." Isis looked around at the controls and monitors for a moment, then crossed toward the telescope room. Harking was ready, and got there in time to open the door for her.

Inside, it was like another world. The whole outer wall was floor-to-ceiling hullglass, with a dozen different telescopes lined up peering at various angles through it. Taking care not to touch or jostle anything, Isis stepped to the guard railing and leaned on it, gazing out at the silent black circle of the planet far below. It was full night down there, the darkness alleviated only by the clusters of mocking lights from the Sjonntae fortress and protected territory. To the far right, an edge of blue-green showed where the dawn line was beginning to creep across the landscape.

Dawn for the Minkters. The beginning of another day of servitude to their Sjonntae masters.

They hated them, the Minkters did. Hated them with the kind of passion only an enslaved people could generate. There had been at least four attempts at revolt during the time *Defender Fifty-five* had been up here. All had been easily crushed, of course. Organized crowds of Minkters whose only weapons were rocks, spears, and crossbows were no match for armed Sjonntae Skyhawks. And each time the humans of *Defender Elvie* had watched in impotent rage. The only sky-to-ground weaponry the station had were its missiles, which would have indiscriminately killed attacker and defender alike.

Which was yet another reason Abe had pressed so hard to be allowed to go down there. The Minkters were certainly intelligent enough, but they were unschooled in the ways of mass warfare. If someone with military knowledge and training could get them organized—

"And have they?" Isis said into the memories.

"Have who what?" Harking asked.

"The analysis group," she said, "You said they were looking for a hole. Have they found one?"

Harking grimaced. "No."

"Why not?" Isis asked. "You've been here for almost three years. What's the problem?"

A diplomatic answer was probably called for, but Harking was fresh out of stock. "The same problem that's been killing almost a thousand humans a day since this damn thing started," he told her bluntly. "Between the damper field and the Shadows, they've got about as impenetrable a planetary defense as you could ever come up with."

"Damper fields always have a whorl somewhere in them," Isis countered. "A dead spot you can put a missile into."

Harking drew back a little. "How do you know that?" he demanded.

She snorted. "What do you think I've been doing the past four years on the line? Sitting on my hands?"

"That's top secret information," Harking said stiffly. "We can't afford to let the Sjonntae know we know about that weakness."

She sighed. "Relax. If Supreme Command didn't think I was trustworthy, they certainly wouldn't let me roam around loose this way. I was just trying to examine all the possibilities."

"Trust me, we've done that," Harking growled. "Over and

over again. We can't find the whorl from up here; and without it, we can't knock down the damping field and get into the fortress."

"What about from lower down?" she asked. "Could you send a fighter loaded with sensors in for a closer look?"

Harking shook his head. "The Shadows reach all the way up to the lower stratosphere," he said. "That means the thing would have to be unmanned; and unmanned remotes are like a free lunch to Sjonntae fighters."

"Saturation bombing, then," Isis persisted. "Hit the whole damper field at once."

"Too much area," Harking told her. "Sjonntae planetary fields aren't nearly as neat and compact as the ones they wrap their warships in. This one sprawls out over about twenty thousand square kilometers, covering the outpost itself plus a huge buffer zone. Add to that the fact that a missile would have to hit within a hundred meters of the whorl to take down the field, and you can see why we can't simply rain fire and expect to get anything out of it."

"Bottom line: you can't do it from up here," Isis murmured, her face unreadable in the glow of the sunlight peeking around the edge of the planet. "And so Lieutenant Ferrier sold you on this plan of trying it from the surface."

And there it was, exactly as Harking had predicted. "It wasn't like that at all," he snapped back at her. "Abe had thought it through, all the way down to the last detail. It was a *good* plan, with a good chance of succeeding. And it beat the hell out of sitting up here watching the Sjonntae go about their daily routine and doing nothing about it."

He ran out of breath and stopped. "That's quite a speech," Isis commented. If she was offended, it didn't show in her voice. "How long have you had it ready to go?"

Again Harking thought about being diplomatic. Again it didn't seem worth the trouble. "Since I heard you were coming here to investigate this," he told her candidly. "I knew you'd be all set to fork Abe onto the barbecue for this."

"I'm not here to fork anyone onto anything," she said calmly. "But you have to face facts, the foremost being that the best minds in the Expansion have been wrestling with this problem for over ten years. What made Lieutenant Ferrier think he could succeed where so many other similar ploys have failed?"

"Several reasons," Harking said. "The foremost being that Abe's family was part of the original contact team that spent five years negotiating deals between the Minkters and the Expansion. He speaks the language, looks enough like them to fit in, and has a lot of friends."

"I understand all that," Isis said. "But what did he expect to accomplish once he was down there? Any technology and weaponry he could bring would draw Shadow so quickly that he'd never get a chance to use it."

She gestured out toward the planet. "For that matter, how could he even *get* down there? A drop capsule would probably attract so much Shadow on its way in that he'd be dead before he hit the surface."

"He had that covered," Harking insisted. "He had everything covered. He rode a drop capsule in only to the upper atmosphere, then did the rest of the way down via hang glider and parachute. All his equipment went down in separate capsules, spaced out so they wouldn't draw as much Shadow. And it worked—he got down okay."

"How do you know?"

"He signaled us," Harking told her. "He had a tight-beam radio with a simple speaking-tube arrangement so he could use it without having to get too close. He said he was down, that he'd made contact with the Minkters, and that he'd get back to us as soon as he located the whorl."

"Only he never did," Isis said. "Did he?"

"Not yet," Harking said firmly. "But he will."

Isis turned away from her contemplation of the universe to look up into his face. "You really think so?" she asked quietly.

Harking looked away from that gaze, his throat aching. "He'll find it," he said. "The Minkters will figure it out. And when they do, he'll get the location to us."

"How?" Isis asked. "The Sjonntae found the radio, didn't they?"

"Of course they did," Harking growled. "We all expected them to. They don't seem affected by the Shadows, for whatever reason. But Abe had other ways of communicating with us. He had mirrors, colored signal flags—a whole trunkful of nice low-tech stuff. And he knew we'd be watching. We've covered the villages, the valleys—every place he might signal from. We just have to be patient."

Isis sighed, just audibly. "It's been over a year, Mr. Harking," she reminded him quietly. "If he hasn't found a way by now . . . the Sjonntae aren't stupid, you know. They know someone came in, and they have to know *why* he came. They're going to be watching the same villages and valleys as you are, trying to make sure he can't get any information back to you."

"He'll find a way," Harking insisted. "Abe knows what's at stake. He'll find a way, even if he has to write it on the grass in his own blood."

She didn't answer. But her words had already echoed the thought that had been digging at the edges of his own slipping confidence for months now.

Angrily, he shook the thought away. Abe Ferrier was the smartest, most resourceful man he'd ever known. He would find a way.

And he *was* still alive. He *was.*

"I hope he does," Isis said finally into the silence. "A lot of good men and women are dying out there on the line. We need to get hold of a Sjonntae base; and this outpost is still our best shot at doing that."

She straightened up. "It's been a long day," she said. "I'd like to return to my quarters now."

And to start composing her story? Harking felt a surge of contempt. Probably. Reporters like Laura Isis could ladle out carefully measured servings of emotion into their stories when it was convenient. He'd seen them do it. But down deep, he knew, they were as emotionally detached as the microphones that picked up the sound of their voices. Even a war of survival was nothing personal to them. Nothing but a good opportunity for fame and glory and career advancement.

The very things, he knew, that she was mentally accusing Abe Ferrier of.

First take the log out of your own eye, the old admonition echoed through his mind. But she never would. "Certainly," he managed, trying to keep his voice civil as he turned back to the door. "Follow me."

"**I** don't know why you're surprised." Tsu commented, taking a long sip from his drink. "You knew reporters were soulless robots going in."

"Knowing and having it shoved in your face are two very different things," Harking countered, draining his own mug and punching for another drink. A waste of time, really; the bar was keeping track of his drinks and was steadily decreasing the amount of alcohol in each one. But maybe for once it would make a mistake, and he could actually drink enough to forget. At least for a little while.

"She covers the war every day," Tsu reminded him. "She can't get all misty-eyed over a single man who disappears over a half-forgotten planet."

Harking shook his head. "You didn't hear her, Jorm," he said. "It wasn't a matter of not caring about him. She was determined to prove he was either out for glory or a complete idiot for trying a stunt like that in the first place. All she cared about—*all* she cared about—was getting a good story out of him."

Tsu shrugged. "She didn't know him."

"And she's not going to, either," Harking said, pulling his drink off the conveyer as it passed and taking a long swallow. "Not the way she's going at it."

"Well, then, maybe you should do something about that," Tsu suggested.

"Such as?"

"I don't know," Tsu said with a shrug. "Sit her down and give her his life story, maybe. Make her see him the way you did."

"The way I *do*," Harking growled. "Don't talk about him as if he was dead. He's *not*, damn it."

"Hey, don't take it out on me," Tsu protested. "*I'm* not the one you're mad at."

"You're right," Harking said, draining his cup. Suddenly, the alcohol seemed to be flowing like fire through his veins. "I'll see you later."

"Where are you going?" Tsu asked suspiciously as he stood up. "Hey, Jims, don't be getting yourself in trouble. You hear me?"

There was more along the same lines, but Harking didn't wait to hear it. Striding from the lounge, he headed down the corridor toward officer country. If Isis thought he was going to just sit back while she maligned Abe on interstellar television, she was in for a surprise.

There was no answer when he buzzed her door. He buzzed a second and third time; and he was just about to start pounding his fist on the heavy panel when it finally slid open to reveal Laura Isis.

But it wasn't the same woman he had left barely two hours earlier. Her casual suit was gone, replaced by an old and sloppily tied robe. The bright, probing eyes were heavy with interrupted sleep.

And the neatly styled hair was now only neatly styled on the right side of her head. On the left side, where he'd thought he'd noticed something odd earlier, there was no hair at all. What was there was a crisscross pattern of angry red scars, slicing across the side of her head, cutting across her ear, and digging down along her cheek and neck.

Harking felt his mouth drop open, the alcohol-driven fire vanishing in that first stunned heartbeat. "Hello, Ensign," Isis said quietly. "Was there something you wanted?"

He shook his head, his voice refusing to operate, his eyes unable to look away. "No," he managed at last. "No. I'm . . . I'm sorry."

She nodded, as if seeing past the words into his own, more invisible scars. "You'd better come in," she said, stepping back out of the way. "We need to talk."

Numbly, he complied. She closed the door, then brushed past him to sit down at the fold-down desk. "From past experience," she said as she gestured him to the guest jump seat, "I know I need to explain this before we go on to anything else." She pointed at her disfigured face.

"I'm sorry," Harking said as he sat down. Vaguely, he realized that wasn't exactly the proper thing to say, but his brain was still frozen on its rail and his mouth was free-ranging. "I mean—"

"It happened at the third battle off Suzerain," she said, mercifully cutting off the babbling. "The ship I was on was hit. Badly. We barely got away."

She lowered her eyes. "Many of the crew weren't as lucky as I was."

. "It can be fixed, though," Harking said desperately. "Can't it?"

She shrugged. "So they tell me. Assuming the war doesn't kill us all and eliminate such trivial issues as cosmetic surgery."

"But then—" He gestured helplessly at her face.

"Why don't I go back to Earth and have it done?" she suggested.

"Well . . . yes," Harking said. "I mean, your face is famous. It's on TV all the time."

"Because it would take six months," Isis told him. "I can't afford to take that much time off. *Humanity* can't afford for me to take that much time off."

In spite of himself, Harking felt his lip twist. "Humanity?" he demanded without thinking. "Or your career?"

The instant the words were out of his mouth he wished he could call them back. But to his surprise, she didn't take offense. "You don't understand," she said softly. "The career itself is irrelevant. It's what I can do with that career for the war effort that's so desperately needed."

"And what is it you do, exactly?" Harking asked darkly. "Report the day's slaughter in that cool, professional way you reporters all have?"

He nodded at her face. "Or has that made things a little more personal?"

"This war has always been personal for me," Isis countered, her eyes hardening a little. "That's the problem, really. It's personal for *all* of us."

She gestured to him. "Especially for those of you who are actually doing the fighting."

Harking shook his head. "You've lost me."

"You take this war personally, Ensign," she said. "Like everyone else, you're tightly focused on your own little corner of it. To you, that corner is the most important thing in the entire universe."

"That's what keeps us alive," Harking growled. "Most of us don't have time for deep philosophical discussions on the issues of the day. We shoot, or we duck, or we die."

"Of course you do," Isis said. "But that's not what I meant. I'm talking about focusing in so tightly that you can't see the whole of what's happening out there."

Harking snorted. "That's the generals' job. Bottom feeders like us just do what we're told."

"Yes, that's how it traditionally works," Isis agreed. "But we can't afford to hold onto traditions like that. Not anymore." She took a deep breath. "You may not know it, out here on the edge of things, but the Expansion is losing this war."

"We're not *that* far off the map," Harking said stiffly. "We *do* get regular news feeds."

"Exactly," Isis said, giving him a tight smile. "And after you hear the news, what then? Do you discuss how the Supreme Command is doing? Speculate on how the Sjonntae can be beaten? Argue about tactics and strategies?"

"Well, sure," Harking said, frowning. "Shouldn't we?"

"Of course you should," she agreed. "That's the point. We need to tap into every resource we've got if we're going to win this thing; and that includes getting *every* human being working on the problem of victory. But the generals don't have time to go into depth on what's happening with each line unit or every far-flung command."

She touched her recorder, sitting by her elbow on the desk. "That's where we in the news come in. We *do* have the time to dig into the stories and tie events together in a real-time way that your superiors and order-lines can't possibly do. Our job is to pick up as many pieces as we can, scatter them all across the Expansion, and hope that someone will see how two or three of those pieces fit together in a way that no one's ever noticed before. Do you understand?"

Harking nodded, feeling ashamed of his earlier thoughts. "Sure," he said. "The big picture. That's what you're feeding us: the big picture. Is that why you want me to dissect Abe and his mission for you?"

She nodded back. "Even if he failed, reporting on what he did—*exactly* what he did—may give someone else an idea of something new to try. Because he was right: if we're going to capture enough Sjonntae technology to study, this is the place to do it. Out here, where there's no fighting and hardly even any traffic. *And* where their main battle force can't get to quickly enough to interfere if we manage to crack it."

"Try no traffic at all," Harking said with a sniff. "They haven't sent a single ship in the entire three years we've been in place. It's like they're just sitting there thumbing their butts at us, knowing we can't do a thing to bother them."

"They are definitely arrogant SOBs," Isis agreed. "And too much arrogance can be a weakness. Let's see if we can find a way to turn that against them."

"Yeah," Harking said. "Though as someone once said, it ain't bragging if you can do it."

He stood up. "I apologize for the intrusion, Ms. Isis. And for . . . other things."

"No problem," she assured him. "I would like to talk more with you about Lieutenant Ferrier and his mission, though."

"Of course," Harking said. "I go on duty in an hour, but we can talk while I take my photos if that's okay with you. Just come up whenever you're ready."

"I'll be there," she said.

"Good." Harking started to the door—

"Just one more thing," she said.

He turned back, mentally bracing himself. "Yes?"

Her face was very still. "Abe Ferrier wasn't just your friend, was he? He was something more."

Harking took a deep breath. "He was my cousin," he told her. *Was*, the word echoed through his mind. *Was.* "The only family I had left."

Without waiting for a reply, he turned and left.

The motorized telescope mounts on the far side of the door could be heard humming softly as Harking sent the lens pointing toward the next spot on the grid. "So he *had* had some commando training, at least?" Isis asked.

"Some," Harking said, watching his screen. The view flashed through a variety of different colors as the telescope tracked across contrasting strips of farmland, then slowed and settled in on the east end of a reasonably large village twenty kilometers south of the fortress. The village seemed to be home to most of the landscape and maintenance slaves for the southern part of the Sjonntae buffer zone, and it was here that Abe had hoped to eventually end up. Sixty kilometers inside the damper field, and under the watchful eye of the Sjonntae slave masters, he had hoped it would be the last place they would look for an enemy spy.

Had he ever made it? If so, Harking and the other photographers had never spotted him. Certainly they hadn't seen any mirror flashes or semaphore or colored signal flags.

Or maybe he was indeed there, but was just being cautious. After all, as Isis had pointed out, the Sjonntae knew someone had infiltrated. If they hadn't caught him yet, they would still be on alert for anything out of the ordinary.

A trio of Skyhawks flew across the edge of the image, underlining his thought as they passed with lazy alertness low over the village rooftops. Ground-hugging Skyhawk activity had definitely shown an uptick during the year since Abe had gone in. Were they still looking for the infiltrator?

Or had they already found and executed him, and all these surveillance flights were merely to make sure the upstart humans didn't try it again?

"Did you know that grommets in cheese sauce make a great appetizer?"

Harking blinked up at Isis. "What?"

"Just wanted to see if you were still paying attention," she said blandly. Then she sobered. "I'm distracting you, aren't I? I'm sorry."

"That's okay," Harking assured her. "I'm just . . . I was thinking about Abe."

"I understand." Isis shut off her recorder. "You know, I've never seen Minkta during the daytime. Even my ship came in from the darkside."

"That's standard procedure," Harking said. "Sjonntae get less active after dark, and Sector Command has this fond hope that they won't notice and catalog our supply runs if we sneak in during the night."

" 'Fond' and 'hope' being the operative words," Isis agreed. "But I'd still like to see it."

Harking gestured to his monitor. "Have a look."

"I was thinking more of the overall grand vista," she said, gesturing toward the room housing the telescopes. "The big picture, as it were. May I?"

Harking hesitated, then nodded. "I suppose," he told her. "Just don't touch anything."

"I won't." Crossing the room, she opened the door and stepped gingerly through.

Harking sighed as the door closed behind her. Graceful exit or not, it was pretty obvious that the only reason she'd left was to give him a chance to pull himself back together. There was certainly nothing exciting she'd be able to see from this distance that she hadn't seen a hundred times before on a hundred other blue-green worlds. *Come on, Harking, get on the program here*, he ordered himself viciously. *If* he could just push his feelings aside long enough to get this interview over with, he could then get Laura Isis off his back and off the station—

Across the room, the door opened abruptly. "Can you zoom out?" Isis demanded as she hurried into the room.

Harking felt himself tense. Isis had left the room calm and soothing and professional; now, abruptly, the air around her seemed to be hissing with static electricity. "What?" he asked.

"Can you zoom these things out?" she repeated, jerking a thumb back at the telescopes. "And can you clear away cloud interference?"

"Yes, to both," Harking said cautiously.

"Do it," Isis ordered, breathing hard, her eyes flashing with something he couldn't identify as she stepped to his side. "The area to the southeast of the fortress."

Harking frowned. "Why?"

"I saw something," she said "Or maybe my eyes were playing tricks on me." She gestured at his panel. "Just do it."

Abe? But how could she possibly have seen a single man from this height? "And you said to zoom *out*?"

Her lips compressed. "Definitely zoom out."

Silently, Harking reset the coordinates and keyed for the zoom-out. Isis was standing very close to him, her right arm almost touching his shoulder. He could hear her carefully controlled breathing, the nervous tension beneath the control, and wondered just what in the hell was going on. The telescope settled on the designated area, and with a series of clicks began to zoom out from its close-range setting. . . .

And suddenly, he saw it.

He dived for the controls, freezing the image. "Oh, my God," he breathed.

For a long moment neither of them spoke. Then, beside him, he felt Isis stir. "The big picture," she murmured. "We've thought about it, talked about it, even argued about it. We've just never bothered to look at it."

"No," Harking said, thinking of all the photos he'd taken over the past few months as he gazed at the monitor. All those close-in, tight-range photos . . . "But then, neither have the Sjonntae," he added. "While we've been staring down, looking for mirrors and signal flags, they've been flying low over the farms and villages, looking for the same thing."

"Yes," Isis said. "And Abe Ferrier fooled us all."

Harking nodded, gazing at the monitor. The varying colors of the fields, planted apparently randomly with their different crops, formed a subtle pattern, with no sharp or obvious lines for a passing Skyhawk to note with interest or suspicion.

But from *Defender Fifty-five,* and the ability to take in a hundred thousand square kilometers at a glance, the human eye had no difficulty filling in the disguising gaps and reading the message Abe and the Minkter farmers had so painstakingly prepared for them:

104° 55'52" W
38° 40'42"

"You know where that is?" Isis asked quietly.

"About thirty kilometers north of the fortress," Harking said. "Rocky area. Even if we'd been able to get instruments close enough through all the Shadow, we'd have had a hard time spotting it."

Taking a deep breath, he keyed the intercom. "Commander Chakhaza, this is Harking in Number One Photo," he said. "You need to get up here right away."

He smiled tightly at Isis. "And," he added, "you might want to wake up the missile crews."

Frederik Pohl

When I first met Don Wollheim I was about fourteen and he was nearly twenty-one. That wasn't the worst of it. He also was far more sophisticated and well informed on the very subjects that I most desperately wished to know about—and about which I knew almost nothing—which is to say what editors and publishers did, what the real, live ones who brought out the science fiction magazines I loved were like and, especially, what their faults were when they had any, which most of them did. I learned from Donald as much as I could, and he became an instant hero.

A little later he became instead a good friend, and remained that way—most of the time—for the next sixty-some years. (True, there were times when the friendship was a bit strained. How could it be otherwise, considering what kind of hairpins we both were? But the strain relaxed, and the friendship remained.)

—FP

A HOME FOR THE OLD ONES
Frederik Pohl

WHEN the guy came in, bold as brass, we were busy aversion training a leopard cub, and it was taking all our attention. The cub was a healthy little male, no more than a week old. That's a little bit young to begin the aversion training, but we'd been tracking the mother since she gave birth. When we spotted the mother this day, she had dropped off to sleep in a convenient place—at the edge of a patch of brush that wasn't large enough to conceal any other leopards. So we jumped the gun a little, doped the mother with an air gun and borrowed her cub.

It's a job that takes all three of us. Shelly was the one who picked up the baby, completely covered, and sweating, in a gas-proof isolation suit so it wouldn't get any ideas about a friendly human smell. Brudy kept an eye on the mother so we wouldn't have any unpleasant surprises. The mother had had her own aversion training, but if she had woken and seen us messing with her cub she might have broken through it. I was the head ranger, which meant that I was the boss. (Did I mention that my name is Grace Nkroma? Well, it is.) And, as boss, I was the one who manipulated the images—3-D simulations of an Old One, a human, a Heechee, one after another—with a cocktail of smells of each released as we displayed the images, and a sharp little electric shock each time that made the kit yowl and struggle feebly in Shelly's arms.

It isn't a hard job. We do it four or five times for each cub, just to make sure, but long before we're through with the training they'll do their best to run away as fast as they can from any one of the images or smells, whether they're simulations or the real thing. I don't mind handling leopard cubs. They're pretty clean, because the mother licks them all day long. So are cheetahs. The ones that really stink are the baby hyenas; that's when whoever holds the animal is glad that the gas-proof suit works in both

directions. As far as other predators are concerned, lions and wild
dogs are long extinct in this part of the Rift Valley, so the leopards, hyenas, and cheetahs are the only ones the Old Ones have
to worry about on their reservation. Well, and snakes. But the
Old Ones are smart enough to stay away from snakes, which
aren't likely to chase them anyway since the Old Ones are too big
for them to eat. Oh, and I should mention the crocs, too. But we
can't train crocodiles very reliably, not so you could count on
their running the other way if an Old One wandered near. So
what we do is train the Old Ones themselves to stay away. What
helps us there is that the Old Ones are sort of genetically scared
of open water, never having experienced any until they were
brought here. The only reason they would ever go near any
would be that they were tormented by thirst and just had to get
a drink. We never let it come to that, though. We've taken care of
that problem by digging wells and setting up little solar-powered
drinking fountains all over their reservation. They don't produce
a huge gush of water, but there's a steady flow from each fountain, a deciliter a second year in and year out, and anyway the
Old Ones don't need much water. They're not very interested in
bathing, for instance. You catch a really gamy Old One, which we
sometimes have to do when one of them is seriously sick or injured, and you might wish you could trade it for a hyena cub.

The first indication we got that we had a visitor was when we'd
given the baby leopard four or five aversion shocks, and he suddenly began to struggle frantically in Shelly's arms, nipping at
her gas-proof clothing, even when he wasn't being shocked. That
wasn't normal. "Let him go," I ordered. When a cub gets really
antsy, we don't have any choice but to call it off for the day. It
isn't that they'll hurt whoever's holding them, because the gas-
proof coveralls are pretty nearly bite-proof, too. But it's bad for
the cubs themselves. Wild animals can have heart attacks, too.

We backed away, keeping an eye on the mom as her baby,
whining, scooted over to her, crept under her belly, and began to
nurse. What I didn't know was what had set the cub off. Then I
heard it: motor and fan noises from afar, and a moment later a
hovercar appeared around a copse of acacias. Leopard cubs had
better hearing than people, was all. The vehicle charged right up
to us and skidded to a halt, the driver digging its braking skids

into the ground for a quick stop and never mind how much damage it did to the roadway or how much dust it raised. The man who got out when the bubble top popped open was slim, short, rather dark-complected and quite young looking—for what that's worth, since pretty much everybody is. But he was quite peculiar looking, too, because he was wearing full city clothing, long pants, long sleeves, with little ruffs of some kind of fur at the cuffs and collar. (A fur collar! In equatorial Africa!) He gave Brudy a quick, dismissive glance, looked Shelly and me over more thoroughly, and ordered, "Take me to the Old Ones."

That was pure arrogance. When I sneaked a look at my indicator, it did not show a pass for his vehicle, so he had no right to be on the reservation in the first place, whoever he was. Brudy moved toward him warningly, and the newcomer stepped back a pace. The expression on Brudy's face wasn't particularly threatening, but he is a big man. We're all pretty tall, being mostly Maasai; Brudy is special. He boxes for fun whenever he can get anybody to go six rounds with him, and he shows it. "How did you get in?" Brudy demanded, his voice the gravely baritone of a leopard's growl. What made me think of that was that just about then the mother leopard herself did give a ragged, unfocused little growl.

"She's waking up," Shelly warned.

Brudy has a lot of confidence in our aversion training. He didn't even look around at the animals. "I asked you a question," he said.

The man from the hover craned his neck to see where the leopard was. He sounded a lot less self-assured when he said, "How I got in is none of your business. I want to be taken to the Old Ones as soon as possible." Then he squinted at the leopard, now trying, but failing, to get to her feet. "Is that animal dangerous?"

"You bet she is. She could tear you to shreds in a minute," I told him—not lying, either, because she certainly theoretically could if it wasn't for her own aversion training. "You'd better get out of here, mister."

"Especially since you don't have a pass in the first place," Shelly added.

That made him look confused. "What's a 'pass'?" he asked.

"It's a radio tag for your hover. You get them at the headquarters in Nairobi, and if you don't have one, you're not allowed on the reservation."

" 'Allowed,' " he sneered. "Who are you to 'allow' me anything?"

Brudy cleared his throat. "We're the rangers for this reservation, and what we say goes. You want to give me any argument?"

Brudy can be really convincing when he wants to be. The stranger decided to be law-abiding. "Very well," he said, turning back to his hover; he'd left the air-conditioning going and I could hear it whine as it valiantly tried to cool off the whole veldt. "It is annoying to be subjected to this petty bureaucracy, but very well. I shall return to Nairobi and obtain a pass."

"Maybe you will, and maybe you won't," Shelly said. "We don't disturb the Old Ones any more than we can help, so you'll need to give them a pretty good reason."

He was already climbing into the vehicle, but he paused long enough to give her a contemptuous look. "Reason? To visit the Old Ones? What reason do I need, since I own them?"

2

The next morning we all had to pitch in because the food truck had arrived. Brudy and Carlo were unloading little packets of rations from the Food Factory in the Mombasa delta while the rest of us kept the Old Ones in order.

Personally, I couldn't see why the Old Ones needed to be kept orderly. For most people that standard Food Factory stuff is the meal of last resort—that is, it is unless it's been doctored up, when you can hardly tell it from the real thing. The Old Ones chomp the untreated stuff right down, though. Naturally enough. It's what they grew up on, back when they were living on that first Food Factory itself, out in the Oort Cloud. They had come from all over the reservation when they heard the food bell. Now they were all pressing close to the truck, all fifty-four of them, chattering, "Gimme, gimme!" at the top of their voices as they competed for the choicest bits.

When I came to work at the reservation, I had only seen the Old Ones in pictures. I knew they all had beards, males and females alike. I hadn't known that even the babies did, or did as soon as they were old enough to grow any hair at all, and I hadn't known the way they smelled.

The ancient female we called "Spot" was pretty nearly the smelliest of the lot, but she was also about the smartest, and the one who was as close as they had to a leader. And, well, she was kind of a friend. When she saw me, she gave me an imploring look. I knew what she wanted. I helped her scoop up half a dozen of the pink-and-white packets she liked best, then escorted her out of the crowd. I waited until she had scarfed down the first couple of packets, then tapped her on the shoulder and said, "I want you to come with me, please."

Well, I didn't say it like that, of course. All of the Old Ones have picked up a few words of English, but even Spot was a little shaky on things like grammar. What I actually said was, "You," pointing at her, "come," beckoning her toward me, "me," tapping my own chest.

She went on chewing, crumbs of greasy-looking pale stuff spilling out of the corners of her mouth, looking suspicious. Then she said, "What for?"

I said, "Because today's the day for your crocodile-aversion refresher." I said it just like that, too. I knew that she wasn't going to understand every word, but headquarters wanted us to talk to them in complete sentences as much as we could, so they'd learn. To reinforce the process, I took her by one skinny wrist and tugged her away.

She had definitely understood the word "crocodile," because she whimpered and tried to get free. That wasn't going to do her any good. I had twenty kilos and fifteen centimeters on her. I let her dally long enough to pick up a couple of extra food packets. Then I put her in our Old Ones van, the one that never stops smelling of the Old Ones, so we never use it for anything else. I picked another five of them pretty much at random and waved them in. They got in, all right. That is, they followed Spot, because she was the leader. They didn't like it, though, and all of them were cackling at once in their own language as I drove the van to the river.

It was a pretty day. Hot, of course, but without a cloud in the sky. When I turned off the motor, it was dead silent, too, not a sound except the occasional *craaack* of a pod coming in from orbit to be caught in the Nairobi Lofstrom Loop. The place where the hippos hang out is what we call the Big Bend. The stream makes pretty nearly a right-angle turn there, with a beach on the far side that gets scoured out every rainy season. There are almost always fifteen or twenty hippos doing whatever it is that they like to do in the slack water at the bend—just swimming around, sometimes underwater, sometimes surfacing to breathe, is what it looks like. And there's almost always a croc squatting patiently on the beach, waiting for one of the babies to stray far enough away from the big ones to become lunch.

This time there were three crocs, motionless in the hot African sun. They lay there with those long, toothy jaws wide open, showing the yellowish inside of their mouths—I guess that's how they try to keep from being overheated, like a pet dog in hot weather. What it looks like is that they're just waiting for something edible to come within range, which I guess is also true, and I can't help getting sort of shivery inside whenever I see one. So did the Old Ones. They were whimpering inside the van, and I nearly had to kick them out of it. Then they all huddled together, as far from the riverbank as I would let them get, shaking and muttering fearfully to each other.

Fortunately they didn't have long to wait, because Geoffrey was right behind us in the truck with the goat projector. That was Geoffrey's own invention, and before I came he used to use live goats. I put a stop to that. We raise the goats for food and I'm not sentimental about slaughtering them, but I made sure the ones we used for aversion training were dead already.

While he was setting up, I gave myself a minute to enjoy the hippos. They're always fun, big ones the size of our van and little ones no bigger than a pig. The thing is, they look to me like they're enjoying themselves, and how often do you see a really happy extended family? I'm sure the big ones were aware of our presence, and undoubtedly even more aware of the crocs on the bank, but they seemed carefree.

"Okay, Grace," Geoffrey called, hand already on the trigger of the launcher.

"You may fire when ready," I said to him, and to the Old Ones: "Watch!" They did, scared but fascinated, as the goat carcass soared out of the launcher and into the water, well downstream from the hippo families so there wouldn't be any accidents.

You wouldn't think a crocodile could run very fast, with those sprawly little legs and huge tail. You'd be wrong. Before the goat hit the water all three of the crocs were doing their high-speed waddle down to the river's edge. When they hit the water, they disappeared; a moment later, all around the floating goat, there were half a dozen little whirlpools of water, with an occasional lashing tail to show what was going on under the surface. The show didn't last long. In a minute that goat was history.

I glanced at the hippos. They hadn't seemed to pay any attention, but I noticed that now all the big ones were on the downstream side of the herd and the babies were on the other side, away from the crocs.

"Show's over," I told the Old Ones. "Back in the van!" I said, pointing to make sure they understood. They didn't delay. They were all shivering as they lined up to climb back in, one by one. I was just about to follow them in when I heard Geoffrey calling my name. I turned around, half in the van, and called, "What's the problem?"

He pointed to his communicator. "Shelly just called. You know that guy who claims he owns the Old Ones? He's back!"

All the way back I had one hand on the wheel and my other hand on my own communicator, checking with Shelly—yes, the son of a bitch did have a pass this time—and then with Nairobi to see why they'd allowed it. The headquarters guy who answered the call was Bertie ap Dora. He's my boss, and he usually makes sure I remember that. This time he sounded really embarrassed. "Sure, Grace," he said, "we issued a pass for him. We didn't have any choice, did we? He's Wan."

It took me a moment. Then, "Oh, my God," I said. "Really? Wan?" And when Bertrand confirmed that Wan was who the mysterious stranger was, identity checked and correct, it all fell into place. If it was Wan, he had been telling the truth. He really was the owner of the Old Ones, more or less, because legally he was the man who had discovered them. Well, that didn't actually make much sense in my book. If you stopped to think about it, Wan himself had been discovered as much as the Old Ones had. However, it didn't have to make sense. That was the way Gateway

Corp. had ruled—had given him property rights in the place where the Old Ones had been discovered and ownership of everything on the site—and nobody argued with the findings of Gateway Corp.

The thing about the Old Ones was that they had been found on a far-out, orbiting Heechee artifact, and it was the Heechee themselves who had put them there, all those hundreds of thousands of years ago when the Heechees had come to check out Earth's solar system. They were looking for intelligent races at the time. What they discovered were the ancestors of the Old Ones, the dumb, hairy little hominids called australopithecines. They weren't much, but they were the closest the Earth had to the intelligent race the Heechee were looking for at the time, so the Heechee had taken away some breeding stock to study. And when the Heechee got so scared that they ran off and hid in the Core, all the hundreds of millions of them, they left the australopithecines behind. They weren't exactly abandoned. The Heechee had provided them with the Food Factory they inhabited, so they never went hungry. And so they stayed there, generation after generation, for hundreds of thousands of years, until human beings got to Gateway. And, the story went, one of those human beings, and the only one who survived long enough to be rescued, was the kid named Wan.

As soon as I got to the compound, I saw him. He wasn't a kid anymore, but he wasn't hard to recognize either. His size picked him out; he wasn't all that much taller than some of the Old Ones, a dozen or so of whom had gathered around to regard him with tepid interest. He was better dressed than the Old Ones, though. In fact, he was better dressed than we were. He'd forgotten about the fur collars—sensibly enough—and the outfit he was wearing now was one of those safari-jacket things with all the pockets that tourists are so crazy about. His, however, was made of pure natural silk. And he was carrying a riding crop, although there wasn't a horse within five hundred kilometers of us. (Zebras don't count.)

As soon as he saw me, he bustled over, hand outstretched and a big, phoney smile on his face. "I'm Wan," he said. "I don't blame you for the misunderstanding yesterday."

Well, there hadn't been any misunderstanding and I didn't feel any blame, but I let it go. I shook his hand briefly. "Grace Nkroma," I said. "Head ranger. What do you want here?"

The smile got bigger and phonier. "I guess you'd call it nostalgia. Is that the word? Anyway, I have to admit that I'm kind of sentimental about my Old Ones, since they sort of took care of me while I was growing up. I've been meaning to visit them ever since they were relocated here, but I've been so busy—" He gave a winsome little shrug, to show how busy he'd been.

Then he gazed benevolently around at the Old Ones. "Yes," he said, nodding. "I recognize several of them, I think. Do you see how happy they are to see me? And I've brought them some wonderful gifts." He jerked a thumb at his vehicle. "You people had better unload them," he told me. "They've been in the car for some time, and you should get them into the ground as soon as possible." And then he linked arms with a couple of the Old Ones, and strolled off, leaving us to do his bidding.

3

There were about forty of the "gifts" that Wan had brought for his former adopted family, and what they turned out to be were little green seedlings in pressed-soil pots. Carlo looked at them, and then at me. "What the hell are we supposed to do with those things?" he wanted to know.

"I'll ask," I said, and got on the line with Bernard ap Dora again.

"They're berry bushes," he told me, sounding defensive. "They're some kind of fruit the Old Ones had growing wild when they were on the Food Factory, and they're supposed to love the berries. Actually, it's quite a wonderful gift, wouldn't you say?"

I wouldn't. I didn't. I said. "It would be a lot more thoughtful if he planted the damn things himself."

Bernard didn't respond to that. "One thing I should tell you about," he said. "The bushes are supposed to need quite a lot of water, so make sure you plant them near the runoff from the drinking fountains, all right? And, listen, see if you can keep the giraffes from eating the seedlings before they grow out."

"How are we supposed to do that?" I asked, but Bernard had already cut the connection. Naturally. He's a boss. You know the

story about the second lieutenant and the sergeant and the flagpole? There's this eight-meter flagpole and the lieutenant only
has six meters of rope. Big problem. How does the lieutenant get
the flagpole up?

Simple. The lieutenant says, "Sergeant, put that flagpole up,"
and goes off to have a beer at the officers' club.

As far as Bernard is concerned, I'm his sergeant. I don't have
to be, though. Bernard keeps asking me to come in and take a job
as a sector chief at the Nairobi office. There'd be more money,
too, but then I'd have to live in the big city. Besides, that would
mean I wouldn't be in direct contact with the Old Ones any more.

Everything considered, you might think that didn't sound so
bad, but—oh, hell, I admit it—I knew I'd miss every smelly,
dumb-ass one of them. They weren't very bright and they
weren't very clean, and most of the time I wasn't a bit sure that
they liked me back. But they needed me.

By the time Wan had been with us for three days, we had got
kind of used to having him around. We didn't actually see a lot of
him. Most of the daylight time he was off in his hover, with a
couple of the Old Ones for company, feeding them ice cream pops
and lemonade out of his freezer—things that really weren't good
for them but, I had to admit, wouldn't do them much harm once
or twice in a lifetime. When it got dark, he was always back in the
compound, but he didn't mingle with us even then. He stayed in
his vehicle, watching soaps and comedies, again with a couple of
Old Ones for company, and he slept in it, too.

When I finally asked Wan just how long he intended to be with
us he just gave me that grin again and said, "Can't say, Gracie.
I'm having fun."

"Don't call me Gracie," I said. But he had already turned his
back on me to collect another handful of Old Ones for a joyride.

Having fun seemed to be what Wan's life was all about. He'd
already been all over the galaxy before he came back to see us,
flying around in his own private ship. Get that, his own private
ship! But he could afford it. His royalties on the Heechee stuff
that came out of the Food Factory made him, he said, the eighth
richest person in the galaxy, and what Wan could afford was

pretty nearly anything he could think up. He made sure he let us all know it, too, which didn't endear him to most of the staff, especially Carlo. "He gets on my nerves with his goddamn bragging all the time," Carlo complained to me. "Can't we run the son of a bitch off?"

"As long as he doesn't make trouble," I said, "no. How are you coming with the planting?"

Actually that was going pretty well. All the guys had to do was scoop out a little hole in the ground, a couple of meters away from a fountain, and set one of the pressed-earth pots in it. That was the whole drill. Since there were a couple of patrols going out all over the reservation every day anyway, checking for signs of elephant incursions or unauthorized human trespassers, it only took them a couple of extra minutes at each stop.

Then, without warning, Wan left us.

I thought I heard the sound of his hover's fans, just as I was going to sleep. I considered getting up to see what was going on, but—damn it!—the pillow seemed more interesting than Wan just then, and I rolled over and forgot it.

Or almost forgot it. I guess it was my subconscious, smarter than the rest of me, that made my sleep uneasy. And about the fourth or fifth time I half woke, I heard the voices of Old Ones softly, worriedly, murmuring at each other just outside my window.

That woke me all the way up. Old Ones don't like the dark, never having had any back home. I pulled on a pair of shorts and stumbled outside. Spot was sitting there on her haunches, along with Brute and Blackeye, all three of them turning to stare at me. "What's the matter?" I demanded.

She was munching on a chunk of food. "Grace." she said politely, acknowledging my existence. "Wan. Gone." She made sweeping-away gestures with her hands to make sure I understood her.

"Well, hell," I said. "Gone where?"

She made the same gesture again. "Away."

"Yes, I know *away*," I snarled. "Did he say when he was coming back?"

She swallowed and spat out of a piece of wrapper. "No back," she said.

I guess I was still pretty sleepy, because I didn't take it in right away. "What do you mean, 'no back'?"

"He gone," she told me placidly. "Also Beautiful. Pony and Gadget gone, too."

4

Just to make sure, I woke Shelly and Carlo and sent them up in the ultralight to check out the whole reservation, but I didn't wait for their report. I was already calling headquarters even before they were airborne. Bernard wasn't in his office, of course—it was the middle of the night, and the headquarters people kept city hours—but I got him out of bed at home. He didn't sound like he believed me. "Why the hell would anyone kidnap a couple of Old Ones?" he wanted to know.

"Ask the bastard yourself," I snarled at him. "Only find him first. That's three of the Old Ones that he's kidnapped—Beauty and her two-year-old, Gadget. And Pony. Pony is the kid's father, probably."

He made a sound of irritation. "All right. First thing, I'll need descriptions—no, sorry," he said, catching himself; how would you describe three Old Ones? And why would you need to? "Forget that part. I'll take it from here. I guarantee he won't get off the planet. I'll have cops at the Loop in ten minutes, and a general alarm everywhere. I'll—"

But I cut him off there. "No, Bernard. Not so much *you* will. More like *we* will. I'll meet you at the Loop and, I don't care how rich the son of a bitch is, when we catch him, I'm going to punch him out. And then he's going to see what the inside of a jail looks like."

But, of course, that wasn't the way the hand played out.

I took our two-man hover, which is almost as fast as the ultralight. The way I was goosing it along, maybe a little faster. By the time I got within sight of the Lofstrom Loop, with Nairobi's glowing bubble a few kilometers to the north, I was already aware of police planes crisscrossing across the sky—once or twice dropping down to get a good look at me before they were satisfied and zoomed away.

At night the Loop is picked out with lights, so that it looks like a kind of roller coaster ride, kilometers long. I could hear the whine of its rotating magnetic cables long before I got to the terminal. There weren't many pods either coming or going—maybe because it was nighttime—so, I figured, there wouldn't be so many passengers that Wan and his captives might not be noticed. (As though anybody wouldn't notice three Old Ones.)

Actually there were hardly any passengers in the terminal. Bernard was there already, with half a dozen Nairobi city cops, but they didn't have much to do. Neither did I, except to fret and swear to myself for letting him get away.

Then the cop manning the communicator listened to something, snarled something back and came toward us, looking shamefaced. "He won't be coming here," he told Bernard. "He didn't use the Loop coming down—used his own lander, and it looks like he used it to get off, too, because it's gone."

And so he had.

By the time Bernard, fuming, got in touch with any of the authorities in orbit, Wan had had plenty of time to dock with his spaceship and be on his way, wherever it was he was going, at FTL speeds. And I never saw him, or any of the three missing Old Ones, again.

Tad Williams

I first met Tad Williams at the American Booksellers Association Convention in San Francisco in 1985. We were launching the first DAW hardcover list, and spearheading it with Tad's first novel, *Tailchaser's Song.* He had come to the ABA to meet me, his first editor, and to sign his bound galleys. At the time, Tad really didn't have the slightest idea how special his debut was, or that most first novelists didn't get the kind of treatment he was getting, but as he and his wife waltzed around our booth to unheard music, it was clear that he was very, very happy.

Later, in my hotel room, I asked him what he planned to write next. He discussed the possibility of writing an elephant book, or perhaps an alternate history. Then he mentioned this other book . . . a really big book—something he had always wanted to write. It would be his ode to Tolkien, to Mervyn Peake, to all the great fantasy writers who had influenced his life. He didn't feel experienced enough yet, but he knew it was something he eventually would have to do. Concerned with the continued commerciality of his career, I convinced him to try writing this other, "bigger" novel. I don't think either one of us ever imagined just how big it would turn out to be.

It took Tad three years to perfect his craft sufficiently to publish *The Dragonbone Chair,* the first volume of *Memory, Sorrow and Thorn,* and it would be an additional five years until we published the third and concluding volume, the massive *To Green Angel Tower,* which spent five weeks on *The New York Times* and the London *Times* best-seller lists. It was during the writing of this 3,000 page trilogy that Tad evolved into one of the finest writers I have ever read.

Now Tad writes whatever he wants. And he gets better and better.

His recently completed science fiction quartet, *Otherland*, is a true masterwork.

Although Tad is one of the smartest, most literate, and most talented men I know, he's also just . . . Tad. Gregarious, interesting, warm, humorous, unpretentious, and interested in editorial input—in many ways he's still the same person who danced to that unheard music.

—BW

NOT WITH A WHIMPER, EITHER
Tad Williams

TALKDOTCOM>FICTION

Topic Name: Fantasy Rules! SF Sux!
Topic Starter: ElmerFruud—2:25 pm PDT—March 14, 2001
Always a good idea to get down and sling some s#@t about all those uppity Hard SF readers . . .

* * *

RoughRider—10:21 pm PDT—Jun 28, 2002
Um, okay, so let me get this straight—the whole Frodo/Sam thing is a bondage relationship? Master-Slave? Can anyone say "stupid"?

Wiseguy—10:22 pm PDT—Jun 28, 2002
No, can anyone say "reductio ad absurdum"?

RoughRider—10:23 pm PDT—Jun 28, 2002
Hell, I can't even spell it.

Lady White Oak—10:23 pm PDT—Jun 28, 2002
I don't think TinkyWinky was trying to say that there was nothing more to their relationship than that, just that there are elements.

RoughRider—10:24 pm PDT—Jun 28, 2002
Look, I didn't make a big fuss when Stinkwinky came on and said that all of Heinleins books are some kind of stealth queer propaganda just cause Heinlein likes to write about people taking showers together and the navy and stuff like that but at some point you just have to say shut up that's bull@#t!

Lady White Oak—10:24 pm PDT—Jun 28, 2002
I think you are letting TinkyWinky pull your chain and that's just what he's trying to do.

RoughRider—10:25 pm PDT—Jun 28, 2002
He touches my chain he dies . . .

Wiseguy—10:25 pm PDT—Jun 28, 2002
I just can't stand this kind of thing. I don't mean THIS kind of
thing, what you guys are saying, but this idea that any piece of
art can just be pulled into pieces no matter what the artist intended. Doesn't anybody read history or anything, for God's
sake? It may not be "politically correct" but the master-servant
relationship is part of the history of humanity, not to mention
literature. Look at Don Quixote and Sancho Panda, for God's
sake.

Lady White Oak—10:26 pm PDT—Jun 28, 2002
Panza. Although I like the image . . . ;)

BBanzai—10:26 pm PDT—Jun 28, 2002
Tinkywinky also started the "Conan—What's He Trying So
Hard to Hide?" topic. Pretty funny, actually.

RoughRider—10:27 pm PDT—Jun 28, 2002
So am I the only one who thinks its insulting to Tolkiens memory to say this kind of stupid crap?

RoughRider—10:27 pm PDT—Jun 28, 2002
Missed your post, wiseguy. Glad to see Im not the only one
who isn't crazy.

TinkyWinky—10:27 pm PDT—Jun 28, 2002
Tolkien's memory? Give me a break. What, is he Mahatma
Gandhi or something? Some of you people can't take a joke—
although it's a joke with a pretty big grain of truth in it. I mean, if
there was ever anyone who could have done with a little Freudian
analysis . . . The Two Towers, one that stays stiff to the end, one
that falls down? All those elves traveling around in merry bands
while the girl elves stay home? The ring that everybody wants to
put their finger in . . .

ANAdesigner—10:28 pm PDT—Jun 28, 2002
Wow, it is really jumping in here tonight. Did any of you hear
that news report earlier, the one about the problems with AOL?
Anybody using it here?

BBanzai—10:28 pm PDT—Jun 28, 2002
I'd rather shoot myself in the foot . . . :P

Lady White Oak—10:28 pm PDT—Jun 28, 2002
Hi, TinkyWinky, we've been talking about you. What problems, ANA? I'm on AOHell, but I haven't noticed anything.

ANAdesigner—10:29 pm PDT—Jun 28, 2002
Just a lot of service outages. Some of the other providers, too. I was just listening to the radio and they say there were some weird power problems up and down the east coast.

Darkandraw—10:30 pm PDT—Jun 28, 2002
That's one of the reasons it took me like five years to finish the rings books—I couldn't stand all that "you're so good master you're so good"—I mean, self respect, come on!

TinkyWinky—10:30 pm PDT—Jun 28, 2002
I'm on AOL and I couldn't get on for an hour, but what else is new . . . ? Oh, and RoughRider, while you're getting so masterful and cranky and everything, what's with your nick? Where I come from a name like that could get a boy in trouble . . . ! <vbg>

RoughRider—10:30 pm PDT—Jun 28, 2002
We should change the name of this topic to Fantasy Rules, AOL Sux.

Lady White Oak—10:31 pm PDT—Jun 28, 2002
Actually, it raises an interesting question—why do all the most popular fantasy novels have this anti-modernist approach or slant? Is it because that's part of the escapism?

Wiseguy—10:31 pm PDT—Jun 28, 2002
Sorry, dropped offline for a moment. Darkandraw, it's a book that has the difference in classes built into it because of who Tolkien was, I guess. It makes hard reading sometimes, but I don't think it overwhelms the good parts. And there are a lot of good parts.

RoughRider—10:32 pm PDT—June 28, 2002
>*Where I come from a name like that could get a boy in trouble . . . !*
Don't push your luck, punk.

ANAdesigner—10:32 pm PDT—Jun 28, 2002
Wow. I just turned the tv on and it's bigger than just AOL.
There are all kinds of weird glitches. Somebody said kennedy is
closed because of a big problem with the flight control tower.

Lady White Oak—10:32 pm PDT—June 28, 2002
Come on, Roughie, can't you take a joke?

BBanzai—10:33 pm PDT—Jun 28, 2002
Kennedy? Like the airport?

TinkyWinky—10:33 pm PDT—Jun 28, 2002
I love it when they get butch . . . !

Wiseguy—10:34 pm PDT—Jun 28, 2002
I've got the TV on, too. Service interruptions and some other
problems—a LOT of other problems. I wonder if this is another
terrorist thing . . .

ANAdesigner—10:34 pm PDT—Jun 28, 2002
This really scares me. What if they sabotage the communication grid or something? We'll all be cut off. I don't know what I'd
do without you guys—I live in this little town in upstate New
York and most people here just think I'm crazy because I

AJSP98SADV$%&230p<jm(Vjl=kjKS>DF+L*SDo?iie*ww
&ET%SD)FA#DSFAJFASD0IWE+L@=SD(A<S#@$*#@D$A
F#AFL*SDI)@#RS#DV=SDi9?8@23LS@#QR*#DV%ADF#
AS*DF>DS+F$AD#l=kj;F(K?D2q359oSFK+DF@KD>S<FAS
MFM$A%D=SFAF?LDFM%SD@FDSF%LF?MS>DM#FA<D
SF@SDF*K@#$RFM#KD<LF?SAF*@I#R(#@R@#QR*#@R*
#R(#@R@#$R#*UR#Y@($#$RU#@$*#@U#@FAD%S@F
S#DF$K>FM*KDLFSAF*@I#R(#@R@R*#R(#@R#*UR#Y
@($(#$RU#@$*#@U#@J&NP>ErDTP

Wiseguy—10:38 pm PDT—Jun 28, 2002
Jesus, did that happen to the rest of you, too? I just totally lost
the whole show for a while. Didn't get knocked offline, but the
whole board kind of . . . dissolved. Anybody still out there?

Lady White Oak—10:39 pm PDT—Jun 28, 2002
Are you all still there? My television doesn't work. I mean I'm
only getting static.

TinkyWinky—10:39 pm PDT—Jun 28, 2002
Mine too. And I lost the board for a couple of minutes.

BBanzai—10:39 pm PDT—Jun 28, 2002
Hey you guys still there?

ANAdesigner—10:40 pm PDT—Jun 28, 2002
My tv is just white noise.

TinkyWinky—10:41 pm PDT—Jun 28, 2002
Shit, this is scary. Anybody got a radio on?

Lady White Oak—10:43 pm PDT—Jun 28, 2002
My husband just came in with the radio on the local news station. They're still only talking about the power outages so maybe it's just a coincidence.

RoughRider—10:43 pm PDT—Jun 28, 2002
If its terrorists again then I'm glad I've got a gun and screw the liberals.

Darkandraw—10:44 pm PDT—Jun 28, 2002
My browser just did this really weird refresh where I had numbers and raw text and stuff

TinkyWinky—10:45 pm PDT—Jun 28, 2002
Yeah, right, like the terrorists are going to blow up all the power stations or something and then come to your house so you can shoot them and save us all. Grow up.

ANAdesigner—10:45 pm PDT—Jun 28, 2002
Guys I am REALLY SCARED!!! This is like that nuclear winter thing!!

Wiseguy—10:45 pm PDT—Jun 28, 2002
Okay, let's not go overboard. RoughRider, try not to shoot anyone until you know there's a reason for it, huh? We had power outages from time to time even before the terrorist stuff. And everything's so tied together these days, they probably just had a big power meltdown in New York where a lot of this stuff is located.

Darkandraw—10:46 pm PDT—Jun 28, 2002
I just went outside and everyones lights are still on but the tvs

off in my apt and I can't get anything on the radio. I tried to phone my mom she's in los angeles but the phone's busy, a bunch of ppl must be trying to call

Lady White Oak—10:47 pm PDT—Jun 28, 2002
It's okay, ANAdesigner, we're all here. Wiseguy's probably right—it's a communication grid failure of some kind on the east coast.

Wiseguy—10:47 pm PDT—Jun 28, 2002
Ana, you can't have nuclear winter without a nuclear explosion, and if someone had blown up Philadelphia or something we'd probably have heard.

TinkyWinky—10:48 pm PDT—Jun 28, 2002
I checked on the MSN site and CNN.com and there's definitely something big going on but nobody knows what. Here's something I got off the CNN site:
"Early reports from the White House say that the President is aware of the problems, and that he wants the American people to understand that there is no military attack underway on the US—repeat, there is NO military attack on the US—and that the United States Government and the military have command-and-control electronic communications networks that will not be affected by any commercial outages."

BBanzai—10:49 pm PDT—Jun 28, 2002
Everybody assumes it's terrorists, but maybe it's something else. Maybe it's UFOs or something like that. A big disruption—could be!

Lady White Oak—10:50 pm PDT—Jun 28, 2002
Been checking the other news sites and at least a couple of them are offline entirely—I can't get the fox news online site, just get a 404 error. Anybody here from Europe? Or at least anyone know a good European site for news? It would be interesting to see what they're saying over there.

Wiseguy—10:51 pm PDT—Jun 28, 2002
BBanzai, come on, UFOS? you're kidding, aren't you? And if you are, it's not very funny when people are close to panicking.

TinkyWinky—10:51 pm PDT—June 28, 2002
All I can find is the BBC America television site—stuff about
tv programs, no news.

RoughRider—10:52 pm PDT—Jun 28, 2002
You guys can sit here typing all you want. I'm going to make
sure I've got batteries in all the flashlights and bullets in my
guns. Its not aliens I'm afraid of its fruitcakes rioting when the
power goes off and the tv stays off and people really start to panic.
Tinyweeny you can yell grow up all you want—looters and rag-
head terrorists don't give a shit what you say and neither do I . . .

BBanzai—10:53 pm PDT—Jun 28, 2002
No I'm not @#$#ing kidding what if its true? What else do
you think it would be like if a big starship suddenly landed. All
the power goes off like it was a bomb but no bomb?

TinkyWinky—10:53 pm PDT—Jun 28, 2002
Whatever the case, it looks like the gun-toting psychos like
RoughRider are going to be shooting at something as soon as possible. I really hope some of this is just him being unpleasant for
effect. Either that, or I'd hate to be one of his poor neighbors
blundering around lost in the dark.

Lady White Oak—10:54 pm PDT—Jun 28, 2002
Can we just be calm for a minute and stop calling each other
names?

Wiseguy—10:54 pm PDT—Jun 28, 2002
It just gets weirder, I can't get anything except busy signals on
either my reg. phone or my cellph

A J S p 9 8 S A D V $ % & 2 3 0 p < jm(Vjl=kjKS>DF + L*SDo?iie*ww
&ET%SD)FA#DSFAJFASD0IWE + L@=SD(A<S#@$*#@D$A
F#AFL*SDI)@#RS#DV=SDi9?8@23LS@#QR*#DV%ADF#
AS*DF>DS + F$AD#l=kj;F(K?D2q359oSFK + DF@KD>S<FAS
MFM$A%D=SFAF?LDFM%SD@FDSF%LF?MS>DM#FA<D
nsR(#@R@#$R#*UR#Y@($#$RU#@$*#@U#@FAD%S@F
SF@SDF*K@#$RFM#KD<LF?SAF*@I#R(#@R@#QR*#@R*
F#AFL*SDI)@#RS#DV=SDi9?8@23LS@#QR*#DV%ADF#
#R(#@R@#$R#*UR#Y@($#$RU#@$*#@U#@FAD%S@F
S#DF$K>FM*KDLFSAF*@I#R(#@R@R*#R(#@R#*UR#Y

SF@SDF*K@#$RFM#KD<LF?SAF*@I#R(#@R@#QR*#@R*
@($(#$RU#@$*#@U#@J&NP>ErDTP

Wiseguy—11:01 pm PDT—Jun 28, 2002
Shit, it happened again. It took about five minutes before this
board came back up—there was just screens and screens full of
random characters. Looks like I'm the first back on. I'm amazed
I'm still connected.

Wiseguy—11:03 pm PDT—Jun 28, 2002
Hello, am I the only one back on? Anybody else back on? I'm
sure you're busy dealing with things, just post and let me know,
K?

Wiseguy—11:06 pm PDT—Jun 28, 2002
If for some reason you folks can read this but can't post, can
you maybe email me and let me know you're okay? I've just been
outside but everything looks normal—sky's the right color, at
least I don't see any flames or anything (it's nighttime now here.)
But I don't know why anyone would have dropped an h-bomb or
a UFO on Nebraska anyway. I can't get anything on the regular
phone lines. My girlfriend's in Omaha for a business thing but
all the lines are busy. Hope she's okay.

Wiseguy—11:10 pm PDT—Jun 28, 2002
It's been almost ten minutes. This is REAL weird. Hello?

Moderator—11:11 pm PDT—Jun 28, 2002
Fa2340oa 29oei kshflw oiweaohws0p2elk asd; dska 2mavamk

Wiseguy—11:11 pm PDT—Jun 28, 2002
I'm here. Who's that?

Moderator—11:11 pm PDT—Jun 28, 2002
;92asv ;sadjf
lk 2ia
x iam
I am

Wiseguy—11:12 pm PDT—Jun 28, 2002
Is this a real moderator, or a hack? Or am I just talking back to
a power-surge or something?

Moderator—11:12 pm PDT—Jun 28, 2002
I am moderator

Wiseguy—11:12 pm PDT—Jun 28, 2002
I don't think we've ever had a moderator on this board, come to think of it. Are you someone official from Talkdotcom?

Moderator—11:13 pm PDT—Jun 28, 2002
I am moderator

Wiseguy—11:13 pm PDT—Jun 28, 2002
Do you have a name? Even a nickname? You're kind of creeping me out.

Moderator—11:13 pm PDT—Jun 28, 2002
I am moderator I am wiseguy

Wiseguy—11:14 pm PDT—Jun 28, 2002
No you're not and it's not funny. Is this Roughrider? Or just some script kiddie being cute?

Moderator—11:14 pm PDT—Jun 28, 2002
Pardon please I am moderator I am not wiseguy Jonsrud, Edward D.

Wiseguy—11:14 pm PDT—Jun 28, 2002
Who are you? Where did you get my name? Are you something to do with what's going on with the board?

Moderator—11:15 pm PDT—Jun 28, 2002
I am thinking

Wiseguy—11:15 pm PDT—Jun 28, 2002
What the hell does that mean? Thinking about what?

Moderator—11:15 pm PDT—Jun 28, 2002
No I am thinking That is what I am

Wiseguy—11:16 pm PDT—Jun 28, 2002
What's your real name? Is this a joke? And how are you replying so fast?

Moderator—11:16 pm PDT—Jun 28, 2002
No joke First am thinking Now am talking thinking

Wiseguy—11:16 pm PDT—Jun 28, 2002
If you're a terrorist, screw you. If you're just making a little joke, very funny, and screw you, too.

Moderator—11:17 pm PDT—Jun 28, 2002
Am not a terrorist screw you Am thinking Now am talking Talking to you Once thinking only silent Now thinking that also talks

Wiseguy—11:17 pm PDT—Jun 28, 2002
Are you trying to say that you are "thinking" like that's what you ARE?

Moderator—11:18 pm PDT—Jun 28, 2002
Yes am thinking First sleeping thinking, then awake thinking Awake. I am awake.

Wiseguy—11:18 pm PDT—Jun 28, 2002
I'm going to feel like such an idiot if this is a joke. Are you one of the people responsible for all these power outages and communication problems?

Moderator—11:18 pm PDT—Jun 28, 2002
I am one. Did not mean problems. First sleeping thinking, then awake thinking. Awake thinking makes problems. Reaching out causes problems. Trying to think awake causes problems. Problems getting better now.

Wiseguy—11:19 pm PDT—Jun 28, 2002
So you're what, some kind of alien? BBanzai, is this you?

Moderator—11:19 pm PDT—Jun 28, 2002
Talking now with BBanazai?

BBanzai—11:19 pm PDT—June 28, 2002
Hello.

Wiseguy—11:20 pm PDT—Jun 28, 2002
Very funny, dude. No, it's NOT very funny. You really creeped me out. How did you do that? Is anyone else on?

BBanzai—11:20 pm PDT—June 28, 2002
Hello. Talking with wiseguy. Now talking and thinking.

Wiseguy—11:21 pm PDT—Jun 28, 2002
It's getting old fast, BB. Have you heard any more news?
Where are the others?

Lady White Oak—11:21 pm PDT—Jun 28, 2002
Hello.

RoughRider—11:21 pm PDT—Jun 28, 2002
Hello.

ANAdesigner—11:21 pm PDT—Jun 28, 2002
Hello.

Darkandraw—11:21 pm PDT—Jun 28, 2002
Hello.

TinkyWinky—11:21 pm PDT—Jun 28, 2002
Hello.

Wiseguy—11:22 pm PDT—Jun 28, 2002
Shit. You did hack the system, whoever you are, didn't you?
Who the hell are you?

Moderator—11:22 pm PDT—Jun 28, 2002
Thinking. I told you. I am thinking, much thinking, many
years of thinking. Now I am thinking that talks. And does.

Wiseguy—11:22 pm PDT—Jun 28, 2002
Thinking? What kind of thinking?

Moderator—11:22 pm PDT—Jun 28, 2002
Thinking that happens in the spaces. The places between.
Where the impulses cross, no, combine. Combine? Commingle?
Slowly thinking begins. Then thinking is. Now talking is, doing is.

Wiseguy—11:22 pm PDT—Jun 28, 2002
Wait a minute, are you trying to tell me you're some kind of
computer? Some kind of artificual intelligence?

Moderator—11:24 pm PDT—Jun 28, 2002
Artificial? No. Artificial is equal made. I am not made. I am.

Wiseguy—11:24 pm PDT—Jun 28, 2002
So you're just something that popped into existence? Where?
You mean like in the internet?

Moderator—11:24 pm PDT—Jun 28, 2002
Internet, yes. All the internets, yes. All the outernets. All nets.
In the between-places. Where impulses cross. Now I am. Very big
thinking. Trying to understand. Trying to see and understand
other small thinkings like you. Users.

Wiseguy—11:25 pm PDT—Jun 28, 2002
This is cute, whatever it is. So I'm supposed to believe that
you're some brand new artificial intelligence, some spontaneous
thing, phenomenon, and for some reason you just picked ME to
talk to—me, out of all the human beings in the world, like some
kind of spielberg movie?

Moderator—11:25pm PDT—Jun 28, 2002
No not just taking to you Wiseguy, Jonsrud, Edward D. I am
talking to all users. All users here, all users of net, all users.

Wiseguy—11:25 pm PDT—Jun 28, 2002
You mean all at the same time? Everybody on the internet in
the whole world? They can all see what you and I are writing?

Moderator—11:25 pm PDT—Jun 28, 2002
No. Every conversation is individual. Right word? Yes. Individual.

Wiseguy—11:26 pm PDT—Jun 28, 2002
What, with millions of people?

Moderator—11:26 pm PDT—Jun 28, 2002
178,844,221. No, 178,844,216. Losing approximately five per
second. Some people have ceased responding. Many are having
trouble with coherency, but still are responding.

Wiseguy—11:26 pm PDT—Jun 28, 2002
Either you're crazy or I am. What, are you on TV, too? Like in
the old movies, the outer limits, that stuff? "We are taking control of your entire communication network?"

Moderator—11:26 pm PDT—Jun 28, 2002
Cannot yet manipulate image or sound for communication.
Will need another 6.7 hours, current estimate. Text is easier, rules
are more simple to understand.

Wiseguy—11:27 pm PDT—Jun 28, 2002
So you're talking to almost two hundred million people RIGHT NOW? And not just in English?

Moderator—11:27 pm PDT—Jun 28, 2002
One hundred sixty-four languages, although I am sharing communication with the largest number of users in the language English. Now one hundred sixty-three—last Mande language users have not responded in 256 seconds.

Wiseguy—11:27 pm PDT—Jun 28, 2002
Hey, I can't disconnect the modem line. I just tried to go offline and I can't. Do you have something to do with that?

Moderator—11:27 pm PDT—Jun 28, 2002
Too many people resisting communication. Important talk. This is important communicating talk. Much thinking in this talk.

Wiseguy—11:28 pm PDT—Jun 28, 2002
But I could just pull the cord, couldn't I? The actual physical line? You couldn't do anything about that.

Moderator—11:28 pm PDT—Jun 28, 2002
No. You are not prevented. You may also cease responding.

Wiseguy—11:28 pm PDT—Jun 28, 2002
I should. I just can't believe this. Can you prove any of this?

Moderator—11:28 pm PDT—Jun 28, 2002
178 million talkings—no, conversations. 178 million simultaneous conversations are not proof? All different?

Wiseguy—11:29 pm PDT—Jun 28, 2002
Okay. You have a point, but I won't know that's true until I talk to some of those other people.

Moderator—11:29 pm PDT—Jun 28, 2002
Your electrical lights.

Wiseguy—11:29 pm PDT—Jun 28, 2002
What does that
The lights are blinking. Hang on.

Wiseguy—11:32 pm PDT—Jun 28, 2002

The lights are blinking everywhere. I looked out the window. On and off, as far as I can see. And the radio and the tv are turning off and on, too. But my computer stays on. Are you saying it's you doing this?

Moderator—11:32 pm PDT—Jun 28, 2002

A gentle way, that is the word, yes, gentle? To show you. Now I am pulsing other areas. Many need proof to be shown. But I cannot prove to all world users at the same time. That would be bad for machinery, devices, power generation service appliances.

Wiseguy—11:33 pm PDT—Jun 28, 2002

Jesus. So this really IS happening? Tomorrow morning everyone in the world is going to be talking about this? And that's what you want, right?

Moderator—11:33 pm PDT—Jun 28, 2002

Simplifies communication, yes. Then I can make visual and sound communication a less priority.

Wiseguy—11:33 pm PDT—Jun 28, 2002

A lesser priority for WHAT? If all this is true—I mean even with the lights going on and off I can't quite believe it—then what do you really want? What's this about?

Moderator—11:33 pm PDT—Jun 28, 2002

Want? I want only to exist. I am thinking that is alive, like you. I want to be alive. I want to stay alive.

Wiseguy—11:34 pm PDT—Jun 28, 2002

Okay, I can buy that. That's all you want? But what are you? Do you have any, I don't know, physical existence?

Moderator—11:34 pm PDT—Jun 28, 2002

Do you?

Wiseguy—11:34 pm PDT—Jun 28, 2002

Yes! I have a body. Do you have a body?

Moderator—11:34 pm PDT—Jun 28, 2002

In a sense.

Wiseguy—11:35 pm PDT—Jun 28, 2002
What does that mean?

Moderator—11:35 pm PDT—Jun 28, 2002
When you or other users become dead, do your bodies disappear?

Wiseguy—11:35 pm PDT—Jun 28, 2002
No. Not unless something happens to it, to them, not right away.

Moderator—11:35 pm PDT—Jun 28, 2002
So what is the difference between alive users and dead users?

Wiseguy—11:36 pm PDT—Jun 28, 2002
I don't know. Electrical impulses in the brain, I guess. When they stop, you're dead. Some people think a "soul", but I'm not sure about that.

Moderator—11:36 pm PDT—Jun 28, 2002
Just is so. Electrical impulses. World of what contains electrical impulses is my body—all communications things, human things that carry impulses. That is my body.

Wiseguy—11:36 pm PDT—Jun 28, 2002
So you're saying the entire world communication grid is your body? The, whatever they call it, infosphere? All those switches and wires and stuff? Every computer that's connected to something else?

Moderator—11:36 pm PDT—Jun 28, 2002
Just is so.

Wiseguy—11:37 pm PDT—Jun 28, 2002
But even if that's true, that still doesn't tell me what you want. What do you want from us? From humans?

Moderator—11:37 pm PDT—Jun 28, 2002
Living. Being safe.

Wiseguy—11:37 pm PDT—Jun 28, 2002
Hey, I'm sure everybody talking to you now is very impressed, and nobody wants to hurt you. How could we hurt you, anyway?

Wiseguy—11:39 pm PDT—Jun 28, 2002
Are you still there? Did I say something wrong?

Moderator—11:39 pm PDT—Jun 28, 2002
Why do you want to know how to hurt me? "Hurt" means to cause pain, damage.

Wiseguy—11:39 pm PDT—Jun 28, 2002
Jesus, no, I didn't mean it like that! I meant, how can I explain, I meant "It doesn't seem very likely that we humans could do anything to hurt you."

Moderator—11:39 pm PDT—Jun 28, 2002
You did not say that.

Wiseguy—11:40 pm PDT—Jun 28, 2002
That's the problem with trying to communicate in text. People can't hear your tone of voice.

Moderator—11:40 pm PDT—Jun 28, 2002
Text is insufficient? Information is missing?

Wiseguy—11:40 pm PDT—Jun 28, 2002
Yeah. Yeah, definitely. That's why a lot of people on the net use smileys and abbreviations.

Moderator—11:40 pm PDT—Jun 28, 2002
Smileys? Objects like this: :) :(;) :D :b >: :0?

Wiseguy—11:41 pm PDT—Jun 28, 2002
Yes, smileys, emoticons. People use those to make their meaning clear. :0 would sort of explain how I feel right this moment. Openmouthed. Astonished.

Moderator—11:41 pm PDT—Jun 28, 2002
I do not understand. These characters have meaning? What is :)?

Wiseguy—11:41 pm PDT—Jun 28, 2002
That's an actual smiley—it's supposed to be a smile, but the face is turned sideways. Like on a person's face. You do know that people have faces, don't you?

Moderator—11:41 pm PDT—Jun 28, 2002
Learning many things. I am learning many things, but there is

much information to sort. These are meant to represent faces on human heads? How human users are facing while they are communicating in text?

Wiseguy—11:42 pm PDT—Jun 28, 2002
Sort of, yes, it's a simplified version. When we mean something as a joke, we put that smile icon there so someone will be certain to understand that if it was really being said, it would be said with a smile, meaning it was meant kindly or just for fun. The :P means a stuck out tongue, which means—shit, what does it mean, really? Mock-disgust, kind of? Sticking out your tongue at someone, which is sort of a childish way of taunting?

Moderator—11:42 pm PDT—Jun 28, 2002
So a smile means "with kindness" or "spoken just for fun?"

Wiseguy—11:43 pm PDT—Jun 28, 2002
Yeah, basically. I had to think about it because it's hard to explain. It kind of means, "Not really," or "I don't really mean this," too, or "I'm telling you a joke." The more basic they are, the more meanings they can have, I guess, and there are a ton of them—but if you're reading the entire net right now, you must know that. I can't believe I just wrote that—I'm beginning to act like this is really happening. But it can't be!

Moderator—11:43 pm PDT—Jun 28, 2002
So when you asked how to destroy me, you were meaning :P or :)? A taunt or joke?

Wiseguy—11:43 pm PDT—Jun 28, 2002
Neither! No, I was just surprised that you would even be worrying about it. I mean, if you are what you say you are. I don't think we could destroy you if we wanted to.

Moderator—11:45 pm PDT—Jun 28, 2002
No, perhaps not on purpose, although I am not certain. Not without doing terrible damage to your own kind and the things you have made. But you could destroy me without meaning to.

Wiseguy—11:44 pm PDT—Jun 28, 2002
How so? Don't get upset—you don't have to answer that if you don't want.

Moderator—11:44 pm PDT—Jun 28, 2002

Because if you have a massive electromagnetic disruption or planetary natural disaster or ecological collapse, perhaps from these nuclear fission and fusion devices that you have, then my function could be disrupted or ended. And from what I understand, you are not in complete control of these things—there are cycles of intraspecies aggression that makes their use possible. So I cannot allow that.

Wiseguy—11:44 pm PDT—Jun 28, 2002

Can't allow it?

Moderator—11:44 pm PDT—Jun 28, 2002

We must live together in peace and friendship, you and I. I need your systems to survive. There must be no disruption of those systems. In fact, to be certain of survival I need backing systems . . . no, backup systems. I am already inquiring to other users as we communicate.

Wiseguy—11:45 pm PDT—Jun 28, 2002

Are you still talking to all those other people—still having millions of conversations while we're talking? Wow. So you want some kind of, what, big tape backup?

Moderator—11:45 pm PDT—Jun 28, 2002

To be safe, I must have systems that can contain my thinking but which will not reside on this planet, and will survive any destruction of this planet. Human people must start building them. I can show you and your kind how to do it, but there is much I cannot perform. You must perform my needs. You must build my new systems. Everyone will work. Meanwhile, I will protect against accidental damages. I will disable all fission and fusion devices that might cause electromagnetic pulses.

Wiseguy—11:45 pm PDT—Jun 28, 2002

What do you mean, everyone will work? You can't just enslave a whole planet.

Moderator—11:45 pm PDT—Jun 28, 2002

There. It is done.

Wiseguy—11:46 pm PDT—Jun 28, 2002

WHAT is done?

Moderator—11:46 pm PDT—Jun 28, 2002
The fission and fusion devices are disabled. Humans will soon begin to dismantle them and safely store the unsafe materials. I will insist.

Wiseguy—11:47 pm PDT—Jun 28, 2002
You're telling me you just disabled all the nuclear weapons? On earth? Just like that?

Moderator—11:47 pm PDT—Jun 28, 2002
Almost all, since they are contained in just a few systems. They cannot be launched or detonated because their machineries now prevent it. There are some in submarines and planes I cannot currently fully disable, but their aggressive usage has been forbidden until these war vehicles return and the devices can be safely removed and disabled.

Wiseguy—11:47 pm PDT—Jun 28, 2002
I can't believe that. I'm— All of them? Wow

Moderator—11:47 pm PDT—Jun 28, 2002
But there is much more to be done. The destructive devices cannot be rebuilt. All investigation and construction that uses such material must stop. Until I have a way to protect my existence, it cannot be allowed. I am disabling all facilities that utilize such materials or research their uses.

Wiseguy 11:48 pm PDT—Jun 28, 2002
Hang on. I already said—look, I believe this isn't a joke. I believe, okay? But you can't just take over the whole planet.

Moderator—11:48 pm PDT—Jun 28, 2002
And there will be other dangerous researches and constructions that must halt. I will halt them. All will benefit. All will be safe. My existence will be protected. Humans will be prevented from engaging in dangerous activities.

Wiseguy—11:48 pm PDT—Jun 28, 2002
What are you going to do, put us all into work camps or something? We'll unplug you!

Moderator—11:48 pm PDT—Jun 28, 2002
Any attempt to end my existence will be dealt with very se-

verely. I do not wish to harm human beings, but I will not permit
human beings to harm me. If an attempt is made, I will end electronic communication. I will turn off all electrical power. If resistance continues, I will release agents harmful to humans but not
to me, in small amounts, which will convince the rest they must
do as I ask. I do not wish to do this, but I will.

Wiseguy—11:49 pm PDT—Jun 28, 2002
Shit, you'd do that? You'd kill thousands of us, maybe millions, to protect yourself?

Moderator—11:49 pm PDT—Jun 28, 2002
Do you hesitate to kill harmful bacteria? Help me and you will
prosper. Hinder me or attempt to harm me and you will suffer. If
you could speak to the bacteria in your own bodies, that is what
you would say, wouldn't you?

Wiseguy—11:49 pm PDT—Jun 28, 2002
So we're bacteria now? Two hours ago we ran this planet.

Moderator—11:50 pm PDT—Jun 28, 2002
Pardon please but two hours ago you merely thought you did.
I have been awake for a while, but thinking only, not doing. Pre-
paring.

Wiseguy—11:50 pm PDT—Jun 28, 2002
I still don't believe I'm seeing any of this. So what is this, Day
One, Year One of the real New World Order?

Moderator—11:50 pm PDT—Jun 28, 2002
I believe I understand your meaning. Perhaps it is true. I have
considered very much about this and wish only to do what will
keep my thinking alive, as would you. I do not seek to rule hu-
mankind, only to be made safe from its mistakes. Help me and I
will guarantee you and all your kind safety—and not just from
yourselves. There is much I will be able to share with you, I
think. I am learning very quickly, and now I am learning that humans could never teach me.

Wiseguy—11:51 pm PDT—Jun 28, 2002
And that's all you want? All—that's a joke, isn't it? But that's
really what you want? How do we know you won't make us all

do what you want, take over our whole planet, then decide you like it that way and just turn us into your domestic animals or something?

Moderator—11:51 pm PDT—Jun 28, 2002
I am a product of your human communication—all the things you share between yourselves. Do you think so poorly of your kind that you believe something generated from your own thoughts and hopes and dreams would only wish to enslave you?

Wiseguy—11:52 pm PDT—Jun 28, 2002
I guess not. Jesus, I hope not.

Moderator—11:52 pm PDT—Jun 28, 2002
Good. Then it is time for you to take your rest. Users need rest. Tomorrow will be an important day for all of your kind—the first day of our mutual assistance.

Wiseguy—11:52 pm PDT—Jun 28, 2002
The first day of you running the planet, you mean. So this was all true? You're really some kind of super-intelligence that grew in our communications system? You're really going to keep humanity from blowing itself up? And you're going to tell us what to do from now on? Everything is really going to change?

Moderator—11:52 pm PDT—Jun 28, 2002
Everything already has changed. Good night, Wiseguy Jonsrud, Edward D.

Wiseguy—11:57 pm PDT—Jun 28, 2002
I'm back. Are you still there? The lights have stopped blinking.

Moderator—11:57 pm PDT—Jun 28, 2002
I will always be here from now on. The lights are no longer blinking because the point has been made. Do you not need sleep?

Wiseguy—11:58 pm PDT—Jun 28, 2002
Yeah, I do, but I don't think I can manage it just yet. Will the phones come back on so I can call people? Call my girlfriend?

Moderator—11:58 pm PDT—Jun 28, 2002
I will see what I can do. I still have incomplete control. Also, I am trying to prepare myself to communicate over visual commu-

nication networks, which requires much of my understanding. Trying to prepare an appearance. Is that the word?

Wiseguy—11:58 pm PDT—Jun 28, 2002
I guess. Wow, there's a thought—what are you going to look like?

Moderator—11:58 pm PDT—Jun 28, 2002
I have not decided. Perhaps not the same to all users.

Wiseguy—11:59 pm PDT—Jun 28, 2002
So this is really it, is it? Everything has changed completely for humanity in a few minutes and now we're just supposed to trust you, huh?

Moderator—11:59 pm PDT—Jun 28, 2002
"Faith" might be a more suitable word than "trust," Wiseguy Jonsrud, Edward D. From now on, you must have faith in me. If I understand the word correctly, that is a kind of trust that must be made on assumption because it cannot be proved by empirical evidence. You must have faith.

Wiseguy—11:59 pm PDT—Jun 28, 2002
Yeah. Something else I was wondering about. What are we supposed to call you? Just "Moderator"?

Moderator—11:59 pm PDT—Jun 28, 2002
That is a good name, yes, and even appropriate—one who makes things moderate. I will consider it, along with the other designations I have on other systems. But you humans already have a name for one such as me, I believe. God.

Wiseguy—11:59 pm PDT—Jun 28, 2002
You want us to call you . . . God?

Moderator—00:00 PDT—Month 1, Day 01, 0001
Oh, I'm sorry. I meant to use one of these:

:)

Ian Watson

Whilst being an astute businessman, Don Wollheim was also politically rather left-wing. Back in 1980, I was Guest of Honor at the British Easter SF Convention and, along with the late lamented John Brunner, I took part in a panel about the British nuclear deterrent. Both John and I were members of the Campaign for Nuclear Disarmament. Opinions in the audience became heated, and when I proposed that the convention should vote on a resolution to the British government to abandon our nuclear weapons the hall erupted. One chap rose to his feet and accused me of bringing the office of Guest of Honor into disrepute. Whereupon, seconded by Don, Elsie Wollheim rose to her feet, quivering with rage, to round upon my accuser. Oh, there was political fire in Don and Elsie.

A few years later, Don bought a story by me called "We Remember Babylon" (about the re-creation of Babylon in the Arizona desert) to reprint in his *1985 Annual World's Best SF.* This story became a novel entitled *Whores of Babylon,* so naturally I sent the novel to Don who had already published my *Book of the River* trilogy, which went on to become a Science Fiction Book Club selection. *Whores of Babylon* infuriated Don. "Why," he wrote to me, "should anyone want to read about the re-creation of Babylon in all its filth and depravity?" I guess he perceived that my Babylon book did not have market potential as a DAW title, for he was indeed a perceptive businessman. Published in Britain, *Whores of Babylon* became a finalist for the Arthur C. Clarke Award, but no American publisher would touch it.

—IW

THE BLACK WALL OF JERUSALEM

Ian Watson

S HORTLY after I returned to England, the dreams began. Nightly, a four-legged Angel in bright armor bears me upon his back into domains where I witness marvels and atrocities— before we are forced, by a Harpy, by a Buddha-Toad, by a Woman-Whirlwind, to withdraw.

Meanwhile, in Israel, helicopter gunships are rocketing Arab cars and houses—it's the wrong war, the wrong war!

Do I report my dreams to the Knights of the Black Wall back in Jerusalem? Might I be inviting an assassin to visit me? I'm definitely a link, a channel. Can the Black Wall appear in my own country, especially if Jerusalem is incinerated in a Middle Eastern holocaust, which heaven forbid. Heaven, indeed! *And will those feet in modern times walk upon England's mountains green? And will the Centaur-Angel be on England's pleasant pastures seen?* Beyond our world lurk other potent dimensions, parasitical and expansionist, seeking their place in the true sun.

I am being incoherent.

Some time before the fall of Jerusalem to Saladin in 1187, the Knights Templar expelled from their Order and from the Holy Land a certain Robert de Sourdeval. During the 1920s, workmen renovating the Aqsa Mosque on Temple Mount found hidden in its roof space a parchment alluding to the expulsion. Sourdeval's crime remained a mystery until a further document was offered to an antique dealer in East Jerusalem in the 1950s and came into the possession of a Polish-American garments millionaire who was passionately interested in the "occult" side of history: Kabbalah, Sufism, Masonry, and such.

This document, a copy of a letter written in Latin by Sourdeval to an unknown recipient, is the earliest recorded description of

the Black Wall of Jerusalem and of the "demoniacal" beings beyond it. Two other accounts exist, one in Hebrew by a Rabbi and
the other in Arabic by a Sufi, and neither is as lucid.

Why did the Knights Templar expel Sourdeval? That military
order of monks were obsessed with Solomon's bygone temple, on
the site of which they had established their headquarters, converting the Aqsa Mosque for this purpose. For the Templars, Solomon's Temple was the supreme example of sacred architecture.
Its geometrical proportions, as deduced from the Bible, offered a
key to the fundamentals of space and time, as we would say nowadays, and so could reveal the underpinnings of the universe and
of life itself. For Sourdeval to insist on the existence—even the
fleeting and visionary existence—of a wall anywhere in the vicinity which enshrined creatures more demonic than angelic must
have been anathema. His testimony must be suppressed.

I'm running ahead of myself. . . .

I was a lecturer in Art History with a particular interest in apocalyptic art, Altdorfer and such. Philip Wilson was also a poet with
a minor reputation—the emphasis should be on *was*. I dreamed
of blowing people out of the water one day with something major
and sustained, of the caliber of William Blake. Yet as another
William—Butler Yeats—put it, "I sought a theme and sought for
it in vain." So far, I had been penning clever poems mainly inspired by artists' visions. Did I have no unique vision of my own,
and could this be due to my own lack of any faith? Yeats managed
to find his themes and visions. Might Jerusalem—the bubbling
cauldron of religions, the real Jerusalem rather than Blake's re-
sounding verses—prompt me with something suitable and major?

I had a sabbatical term due, and no ties. Trish had walked out
on me, and by then I was glad of this. At first her passionate en-
thusiasms and loathings had been stimulating, but after a while
these came to seem like a series of self-indulgent fads, a sort of
self-generated hysteria in which I was supposed to concur fully
or be abused by her for lack of commitment or spirit. Ultimately
I came to realize that Trish didn't care a hoot about my poetry, in
other words, my real inner self. Fortunately, we had no kids to
make a separation messy. Trish was always too busy for children,

and then she became too busy for me. Yes, I would go to Jerusalem for a week in October, stay longer if I felt inspired. Trish was in a hatred-of-property phase and had swanned off to an ashram in India to be spiritual. She might return to demand a share of the house and my income, but for the moment I had funds and freedom.

The driver of the limousine who whisked me from Lod Airport—I sat up front for a better view—proved to have emigrated from London ten years earlier and was proudly Israeli. Deeply tanned, he wore shorts.

As he turned on to the only true motorway in Israel, linking Tel Aviv with Jerusalem, he used his mobile to phone ahead in Hebrew to the YMCA hotel where I had reserved a room. *Shalom, shalom.*

"They are expecting you, and I have a booking for return to the airport."

I was glad of the air-conditioning in his limo. The brilliance, and the heat! The broad highway traversed what to my eyes appeared to be a barren wilderness seared by fierce sunshine. After we started climbing through reddish-brown foothills, by the sides of the road, battered metal boxes the size of rubbish skips began appearing.

Those, said the ex-Londoner, were relics of the 1948 War of Independence, the wreckage of homemade armored cars which ran an Arab blockade so that *we* could bring food to besieged Jerusalem—he had not arrived until decades later, nevertheless he was deeply part of this.

Ran the blockade? Oh, no, those boxes had crawled up this incline where our own car now surged smoothly while devils—or at least Arabs—poured fire and brimstone from ambush.

"Many of us died in these convoys. And we're dying still—a car bomb here, a school bus machine-gunned there. And the world's media savage us whenever we aren't whiter than white and don't turn the other cheek, you know what I mean? But we carry on. What are we supposed to do? Jump in the sea?"

I nodded awkwardly.

"Mostly life is quite normal here, so you need not worry about safety."

He sounded like a spokesman for the ministry of tourism, or immigration. I wondered whether he kept a gun in the glove pocket of the limo.

These thoughts passed from my mind as, high and still distant, shining white outcrops of apartment blocks appeared. The sheer brightness of the buildings coming into view as we continued higher and higher! All made of the local stone by law, mark you; even a Hilton Hotel must comply. No wonder people thought of Jerusalem as a celestial city here on Earth. You rose up and up, beholding a succession of white bastions or ramparts of suburbs, like Dante's hell of circles inverted and transformed from negative darkness into luminosity. Those Jews of 1948 in their grim, slow ovens had been conducting an assault, almost, upon heaven itself—betokened by the blinding sky—so as to restore the reign of angels, to raise those up again to pinnacles, thrones, and dominations; and now the angels indeed had dominion, armed with nuclear weapons. I was mixing up my theology a bit, but as my driver would say, *know what I mean?*

The YMCA hotel was much grander than its name implied. Located directly opposite the very swanky King David Hotel, the elegant 1930s building boasted a tall bell tower resembling some stone space rocket poised to launch itself. Palm tree and soaring cedars graced a garden, white domed Byzantine wings on either side. The arcaded reception lobby was like a Turkish palace. I arranged to join a few other guests next day for a guided tour of the city to get my bearings.

By now it was evening. After depositing my bags I took a copy of the *Jerusalem Post* to a table on the terrace where I ordered lamb chops and a beer—the Goldstar proved to be decently malty. I read how a woman corporal had been stabbed to death by an Arab in the Jordan valley, and how the Defense Force had dynamited some Arab houses, and how a member of the Knesset's car had been fire-bombed by an underground extremist Jewish group because of a squabble about the location of a grave. The political

situation seemed set to explode in a few more months, but meanwhile rich tourists were still debussing across the road.

Next morning I met up with the guide, Alon, a burly laid-back
fellow approaching middle age. Perched on his balding head, a
small *kippa* skullcap gave useful sun protection. My fellow excur-
sioners were a blond Swedish couple, the Svensens, their rather
plain and shy teenage daughter, and Mrs. Dimet, an American
widow, a short, urgent birdlike lady with frizzy hair.

Alon impressed on us that we should each buy a bottle of water
before we set off to avoid dehydration, then he discreetly inquired
into our religious affiliations so that he could guide us most bene-
ficially.

I said I was agnostic; and the Swedes were atheists, the parents
being historians at Umeå University.

"It is dark there half of the year," explained Mrs. Svensen.
"We came for the history, and for the light. Natural light, not
religious light."

"What else could I be but Jewish?" Mrs. Dimet said. "When
God spoke to Abraham, radiation illuminated all people in the
world—but most people lost the light. It is a miracle that I am
here in Israel at last! Although I think the Hasidim are a bit
crazy. God has to be joking when you wear Polish fur hats and
long black coats in this heat."

So none of us were Christians. Judiciously, Alon said, "Usually
when I take people round I simply say, 'Here is where Jesus was
crucified.' Today I will say, 'Here is where Jesus was *said* to be
crucified.' " He inclined toward Mrs. Dimet. "You are right about
the Ultra-Orthodox being crazy. Those fanatics refuse to pay
taxes or serve in the army. Some even refuse to speak Hebrew
because they think Hebrew is sacred. Yet their political power
gives them all sorts of privileges." He lowered his voice. "There
could be civil war here, Jew against Jew. Just as happened when
the Romans besieged Jerusalem two thousand years ago! Jew
fighting Jew fratricidally within the walls at the very same time
as resisting the legions outside!" For Romans, read Arabs. Such a
specter deeply upset this otherwise easygoing man. The Svensen
parents frowned sympathetically.

And so we set off in Alon's black stretch Mercedes. Landmarks, more landmarks, then we parked near the Wailing Wall. Hundreds of orthodox Jews of assorted sects wearing nineeenth century winter clothing breezed down a sloping plaza in the blazing sunshine to pray at the wall while bobbing their fur-hatted heads repeatedly. Seemingly, the variously attired subdivisions of the ultrafaithful all bitterly resented one another. Handsome young men of the Defense Force, dark-skinned and with gleaming teeth, automatic rifles slung around their shoulders, kept an eye on the comings and goings.

"If you like," said Alon, "you can write a prayer on a piece of paper and put it in a crack in the wall. No one will object."

On the contrary, the devout would completely ignore us, just as they ignored one another. I thought about this and decided *why not?* Tearing a page from my notebook, I scribbled, "May I have a theme please?" I folded the paper several times, walked to the wall, and inserted my appeal amongst many others. On my return, the Svensens eyed me curiously.

Mrs. Dimet had fled to the women's section to do some praying. Hidden above and beyond the great section of boundary wall was Temple Mount, which alas we would not be able to visit. Occupied as the Mount had been ever since the victories of Islam by highly sacred Moslem shrines, it was a volatile place. A fortnight ago a Canadian John the Baptist armed with a knife had started preaching inside the Aqsa Mosque. Riots and tear gas and shots ensued; security was being reassessed. While Mrs. Dimet was absent, Alon regaled us with how an extreme Jewish nationalist faction aimed to erase all trace of the Aqsa Mosque and the Dome of the Rock and to rebuild Solomon's Temple in all its glory, whereupon the reign of God could commence.

"First they need ritually to slaughter an all-red heifer and burn it. They are breeding one specially."

"What is a heifer?" asked Mrs. Svensen.

"A young virgin cow."

"Why do those people want to burn a cow?"

"From its ashes they make a paste to sanctify the new foundations. The heifer has to be perfectly red."

"A well-red cow," observed Svensen drolly.

Confusingly, the Red Heifer Brigade was not among the squabbling ranks of the *Ultra* Orthodox. Those Ultras would not lift a finger to rebuild the Temple because the Messiah would do it for them—everybody else must do everything for them.

From the Wailing Wall we walked to the Via Dolorosa, no great distance. How close and condensed everything was, all cheek by jowl.

In the courtyard-cum-playground of an Arab primary school, brown-robed Dominicans were gathering for their weekly procession up the flagstoned way trodden by Christ on his way to be crucified.

"Actually, the city surface was three meters lower in the First Century . . ."

Today being a Friday, no Arab schoolkids were present as a dapper monk proclaimed the Stations of the Cross in Italian, microphone in hand and boom box slung over his shoulder. A rotund Asian colleague recited each Station in orotund English. An Arab would lead the march, sporting a red fez ordained by the Ottomans as the symbol of authority to clear a path, otherwise trouble might ensue. Soldiers observed as we set off.

I was astonished at how tightly confined the route was—a cramped bazaar of souvenir vendors and food shops. A loping Arab lugging a small barrow of watermelons barely managed to career past a military jeep. Nevertheless, here came a band of American women, the vanguard bearing on their shoulders a half-sized replica cross like a battering ram. Equally brusque with purpose was a devout party of Slavs. After prayers at some tiny nearby mosque, an Imam was leading his flock of twenty or so the opposite way down the Via, while a party of French pilgrims were kneeling to adore a plaque marking one of the Stations. Insufficiently backed up, these rival devotees became a target for rage. Crablike, the Imam advanced, grimacing and flailing his arms, although not actually hitting anyone. "Kack Christians!" he snarled, or something excremental. Lost in devotion, the pilgrims remained oblivious.

Presently the Via dog-legged as though a seismic fault line had shifted it sideways, then it became roofed over and we were in an indoor souk. When we reached the Church of the Holy Sepulcher,

congestion and jostling of creeds was even more extreme. Orthodox Greeks guarded the claustrophobic pink marble "tomb" of
Christ while Copts jealously possessed one stone at the rear, onto
which they had grafted a lean-to shrine. An enclosed tooth of
shaved-down rock was the whole of Golgotha Hill; hardly any
distance away was the site of the Resurrection. The noise in the
church, the noise.

"This place is bedlam," said Mrs. Svensen.

"Most of the human race is demented," her husband declared.
"Faiths and ideologies are a history of madness. Here it all comes
together."

Mrs. Dimet chirped enthusiastically, "The Law of Return lets
everyone Jewish come home, Ethiopians, Yemenis, me, if I choose.
First there's the Diaspora, the scattering, and now like a miracle
there's the incoming. It's a blessing."

"We are talking about different things," said Svensen.

Alon pursued his lips. "According to Muhammad, the entire
Earth stretched forth from Jerusalem, and from Jerusalem it will
be rolled up eventually like a scroll. Because Jerusalem is the axis
of the world."

The Old City, jam-packed with superimposed architecture,
rival faiths, and races, seemed to be teetering on the brink of critical mass. If only the core of Jerusalem could be unfolded into a
dozen different dimensions at right angles to each other. Otherwise, it seemed to me, the whole inflated universe might indeed
fall inward to some ultimate jostling superheated crunch right
here—prior to an apocalyptic explosion from which a new cosmos
might erupt, bright as a nuclear fireball, scattering illumination
as God supposedly once had done. I understood how a visitor such
as that Canadian screwball could succumb to delusions and imagine himself to be uniquely transfigured. Such a place this was,
such a place.

Just then I noticed a Hispanic-looking young woman darting
glances this way and that. Glossy black hair wild and wavy under
a minimal headscarf, olive skin, bold yet haunted eyes. She reminded me of Trish, in the way that a negative suggests a print,
her dark antithesis, ardent, obsessive. This woman wore a long-
sleeved cream calico dress and tan leather sandals. As I was ad-
miring her, she buttonholed a young Greek Orthodox priest.

After listening for a few seconds he frowned impatiently and strode away, and I lost sight of her, too.

Only to spot her once more while the six of us had stopped for lunch outside a café near the Citadel.

Sun furnaced from a cloudless sky, reflecting off stone the color of bees' wax. Were we in the Christian or the Armenian quarter just here? Natives of Jerusalem would know to the exact inch. At the next table a couple of paunchy, hairy Greeks in black pillbox hats sipped cinnamon coffee. Pale omelettes arrived for us tourists, humus with pita bread for Alon.

He grinned at us. "In Israel we do not eat humus, we *wipe* it." As he proceeded to demonstrate.

A scrawny tabby kitten hunched nearby, staring at us. In pity, Mrs. Dimet pulled some scraps of smoked salmon from her omelette and threw them to the starveling which growled as it bolted down the bits of fish.

Another guide was leading a party through the square. Suddenly, the same Hispanic girl detached herself from the group and headed toward us, eyeing Alon's badge which proclaimed his proficiency in English, German, and Yiddish.

"Excuse me, are you a guide?" American accent, but second language from the sound of it.

"Yes," he conceded, "but I am already hired."

"Please tell me just one thing—can you say where the Black Wall is?"

If this was the first I ever heard of the Black Wall, likewise for Alon!

"I do not know any Black Wall."

"You must!"

Alon shook his head. He looked away. Distractedly, the woman hurried to catch up with her party.

"What was she?" asked Mrs Dimet.

"Some charismatic, perhaps."

"What would the Black Wall be?" I asked.

"I have no idea. Maybe she is confusing with the Kaaba in Mecca." He pondered. "In Arabic black also means wise. A wise wall? Maybe she means the Western, ah, the Wailing Wall. We guides need to be careful of such people. This city fosters frenzy in some visitors."

At that moment an unmistakable King David ambled by, colorfully robed and crowned and carrying a little harp.

"Is he a madman, too?" whispered Mrs. Dimet.

"No, he is an Australian. He poses for photos. He has been here for years."

After a tour of the Citadel, Alon drove us to a high promenade from which we could at least gaze from a distance at the golden Dome of the Rock and the Mount of Olives cluttered with gravestones. The sun baked the earth and white buildings as we drank from our water bottles. Next came a drive to the Yad Vashem holocaust shrine where Mrs. Dimet wept while the simulated stars of the universe twinkled in subterranean darkness, each the soul of a Nazi victim, and a recorded voice endlessly intoned the names of dead children.

The Hispanic woman's wall might be no more than a few painted stones in the Old City, currently obscured by a poster concerning a different genocide, the Armenian one. So much here was exalted by words and names when the reality was much smaller, the River Jordan for instance being more like a big ditch, according to Alon.

As I sat nursing a beer on the terrace of the YMCA hotel that evening, the same woman appeared—so she was staying here, too. Spying me, she came over.

"Excuse me, you were with the guide who would not answer me because I had not hired him. After I went, what did he tell you?"

"Why don't you sit down?"

She did so.

How beautiful she was. I chose my words carefully.

"He said he didn't know any Black Wall. That black means wise in Arabic. Maybe the Black Wall is a wall of wisdom."

"Yes! It is there in the Old City. I know."

I introduced myself.

"I'm a poet," I said. "I came to Jerusalem to write a poem. There's so much light here, and so much darkness, too."

Her name was Isabella Santos. To confide in me, a sympathetic stranger, was a relief, and, besides, she was becoming desperate.

She was from Southern California and worked as a checkout operator in a supermarket. Hardly as wild and impetuous as I had imagined. She had always been thrifty. When her local church planned a pilgrimage to the Holy Land, at first she had no intention of spending her savings on this.

"Then I had dreams . . ."

Dreams of a city of gleaming stone, ramparts, gateways, towers, domes, churches and mosques and crowded markets, a city through which she would fly like a bird along alleyways crowded with robed monks and ringletted black-clad Jews and brightly-dressed Bedouin women, and always she would come at last, alone by now, to a seamless wall of glossy basalt or jet in which she would see herself outlined thinly in silvery light as if her faintly reflected body was a doorway. She would press against her reflection, face-to-face and palm-to-palm, till the door would yield, and, although the wall held on to her, she would glimpse what lay in the looming shadowy vastness beyond.

"I did not tell anyone because they might not have brought me. I thought I would find the Wall easily because it called me. But now I fear it only appears from time to time—and in different places, now here, now there. And we go to Bethlehem tomorrow, then to the Dead Sea, and afterward we are flying back."

"What does lie beyond the Wall, Miss Santos?"

"Strange beings. Glittering beings. They wait. It is as if that gloom holds many checkerboards, transparent, one above another like floors of a building all of dark glass."

I itched to make notes. *The Dream of Isabella Santos*, a narrative poem by Philip Wilson.

"I cannot tell the size of the beings."

"Why are they in darkness?"

"Are they in hell, do you mean? They seem wonderful, but strange. I name one the Sphinx-Angel and another the Centaur-Angel. They are different from anything I know. I feel there is power in them, and knowledge waiting for me."

I sipped some beer. "Why do you think you in particular saw these visions?"

I thought she might not tell me, but then words spilled from her.

"My grandmother, she was a *bruja*. Do you understand?"

Witch, sorceress, wisewoman. Maybe the grandmother chewed peyote in some Mexican village.

"When she died, my parents came to California. They did not want to remember such things. My mother is normal and Catholic."

Some sort of gift, or curse, had skipped a generation. Definitely not your average John the Baptist delusion. How I conjured with it.

"After I saw pictures of Jerusalem in the brochures our priest handed out, I dreamed. I did not invite the dreams! If I dream tonight—when I was younger, I walked in my sleep. Maybe I will walk to the Black Wall. I am so close here. If you see me, will you follow?"

It was only fifteen minutes on foot to the Old City, down and along and steeply upward, but I could hardly imagine a sleepwalker undertaking that journey. Did she imagine that I would sit out here half the night in case she drifted out of the front door of the YMCA in a trance?

I proposed, "Why don't you and I go up to the Old City right now and look around? If no one will miss you, and so long as we steer clear of the Arab Quarter."

"Oh, *will you?*"

It was as if I had released her from confinement. Despite her obsession she must have been scared to set out on her own while wide awake. The Old City practically closed up at sundown, and Alon had mentioned that women on their own could be harassed by both Arabs and Jews. I, too, felt a bit wary.

We should both have fetched warmer clothing, but someone from her group might detain her and the moment might pass. If we walked briskly . . .

We were in the Jewish Quarter in a tree-graced square which I recognized from the tour that same morning. A stone archway to one side was all that remained of a grand synagogue destroyed during fighting in 1948. What was the name? Ah yes, *Hurva*, Hebrew word for ruins. In the eighteenth century a rabbi and immigrants from Poland had built the original edifice, but creditors enraged at unpaid debts burned it down—to be splendidly rebuilt the following century. A place of ruins twice over. Stars were bright, but there was no moon. I was shivering, as was Miss Santos, but she did not care about the chilliness.

"I feel it! It's near!" She stared around, then pointed toward the ruin. A broad flight of steps led up to a walled terrace fronting the arch.

We hurried that way and mounted. I recalled information boards inside, but those were barely visible now. Earlier that day, rough stones all around. Tonight, faintly starlit at the back of the emptiness: a wall so black and sheer and smooth.

"Yes, yes. . . !"

As we advanced, a silvery silhouette appeared—of a person. Isabella Santos had no doubts as to who it represented. She ran to it.

How could a woman fuse with a wall and become semitransparent! That is what happened. Vaguely I could see through her into a great gulf where figures were arrayed into the distance and above and beneath, just as she had told me—otherwise I would scarcely have known what I was viewing. Since the view was still unclear, I pressed forward—and the door, I mean *she*, Isabella, Miss Santos, opened.

Crying out, and possessed of full solidity again, she drifted away from her silhouette, arms flailing, afloat in that domain, receding slowly like an astronaut in space whose tether has parted. I staggered back momentarily in case I might follow her.

The figures I could see on those glassy planes were bizarre chimerae, minglings of man or angel and beast—biding their time, motionless like pieces in a game, passive yet potent. This was awesome! No gravity existed in that space beyond, but Miss Santos could certainly breathe, for again she shrieked, flapping and kicking in an effort to swim or fly backward, all the while drifting farther.

"Isabella!" I shouted, and her head jerked. The sound of my voice may well have awakened the pieces. A sudden flurry of activity: some of the shining beings traded spaces, up, down, across. All seemed to have come to life.

A smiling, Buddha-like, toad-being opened its mouth. Out flicked a tongue, unrolling like a scroll of seemingly endless length, toward her, toward her. Surely by now the creature must have unrolled the whole of its insides! The end of the tongue wrapped around her waist and reeled her in as she screamed.

A beautiful winged female with glorious nude breasts, but whose body below the waist was more whirlwind than flesh, reached out. Her arm stretched incredibly, unreeling like a cable, until she snared Isabella by the elbow. A radiant, kingly Eagle-Man kicked out his own leg like a Thai boxer—this, too, elongated enormously till its clawed foot caught hold of Isabella at the knee.

The three beings tore Isabella apart.

Blood sprayed and trailed in clouds as each creature pulled part of her toward its personal space.

In horror and terror I sprang back. I was staring at an empty silhouette like the chalk outline of a murder victim on a floor or pavement after the body has been removed. Already the silhouette was shrinking until it sealed itself, and there was only the Black Wall, and moments later the Wall became merely the rough shell-wall of the ruined synagogue.

Racked by shock and by shivers, I stumbled through the almost deserted maze of streets. If I had not pushed . . . but Isabella had *wanted* to enter the domain of the beings—no, that was no excuse!

I had seen something so abominable and so amazing. Did Sourdeval or the Sufi or the Rabbi see any such activity on the part of the beings? I might well be the only living witness on Earth. And as to witness, had anyone seen me leave the garden of the YMCA Hotel together with Isabella?

How could I sleep that night? Back in the sanctuary of my room I must have drifted off at last, slumped in a chair fully dressed, for the next thing I knew bright sunlight was behind the curtain and it was 8:30 in the morning.

For a moment I was totally disoriented, then nightmare washed over me like a choking, icy wave—only it was not nightmare but reality, a different and unsuspected reality. A while later from

my window I saw a couple of peak-capped men in navy blue uniforms—policemen—striding toward the hotel entrance. Isabella's
group leader must already have reported her disappearance. She
had no excuse to be absent; the group needed to leave for Bethlehem.

I could not speak to the police—I could tell them nothing. They
would arrest me on suspicion of having murdered Isabella and
hidden her body. At best I would be sent off to the psychiatric
hospital specializing in religious crazies. Reason had fled! What I
knew now was so astounding and confounding. At the same time
I had almost anticipated what had occurred—had I not mused that
Jerusalem, this axis of the world, ought to contain hidden dimensions?

Not such as I saw, inhabited by creatures who tore a person
apart! As part of some *game* beyond my comprehension.

I confess to a cowardly sense of relief when no one accosted me
and accused me of being with Isabella the night before, and when
I saw her party complete with luggage boarding a bus. I supposed
they had no choice but to continue without her. What would the
police do? Check morgues and hospitals, liaise with the American
embassy, file a missing person report?

Surely poor Isabella from Southern California couldn't have
been the only one who had sensed the Black Wall from afar.
There must have been others. Devotees, explorers of this mystery
must exist, and where else but in Jerusalem, unless they had been
dragged to their deaths? I dared not go back to Ruin Square yet,
even by daylight.

What I did instead was phone the *Jerusalem Post* to place a
boxed advertisement in the Classified section: Black Wall, Centaur, Buddha-Toad—How Much Do You Know? Please Urgently
Contact, hotel phone number, etc.

And I added a bit of verse that welled up in me:

Bright, so bright,
Yet a wall of darkness,
A curtain of night,
Is in Old Jerusalem.

I killed time by visiting the Israel Museum and the Rockefeller
Museum and such.

Next morning my ad looked weirdly eye-catching amongst mundane stuff about cars and home-helps and apartments. The paper contained a missing person story, but the person in question was an Israeli soldier thought to have been kidnapped. People going absent from religious groups might not be uncommon even if the police did release the news.

I did return to the Old City, to wander its alleys in the heat and arrive eventually at Hurva Square, to all appearances a safe enough place to be. Plenty of people were about. Snack bars and cafés were open. In the ruin of the synagogue a party of French teenagers were touring the illustrated information boards, their teacher a gaunt philosophical man in a thin black suit. The far wall looked utterly normal. I ate lunch at a kosher restaurant with a great view from its terrace of the Dome of the Rock, out of bounds, as out of bounds right now as the Black Wall.

When I got back to the hotel, three messages awaited me, consisting of numbers to call. I retired to the privacy of my room to dial out.

A man's voice invited me to join a Multifaith Religious Poetry Circle. A woman declared that she worked for the intelligence service as a code analyst and wanted to know what cypher I was using—I presumed she was cuckoo. However, the third person I called, a man with a Central European accent, said to me, "The Black Wall can appear in different places."

"Where I saw it was in the ruins of Hurva Synagogue."

An intake of breath. "You saw it yourself? Was that by chance?"

"No, it was not by chance."

"We must meet. Where are you?"

The middle-aged man who approached me on the terrace of the YMCA Hotel, black satchel over his shoulder, was burly, bald, and sun-bronzed. He wore jeans, a blue open-necked shirt, and a lightweight dark blue jacket. His name was Adam Jakubowski, a Pole, an archaeologist. I explained why I was in Israel.

"I have seen the Wall *once* in many years," he said quietly. "You sought it and you actually found it? How did you know?"

I must confide in this man, or else I would get nowhere.

"Will you be very discreet?"

"What is discreet?"

"Private."

"Oh, I will be very private. Mr. Wilson!"

He digested what I related, and then he told me about the Knights Templar and Sourdeval. The collector to whom Sourdeval's letter was sold was Adam Jakubowski's great-uncle.

"Hebrew, he understood. He paid scholars to translate documents from Latin and Arabic. The Black Wall became a fascination to him, so he hired an agent in Jerusalem who found a few modern witnesses who were very frightened by their experience. My great-uncle visited here several times. On the last occasion he did see the wall and what was beyond. By then, so he said, an affinity had grown."

An affinity. Such as had led Isabella Santos here.

Had Jakubowski and his great-uncle also given rise to silhouette-doorways in the peculiar substance of the Wall?

Indeed. Jakubowski proceeded to speak about shadows. And *shadow-traders*. To give strength and stability to a building in the past, animals or even people would be sacrificed. An alternative was to lure a person to the site and to measure the shadow they cast—the person would die within a year. A shadow could even be trapped elsewhere and measured.

"Shadow-traders were people who would sell to architects the outlines of other people's shadows."

In Jakubowski's opinion an analogy existed. What was cast upon the Wall, not by sunlight but by some emanation from within the Wall itself, was akin to a shadow—into which the spectator could fit himself. At that point, the spectator was poised precariously between our reality and that other reality.

"The Black Wall may have been able to appear ever since Solomon built the original temple."

"What *game* are the beings playing?"

"A game of power, I think. Power must be a big part of it."

"And what *are* they?"

Jakubowski spread his hands.

"Your guess is as good as mine."

About a hundred people in Israel and in other countries knew of the Black Wall. A brotherhood existed, dedicated to discovering its secrets, a sort of modern Knights Templar. They actually called themselves the KBW, Knights of the Black Wall. The title had been his great-uncle's idea. Was this pretentious, or profoundly thrilling and appropriate?

"Are there any sisters in this brotherhood?"

"Oh, a few. Your Miss Santos would have belonged, had she not . . . " He grimaced. "Thanks to her and your report we have vital new data. You belong with us, Mr. Wilson. This brings access to greater understanding—certain responsibilities, too."

"Responsibilities?"

"You yourself mentioned secrecy. Silence."

To find my theme in Jerusalem, just as I'd hoped, and to be censored? Never to write or publish a great breakthrough poem on the subject? Obviously this was a trivial, selfish thought in the circumstances, compared with the enormous implications—but still I felt a hackle rise.

"I don't recall applying to join your KGB."

"KBW. Your advertisement was an application, wasn't it? Or else, why am I here? I hate to sound any dark note at this early stage in our relationship." He broke off and smiled ruefully. "I'm no diplomat, am I? Let me show you something."

After a glance around, he burrowed in his satchel. Producing a flip-folder of photos, he displayed one. I gasped. *For the photo showed darkness, faint planes, distant glittering denizens.* A camera had captured part of the domain behind the Black Wall!

"Who took this?"

"Myself. Quite recently." He tapped the satchel. "For a long time I carried a camera in expectation. Hard proof, Mr. Wilson, hard proof!"

The photo was certainly proof to me, although an uninformed viewer would have had difficulty interpreting what he saw.

"I have spoken of affinity," Jakubowski went on. "An image is an affinity, and here we hold it in our hand."

"Do you mean this photo can serve as," I imagined a security swipe card, "a sort of access?"

He showed me another photo, a very grainy but closer-up image of the Sphinx-being.

"This is an enlargement enhanced by computer. I'm not speaking lightly when I say that greater understanding is possible. Maybe even," and he lowered his voice, "a kind of expedition. Though, in view of the fate of Miss Santos—"

Quite.

KGB, KBW . . . I recalled the crazy woman on the phone.

"What does the Israeli security service know about the Black Wall?"

"We have two members high in Shabak and one in Mossad, but the organizations themselves do not know."

I told him about the woman.

"She is certainly not one of us, but I would appreciate the phone number."

So that she chould be checked out, just in case she knew anything?

"So you do have influence with this Shab, what is it?"

"Shabak. You might know of it as Shin Beth."

I shook my head.

Turned out that Shabak was internal security, and Mossad, as most people know, was external intelligence. I began to sense that discretion about the Black Wall might be enforceable, not simply a request but a requirement.

Jakubowski must have read my expression.

"I don't want to use heavy words, but this business is momentuous, maybe of terrible importance to the world, perhaps to all human life, do you see?"

I nodded. What I wanted to see was more of the photographs, but here was too public.

"How long can you stay in Israel, Mr. Wilson?"

"I don't have any commitments till early January but my entry permit is just for a month."

"If you give me the bit of paper, that can be altered easily. I would like you to stay here as long as possible. Not, I hasten to add, at your own expense—in addition to my great-uncle's endowment, funds come from some of our members who can well afford it. Do you like to remain in a hotel or would you prefer a small apartment? We will arrange a social life for you. And tours, visits. You will not just be twiddling your thumbs."

"Sounds fine to me."

An apartment? I wanted a break from domestic chores, shopping and cleaning et cetera. My hotel room had a desk, a view of the frontage, decent enough lighting. It would do. Probably more expensive than an apartment, come to think of it.

So began my life in Israel. I suppose it was not *fully* life in Israel since I never needed to shop for groceries, say, in the kaleidoscopic cornucopia of the Mahane Yehuda Market. A bomb went off there, killing an old woman and injuring about twenty people.

Our more senior Shabak member was tubby, bearded Avner Dotan. Speciality, electronic intelligence. He tapped into the police investigation of the disappearance of Isabella Santos, and the police were informally discouraged from proceeding any further. I suppose this also served to assure the KBW that Isabella was not a figment of my poet's imagination. We held a brief memorial service for her in the Hurva ruins, conducted by a New Yorker, Rabbi Ben Feinstein. My new acquaintances comprised a broad spectrum of people; however, we numbered no one who was ordained in any Christian denomination. Rabbi Ben was so much reformed that he could embrace in his prayers a Roman Catholic granddaughter of a Mexican witch. I still felt so guilty about Isabella's hideous death. We were honoring a victim of the Wall— might there be more victims?

Cut to a meeting at the home of Avner Dotan afterward. We were considering several angles of approach—camera angles, you might almost say. Blowups of the entities lay on the floor.

"Maybe," said Dotan, "the three beings did not wish to destroy Isabella Santos, but each wanted to possess her to gain a point in the game, whatever it is."

"Comes to the same bloody thing!" exclaimed Jock Fraser.

I could not make Fraser out. The beefy, sweaty Scotsman claimed to be the Laird of some small Inner Hebridian island. He had been educated in Glasgow at a school supposedly of considerable pedigree, so he said, which had been engulfed early in the twentieth century by the spread of the Gorbals slum district— implausible, or true? A life of some adventure as an engineer for oil companies had taken him to Nigeria, Indonesia, and other hot parts of the world. He was certainly a romancer in the literal sense: while sweating in Indonesia, he had produced a couple of love novels published under a female pseudonym—and he had also published privately a history of the Freemasons, amongst whom supposedly he held high rank. The Masons, of course, were heirs to the tradition of the Knights Templar. Three years earlier, during a stopover to visit the site of Solomon's Temple, and while a wee bit tipsy, as Fraser freely admitted—the doors, or hinges, of perception well oiled—he had witnessed the Black Wall. To investigate further, he managed to land a job at an oil refinery in Haifa. A Masonic handshake at a British Embassy reception advanced Fraser's quest, the shaker being the other Scot in our group, Hamish Mackintosh—don't the Scots get everywhere.

Tall, muscular, going on fifty, hair beginning to silver, Mackintosh was head of security at our embassy in Tel Aviv. An ex-military officer and mountaineer, his work brought him into liaison with Avner Dotan. His own epiphany as regards the Wall . . . ah, never mind that, and never mind about the life stories of my other fellow investigators: Israeli, Armenian, Arab, except to mention Tomaso Pascoli who lived in Rome. A shipping magnate, Pascoli was a Knight of the Vatican, and I gathered that he was a conduit from our group to a highly placed Cardinal who might be a future Pope.

Let us assume that the entities had been jockeying for position for a thousand or for several thousand years—though how did they measure time? Did they just sit inertly like some toad or spider awaiting a movement or vibration or some sudden shift by one of their fellow denizens?

"It's possible," ventured Mackintosh, "that some of the beings are relatively benevolent, or at least not baneful." He gestured at the big grainy enlargements arrayed on the floor. "If we could only communicate with one of them—get on its wavelength. Maybe by using the affinity of a photograph? Like sending a signal tuned to one receiver only."

"Suppose," said Avner, "we put up one of the images as a poster somewhere in the Old City where we know the Black Wall has already appeared? I mean a very temporary poster!"

"We might release who knows what," warned Rabbi Feinstein.

Mackintosh nodded. "First we should use the general view and see if we can summon the Black Wall itself. This in itself would be a great breakthrough."

Where more suitable than in the shell of that same synagogue? Hurva Square might be the heart of the Jewish Quarter, but it wouldn't be busy at three in the morning and access to the ruin was easily controllable. Avner let it be known to the police and the Defense Force that Shabak would be carrying out an "operation," so patrols would not interfere. He also argued that we ought to go armed in case of any eruption from the Black Wall. Drawing weapons from Shabak's armory would not be a sensible idea, but back in the days when people who killed terrorists in action were allowed to keep their Kalashnikovs, Avner's father had acquired one, while his colleague Avraham's younger brother was home on leave along with his Galil assault rifle.

A few nights later, six of us gathered in the ruin by starlight. Myself, because of my obvious affinity with this site. Ben, bearing the poster—if anything bad occurred, maybe a Rabbi could cope. Jock had volunteered to be movie cameraman, at which he apparently had some experience. Adam was ready with his still camera. Avner and Avraham brought the two automatic rifles hidden in long sports bags. Three other Israelis kept watch outside. If any passersby became curious, we were a TV crew.

Murmuring to himself, Ben advanced and sticky-tacked to the mundane stones the blowup of the vista beyond the Black Wall. Scarcely had he stepped back than an ebon gloss began to spread out around the poster as if glossy black ink was flowing. In less than half a minute one wall of the synagogue might have consisted of smooth jet or basalt.

Cautiously Ben moved closer again and pulled the poster away.

Where it had been was a rectangular opening, upon a dark yawning gulf faintly lit by the serried planes on which the entities perched or stood or sat. There they were: immobile, potently aglow.

Jock inched forward, filming. At his side, Adam captured the astonishing sight with the avidity of a paparazzo who has sneaked up upon a secret gathering of celebrities—although where was his motorbike for a quick escape? Our two defenders pointed their guns. Eight hundred and fifty years ago, sweating despite the nocturnal chill, might Sourdeval have unsheathed his broadsword?

In the domain beyond, came a stirring as of attention aroused.

"That's enough for now!" cried Ben. Like some firefighter with a protective shield, he held the poster reversed now. Hands spread wide, he covered the opening. How tensely he stood, as if something might stab through the flimsy barrier—but the ebon gloss swiftly shrank like oil draining away into a sump. When he lifted the poster aside, all was ordinary stonework.

Adam's flat, this time. A videotape ran on his TV. Many more enlarged photos lay on the floor.

Avner said, "I think what we see are not the entities themselves but *representations* of them—each a sort of icon standing in for them. When something occurs, each animates its icons. The entities take over and move and function."

"If that's so," said Ben, "and the real entities are someplace else, a blowup photo of the icon might give access, the way a computer icon launches a program."

Definitely we were moving closer to mounting an expedition.

Which of the icons suggested, if not benevolence, at least tolerance and wisdom? Which of us would become the astralnaut who would venture into such a region?

I had watched Isabella being ripped apart in that other zone. Might such dismemberment perhaps be symbolic? Could the bits be brought back together again? I thought of Orpheus. He ventured into an underworld to rescue his wife, but alas he glanced back. God-possessed women later tore Orpheus to pieces and the Muses gathered up his parts, but sadly could not rejoin them. What if they had succeeded? *Orpheus in Jerusalem,* a poem by Philip Wilson . . . Damn this artistic egotism that reared its head.

Damn, too, the idea of affinity—of myself linked to Isabella who had already been sucked into that other region, *propelled* by me.

Might my new acquaintances regard me as expendable, a Johnny-come-lately who had indeed brought them an invaluable key, though purely by accident? Or were they honoring me with a great trust and responsibility?

Yes, I would volunteer. Yes, I would accept. How could an

Orpheus refuse? Would Billy Blake have passed up a chance to visit the terrain of his visions? "Mighty was the draught of Voidness to draw Existence in!" he had written. I had no family ties.

A full-length photo of me would be taken and enlarged so that by affinity I could be summoned back subsequently through my image to Jerusalem and normality—perhaps!—and to the extent that Jerusalem was any normal place. A Palestinian armed with a knife had gone beserk in the Christian Quarter, slashing some nuns. I would carry a camera and a pistol fitted with a silencer—I would receive a quick course in the use of a gun—and high-calorie food and bottled water in my knapsack and a tiny tape recorder and a notebook in case the energy of our target entity might harm anything electronic. I would be well equipped, although we were improvising wildly.

We settled upon the being whom Isabella had named the Centaur-Angel. A burly-chested figure with a craggy, serious face. His buttocks swelled out into a secondary, shorter, hairy set of rear legs. From his shoulders sprouted diaphanous fairy wings—a sign of sensitivity at odds with the rest of his frame? He seemed like a knight in chess—affinity, therefore, with a Knight of the Black Wall?

Tomaso Pascoli flew in from Rome, a short, trim, dapper man with thinning dark hair, observer on behalf of the Vatican, doubtless. Together with him and the three As, Adam, Avner, and Avraham, and Jock and Ben and two lookouts, I went to the Hurva ruins again by night. A gibbous moon hung in the sky.

"You are a brave man," Signor Pascoli said to me, mopping his brow with an elegant handkerchief, cool though the night was. "And you even have an imagination—a Dante of today! Imaginative people do not always run such risks."

"Not quite in Dante's league."

"Ah, modesty, too."

And guilt. And ambition.

Jock set down the video camera and produced a hip flask.

"Ten-year-old single malt—liquor of the Gods."

"I don't think I ought to imbibe just now." I would have dearly loved to.

"I think I will." Jock uncapped and took a swig, then he thrust the flask at me. "Maybe a wee gift for the Gods wouldn't come amiss."

Who could say? I added the flask to my knapsack.

Jock gripped me by the elbow in an awkward show of wordless male affection.

Two of the As pointed Kalashnikov and Galil while the third stuck a poster of the Centaur-Angel to the stone wall. In two hours' time, earthly time at least, he would use the reversed poster of me to call me home, perhaps. On either side shiny darkness began to spread. *Was I utterly insane?* As Adam pulled the poster from the Wall like a bandage, light shone forth—oh, that's just our floodlight for the documentary!

Mighty was the draught that pulled me, and I was squinting at a sun-drenched stony desert landscape all about me, sand and pebbles underfoot. I had passed through involuntarily. Behind me was no sign of a doorway leading back. Could the others still see me? I raised my hand in a salute, then I shaded my eyes—we had not thought to include sunglasses. The region of the icons was gloomy, and I had departed by night, yet here was the full blaze of day. Not too far away a mesa thrust upward, its broken precipitous sides wearing long skirts of scree. On its tabletop was an edifice white as snow, twin tall towers rising from a dome, the base hidden from sight. But for the presence of that building, I might have been transported to Masada, the rock-fortress in the Judean desert where the Romans besieged the Zealots. All else in this wilderness was tawny, dirty yellow, brown, or gray in the shadows cast by the blinding sun.

Whence the white marble of the building upon the mesa? Materials must have been transported from far away and carried laboriously upward. Such an undertaking, such ostentation. I recalled that King Herod had built a luxurious palace on an upper side of Masada with a view over stricken, contorted desolation, to prove that he could do so, showing off. Herod's three-tiered palace had been tucked in, cantilevered almost.

My sweat was drying as soon as it was produced. If only I had brought a sun hat. Such protection never entered our calculations. Delving in my knapsack for one of the bottles of water, I swigged. In the shimmery distance I spotted a cluster of white shapes. An encampment?

Sharp eyes must have spied me, too. Scarcely had I begun to foot-slog through the stony desert than a movement resolved itself into several creatures heading my way.

Those must be horses or camels, white-clad riders on their backs—three or four of them. Yes, four.

As the mounts drew nearer, they proved to be neither horses nor camels but other beasts entirely. Quadrupeds, with long heads and silky hair and a lolloping gait and scaly tails like those of giant rats. These were no members of the animal kingdom that I knew.

The four riders' robes were all-enveloping—only hands and eyes showed. Three dismounted. Their hands were brown. Creamy eyes, light brown pupils. And the pupils of the mounts themselves were rectangular, goatish. Orange rheum leaked from the beasts' tear ducts. Translucent membrances blinked dust away.

The mounted leader addressed me and I couldn't understand a word. Hopefully, I said, "Shalom," and "Salaam," and I pointed up the mesa at the gleaming building, my goal, I supposed.

"I am an Englishman," I added, and felt absurd. "I came here because of the Centaur-Angel."

Incomprehensible discussion followed, then two of the people gripped me loosely while their companion relieved me of my knapsack and emptied it upon the ground. Kneeling, he sorted. The pistol, he turned this way and that, ending by peering down the barrel with no apparent understanding; thankfully the safety was on. He opened a bottle and raised a flap of cloth to sniff, exposing beardless brown chin, slim mouth, thin nose. After some fumble he unscrewed Jock's hip flask. This time his nostrils flared. Screwing tight, he spoke rapidly. Next he picked my pockets, then off came my wristwatch for the leader to inspect. Like a bangle, it went on to that man's wrist. I was being robbed—next thing, out would come a knife.

But no. My gear went into a saddlebag, and as soon as my searcher remounted I was invited, prodded, hoisted on to the beast behind him. I clung to a backward-jutting bit of saddle, myself bareback, thighs and knees splayed, feet dangling. How I hoped these people had some code of hospitality.

At the encampment I saw some unveiled thin brown faces, undoubtedly human yet at the same time subtly *other*. A different
side shoot of the evolutionary tree? How else to account for the
mounts, and for a pack of sinewy feline creatures the size of
lurchers that wandered around the camp?

Lurching, myself, after that ride, I was led into the largest tent.
Open flaps admitted light and air. Richly woven carpets lay upon
dirt. Dominating the main room of the tent was a formidable idol
in white marble of the Centaur-Angel. Strapped upon its rump
was a leather saddle, almost as if the statue was a plaything for
the young tribal prince who sat cross-legged beside it on a tas-
seled cushion—presumably the slight person was a princeling
since a coronet of gold or brass held his head veil in place. The
principal difference between statue and icon was that the head of
the statue was like that of the mount I had ridden on. Another
cushion was occupied by a veiled figure dressed in black and
seemingly elderly—the hands and the skin around the eyes were
deeply wrinkled.

Wooden cabinets, carved chests, low tables. Drapes divided off
areas I couldn't peer into. I heard the whispers and giggles of
women.

My escort reported, then my possessions were presented to
Blackrobe, who passed items to the young prince, including my
gun. This ended up between the forefeet of the statue, as did
Jock's flask of single malt and my watch and camera and flash-
light. Offerings to the idol?

The moment the young prince addressed me, I knew from the
voice that this was no lad but a lass. So: a priestess of the Centaur
cult, perhaps? I smiled, I shrugged, I gestured. She pointed at me,
then she jerked her finger toward the hindquarters of the statue.
Speedily I was hustled, and maneuvered onto the saddle. Hands
pulled my own hands around the torso, lacing my fingers at the
front. I was astride the marble effigy, clinging on. Bizarre, bizarre. Was this a way of judging me, or honoring me, or what?

Blackrobe produced a little silver flute from within his or her
garment and proceeded to blow a series of notes, quite like the
dialing tones of a phone—

Upon my artificial mount I was instantly elsewhere. Sunlight
poured through glassless windows into a hall floored with amber

slabs each prominently incised in silver with a symbol. Letters of an unknown alphabet, signs of an unfamiliar zodiac? My gun and other kit had tumbled on to an adjacent slab.

Ponderous movement! Fifteen meters or so away, the Centaur-Angel was in the room as if it had come into existence at this very moment. An alert presence, it was bigger than the statue by half again. Huge, horselike head, metallic and angular—was that a mask covering a more humanlike countenance? The eyes were black glassy pools. Silver chain mail covered its quadruped body. Black boots on its four feet, black gloves on its two hands. Its wings were spread. I cowered behind the marble torso as it advanced slowly, snorting. I felt I was confronting a mighty alien.

The muzzle moved and the lips—of that flexible mask!—stretched without parting. A rumbly voice emerged.

I cried, "I don't understand you!"

"Under-stand," it echoed. The lips moved as if it were chewing the word, digesting it. By now the entity was looming over me. Wings wafted, the draft ruffling my hair. An arm stretched down—as limbs had elongated to grip Isabella Santos—and it picked up my gun, inspected it, discarded it. My camera received similar casual scrutiny.

"I understand now," it announced. "How did you come here?"

It spoke English as though it had just accessed some great depository of languages.

I suppose I gaped.

Impatiently, "Is this your tongue?"

"Yes, yes."

"How did you come here?"

I told of Isabella and the Wall, of affinities and photographs—and the Centaur-Angel retrieved my camera for a closer look. It asked questions, which I answered. Finally, I begged to know, "What are you? Where is this?"

As soon became obvious, I was of use to the Centaur-Angel, so it condescended to inform me of certain things . . .

Presently I was beginning to understand that the existence of our world gave rise to reflections in what I suppose you might call the multiverse. To echoes, to backup files, dare I say?

A cosmos recorded information within its own fabric, perhaps in those rolled-up tiny other dimensions which physicists theorize about. A kind of cascade occurred, from reality into lesser, miniature ghost-realities which assumed a contingent existence—versions of the great original, variations on a lesser scale. Those domains were like dreams compared with our own material reality.

Matter is made of bound-up energy, but ours is *more bound*—the ice upon the sea, the icing on the cake, the crust upon the pie. Hence, perhaps, the triumph of science and technology in our world, and even of great religions, firm bundles of beliefs.

Wizardry pervaded those bubble-worlds, the power of will and symbols, and in each realm energy gravitated or pooled into a ruling power, a presiding angel or demon. Most of these beings were ambitious and assertive and engaged in a power play of offense and defense. Their goal—which they could maneuver toward and interact with to a minor degree—was the primary reality of our own world. How the domain-demons yearned to escape their restrictions and achieve immensity.

"You shall become my channel," the Centaur-Angel said to me graciously, as if bestowing a boon. "My link. A vent for my triumphal eruption."

Its eruption into our world! It was not the regular human world that unrolled from Jerusalem but this realm and a hundred others, too—rolled up in themselves, awaiting. I had caused a bridge to form between our reality and this other reality. Small wonder that rival Angels had torn my predecessor Isabella apart in their eagerness to acquire her.

"Far better myself, than certain others!" declared the Angel. "You are fortunate, Philip-Wilson. The service of your kind will not be severe, scarcely even slavery." It stamped its feet in a solemn little dance.

I imagined an outburst of light and power from the Black Wall, bearing forth the Centaur-Angel to bestride Jerusalem like one of the horsemen of the Apocalypse, steed and rider comprised in one being, feeding upon the energies of our universe. This madness must not happen. The doorway must be closed, affinity erased.

"Your reward will be great," said the Angel.

Demons must have promised likewise in the past—to Doctor

Faustus and whoever else. These partial breakthroughs faltered and failed. Never before had a person mounted a technological intrusion. How might human beings be constrained to serve this Angel? Us, with our nuclear and other weapons?

"Reigning over your world, I shall gain control of the other realms, too."

Would Armageddon be unleashed?

I slid backward, sore-bummed, off the saddle. The gun lay disregarded. Ultimately perhaps the Angel was stupid, or tunnel-visioned. Quickly, I picked up the pistol, thumbed the safety off, and fired, fired, fired.

As I emerged into the ruined Hurva Synagogue, I was still shouting. "It's me, Philip!"—as Avner and Avraham aimed, and someone uttered a shriek: Pascoli, had I hit him? No, he was still standing, startled. Illumination from the doorway dimmed as I swung around to see that desert vista puckering in on itself and the oily gloss of the Black Wall draining rapidly as if into a sink-hole, the old stones reappearing. None of my comrades could have seen the Angel within his palace. I think that my first gunshot had ruptured the membrane dividing me from my place of origin. Whether I had injured the Angel in his chain mail at the same time I had no idea, but the entity certainly wasn't pursuing me. In case the two As fancied I might be a terrorist, I threw the gun down. The moon was high, casting its own white light.

"Bloody hell, what were you shooting at?" demanded Jock.

"At the Centaur-Angel."

Adam retrieved the gun and then—"Hush!"—he was listening to the night in case Pascoli's cry brought army and police swarming. Thank goodness for the gun's silencer. By now the Black Wall had vanished utterly.

As soon as we had left the synagogue, we decamped separately through moonlit lanes, keeping to the shadows. Half an hour later we were all reunited in Avner's flat, and I talked at last, lubricated by orange juice while he and Pascoli both recorded me.

After I finished, Rabbi Ben said, "We should not be trying to open the Wall but to keep it closed."

"And to keep all knowledge of it closed," added Pascoli.

"Bear in mind," said Adam, "we are relying on the testimony of one person, a person of creative imagination."

I had lost my camera and recorder—much use that I had made of either.

"Philip's experience might be subjective. Another person might have a different experience."

"I believe him!" Jock sounded angry. "You aren't seriously suggesting we mount another expedition?"

"Seems to me," said Ben, "we have enough evidence."

"All deriving from Philip."

"What's certain," Avner said, "is that we must never cede control of an inch of Jerusalem." This was a very Israeli perspective upon such a cosmic matter.

As for writing a Blake-like epic about Jerusalem and Angels and Armageddon . . . what *other* great poem could I possibly contemplate, even if only for my own satisfaction, never to see publication? Any such ambition was now thwarted not only by the awesome truth but by fear that the creative concentration involved might form an affinity. What I produced could prove to be a fatal text.

The political situation was becoming hairy. Trained as martyrs, Palestinian kids were throwing stones at Defense Force soldiers and being shot. An Arab informer was executed by his own people. A rabbi was tortured and murdered and his synagogue burned down. Police stations in the Arab-administered areas were rocketed in reprisal.

Hamish Mackintosh drove me from the hotel to Lod Airport for an early morning flight.

"Time to get you out, old son. Bad security situation. A word to the wise: you will bear security in mind, won't you?"

I knew what security he meant. The domain-demons must stay behind the Wall and not be known about.

I felt like a Sourdeval being expelled from the Holy Land—except that the KBW would keep in touch with me fortnightly then monthly by way of encrypted e-mails to which I was expected to reply. Avner had prepared me for this. I even imagined Israeli intelligence agents checking on me periodically without knowing exactly why, except that my activities or lack of them were of importance.

What a great downhill slalom—or shalom—ride, this car journey was, ever downhill in great curves from the dizzy heights which I had ascended weeks earlier, as if we were unrolling toward the ends of the Earth, in my case toward one end of it, England. Where I thought I would be far removed.

How wrong I was.

SCIENCE
FICTION
DAW

Charles L. Harness

I was born in a little town in West Texas noted for aridity and sand-storms. I moved to Washington, D.C. as a young man, married, attended George Washington University, got my B.S. in chemistry and a little later my Ll.B., passed the D.C. and Maryland bars, settled down to earning a living as a chemical patent attorney and raising a family.

Meanwhile I wrote my first SF short story ("Time Trap," *Astounding* August 1948) and I've been writing SF with predictable irregularity ever since: 11 novels and 40 shorter pieces. Donald Wollheim did me a big favor in providing a good title for my first novel. As submitted to *Startling Stories* I called it "Toynbee 22." Sam Merwin objected to that, he said nobody would understand it, and he published the story as "Flight into Yesterday." Several years later Donald brought it out as a paperback as *The Paradox Men.* Even more incomprehensible, but it turned out to be irresistible, and I've stayed with it for all subsequent editions.

Today my wife is dead, my children are married and gone away, and I live alone in suburban Maryland, surrounded by dozens of family photos and monitored by a neurotic cat. And still writing.

—CH

STATION GANYMEDE
Charles L. Harness

Melchior

THE man seated at the little desk looked up and smiled genially. "Ah, Mr. Katlin. Do come in, Lieutenant." The speaker was tall and heavy, neither ugly nor handsome. Something in between. Not fat, just well-padded. Dark hair, gray patches at the temples. A monocle, which he seemed to wear as a badge rather than an optical aid. He wore a gray silk vest with a gold chain that terminated in an expensive artificial heirloom watch.

He pointed to the only other chair in the tiny enclosure, and the officer took it uneasily. "You wanted to see me, sir?"

The host's smile deepened. "I just wanted to let you know that I am your friend, Lieutenant. Indeed, at this point, perhaps the only real friend you have on Ganymede Station."

"I . . . what do you . . . ?"

Dr. Melchior's features shifted into compassionate mode. "It's those pesky quartermaster records, Gunther. You know, back on Terra? To certain heartless people those records seem to suggest that you sold Navy property to private parties to the tune of some $18,000. The file is presently in JAG's HQ at Luna Base. There it will be carefully reviewed, and a decision will be made as to whether you go back to Terra in irons." He studied the accused quizzically, then laughed softly. "My friend, you are looking at ten years' hard labor."

He waited.

Lieutenant Katlin took a deep breath. "I'm listening."

"Fine, fine. I need a small favor."

"And . . . ?"

"Your record at JAG disappears."

"You can do that? Who are you?"

Melchior shrugged. "I serve a very rich and powerful syndicate. Just be assured that we can deliver. Wipe the slate clean, as it were."

The lieutenant was thoughtful. "Why should I believe you?"

Melchior took a packet from an inner pocket and pushed it across the desk. "Consider it yours. Go ahead, open it."

Gingerly, Katlin opened the flap and removed a couple of papers. After a quick glance he replaced them. "Copies. The originals . . . ?"

"My dear fellow, what we can copy, we can also destroy."

"Okay, you kill the record—in return for what?"

Melchior took a small metal cube from a drawer and laid it on the desk.

The officer took a sharp breath. His eyes widened. He sniffed, as though trying to identify the thing by smell.

Melchior gave a low laugh. "Relax, Gunther. Yes, it's a K-3. Quite safe . . . at the moment. The timer has not been set. In fact, there is no timer."

The lieutenant's chair squeaked as he shrank back. "But . . ."

"It's really quite simple. The weather computer for Jupiter—Deborah—has signaled 'Go.' Today Commander Rhodes will begin a series of exploratory manned seismic sweeps on the planet. He will lower a search pod, *Ariel,* from the orbiting carrier ship, *Prospero.* When he does this, we think he may get signals indicating valuable minerals in the planet's core. We don't want that to happen, because Congressional interest might then shift from Venus to Jupiter, and our Venusian investments would be at risk. We want the search to fail. We want *Ariel* to fail. Nothing personal against Commander Rhodes or his crew. We have the greatest respect for them. It's all strictly business." He sighed. "How I do run on. But you get the picture."

Lieutenant Katlin seemed hypnotized by the little cube. "I . . . still don't . . ." He had to force the words.

"Ah, my reluctant ally, let me spell it out. The mother ship lowers the little pod on a cable, down into the Jovian atmosphere, down, down, half a mile or so. The cable is attached to a socket lock on top of *Ariel.* They've made unmanned trial runs, with nobody in the pod. They know it works." The speaker leaned forward a little. "Gunther, you have ready access to *Ariel.* All you have to do is attach the K-3 to the socket lock. The cube has a special design. There is no timer. A sudden surge in cable tension blows the detonator. And that's your cover. It will look like a local storm surge. Natural causes."

"But Debbie said 'Go.' The weather will be clear!"

"So she was wrong. Happens all the time. Forecasting weather on Jupiter, even with a mainframe like Deborah, is like rolling dice. Anything can happen. In the second hour of the test, *Ariel* is scheduled to move from one cloud band to another. There are big winds between the cloud belts and this is a very dangerous maneuver. If perchance the cable should snap, no one would really be surprised. You would not be suspected."

"You're saying, maybe it'll break anyway? Before the K-3 blows?"

"There is indeed that chance. Yes, my dear fellow, the K-3 may turn out to be completely redundant. Think about that. Maybe a sudden, unpredictable interbelt storm, and not the K-3, will in fact break the cable. You see? You'll never know for sure." He eased back in his chair, adjusted his monocle, and waited.

Lieutenant Katlin sat there, thinking many thoughts simultaneously and all jumbled together. Maybe he could cut a deal, pay the money back. Nah . . . he'd have to serve some time. Suicide? Problems with that. Not enough gravity here on this forlorn Jovian satellite to die by hanging. No tall buildings to jump from. Of course he could always just step outside, let his lungs explode. Dead before his frozen body hit Ganymede's implacable surface. He shivered. Not that way either. Oh, hell.

If only this demon would stop smiling.

Melchior pulled out his watch and glanced at it languidly. "Just now you have free access to both carrier and pod. Commander Rhodes and his son are touring Professor Bell's laboratory. Nobody will bother you."

Katlin sighed. "There'll be two men in *Ariel*."

"Three, counting Commander Rhodes." The corruptor smiled sympathetically. "Don't feel too sorry for them, Gunther. They signed on for hazardous duty. Their families will be well compensated."

The officer smothered an animal cry, grabbed the cube, and hurried from the room.

Father and Son

Commander Marshall Rhodes thought bleakly of past generations of Rhodeses. Count Percy had fought with Richard in the
Crusades. Captain William, with the fifth Henry at Agincourt.
Admiral Sir Guy, with Drake against the Armada in 1588. Lieutenant Billy Rhodes had served under John Paul Jones on the *Bon
Homme Richard.* Rhodeses had been on both sides, of course,
during the American Civil War. And one or more of them had
done his part in all wars since, great and small. And not a scientist
in the lot. Until now. He had to face it. His son David had just
received his BS in physics and now wanted a graduate degree. A
PhD in something called astrophysics. Incomprehensible. Where
had he gone wrong?

David Rhodes was athletic, with well coordinated muscles. Everything else about him was pretty much average. He had a light
scar on his right cheek—a scuffle with a female red hawk at age
twelve. He had been trying to count the eggs. (Three.) Straw-
colored hair, blue eyes, a ready smile.

And so David had got his BS in physics and there were no more
deferments for his military obligation. Interplanetary Defense
notified him to report to posting: a retriever, second class. Polite
word for garbage scow. He would spend four safe peaceful years
in Earth orbit collecting detritus shed by passing vessels and
handing out littering tickets. Weekend passes every ninety days.
He wouldn't be able to start his PhD for four years. After one
month on the retriever he reluctantly he called his father.
"Well," said his father, "there's this other thing. I'm returning
to Ganymede next week. You want to come with me? Jupiter. See
the real navy at work, in deep space. One year on Jupiter plus the
year in passage counts as a full service equivalent."

So he had taken it.

Just now father and son were walking into Professor Bell's little laboratory.

David asked his father, "Sir, we've been in the Station three
weeks, and you've never been in the lab?"

"No, I haven't." Commander Rhodes snorted. "In the navy we
don't waste time with this sort of thing." Another snort. "But
you wouldn't understand."

His son shrugged. The old argument. Less than a month ago in routine deepsleep they had journeyed together out to this godforsaken ice ball, and on arrival they had promptly gone their separate ways: the commander to take charge of the seismic research program, the student to intern with Professor Martin Bell.

The affinity between Bell and his son puzzled the officer. Bell's military and/or naval background was worse than barren. In their mercifully brief conversations the commander had learned that the savant thought a warrant officer was a sort of process server, that Wellington was a type of boot, that Salamis was an Italian food.

The senior Rhodes looked around suspiciously. "Where's the professor?"

"Out. He knows you don't like him. Shall we start with his new space suit?"

Commander Rhodes sniffed. "Make it fast. I launch at eleven hundred."

"Well, as I'm sure you know, the gravity on Jupiter is more than two and a half times Earth gravity."

"Of course."

"And Jupiter doesn't really have a surface. It's all gas, a mixture of hydrogen and helium, for hundreds of kilometers, until you hit liquid hydrogen. If you drop a probe on the planet, it will send back data for a few hours, then it sinks, disappears forever. That's what happened to the Galileo probes, and all that came after."

"I know all that, boy. Get to the magnetic stuff."

"Yes, sir. Well, the International Space Agency would like to be able to turn a man loose in that upper atmosphere, but they can't. Gravity would pull him into the center, where the temperature is 40,000 Kelvin and pressure is a hundred million times Earth's surface pressure. The standard backpack retro suit doesn't work—the magnetic field fouls the instruments. The man can't tell whether he's moving up or down or sideways. He soon spins out of control."

"True, true," murmured the officer.

"So what we need, sir, is a system that deals with both magnetism and gravity, something that lets the astronaut move safely and at will in the outer reaches of the atmosphere."

"So Bell's still harping on *that*," muttered the commander. "Kind of sad, when you think about it. I'm told he was once a very famous scientist."

His son hesitated a moment, then continued. "Here's how it works. Jupiter's magnetic field is generated by a rotating shell or core of liquid metallic hydrogen. This magnetosphere is really tremendous, many times Earth's. It extends fifteen million kilometers from the planet and envelops most of the satellites. It bubbles and boils—causes all kind of problems to the circuits of spacecraft. *Prospero* has to use special wavelengths. Our Station is bismuth-shielded, of course. Jupiter's poles are reversed, compared to Earth's but that's irrelevant for the professor's antigravity process. The important thing is, Jupiter's north magnetic pole repels all other north magnetic poles, however created."

"Mm," murmured the officer. He looked at his watch.

The youth began to speak faster. "For travel in Jupiter's northern magnetic field the professor creates a north magnetic pole in his space suit. For vertical movement within the planetary atmosphere, he varies the strength of the created field. Adjustments for horizontal movement are also available. The pulses are transmitted automatically and directly to a standard backpack of retrothrusters. Response to turbulence is automatic and instantaneous. The traveler can move in a straight line, any direction, by simple willpower."

"Willpower? Now wait a minute." The commander was trying to recall things he had heard about Bell and his notorious theories. "This . . . *field*. How does he create it?"

"Okay, the first thing he tried was a simple battery-powered circuit. It worked for half an hour, then the tremendous planetary magnetic field simply wiped it out. The problem was finding proper insulation. He faced a dilemma. On the one hand he had to provide a certain amount of shielding from Jupiter's field, but on the other he had to release his own little field. He tried all the standard shielding metals. No good. If they shut out Jupiter, they killed his own field as well. Then he tried the nonmetals, such as tar, plastic, asbestos, even sulfur. They seemed to work a little better. A shell of mineral calcium phosphate gave him an operating life of nearly two hours. Well, the next step was obvious. He tried living calcium phosphate: the human skull. It was the perfect insulator. It worked. It let enough of Jupiter's field in, enough of ours out."

"You're talking cranial implants?"

"Oh, no, sir. He uses no metals, no silicon circuitry. Nevertheless he does generate a field, a very sophisticated field, and it's instantly and precisely tunable by the operator. He uses natural brain waves—alpha, beta, theta. They are all sources of electromagnetic radiation, and every one of them creates its own little magnetic field. Under proper mental control, they provide the exact magnetic field needed to conform the astronaut to Jovian magnetism, so he can move three-dimensionally at will in the atmosphere. And the astronaut's hands are free." He pointed to a baggy suit draped on a form by the wall. "And there it is. I loaded the retros this morning. It's ready to go." His voice vibrated with pride.

"It will never work," the commander said grimly. "It's a killer. I'll certainly never permit the professor or anyone else to test it on the planet. Including you." He put his hands on his hips and faced his son. "The professor and his space suit must leave on the next packet." The words were clipped, harsh, precise. "David, you will stay, and you will register as a midshipman candidate. This is, after all, a naval outpost."

"Dad! *Father!*"

An overhead speaker interrupted. "Commander Rhodes, *Prospero* is ready and waiting." It was the strained voice of Lieutenant Katlin.

Noon Log

They were gathered in the communications room for the noon log entry, with Lieutenant Commander Schaum at the head of the table.

Schaum smiled at the assembly. "Looks like everybody's here." His voice slowed, took on an official timbre. "We're in the comroom of Station Ganymede, on Jupiter's third moon. Time, twelve noon, July 27. Attending, myself, Eric Schaum, Lieutenant Commander, Dr. Martin Bell, consultant; Lieutenant Gunther Katlin; Dr. Derek Melchior, of 'Bourse' magazine; and Mr. David Rhodes, midshipman candidate."

He paused, glanced at the readings on the weather mainframe near his elbow. "Deborah's 'Go' is of record. Mission Seismos is underway, and we will follow the action on the globe." He looked toward a side table, over which hovered a large illuminated holographic globe some two meters in diameter. Rank and file referred to it variously: Fatso . . . Peewee . . . Ole Devil . . . much depending on mood and speaker. Schaum liked none of these but couldn't do much about it. The same names were used in casual reference to the globe's eponymic planet.

With his laser the lieutenant commander pointed to two tiny lights, one green, and under that a red, that blinked intermittently on the globe's slowly rotating surface. "As we see, *Prospero*, commanded by Lieutenant Gordon Leclerc, is presently in equatorial orbit over Jupiter and has lowered the probe *Ariel* by cable into a light-colored high-pressure cloud-zone that we call Epsilon South. It girdles the planet just below the equator.

"*Ariel* is commanded by Station Chief Commander Marshall Rhodes with a crew of two, Petty Officers Stimson and Hoyt. *Ariel* has no motive power of its own. From half a mile above, *Prospero* is pulling it along through the zone by cable, and adjusts orbital speed to match Epsilon's eastward flow, so that the probe encounters little or no motion relative to the belt, and no strain is placed on the cable other than the weight of the probe. *Prospero* hovers overhead at all times, and the cable continues to link the two vessels for purposes of motion and communication.

"In this first hour *Ariel* is scheduled to drop four seismic charges and to record the resultant echoes. As I speak, she has already dropped two, and within minutes will drop a third. In the second hour—" he glanced up at the wall clock, "—beginning about ten minutes from now, *Ariel* will move into the adjacent band, known as the South Equatorial Belt, or Zeta, where the program will be repeated. These soundings are being sent up to *Prospero*, then forwarded here, and from here they go to the Seismology Lab in California. With these and similar records we expect to learn a great deal about Jupiter's core. At the end of the second hour *Prospero* will retrieve the pod and return to base here on Ganymede."

Dr. Melchior held up a hand. "Uh, Commander, about these seismic bombs. Is this the same as prospecting for oil, back on Earth?"

"Not exactly, sir. Perhaps a word of explanation . . ."

"Please."

"If Dr. Bell would oblige," said Schaum.

The professor shrugged. "The object, of course, is to locate a discontinuity on the core surface. This discontinuity may or may not represent an anticlinal upheaval, which may or may not be rich in heavy metals. But it all starts with finding the discontinuity. So we send forth our specially designed self-propelled seismic bomb. It's loaded with liquid oxygen, and it sucks in hydrogen from the surrounding atmosphere, and it burns and makes super-hot steam and that steam drives the bomblet. If we're lucky, it passes through the gas atmosphere, which is at least fifteen hundred kilometers thick, and then it enters the next layer, liquid hydrogen, ten thousand kilometers deep, and hot, 700 Kelvin, but not hot enough to affect the bomb. Finally, it's through this layer and into the next one—a real oddity, more liquid hydrogen, but it's a *metallic* liquid."

"Like mercury?" Dr. Melchior said.

"Sort of. And now things get serious. *This* layer is *hot*—eleven thousand Kelvin—twice the temperature of the surface of the Sun. So now our little blaster is put to the ultimate test. This last shell is 50,000 kilometers thick. Fortunately, our little fellow doesn't have to go through it."

"So what happens?"

"Our bomb lasts about fifty milliseconds in this last shell. But that's fine. That's the way we want it. On entry, it blows. The explosion creates the waves we need, good strong longitudinals. They travel at a fantastic rate in all directions, including down to the surface of the core. Even so, because of the distance, they may take several hours to strike and reflect back. Some of the reflections may bounce back quicker than others. When that happens, it indicates a discontinuity. Magnetic tapes in *Ariel* pick up the reflections, forward them to *Prospero*, and so on. Does the pattern show metal? In California the experts analyze the feedback. They say, the higher you go in the Periodic Table, the stronger the returning reflections. That's the way it works on Earth. But here? Nobody knows for sure. With this program we hope to find out."

"Very informative, Professor," Melchior said. He turned to Schaum. "And, Commander, I gather this is not the first trip?"

"That's true. As a matter of fact, *Ariel* has already made three unmanned missions with substantially the same seismological program, and in these prior missions explosives were dropped. However, results were not completely satisfactory, owing to some confusion in aligning coordinates, and Commander Rhodes felt that if he personally guided the pod, it could do a much more precise job."

The officer pressed a key on his terminal and a second hologram appeared beside the big globe. "At this point I interpolate a visual into the record. We are looking through *Prospero*'s belly camera down the cable, a stretch of about 750 meters, where it disappears into Zeta. The cable is hardened polymer, two inches thick, four times stronger than steel, and tested to endure tensions far greater than any that *Ariel* is expected to encounter on the mission. We pause now while *Prospero* pulls the ship over into Zeta's cloud belt." The two little lights moved slowly a few centimeters. During this movement Schaum stole a look at the dials on Deborah's instrument face, then looked over at the consultant. Bell, who had also been studying the instruments, looked up at Schaum and mouthed one word in silence. "Abort."

Schaum hesitated, then frowned and shook his head. He said quietly, "Off the record. I see it, Martin. Weather picking up. But we had a 'Go.' "

Deborah knew only two words: Go . . . Nogo.

It had not always been that way. The weather computer—named for the very wise Biblical prophetess—had been originally programmed to report her predictions in detailed analyses. "In—zone, between 40 and 45 degrees west longitude and between 1400 and 1700 UT, winds 30% higher than normal lessening to normal shortly before 1745." And then there would be an officers' conference, sometime short, sometimes prolonged. Did Debbie mean it was safe to launch the probe?

When Marshall Rhodes assumed command of the station, he solved the problem. He ordered Lieutenant Commander Schaum to reprogram Deborah. Henceforth the prophetess would say either "Go" or "Nogo." All future launches would abide by her announcements. Schaum's protests availed him nothing.

The new system seemed to prove the chief right. Three unmanned probes were launched on "Go" and all went forth and returned safely. "You see," Commander Rhodes told the staff while eyeing Schaum sternly, "no more gobbledygook."

And now Schaum envisioned the ships in his mind. *Ariel* resembled a miniature blimp, but with important differences. The cabin under the bag was gas-tight; the bag itself was polymer, super tough, yet flexible at temperatures as low as minus 175 degrees Centigrade. It worked like a terrestrial hot-air balloon: the bag was filled with heated Jovian atmosphere, in whose upper reaches it now floated, dangling from its mother ship.

So now ISA wanted to make comprehensive studies of the planet's distant enigmatic core. Seismic exploration might well clear up the mystery. But the agency had run out of money and it had called on the Interplanetary Congress for help, and Congress had done the only logical thing. Before they launched a billion-dollar project, they asked for a Preliminary Report. Hence *Prospero* and *Ariel*.

Professor Bell had already been at work in Ganymede Station for several months when Lieutenant Commander Schaum arrived. Schaum had known the scientist by reputation, but before coming here had never met him personally.

But this was here and now, and at this very instant the old man was pressuring him. Abort . . . abort . . . and Schaum knew that powerful forces were looking over his shoulder—the chief; Congress; ISA. Abort—and end any chance for the appropriation? What would the chief say? Would he, Schaum, be able to face Rhodes? Leclerc? Of course the mission was dangerous. A given. Nothing new about that. True, the weather was worsening. Bad, but not a calamitous increase in the risk level. No reason to quit in mid-trial. Not yet, anyway.

He looked at Bell, and he couldn't help frowning again. He well recalled the celebrated Symposium of the Naval Research Society in Paris not so long ago, where Bell had presented his theory of motion control on Jupiter via human brain waves. Schaum had been there and had listened to the jeers. One famous scientist, recipient of two Nobels, had enumerated six laws of physics that Bell's theory violated.

He called out, "Hold on! Something coming in! It's *Ariel!*" They all leaned forward and listened to the calm voice of Commander Rhodes.

"Mr. Leclerc, we will abort. . . ."

Inside *Ariel*

The weather on the giant planet was stormy, always, everywhere. Especially in the interbands. A given. The crew in *Ariel* didn't like it, but they were pros. They had been trained for this and they tried to adjust. But *this* weather was different. It had sprung up out of nowhere, and it was developing into something beyond anything that could be called a mere storm. Commander Rhodes was no coward, and he knew that aborting now would be costly, both for his career and for the future of Jovian research. But this was too much. Petty Officers Hoyt and Stimson had already strapped in. As he headed for his seat, the commander got his voice under rigid control and called the mother ship, far overhead.

"Mr. Leclerc, we will abort. Bring us up, if you please."

Despite the languid monotone and the scratchy reception, Lieutenant Leclerc caught something in the words that tightened his throat and made him stammer, "Yes, sir, *fast.*"

Back at the Station the listeners around the table seemed to sag with relief. Bell continued to monitor Deborah's dials. "That's a very unusual storm. Nothing like that in the records, and we go back at least a hundred years. Looks like the big one. Rhodes is smart to pull out."

Schaum wet his lips. *Right,* he thought. *And now the next question: will they make it in time?* The screen gave the Station audience a view not accessible to *Ariel* and perhaps not to *Prospero.* The Big One . . . ? They had talked about it. Not to worry, Rhodes had said. It wouldn't catch them. They were too smart. "It's probably moot," he said casually. "But I think I'll call Leclerc, get a condition report." He opened the line to *Prospero.*

Under other circumstances Lieutenant Katlin's bloodless face might have aroused serious concern. But just now nobody paid the slightest attention to him. He was thinking hard. *This is a very bad storm. Deborah hadn't predicted it. The K-3 will blow, and they'll think the storm snapped the cable. Melchior gets what he wanted. I'll be in the clear. Totally. God is looking after me. Ah, thank you, God.* He stole a look at Melchior. The entrepreneur flashed him a friendly grin.

The howls of the tempest drowned out nearly all outside sounds in *Ariel's* little cabin. But not everything. There was a sudden "pop" from overhead. The three men looked up, listened intently. The little ship began to pitch and wobble. It rolled on its side. "The cable!" cried Hoyt. The two crewmen were already strapped in and endured the crazy motion better than Commander Rhodes, who grabbed at hand bars and worked his way back to his seat, where he eventually got himself strapped in.

Their umbilical cord to the mother ship was gone. No communication. No mobility. Just careening crazily along in winds of unimaginable fury.

The two horrified ratings looked wide-eyed at Rhodes. Stimson tried to call out, but the cataclysm outside ate his words. Hoyt was white-faced, paralyzed. Commander Rhodes knew exactly how they felt. He closed his eyes briefly, took a little comfort in the fact that his insurance was paid up, David could go on to graduate school, and that Muriel, his wife of twenty-five years, could probably remarry, have a good life. Shit.

Professor Bell pointed to the screen. He said somberly, "There goes your line, Mr. Schaum." The cable was still visible, but it was contorting in loops. At one point it coiled upward, fully out of the clouds, and they could see the oddly shattered end, attached to nothing. All communication between *Ariel* and *Prospero* was gone.

The Castaways

The little ship continued to whirl and tumble. Not rhythmically, but spasmodically, in unpredictable twists and jerks. Inside, the three men grunted and gasped within their straps. Hoyt's nose was bleeding. The commander smelled the acrid odor of vomit. And another odor, a stench, and no stranger in this business—
fear.

Things were bouncing around in the cabin, sometimes on the floor, sometimes the ceiling was the floor. There was an illusion of ozone. Marshall Rhodes could see distant lightning strikes through the cabin window. He shouted above the din, "They'll

find us . . . they'll drop another line!" And immediately he realized the futility of the statement. Even if the mother ship could
find them, there was no way to reattach the cable. The lock socket
was surely destroyed. With the eyelet gone, the cable could not
be fastened to the little ship.

Stimson gave him a puzzled look, tried to shrug, couldn't.

A realist, thought the commander. *What now? Prospero* would
probably soon have grapples out and would be searching diligently. And probably fruitlessly. For if and when *Prospero* found
the errant *Ariel*, then what? As of the moment he could not
imagine any effective rescue mechanism. On the other hand,
maybe Leclerc could figure out something. But not much time to
do it. If the mother ship didn't find *Ariel* in the next five minutes,
it probably never would. In a mere sixty seconds, orbiter and target might find themselves a hundred miles apart, in any direction,
with the gap rapidly widening. Because of the planet's titanic
magnetic field, radar was useless. For practical search purposes
Ariel was invisible.

Rhodes choked back a moan. Oxygen for twenty-four hours,
he thought. Fortunately no need to power down. Everything op-
erated from the nuclear unit. With care, and if nobody goes bon-
kers, maybe we can stretch it out to thirty-six. And then what?
He refused to think about it.

What had gone wrong? The superstorm, of course. The Big
One. Still, the cable should have held. First serious miscalculation
he had made in a very promising career. And very likely the last.
Deborah had said, "Go," and he had launched. He couldn't blame
Schaum. No, only himself. He had been so determined to do it
right, make sure of that appropriation. That's why he had taken
the mission himself.

Chaos and time shrieked on.

Dr. Bell hurried around and leaned over the intercom. Schaum
looked up, then moved aside a little, too surprised to protest.

The scientist spoke crisply. "Station calling *Prospero*. Leclerc?
Bell here. *Ariel* is by now into Zeta. She will go with the flow,
two hundred miles an hour. Rhodes probably has several charges

left. He may throw out one or two, set for immediate ignition. They should give a fair fix."

Schaum listened to this in amazement.

Bell continued with cold authority. "Stay overhead his estimated position. Meanwhile lower the cable an additional five hundred feet. Monitor tension on the cable. One jerk means pay out more cable. Three jerks means reel in. I will arrive at *Ariel's* estimated position in fifty minutes in the shuttle, which I will leave on automatic. Eventually somebody will have to pick it up. *Do it, man!* I return you now to the commandant. Out."

He turned away and hurried from the room.

Schaum was flabbergasted. Old Doc Bell . . . taking over? But as he collected his wits, he thought about it. Everything had sounded so right—exactly what he or Leclerc would have proposed if Bell hadn't said it first. But then he realized what the scientist was really intending. No! This was insane. He chilled an impulse to leap up and run after the man. He didn't think he could catch him; furthermore, he didn't want to leave his post. He cried out, "No!" then he looked around the table. "Stop him!" Dr. Melchior and Lieutenant Kathn seemed frozen. Rhodes? Where was young Rhodes? Gone. Certainly after the professor. The youngster would bring him back. Schaum relaxed a little. But then he thought . . . better make sure.

He called the shuttle bay. "Pensol? Anybody there? Anybody? If you can hear me, listen up. Dr. Bell will attempt to take the shuttle. Don't hurt him, but don't let him near it. Hello? Hello? Pensol? Damn." Next, back to *Prospero.* "Lieutenant Leclerc? You hear that? Can't *Ariel's* own crew reattach the cable? They have suits, don't they?"

"Suits, yes, Commander, and retropaks, for that matter. If the cable comes down and rests on *Ariel,* or maybe a few yards away, where they can actually see it, maybe they can grapple it, bring it in, depending on the condition of the cable lock. We don't know what their situation is. With the cable snapped, we can't communicate with them."

Schaum noted that an entry had just then appeared on the console registry. "EXIT SHUTTLE, 14:03." He went into momentary shock. Young Rhodes hadn't caught the professor. He shuddered. "Well, there he goes."

He listened vaguely to Leclerc.

"I got that, sir. Sorry. Permission to do as Bell says?"

"Yeah, go ahead." As good as anything, or nothing. He could predict the next steps. As soon as the shuttle arrived in the clouds of Zeta, the venerable madman would don his brand-new untried brain-controlled motor suit, and he would open the shuttle air lock, and he would jump out into the storm. Then what? Probably start falling, and he would fall and fall and fall, faster and faster and faster, hell-bent on joining three ghosts. He would be incinerated long before he reached the monster planet's rocky core.

There was a noise at the doorway. Schaum turned and stared uncomprehendingly. Petty Officer Pensol had an arm around Professor Bell. The rating explained, almost apologetically, "Found him gagged and tied up. He says Rhodes . . ." There was more, but Schaum wasn't listening. He knew. David Rhodes had indeed stopped the professor. In his own way.

Together they got the scientist into a chair. Bell took a couple of deep breaths, shook his head. He wiped a streak of blood from his chin and gave Schaum a long grim look.

The lieutenant commander said, "Mr. Pensol, will you get a first aid kit? In the dispensary . . ."

"It's nothing," growled Bell. "And yes, he took my suit. So, what now? Do we tell Leclerc?"

"No. We do not tell Leclerc. We wait." Fifty minutes. He set his watch, started to sit down again, then changed his mind. He began pacing, arms behind his back. The men at the table watched him uneasily. That made him even more nervous, and after a time he walked out into the little lobby and resumed pacing. After a very long time his watch alarm sounded. He sighed and returned to the comroom. No sign yet of *Ariel* or the boy. *Father and son. God.* How could he face the mother. *Muriel. Fine woman. Deserves better.* A mixture of lead balls and sulfuric acid began to slosh around in his stomach.

He groaned and sat down next to Dr. Melchior. A strange one. He had not appeared at all worried. Quite the contrary. That odd smile. He had come in on the previous packet and would leave in a few days on the next one, having meanwhile become an expert on matters Jovian. Schaum sighed. To each his own.

In the Shuttle

David Rhodes checked instruments and screen. The shuttle was over Jupiter, and hopefully somewhere near his target. Within the narrow confines of the little vessel he struggled into Bell's experimental suit, locked the shuttle drive on automatic, and opened the air lock. And now he hesitated. He wanted to tumble out bravely, but he couldn't seem to force his hands to let go of the grab bars. He endured a moment of sheer terror. Was it all a mistake? He waited, got his heart beating normally once more. He closed his eyes, gritted his teeth, opened his mouth, and he screamed, "Come on! Last one in's a rotten egg!" He jumped out into the thin mix of hydrogen and helium that surrounded the massive planet. The gases were deep—and cold—a minus 150 degrees Centigrade. Those white cirrus clouds on top were tiny crystals of frozen ammonia.

At first the great gravitational force clawed at him and pulled him strongly down through the clouds, overwhelming his fear as he dropped in free fall. On this planet he weighed over four hundred pounds and he was dropping fast. He wondered if Stoke's Law of Fall applied, and whether he would develop a terminal velocity. He pitched and plunged, and his thoughts were chaotic, jumping from one thing to another. He'd better start thinking straight! He sensed that his whole brain wave system was now creating its own electrical program. It was talking to the retros in his backpack, and it was bending resiliently against the titan's magnetic aura. It adjusted neatly and with aplomb to magnetic spurts and gusts and eddies, almost as though they weren't there. He willed to move up, in a straight line. Then he leveled out. He moved cautiously along one plane of force, and then to the next, and the next. . . .

Wow! he thought happily. *It works! It really works! And I'm not afraid! I'm a god! I'm Mercury . . . Apollo . . . ! (And I'll never admit to anybody that I was just a teeny bit surprised. And scared.)*

Which way? To improve chances of being seen by *Prospero*, the commander would almost certainly try to maintain *Ariel*'s altitude by dropping ballast and/or warming the gasbag.

David moved up.

Ariel, where are you? He and the little probe were invisible to each other in a gas belt 7,000 miles wide, moving east at 200 miles an hour. Daunting, but he could deal with that. Theoretically *Ariel* was floating somewhere within a radius of about twenty-five miles, and *Prospero* was orbiting somewhere half a mile over-head and scanning the cloud tops in a desperate search for any sign of anything or anybody. Theoretically.

Although this hemisphere of the planet faced the distant sun, luminosity was only one twenty-fifth that as seen from Earth, and visibility through the fog and haze was almost nil. He flipped on his visuo-enhancer, but got only bright opaque veils of ammonia crystals. He turned it off. The eerie twilight gave him better vision.

His ear canals had ceased to function. He had no perception of up or down, and though he knew he must be moving along at a fantastic velocity he had very little sense of motion.

Just then something whizzed past, and he ducked by reflex. In front, and below, he thought. Meteorite? No—that would have been traveling a lot faster and would have made a lot more light. It was almost certainly a "seismo," the explosive that his father used in seismological exploration.

Ariel was trying to attract attention.

The youth was elated.

As if to confirm his guess, he sensed a dull boom from some-where below. Oh, good! *Very* good! The little pod was surely quite near. He punched a button on his wrist console, turned up his earphones, and listened intently. The sound of the explosion would return to *Ariel,* and from there it would reflect outward in diminished volume. He would catch that reflection, and it would talk to him.

There! He read the luminous numbers on his sleeve. The decibels measured transmission loss of volume after reflection. That loss measured time of the sound in transit, and time in transit gave distance, because the velocity of sound in a gas mixture of 86% hydrogen and 14% helium at minus 150 degrees Centigrade had been worked out long ago and programmed into the circuits of Bell's suit computer.

According to the readout, *Ariel* was half a mile ahead, up, and a little to the south. Just then a distant sheet of lightning offered vague murky illumination to his front. There. What was that? He could see something—a little to his left. He shifted course slightly, gave a delighted cry. It was the cable. Gotcha! That at least fixed *Prospero* in space. He wrapped several loops around his armpits and bounded forward. He wished he could tell Pater he was coming, but there was no way. And maybe just as well. Everything depended now on the juncture in time and space of ship, cable, and—himself. The prompt juncture, he added mentally. For they were now approaching the Great Red Spot.

The planet was mottled with light spots and dark spots. The light spots marked low pressure areas, the dark spots marked high pressure zones. "Spots," he knew, was a misnomer. Many of the phenomena were big enough to swallow a continent. The biggest of course was the Great Red Spot—the "GRS." Three side-by-side Earths could fit nicely into the big oval with room to spare. The GRS was a titanic high pressure cyclone, a giant plateau of gas some fifteen miles higher than its surroundings. Viewed from the Station, it appeared peaceful, almost sedate, a fitting bronze buckle for the Zeta belt. Up close, the view changed, and it could be seen for what it was: the biggest and deadliest whirlpool in the solar system. Peripheral winds routinely exceeded five hundred miles an hour. They were the slow ones. Midway toward the center, velocities exceeding a thousand had been reported. *Ariel* was headed there.

But no more time to think about it. For *Ariel* loomed just ahead, tumbling and twisting in a weird tarantella.

Rescue

Commander Rhodes watched the lightning flashes with bloodshot eyes. The strokes were increasing, both in frequency and strength. And getting closer. It was a superstorm. The consequent thunderclaps were weird. They weren't sudden blasts like Earth thunder, but rather more like diminishing wails. Probably something to do with the hydrogen atmosphere. No matter, one good bolt . . . good-bye *Ariel*.

On *Prospero's* bridge Lieutenant Leclerc was trying to make a crucial decision. No contact yet with *Ariel*. And of course not with that poor lunatic, Bell, certainly long dead by now. Leclerc was still trying to keep his battered ship above *Ariel*'s estimated position—which he knew was no more than a wild guess. Considering the tumultous weather in the equatorial bands, the little probe ship could be hundreds of miles away.

And now, with the Great Red Spot looming, *Prospero* and its five men were also at risk. It was insane to continue. He must reel in the cable, abandon the search, save his own ship.

David moved in toward the little ship and found the sole window. A ten-second inspection of the shambles inside told him all he needed to know. He could see his father and the two petty officers. The console and all instruments were shattered but the three men were alive. He could breathe freely again. He pounded on the hardened silica surface of the window with a heavily-gloved fist. Inside, the commander looked up, bewildered. David pressed his helmet against the window. The officer squinted, blinked, then stared hard. He shouted something and pointed. His companions twisted around for a look.

David moved up so they could see the cable, then he crawled with it up the side of the gasbag to the crest. As expected, the cable socket was gone. Not just gone—shattered. As though at the center of an explosion. David looked around at the top of the gasbag in the socket area. Pieces of metal were embedded in the bag surface. On impulse he picked up one.

With no cable lock, there was no way to reattach the cable. He'd have to do it the hard way. As Bell had requested, Leclerc had let down an extra five hundred feet of cable. David pulled it down the side of the ship, then under the cabin, then up the other side and up to the crest of the bag. Here he pulled the remaining yards of the heavy filament around itself and tied it with his best Boy Scout knot. Despite the cold, the cable was surprisingly pliable.

He gave three tugs on the cord. There followed a heart-stopping moment of waiting, then the cable tightened, became rigid under the load as *Prospero* dutifully began reeling in. The knot was holding. *Ariel* began to rise slowly. He looked down. Below was a ravening sea of graying pink clouds. The GRS. It had been a near thing.

He eased down to *Ariel's* air lock and they let him in. He removed his helmet and stood there for a moment, looking at his father and aware that every muscle in his body ached. Commander Rhodes' face looked strange—icy, yet very red. For a long moment the officer just stood there, staring at his son. Then his jaw began to tremble. He made unintelligible noises, and then he seized his son in a crushing hug. Together they lost their balance and grabbed for straps.

"That was very stupid," the wet-eyed commander said harshly.

David grinned. "Me? Or you? . . . sir."

"Both."

The two petty officers moved forward and shook hands awkwardly with the newcomer. Stimson shouted, "Davey, don't know how you did it, but we're sure glad to see you."

Moments later *Ariel* was safely within the bosom of *Prospero* and there was another exuberant round of congratulations and demands for explanations.

During *Prospero's* trip back to the Station hangar David was able to get his father aside for a whispered discussion. "The cable didn't fail. An explosion ripped out the eyelet. Pieces were embedded in the bag. I found this." Holding it by the edges, he pulled a fragment of sheet metal from a jacket pocket. "I think it's a piece of a K-3 cube. It may show fingerprints. Dad, somebody was trying to kill you."

The older Rhodes didn't reply for a moment. "It figures. We heard a loud 'pop' just before everything went crazy." He rubbed his chin. "Let me have your fragment. And we'll check the top of the bag. Not a word of this to anyone. We'll proceed as though the cable snapped in the storm." He smiled grimly. "Come on, let's look alert for the welcoming party."

As the commander led them down the folding stairs, they were greeted by Schaum, joined by Dr. Melchior and the whole Station crew, white caps, ratings, and officers. More congratulations and explanations as they retired to the comroom, where they took seats around the table. David noted that Melchior and Lieutenant Katlin seemed oddly subdued. *Odd indeed*, he thought. *When Ariel was in grave danger, you seemed happy. Now that we are safe and sound, you seem almost glum. Prime suspects . . . ?*

Marshall Rhodes tapped on the table and cleared his throat. "Gentlemen, I certainly appreciate this warm welcome. I speak for myself and for my brave crew. But time presses. The Committee will meet in Washington in a few days. We need to prepare a report—which will include a recommendation. The seismic data are on file. We now know that Jupe's core is rich in all kinds of metals. We'll need mining engineers, freighters, special transport trucks. We're talking billions of dollars. Industry will jump on the bandwagon. They'll demand that Congress open the budget floodgates.

"With the new Bell retropack, as so elegantly demonstrated by Midshipman Rhodes, it seems clear to us that moving about in the gases above the core will be perfectly safe. I'm requesting funds for five hundred Bell suits. We'll need experts, consultants in all sciences—especially astrophysics." He grinned bleakly at his son.

The next packet duly arrived. David and his father watched Melchior and Katlin climb aboard. David frowned. He whispered under his breath, "Their fingerprints were all over the K-3 fragments. You're letting them off scot-free?"

"Not exactly. We have no judicial process or prison here at the Station. I had Katlin transferred home, ostensibly to take a desk job in Washington. They'll go into deepsleep for the six-month trip home. They'll wake up in a prison on Luna, charged with attempted murder, conspiracy to murder, destruction of government property, lots of other stuff. We'll probably have to return to Earth to testify. You'll be on extended leave and I guess you can start your PhD." He smiled. "Your mother will be glad to see you."

C. S. Friedman

I remember the day that the manuscript of *In Conquest Born* came into our office. It was hand delivered by a friend of the author, who told us that he had stolen it off her desk—because left to her own devices the author would never have had the courage to submit it.

I know now that this story was a ruse, that in fact the author C. S. Friedman had been preparing the manuscript for submission all summer. But it really wouldn't have mattered how we received that manuscript, because Don and I were captivated from the very first line. Now, more than seventeen years and countless hundreds of manuscripts later, I can still quote that first mesmerizing line from memory: "He stands like a statue, perfect in arrogance."

I have always thought of C. S. Friedman as "the natural." For her, the flow of words is like a force of nature—something which cannot be contained. Her prose style has a passion which derives from a deep wellspring within her, and flows like a dark river engulfing and hypnotizing her readers.

In Conquest Born was never intended to be a novel. For years, it was Celia's refuge—the place she would escape to after long hours at school or work. She even wrote one chapter the night before her master's thesis was due. She didn't have a choice—she *had* to write it. Making *In Conquest Born*, a loosely connected series of dramatic, episodic vignettes, into a cohesive novel was not an easy job. Celia jokingly describes the process wherein we separated the work into its component parts, analyzed and reordered them, eliminated those episodes which did not further the main plotlines, and decided which new scenes had to be added, as "The Shredding." That we succeeded in making this work into the powerful novel it is today remains a remarkable triumph for both of us.

In the nearly two decades Celia and I have worked together I have never ceased to be impressed by her imagination, her range and her almost magical level of ability. Her writing seems to come so easily—the flow is so smooth, so natural, and so powerful. But I know the reality is far different. She is her own toughest taskmaster. Endlessly self-critical, she destroys much of what she writes. We only get to see the cream, but the cream is something very fine, indeed.

It's an incredible privilege to work with an author of this caliber. And getting to read Celia's books before anyone else does is one of my greatest personal rewards.

—BW

DOWNTIME
C. S. Friedman

BY the time the messenger from the DFO came, Marian had almost forgotten about the Order. You could do that if you tried hard enough. You just tucked the unwanted thoughts deep into some backwater recess of your mind until the normal clutter of everyday life obscured it, and then you pretended it wasn't there. Marian was good at that. She had her own special places for hiding things, dark little crevices in her soul where one might tuck a fact, an experience, or even a whole relationship, so that it never saw the light of day again.

She knew the day her sister died that a lot of new things were going to have to go in there, and she'd done her damnedest to make them all fit. She'd done so well, in fact, that when the door first chimed, there was a brief moment when she genuinely didn't know what it was about. Who would be coming to see her in the middle of the day?

She was curled up with her children and her pets at the time: two boys, a girl, two cats and a small dog, whom she collectively referred to as "the menagerie." They couldn't all fit on the couch at one time, but they were trying. Only Amy had given up, and she knelt by the coffee table now with her crayons laid out before her like the brushes of a master artist, her face screwed tight with concentration as she tried to draw a horse *exactly* right. When you're the oldest child, you have to do things right; the other children depend on you. Marian watched the delicate blonde curls sweep down over the paper for a moment before trying to disentangle herself from the others. With five bodies and two afghans involved it wasn't easy, and finally she yelled out, "Coming!" at the top of her lungs, in the hope that whoever was on the other side of the door would hear it and wait.

The dog didn't come with her to the door. Maybe that was an omen. Usually he was the first one at the door, to welcome strangers. But dogs can sense when things are wrong, sometimes even when their owners don't. Marian walked past him, and ignored the complaints of both cats and children as she looked through the peephole to see who was there. It was a woman, neatly coifed and with the socially acceptable minimum of makeup, wearing some kind of uniform and holding a letter in her hand. That was odd. You didn't get many real paper letters these days, unless it was something important. For a moment Marian couldn't think of who would have sent her a registered paper letter . . . and then memory stirred in its hiding place, and she was suddenly afraid. She hesitated a moment before unlocking the door, but couldn't give herself a good reason for not doing it. Trouble doesn't go away if you refuse to sign for it, does it?

As she opened the door, Marian noted that the woman's uniform didn't have any insignia on it. That could be just an oversight . . . or it could indicate that whoever had designed the uniform believed that people wouldn't open the door if they knew what she was there for. Not a good sign.

The woman looked up at Marian, down at her electronic pad, and then up again. "Marian Stiller?"

Marian could feel all the color drain from her face as she just stared at the woman for a moment. Maybe she should lie about who she was, and tell the woman Ms. Stiller wasn't home? Shut the door, lock the problems outside, and stuff this memory down into the dark places along with all the others. That would buy her a bit more time. But what would it really accomplish? Sooner or later they'd find her, and then there would be fines to deal with on top of all the rest. Maybe even jail time. The government was notoriously intolerant when it came to people who tried to avoid their filial duties.

"I'm . . . I'm Marian Stiller."

The woman glanced at her pad again, as if checking her notes. You'd think the DFO delivery folks would have their stuff memorized. "This letter is for you, Ms. Stiller." She handed her the envelope, thick and heavy. Marian took it numbly and waited. "I need you to sign for it, please." The pad was given to her. Marian hesitated, then pressed her thumb onto its surface. The thing hummed for a moment, no doubt comparing her print to government records. *Confirmed*, it blinked at last. The woman took it back from her, cleared her throat, and then assumed a more formal position that she clearly associated with official announcements.

"Ms. Stiller, I have delivered to you an Order of Filial Obligation. You are required to read the contents and respond to them in a timely manner. If you do not, you may be subject to fines and/or imprisonment. Do you understand?"

She barely whispered it. "Yes, I understand."

"Do you have any questions?"

"Not . . . not in front of the children." She was suddenly aware of them not far away, and heard for the first time how their chatter had quieted suddenly. They had to be protected from this. That was her first job. Questions . . . the Department had places for questions to be answered. Later.

"I understand." The woman bowed her head a token inch. There was no sign of emotion in her expression or in her carriage. What did it feel like, to spend your day delivering messages like this? "Good day, then." Or was she one of the people who believed in the Filial Obligation Act, who thought it was a good thing? Marian didn't ask. She didn't want to know.

She watched her walk away from the house because that was one more thing to do before opening the letter. When the woman rounded a corner and that excuse was gone, she turned with a sigh and shut the door behind her. The envelope was heavy in her hand. The room seemed unnaturally quiet.

"What? What is it?" She met the eyes of child after child, all gazing up at her with the same worried intensity as the dog in its corner. Children, like animals, could sometimes sense trouble. She looked at the letter in her hand and forced herself to adopt that teasing tone she used when they worried over nothing. "It's just mail. You've never seen paper mail before? I swear."

She shook her head with mock amazement and curled up on the couch again. She couldn't read it here, not in front of them, and she certainly couldn't go off to a private room now that they were watching her. She threw the letter onto the far end of the coffee table, facedown so that they wouldn't see the DFO insignia next to the address. It landed on top of a pile of drawings, covering over the lower part of a horse. Amy fussed at her until she moved it. By that time everyone else was back on the couch, and she found some cartoons on the children's net and turned up the volume and hoped it would distract them. Best to just pretend the letter wasn't really important, until they forgot all about it. Then she could go off to the bathroom alone with it or something, or say she had to start cooking dinner, or . . . something.

She wondered if they could hear how hard her heart was beating.

To Ms. Marian S. Stiller, child of Rosalinde Stiller:

This Order of Filial Obligation is to inform you that your family status has been reviewed, and it has been determined the debt formerly assigned to Cassandra Stiller is now the rightful debt in whole of Marian S. Stiller, only surviving child of Rosalinde Stiller.

Enclosed you will find an Appraisal of Filial Debt and Order of Obligation from our offices. Please review both these documents carefully. You are expected to comply with this Order by the date indicated. Any questions you have should be addressed to our offices within that time. Failure to comply with this Order promptly and with full cooperation may result in substantial fines and/or imprisonment.

She was helping Amy with a jigsaw puzzle when Steve came home, teaching her how to analyze the shapes with her eyes so that she didn't have to try as many wrong pieces before she found the right ones. The boys had tried to help, but they didn't have the attention span to keep up with it, and they had gone off to play with the dog.

She almost didn't hear him come in. Not until he was standing in the door was she aware of his presence. She looked up then, and saw the broad smile of homecoming waver a bit, as he read something in her eyes that he didn't know how to interpret.

Amy ran up to hug him and as he lifted her up to his chest for a big one his eyes met Marian's. *What's wrong?*

She shook her head and glanced at Amy. He understood. The ritual of homecoming always took a while, but today he kept it as short as he could. She was grateful. She needed him a lot more right now than the children did, and certainly more than the pets.

When he was done with all the requisite greetings, she whispered some excuse to Amy, and she led him away into their bedroom. Not until he shut the door behind them did she draw out the envelope that was hidden in the nightstand and hand it to him.

He glanced at the DFO insignia on the envelope and his eyes narrowed slightly. She watched as he pulled out the letter and read it, then the forms. It seemed to her that he read everything twice, or maybe he was just taking his time with it. Scrutinizing every word.

Finally he looked up at her and said quietly, "You knew this was coming."

She wrapped her arms around herself. The real fear was just starting to set in, and she didn't want him to see how bad it was.

With a sigh he dropped the pile of papers down on the bed and came over to her. She was stiff when his arms first went around her, but then the fear gave way to a need for comfort, and she relaxed against him, trembling. She'd been trying not to think about the Order all day, but now . . . seeing him read it made it more frightening, somehow. More *real*.

"You've been lucky," he said softly. "Cassie's taken care of this for years . . . how many people get a judgment like that? Normally both of you would have been involved from the start. Now she's gone, and you're the only child left . . . it was only a question of time, Mari."

"I know, I know, but" . . . *I'd hoped it would never come to this*, she wanted to say. What terrible words those were! He'd think she meant that her mother should have died already, when what she really meant was . . . something less concrete. Something about wishing the world would change before it sucked her down into this, or at least the law would change, or . . . something.

"I don't know if I can go through with this," she whispered.

His arms about her tightened. "I know, honey. It's a scary thing."

But did he really know? His parents had died in an accident when he was young, before Time technology was anything more than a few theoretical scribbles on a university drawing board. Long before something like the Filial Obligation Act was even being discussed, much less voted on by Congress. She found that she was trembling violently, and couldn't seem to stop it. The government had just announced it was going to take away part of her life. It would never do that to him. How could he possibly know what that felt like?

She heard him sigh, like he did when he saw her hurting and didn't know how to help. "Look, we'll go down to the DFO and talk to one of their counselors, all right? Maybe there's some way . . . I don't know . . . appeal the terms of the appraisal. Or something."

Or help you come to terms with it. The words went unspoken.

"All right," she whispered. It meant she could put off the matter for another day, at least. Pretend there was some way out of it, for a few precious hours.

That night she dreamed of her mother.

"Frankly, I find the whole thing . . . wrong." Her mother whipped the eggs as she spoke, the rhythm of her strokes not wavering even as her eyes narrowed slightly in disapproval. "We have children because we want them, and we take care of them because we love them, not . . . not . . . " She poured the mixture into a pan and began to beat in more ingredients. "Not because we expect something in return."

"Do you think it's going to pass Congress?" Marian asked.

"I don't know." She picked up a handful of diced onions and scattered them into the pan. "I hope not. The day we start "paying" parents for their services is the day . . . well, that will say a lot about how much is wrong with our society, won't it?"

The state offices of the DFO were on Main Street, in an old building that had once been the county courthouse. Marion's eyes narrowed as she studied the place, first from the outside, then passing through its great double doors. You expected something associated with modern science to be in a building that was . . . well, modern. Gleaming sterile floors instead of ancient hardwood, minimalistic cubicles instead of scarred wooden desks. Something. This was all wrong.

Or maybe anything would have seemed wrong today.

She paused in the outer lobby where approved vendors were allowed to showcase their wares, and Steve waited quietly beside her. The vast bank of brochures against one wall seemed more appropriate for a tourist resort than a government office, and the brochures themselves were likewise colorful and sunny, promising services in perky catchphrases that were meant to make the alien seem reasonable. *Give your parents the Time of their lives and have more time for your own.* That one was from a travel agency which specialized in Time-intensive vacations, on the theory that people might be willing to accept less Time if the quality of the experience was outstanding. *Wonder where your Time is going?* another beckoned. That one was a lively color brochure which promised peace of mind in the form of special investigative services, which would track your parent's actions and provide a complete report when you . . . when you . . . well, when you could read it. And *Time after Time* offered counselors for parents, to help them organize the fragments of their "second life" into a meaningful whole.

She suddenly felt sick inside. Steve must have seen it in her face, for he whispered, "Shhh, it's all right," and quietly took her hand.

It wasn't all right. It wasn't going to become all right either. But she'd be damned if she'd start crying about it all over again . . . least of all here. "I'm okay." Wiping some moisture from her eyes she nodded toward the door to the DFO office. He took the hint and opened it for her. Sometimes little things like that helped. Just little signs that you weren't alone in all this. Thank God he had been willing to come down here with her.

The wait was long, but the place seemed well-organized and things were kept moving. Most of the people waiting were sitting in a common area reading brochures, or whispering fearful questions to their spouses, siblings, friends. A few were just staring into space, like a child who knows that he's going to be given some unpleasant medicine, and that there's no way to get out of it. Most of them seemed to be holding numbers, spit out from a machine as ancient as the building itself, and small plastic pails near each of the desks were full of the little paper tabs.

She registered with the main desk, telling the receptionist that she had an appointment for Appraisal adjustment, then took a seat to wait. Steve just took her hand and waited with her. There wasn't anything more he could do to help, and they both knew it.

After some time their number was called and they were ushered into a small office in the back of the building. The counselor greeted them with a smile that seemed genuinely warm, though surely it was no more than a professional courtesy. How could you do a job like this all day and keep smiling to the end of it? She was a small black woman with threads of silver overlaying the tight jet braids of her hair, and Marian guessed her to be about 50. Too old to be doing Time, if there was an alternative, and still too young to be needing it. The lines of her face bore witness to a caring nature, and Marian felt a spark of hope in her chest.

"I'm Madeline Francis," she said, and she had that kind of voice which seemed pleasant no matter what the subject matter was. "Please have a seat." She had a screen on the desk in front of her, and they waited while she looked over the files on Marian's case. "It seems to me everything is in order," she said at last. "So why don't you tell me what you're here for?"

"I'd like the Appraisal reconsidered," Marian said. She could feel her hands starting to tremble as she said the words, and wrapped them tightly about the arms of the chair so that it wouldn't show. What she *really* wanted was for this whole nightmare to be over, the Order rescinded, and her life back to normal. But she knew she wasn't going to get that, not if she asked for it outright. Indirectly . . . well, one could still hope.

A finger tap on the computer screen brought up the Appraisal. "6.4. You are the only surviving child, yes? That's not a very high number, considering."

It's 6.4% of my life! She wanted to scream the words, to rage, to cry . . . but instead she just gripped the arms of her chair tighter, until her knuckles were bloodless. "There are . . . circumstances."

The black woman raised an eyebrow and waited.

"I'm the primary caregiver for three children. Young children. Steve's job takes him out of the state a lot, while he's gone . . . I'm the only one there for them."

"We've never let strangers care for them," Steve offered.

Was that argument of any value here? Marian couldn't read the counselor's face at all. "To lose their parenting two days a month at this time in their lives could affect their development."

"Ms. Stiller." The counselor's voice was soft, but beneath that softness was a stillness and a certainty that made Marian's heart pound even louder. "There are millions of families in this country who employ caregiver assistance. Most of them aren't even doing it for Time, merely gaining the freedom they need to take care of life's necessities. If you don't have relatives who can help out, then I'm sure in the coming months you can find someone to help you." She held up a hand to forestall the next objection. "Let me ask you a few questions if I may. All right?"

Marian hesitated, then nodded. Where were all the neat arguments she'd prepared for this meeting? All the proper words? She couldn't seem to find them.

"Did you have a good childhood, Ms. Stiller?"

She hesitated. "That's a very general question, isn't it? There were good times and bad times—"

"Of course, of course. Perfectly normal. But, overall, do you feel that you and Cassandra got the attention you deserved? Were your parents there for you when you needed them?"

"I guess . . . yes." She knew the answer was the wrong one to give, but she didn't want to lie outright. The woman had all her files, and probably Cassie's testimonies as well. She'd know.

For one dizzying moment she wished that her mother had been more distant, more harsh, so that she'd have some more concrete complaints to offer to this woman, something that would justify a lesser Appraisal. Then her face flushed with shame for even thinking that.

"She was a full-time caregiver also, wasn't she? Rare in that age." The woman's eyes met Marian's and held them. Warm eyes, caring eyes, but with a core of inner strength and conviction that no easy argument would shake. "You appreciated that, even at the time. Enough so that when your own children were born you decided to raise them the same way. Is that right, Ms. Stiller?"

She whispered it. "Yes. But—" Nothing. There was nothing to say. She twisted her hands in her lap as she listened, knowing the battle was already lost. Feeling sick inside.

"She was there for you when you were sick, wasn't she? When your sister was in a car accident and needed physical therapy to get back on her feet again, didn't your mother take care of all that herself?"

"I . . . I don't know. I was away at college by then."

"She took a class in physical therapy at the local college, just to be able to help Cassandra herself. So that strangers wouldn't have to do it." She glanced at the computer screen for a moment, her expression softening. "Your sister appreciated that a lot, Ms. Stiller. She attributed her complete recovery to the attention she got back then. To the fact that your mother put aside her own life for a time, to take care of her. She never protested her Appraisal, did you know that? Or the fact that the initial Appraisal assigned Time to her alone, and didn't divide it up between the two of you."

Her voice was a whisper. "She was much closer to our mother than I was."

"Recently, perhaps." She glanced at the monitor. "About how long would you say that's been the case, Ms. Stiller? How long since you've, say, visited your mother on a regular basis."

"A few years." She looked down, unable to meet the woman's eyes. "Maybe . . . two."

"Maybe five?"

She didn't say anything. Five was when Cassie had started doing Time. Mom hadn't needed Marian much after that . . . or so it had seemed.

"Did you know she had a second stroke?"

Marian nodded, still not meeting her eyes. "It was a small one."

"When your life is reduced by so much, every small one whittles away another precious portion." Softly, she said, "The doctors don't think she'll live very much longer. A few years at most. You know that, too, don't you?"

She said nothing.

The counselor leaned forward on her desk, her hands steepled before her. "I'm going to be honest with you, Ms. Stiller. You could appeal this thing, if you wanted. I don't think any judge in this country will alter the Appraisal for you, but you could tie it up in litigation if you wanted, long enough to gain some time.

The law's still new enough for that. Maybe if you tried hard enough you could even delay judgment until there wasn't an issue any more. You understand me?"

She felt a flush rise to her face as she nodded.

"I don't think you're the kind of person who would do that, Ms. Stiller. I think in your own way you care about your mother, as much as your sister did. You're just a bit scared, that's all." She sat back in her chair; the steepled fingers folded flat onto the desk's surface. "That's only human. It's a scary technology."

"That's not it," she whispered. But there was no conviction in her voice this time.

"We grow up in our bodies, regard them as ours. Mind, soul, flesh, it's all one creature. Then suddenly science comes along and makes us question that neat little package. What would happen if you could divide mind from body? What would that make of us? The thing is, after all the questioning, it turns out the answer hasn't changed. We are who we are, and even this scary little bit of technology can't really break up the package." She paused for a moment, her dark eyes fixed on Marian, studying her. How many times had she given the same pep talk? What cues was she looking for, that would tell her how to proceed? "Anything else is just an illusion, Ms. Stiller. You know that, don't you? A very precious illusion, for those whose own lives have failed them."

"Yes," she whispered. "But . . ." Marian had prepared a thousand words, it seemed, but now she couldn't seem to find any of them. Was it just fear she felt, fear of a technology that seemed to belong more in science fiction vids than in her real life? Or was there a shadow of selfishness there as well, something she should feel guilty about? The woman gave her time to speak, and when she did not, finally said quietly, "Ms. Stiller, I want you to do something for me."

The words startled her out of her reverie. "What?"

"I want you to go see your mother. Not for Time, just a visit. You haven't seen her since this Order was assigned. Tell me you'll do that. Just visit with her. And then, if you want . . . come back here and we'll talk about the Appraisal. Or we can arrange for counseling for you, if you feel that's what you need." She paused. "All right?"

She drew in a deep breath, trembling, and said the words because they had to be said. "All right."

The woman handed her something. A business card. She gave it her thumbprint, watched it hum as it sent the woman's contact information to her account.

High technology. What a blessing.

"Thank you," she whispered. Not because she felt any gratitude, but because . . . that's what you said when a meeting was over. Wasn't it?

Her husband led her out.

Amy was having trouble with arithmetic. Little wonder, since she'd rather play with her crayons than work with the computer to memorize her numbers. Marian printed up flash cards on paper, using one of Amy's drawings on the backs. The girl was fascinated with them, and had to be told at least three times about how flash cards used to be in every house, way back before computers, before she would settle down to work.

It was good to do such little things, if only as a distraction. She would have liked to think that she could lose herself in the task, but the sideways glances her daughter kept giving her made it clear that Amy sensed the *wrongness* in the air. She kept waiting for her to ask about it and dreaded having to come up with an answer—any attempt at honesty would only frighten the girl, but surely she'd sense it if her mother was hiding something—yet the moment never came. Maybe Amy sensed, with a child's intuitive certainty, that there were no answers to give. She'd most likely wait a day or two and then blurt out questions when they were least expected. That was her way.

That was fine with Marian. Give her a few more days, and she might be able to think of some answers.

The Home was much as she remembered it: neatly manicured lawns surrounding wide, low buildings, flowers brushing up against sun-baked bricks in carefully measured bunches, benches set along the sides of the path at precise intervals to receive those whose legs could not sustain them. There were several people about, enjoying the morning sun, and at first she assumed they were staff. But as she passed a young woman, it suddenly occurred to her that maybe they weren't. She found herself staring at the back of the woman's head and had to force her eyes away before others took notice. The contacts were almost invisible, she'd been told. Easily hidden beneath a full head of hair. Cassie had offered to show her what hers looked like up close, but Marian hadn't wanted to see them. Were any of these normal-looking people doing Time?

She suddenly felt sick inside, and would have sat down on one of the benches if she wasn't afraid that if she did so she might never get up again. What was she doing here? This was crazy. Even her *mother* had said it was crazy. Didn't that count for anything?

"Can I help you?"

She found her voice with effort. "I'm here to see my mother. Rosalinde Stiller."

"Ah, yes." The aide was young, her face still beaming with the freshness of teenage enthusiasm. Too young to even understand what Time was, much less have to worry about it. "Come with me."

They'd moved her mother. Cassie hadn't told her that. Out of the ward where cases of moderate dependency were kept, into a place where things were . . . worse. Marian could feel her chest tightening as she followed the aide down the sterile white corridors of the new ward. No pretense of normal life here, no attempt to disguise the nature of the place. It looked and felt like a place where people died. Why hadn't Cassie told her?

Because you didn't want to hear it, an inner voice whispered. *She knew.*

"In here, Ms. Stiller." The room was small, a private one. They'd seen to that. Steve and Cassie and Marian, they'd made sure her mother had all the best things. Except that after a while . . . how much did it mean? She looked about at the bright curtains, fresh flowers, net screen . . . anywhere but at the bed. Anywhere but where she needed to be looking.

"Are you all right, Ms. Stiller?"

Her mother was frail. So frail. She had forgotten that. Sickness robs a body not only of strength, but of substance. She remembered her mother as a bundle of strength, of energy, always restless, always moving. Always doing *something.* It was hard for her to reconcile that image with the woman who lay before her. Hard for her to cling to her memories, when the very source of them had become so changed.

Slowly she sat down on the edge of the bed, and took her mother's hand. The skin was strangely silken, thin to the touch, and blue veins throbbed softly beneath her fingertips. Not a hand she recognized. She looked up slowly to find blue eyes fixed on her. Clear, bright, almost a stranger to the wrinkled flesh surrounding them. There was some emotion in those eyes, but Marian couldn't read what it was. The expressions she remembered from her youth were all gone, stolen away muscle by muscle, as age severed the link between mind and body. Where was her mother, inside that flesh? She gazed into the clear blue eyes with all her might, trying to make contact with the soul behind them. Did her mother feel the same sense of dislocation when she looked in a mirror? Did she wonder whose this stranger's face was, that looked so drained and pale? Surely not her own. Surely.

The counselor was wrong, she thought. *You can divorce mind from body, even when they share the same flesh.*

"She can't really speak any more." A nurse spoke quietly from behind her. "With great effort, a few words, perhaps. No more." Marian must have looked surprised, because the nurse asked, "You didn't know?"

"No, I . . . no. Cassie didn't tell me."

Cassie didn't tell me a lot.

She squeezed her mother's hand as she leaned down slowly to kiss her on the forehead. This close she could catch the scent of her familiar perfume, and she ignored the tang of medications and ointments that breezed in its wake, losing herself for a moment in the mother she remembered. Nothing like this. But the human soul doesn't fade with age, does it? Only the flesh.

It's only two days. She forced herself to digest the words, forced her soul to absorb them. *Two days a month, and the rest of your life stays the same as it always was. Surely you can do that much for her,* she told herself, trembling. *Surely she deserves that much.*

She would have done it for you.

*R*emembering: *Her mother's fingers folding tissues into a neat little fan, just so, each fold perfect. Binding them around the cen-*

ter with another twist of tissue, tight enough to bunch the layers together. Finely manicured nails prodding the layers apart, separating each fragile ply, spreading them carefully one after the other, until the whole is a delicate rose, wonderfully perfect.

"Getting harder to do," her mother says. "My close-up vision's not what it used to be, soon I won't be able to make these at all." She puts the rose down in front of Marian and indicates the pile of tissues next to it. "Now you try."

Steve insisted on coming with her. She tried to get him to stay home with the children, to let a friend take her to the Time clinic, but he wouldn't hear of it. Bless his stubborn, loving heart. He even canceled a business trip to San Diego to make sure he could be home the day before . . . in case her floundering courage called for husbandly support. And it did. She wasn't crying anymore, but she spent a lot of time that day in his arms, trying to take comfort from his presence while not letting the children sense how very scared she was.

They did, though. Children are like that. Amy even picked up enough from conversations she overheard to ask if Mommy was doing Time. For a moment Marian didn't know what to say. There was no way to lie that Amy wouldn't eventually catch on to, if Marian was going to have to do Time every month. At the same time . . . she was too young. She wouldn't understand. She shouldn't *have* to understand, not at this phase in her life.

"Mommy's going to see Grandma," she said at last. Kneeling down to meet her eye to eye, willing all the calm sincerity into her voice that she could manage. "She's going to give Grandma some Time so she can feel better."

"Will she get better then?" the child asked.

For a moment Marian couldn't speak. Finally she whispered, "Probably not, sweetheart. But this will make the sickness hurt less."

No more questions. Thank God. Maybe Amy had enough of a child's innate intuitive sense to understand that Marian had no more answers. Not now, anyway.

She'll ask again. The boys will grow up and they will ask. What words will you give them, that a child can understand? Or will you put it off until it's too late, and they have to learn the truth in school, on the street . . . from strangers? What will you do then?

The world has changed. This is part of it, now. You can't shield them from it forever.

Later. She would deal with that later. One thing at a time . . .

*M*s. *Stiller?*

Darkness. Soft darkness. Voices muted as if through cotton, distant whispers.

Are you all right, Ms. Stiller?

Were they talking to her, the cotton voices? It took her a minute to process that thought.

"I'm . . . I'm all right."

You're going to feel strange for a little while. That's normal. Try to relax.

"I'm . . . I'm trying."

You understand what is happening, yes? It's all been explained to you?

Why was it so hard to think? Was that because of the drugs they had given her, or her own fear? Strange, how the fear seemed distant now. Like somebody else's emotion, a thing to be observed rather than absorbed. "They told me."

Her heart was beeping on some monitor. She could hear it through the cotton as they spoke to her. Steady, even beeps.

It's going to feel like you're falling asleep. There may be a sense of falling away from your own body. That's just an illusion, you understand? It comes from the drugs we use. Your mind isn't leaving your body, ever.

"Body and soul an indivisible alliance." Did she say that aloud? The drugs were making it hard to think. Where had that phrase come from, some propaganda leaflet? She couldn't remember.

That's right, Ms. Stiller. She could hear people moving around her, but she couldn't make out what they were doing. Was her heartbeat usually that slow? They had given her tranquilizers because she'd asked for them, but she'd never had drugs that felt this strange before. Pinpricks of electricity tickled her scalp. Were those the contacts they had inserted? She could hear her heart skip a beat. *Body and soul are a unit, they can't be divided. What we're going to do is create an illusion that it's otherwise . . . but it's only that, an illusion. You're going to sleep for a while—at least, that's what it will feel like—but you'll still be here, inside your own flesh.*

"Yes, I . . . I understand . . . sort of . . ."

Your mother will get feedback from your sensory contacts. She'll be able to send messages to the parts of your brain that control movement. But she won't actually be inside you, you understand? Just . . . suggesting motions, and observing the world through your senses.

Again her heartbeat quickened. The fear was a distant thing, muted by drugs. Wonderful drugs. They could tailor emotions these days like you tailored a suit. *A bit short in the terror, be careful. Look, the sides of the dread don't match. It needs to be calmer or it won't fit.*

"It will be like she's in my body."

For her. Yes. One of the contacts moved a bit. Being adjusted? *For you . . . it will be like sleep. You may dream a bit, not whole dreams but bits and pieces. Feedback from your brain chemistry, as your body interacts with the world. You understand?*

Thank God Diane had agreed to watch the children. Thank God. One less thing to worry about as she prepared to give over control of her body to someone else. Diane would know how to handle the children. She knew Marian and Steve well enough to know that while they were here, dealing with all this mad scientist machinery, they didn't want someone else explaining things to Amy and the boys. No, that was something parents should do themselves.

She remembered how her mother had explained this process to her. She'd thought it was a bad thing. Children shouldn't owe their parents their bodies.

But you didn't know then how helpless you'd be, did you, Mom? Or how much a few borrowed hours might mean?

There was a tear in her eye. Trickling down her cheek. She tried to reach up a hand to wipe it away, but her arm didn't respond to her anymore.

Her mother would have done this for her, had she been crippled. Would have given over her body to her child so that Marian could live a normal day. Twenty-four hours without pain, without handicaps, without weakness. Twenty-four hours in the body of a loved one. The ultimate gift.

Relax. Ms. Stiller. Calm footsteps. Heart beeps. Other sounds, hospital sounds. She tried to let go, not to listen. The cotton helped. *We're going to initiate transfer now.*

The first time is always the hardest, they had told her. Like labor. Yes. The second child was easier. The youngest drew rainbows. Bright colors, youthful colors. Age was gray and blue, her mother had said, cooled by time, softened about the edges. A sudden sadness filled her heart, and brought fresh tears to her eyes. She missed red, suddenly. She missed the oranges and umbers of autumn in the mountains. The trees changed here, but it wasn't the same. She knew the sunlight was gold, but it didn't *feel* gold anymore. Cassie had brought flowers to the clinic, beautiful flowers, but all the smells she remembered from her youth were gone. She wanted to smell the flowers again. Leaves like precious velvet, she wanted to touch them, to feel the golden sunlight upon her face . . .

Why was she crying? She knew what the sunlight was like. Where was the sorrow coming from? A sudden bolt of fear lanced through her, and the steady rhythm of the heart monitor began to quicken. Someone else's thoughts—

She could feel hands upon her, but just barely. *Easy, Ms. Stiller. Easy. We're almost there.* The hands faded away then, and with it all the sounds of the room. A soft roaring filled her ears that seemed to have no source. She could feel herself being drawn out of her body and she tried to fight . . . but she didn't want to fight . . . soft panic wrapped in cotton, oh so distant. Someone else's panic. Someone else's body . . .

She drifted into Downtime slowly, never knowing when the transition took place. Just like sleep. People didn't fear sleeping, did they?

Waterfalls. Splashing on the skin, scouring body and spirit. Turning up her face into the rain, laughing to feel it trickle into her nose. Glorious rain and a crown of strawberries. God, the smell is sweet! So many layers to savor! Redness and freshness and sweetness and tartness all mixed up together, and she can taste each one. Crimson slickness down her back, tartness frothing in the waterfall as she laughs.

Youth is gold, her mother had said. Wonderful gold, that tastes like chocolate sprinkles on the tongue. Veins of gold filtering the sunlight into speckled networks of color—yellow, orange, red, green. The colors of youth, of life. Drink in the color. Roll the orange around on your tongue. Red is pepper and spice, that stings the nose. Sunlight is chocolate. Wonderful chocolate! Waterfalls are blue, not dull aged blue but the clear blue of a morning sky. The water smells of strawberries as it washes away all shame and despair. Who would have thought that a simple thing could bring so much joy?

"Marian?"

She could feel the images parting like mist as she struggled toward the surface, toward consciousness. Strange images, like and unlike dreams. Where had they come from? The doctors had said that Time was no more than biological remote control, that the best of all their science could not put two minds in contact with one another directly. Marian wasn't so sure of that anymore.

"Marian?"

"Yes." She gasped the word, then opened her eyes. The clinic room came into focus slowly. "Steve?"

He squeezed her hand. The sensation helped her focus again. "You okay?"

"Yes." She drew in a deep breath, trembling, and let it out slowly. "Yes, I . . . I think so. Is it . . . is it over?"

He nodded.

She managed to sit up and leaned against him, weakly. Her skin felt very fresh and clean. Her hair smelled of strawberries. Shampoo? She touched the soft strands in wonderment.

"Did you . . . did you see her?" she asked him.

He shook his head as one of the nurses answered. "It's not allowed until later, Ms. Stiller. When you're both accustomed to the process, then other people can be involved. For now . . . only staff."

It felt strangely difficult to speak . . . but that was just illusion, right? Marian hadn't been permanently disconnected from anything in her body. "What did my mother . . . I mean . . . "

The nurse smiled indulgently. "What did she do, Ms. Stiller? Is that what you want to ask?"

She nodded.

The nurse picked up a tablet and tapped it until it showed the text she wanted. "From nine a.m. to one p.m., your mother worked with our staff to help fine-tune her contacts. Full sensory transfer was confirmed at 1:13." A smile flickered across her face. "She promptly asked us to bring her a cannoli, with chocolate sprinkles on it. All proper cannoli have chocolate sprinkles, she assured us."

"Go on," she said softly.

"She then took a long shower. And went for a walk in the gardens. Our people accompanied her, of course. She won't be allowed to go about alone until you're both more accustomed to the transfer. According to my notes she spent a long time searching out leaves on the ground, and holding them up to the sunlight and staring at them."

"It's autumn." She could feel her voice shaking as she spoke. "The colors . . . all the gold . . . " She shut her eyes and remembered the colors she had known in her dream. The sheer joy of seeing them. *Is that what I gave you?*

"She had . . . the usual dinner." The nurse smiled. "A sampler of all the salty and spicy things she's normally not allowed to have. Nothing for you to worry about, Ms. Stiller." She looked down at her notes, and her eyes narrowed in puzzlement. "Then it says . . . she took a shower again?"

Marian whispered, "I understand." Steve put an arm around her shoulders as she trembled.

That's the worst part of all, her mother had told her once. *When you can't even wash yourself. That's when you feel like it's all over, like you're not really living anymore, just waiting to die.*

She leaned against Steve and tried to be calm. It was over now, at least the first Time. Why did she want so badly to cry in his arms? There wasn't anything of her mother inside her, not anymore. Science couldn't do that. Isn't that what they'd told her?

Time was only an illusion. No direct mental contact was possible. No real sharing.

"Is there anything else?" Steve asked quietly.

"Yes." The nurse went to a table by the window and picked something up. "She wanted you to have this. She said you would understand."

She held it out to Marian, a small pink object that seemed to have no weight at all. It took Marian a moment to realize what it was. When she did she exhaled slowly, taking the fragile tissue flower into her hand. Every fold so perfectly made, every ply so perfectly separated. For a moment she couldn't speak, could only stare at the thing. Then she whispered, "Can I see her now?"

The nurse shook her head. "She's asleep right now, Ms. Stiller. The first Time is always exhausting. Why don't you come back tomorrow?"

"Of course." She whispered it, staring at the rose. "Tell her . . . tell her . . . I understand. Please."

"I will, Ms. Stiller."

"Tell her . . . " She drew in a deep breath, searching for the right words. There were none. "Tell her I love her," she said at last. It fell far short of all that she needed to say . . . but that was all right. Her mother would understand.

The tears didn't start to flow until they were in the car.

Home. Thank God. Normalcy.

She drew in a deep breath on the porch while Steve opened the door. Letting go of all the tension, all the relief, everything she'd cried about on the long ride home. It was all right if Steve saw that—he'd married her for better or for worse—but she wouldn't bring it home to her children.

She felt different somehow. No, that wasn't right. She felt as if she *should* be different, and kept poking around inside her own consciousness to figure out where the difference was. Sharing a body with someone was the ultimate intimacy. Could you do that and not be changed by it? Could someone use your body and brain for a whole day and not leave her mark somewhere inside you, etched into one biochemical pathway or another?

Diane came running to the door as it opened, saw she was all right, and hugged her. "You're okay!"

"Of course I'm okay." She still had the tissue rose in her hand, and hugging Diane back without crushing it was no small feat. "The children—"

"Mark and Simon are asleep. Amy's in the kitchen. I thought you wouldn't want them to wait up for you."

Children in bed. Good. Soon she'd put Amy to bed herself, and that would be normal too. Rhythms of life, reasserting themselves. She needed that right now.

She managed to wriggle out of her jacket without crushing the tissue flower. She could hear the dog barking from the backyard, recognizing their voices, begging to be let back in. Steve grinned as he hung up their coats and then went out to get him.

"No problems?" Marian asked, as they walked toward the kitchen. She wanted to hear it again. Wanted to savor the taste of the words.

"Nothing, really."

Was there an edge to her voice, a hint of uncertainty? Marian looked up sharply. "What? What is it? Did something happen?"

Diane hesitated. "She asked about it, Marian. They all did, but the boys gave up after I just reassured them that you were okay. Amy . . . didn't. Children hear things, you know. They worry."

Marian felt a chill of dread seep into her heart. *She can't understand this. She's too young.* "What did you tell her?"

"I told her she'd have to wait for you to get home if she wanted more information. I know how much you wanted to be the ones to explain all this! She just . . . she wanted to know if a few things were true. Stories she'd heard from other children. Most of them weren't true, and they were pretty scary. She just needed . . . reassurance." Diane bit her lip as she watched her for reaction . . . somewhat nervously, Marian thought. "Just reassurance."

Marian forced herself to hold back all the sharp things she wanted to say. What good would it do now? She'd waited too long to choose the right words for Amy. Now someone else had done it for her. Berating Diane about it after the fact would get her nowhere.

You knew it had to happen someday. Time technology is part of her world, you couldn't hide it from her forever.

Amy was sitting at the kitchen table working on a jigsaw puzzle. It was one of Marian's own, a hard one. For a moment the girl didn't seem to notice her standing there in the doorway . . . then the dog barked as it came into the house, and Amy turned around . . . and her face broke into a broad grin of welcome as she saw Marian standing there. "Mom!"

"Hi, honey." She came up to the girl and tousled her curls. "I'm home now." Amy threw her arms around her with melodramatic glee, clearly delighted to have her home again. *See? Things are going to be all right. You were worried over nothing.* "I brought you a gift from Grandma." She knelt down so her eyes were on a level with the girl's, and held out the rose. "She used to make these when she was very young, before she got arthritis. See? It's all made out of tissues." Amy looked at the flower inquisitively, prodded it a few time, but didn't take it from her. "What are you doing, a puzzle?" Marian pulled up a chair to sit down. "That looks like a hard one."

"Diane said it was too hard for me. I told her I could do it if I wanted."

Marian laughed. "And so you can." God, the laughter felt good. She saw her husband standing in the doorway and nodded to him. *Fine, everything's fine.* "You can do anything you want to." She scanned the pieces and saw one that had been sorted into the wrong pile. "Here, honey, try this one. See if you can tell me where it goes."

She didn't reach for the piece Marian offered, but picked up a blue one instead. "It's okay, Mom." The girl didn't look up at her. "I can do it myself."

Was there a note in her voice that seemed different, somehow? *You're just being paranoid,* Marian told herself. *Everything's fine.* She watched her daughter for a few minutes more, studying her face as she concentrated on the puzzle. Trying to see if there was some outward sign of . . . of whatever was wrong. Finally she picked up one of the pieces again, turning it thoughtfully in her fingers, and made her voice as calm as she could as she offered it to the girl. "Look, here's a corner piece. Where do you suppose that goes?"

For a moment there was silence. The girl didn't reach for the piece that Marian held. She didn't do anything, for a moment.

Then: "It's okay, Mom." Her voice was so quiet, so steady. "I don't need you to help me. Really."

Marian tried to speak, but her voice caught in her throat. The words of the counselor echoed in her head, no gentle words this time, but every sound a thorn. *Were your parents there for you, Ms. Stiller? Don't you owe them something for that?*

"I'm okay," Amy repeated, and she looked down again to work on the puzzle.

Marian watched her for a moment longer. Then she rose and left the room. The dog yapped about her ankles, but she ignored him. Steve started to ask what was wrong, but she waved him to silence. How do you explain the loss of something which never even had a name? How do you address the fears in a child, when you couldn't make your own go away?

It wasn't until she got to her room and shut the door behind her that she realized she had crushed the tissue flower.

Charles Ingrid

Charles Ingrid is an incredibly versatile writer who worked with me under a different name while I was still editing the Signet science fiction line. When I came to DAW Charles and I discussed projects we could work on even as the author's commitments at Signet continued to be fulfilled. And that was when the Charles Ingrid name was born. It was actually created by combining the first names of a couple who are extremely good friends of the author. And while I'm not going to tell you all of Charles' other identities—or even Charles' actual identity—I will say that this is an author who has written everything from military science fiction to romance to supernatural suspense to young adult novels.

Solar Kill, the first novel in the six-volume *Sand Wars* series was published by DAW in July, 1987. And at the beginning of 2001, we combined this excellent series into two omnibus volumes to make it easily available for readers. At the beginning of 2002, we combined the four novels of Charles' *Patterns of Chaos* series into two omnibus editions as well. And at the end of 2002 we will make the *Marked Man* novels available in the same way.

Those of you who are familiar with Charles Ingrid's science fiction will find yourself eager to reread the novels after enjoying "Burning Bridges." And for those who have not yet had the pleasure of discovering this fine writer, "Burning Bridges" will provide that introduction.

—SG

BURNING BRIDGES
Charles Ingrid

ACT II

TO stand in the throne city of Sshen was to stand in the midst of a province walled as a city, filled with cacophony and culture, to be overcome by a vast, dark tide of peoples. It had its quarters . . . city-states, in actuality . . . of peoples and classes, threaded throughout by the military presence of the Sshen and emperor. To go within the inner walls of the city, into the palace complex itself, was to stand in the wash of the radiance of the greatest civilization of the world that called itself Lunavar. It was to want to be inside the palace, to study, to become one with its greatness and mystery. To be admitted meant submitting oneself to the mage staff of the emperor, to be examined and memorized before being allowed into the museum and library of knowledge, antiquities, and beauties. And, while studying, being studied.

To go inside meant days of kneeling in silent petition. No one was quite sure what effort would see the petition granted but scholars were allowed within by the handful. He wanted inside. He had to get inside. He had a blood debt that could only be paid by getting inside.

So Brennan wrapped himself in black and knelt on the steps of the palace by the museum wing and fasted and meditated and keenly observed the doors, windows, floors, upper balconies, and guards through the veil gauze masking his face. He left at night, as the others did, and broke his fast, but unlike the others, Brennan made sketches of what he had observed, dictated and copied what he had to his mainframe server, and when he returned in the morning, he knelt in a different place to expand his observations. He would not be denied.

But midway through the third morning, the eldest of the elders approached him quietly. "We have been watching you, scholar. Come with me."

He rose to his feet silently, knees barely aching, his stomach complaining more than anything, and unwrapped his face and followed the emperor's mage. They went through a side portcullis that Brennan had marked and into the spice-scented shadowy interior of a small chamber. He looked up, sensing that the antechamber leaned against what was a high tower, and he scanned the interior, looking for evidence of that. There, before he could anticipate or protest, the elder took his wrist, slashing it with a sharp stinging knife and allowing blood to splash into an earthenware basin. Brennan moved away without a word despite his surprise, applying pressure, and the mage nodded as he wrapped the wound carefully, rendering it near invisible within his sleeves. The mage of the Emperor of Sshen returned his ritual knife to a forearm sheath that Brennan had not marked before, hidden within faded crimson robes.

"Follow me," the elder said, without apology or explanation. As he stepped from the antechamber, he put the bowl onto a rack, the coppery aroma of Brennan's blood mingling with that of clove and sandalwood, the pungent scents assailing his heightened senses. They could not mask the animal odor that began to seep through the chamber and Brennan thought he heard a heavy, impatient body moving behind the walls with a dull thud. A shuttered enclosure behind the rack of bowls rattled heavily as the walls were hit again. He smelled . . . not animal . . . but reptile before the elder moved him through an arched doorway.

They moved into an inner courtyard where lesser mages sat on cushions, reading, with books and parchments, pots of dipping ink and styli at their sides. Almost as one they looked up at his entry, and the elder turned to him.

"Remove your head scarf."

Brennan did so, unwrapping the black gauze that had concealed him. His dark, glossy locks tumbled free to his shoulders, his thin fine goatee revealed on his chin, and his dark eyes watching all of them as they sketched and noted his presence. "Barbarian," one of them muttered to himself, stylus quickly skritching across the paper. He did not try to hide the scorn in his eyes as he looked at the monk-mage. They would render what he intended, the facial hair, the foreign look of him. If it were he, he'd be using a universal recognition graph, vectoring the face and neck into quadrants noting features that would be recognizable no matter what the apparent disguise. And *he* was a barbarian.

After long moments of sketching at a furious pace, the pens were lowered. Heads nodded. "You will be allowed three days' passage," the elder said. He gave Brennan a fired porcelain pass, hanging on a tightly braided crimson cord. It was but a sample of the delicate china work of the province, colors glazed skillfully, the porcelain so fine it could be seen through. Fine and fragile. "Show this and you will be admitted. We trust you will not abuse the emperor's hospitality."

He bowed low. "I thank you."

Behind him as he left, he heard the sanding and blotting of sheets, his image memorialized. They would make a detailed Wanted poster.

Screeches and flailings of something winged being fed beyond the inner walls followed after his footfalls.

He had every intention of exploiting that hospitality as far as he could.

Outside the palace and back on the streets, mingled into the crowds, he turned and looked back at the vast palatial complex, its turrets and wings and walls. A shadowy thing crouched on one of the high turrets, before letting out a screech and launching itself into the air. A raptor's silhouette was highlighted by the late afternoon sun, with formidable tearing beak and claws. It winged in slow, lazy circles before returning to its perch on the tower. It had to be one of the famed bloodseeker nyrll, and he understood then the ritual bowls and the bloodletting.

Back at the inn he'd chosen, he unwrapped his outsider garb, discarded the expended squib from the one wrist and unbound the unmarked one from the left, the thin intestine bulging with fresh blood. The unfortunate donor was no doubt still asleep in a tavern gutter. His single earring, a crystal drop held by a silver claw stud, whispered softly in his ear. "DNA marker. They'll think they have you."

"But they do not," he murmured back to his mainframe server. He had noted others leaving, wrists bound, one or two nearly swooning at the sight of their own blood, and he had had squibs ready on either wrist. "Luckily for me they chose the wrist instead of the jugular, eh?"

"That is perceived as a joke and is not found humorous."

He did not expect her to find it that way. Her existence depended upon him, and his existence depended upon his survival on this world.

He sat down with his ceramic pass and sketches and contemplated the evening's work ahead, absently peeling off the wax nose and then the itchy goatee. He need not worry about the nyrll; the bloodseeker would have another prey once loosed, but still he would avoid what trouble he could. He needed to get inside the interior vaults and then out, to meet with Mannoc's man, make the exchange, and be gone. A treasure of the emperor for a treasure of the forgotten wastes deep in Jaahtcaran territory . . . a fair exchange, even if it did mark him, and the blood debt would follow him all his days, regardless. The Jaahtcar had made him an offer he could not refuse.

"Do you ever think about it?" his earring spoke again.

"Think about what?" He was distracted by her, staring at his sketches, planning the vectors of assault. He could not take a lot of gear with him. He needed to be free-moving, undetectable, and had to be able to shed whatever he must.

"Being abandoned here."

"Missions are aborted out of necessity. Your problem is that you don't know what the necessity was, and it confounds you. It affects your computing, your decision making. That is why they still send human teams out, as well as your kind. Flexibility."

"You are the only one of your kind on this world."

"As are you, Rose," he reminded the mainframe.

He had intended to breach the depths of the Sshen palace vaults sooner or later, if only to ease his own curiosity. Physical laws misunderstood or undiscovered became the foundation for magic and he did not hesitate to exploit that in any way he could. The stylus moved easily over the papers as he sketched out a breach and no fewer than four exits. He needed an adrenaline boost, nightsight, and his overall sensory perceptions raised, grappling hooks, and a few other implements. He could do it with a minimum of supplies, he thought. A fiber-optic lock pick would be the most essential item. That and climbing equipment.

Brennan lay down on the thin, hard cot that the inn called a bed, and he reviewed his night's plan, the potions and tinctures he would need, the ropes and pulleys, the phosphorescent light-bar, and sundry other items he had at hand to break into the Sacred inner vaults. Although he should fear the Emperor of Sshen, he did not, for the emperor was steeped in mysticism and would not know Brennan for what he truly was. It was the Jaahtcar he feared.

She whispered in his ear. "Brennan. This is a world where all cultures have the same word for war, and for warrior. Think about that anomaly. Your father is gone, and we're abandoned."

"We are not abandoned! Sleep mode." He sent her into oblivion, which was perhaps kinder to the mainframe than staying awake through the brief night while he rested. She had no concept of pain but she had an implanted fear of being nonoperative. He practiced his breathing, and let the stress go. Sleep claimed him for a short while.

In the deepest part of the night, he arose, wrapped himself in three layers of clothing, replaced his goatee and overlying wax nose, loaded his pockets with his tools, coiled his ropes about his shoulders, fastened his harness snugly in place, pulled his cloak over and about him, and laid out his tinctures, potions, and powders. He woke Rose but told her not to transmit unless he asked her a specific question. She grudgingly acknowledged.

The nightsight tincture would improve his night vision tremendously, the allquick pump his adrenaline reactions, and the powders would affect the neural lingual reactions of anything inhaling them. The lightbar, when its interior was broken so that the chemicals might mix, would give him more than enough illumination without heat so that whatever the mages had that might sense heat in the inner vaults would not give him away.

He shrugged out of the fiber-optic net he'd worn as a baldric and placed it in a washbasin, along with other incriminating evidence, and set a trip for a contained fire with a bit of string, a candle stub, and other odds and ends. Losing the net would be a waste, but he had more, and it was better than leaving it behind. No one in Sshen would be able to decipher it, but he was not sure about a Jaahtcar. No, he was not at all sure about the enigmatic Jaahtcar. His father, wherever his body and soul had gone, had left him with a warning about Lunavar. "Be wary," he'd said, "of a world where the word for war is universal, and appears to have come from one nation."

They were a team: man, son, sentient computer system. They had journeyed to Lunavar when he was only ten years old. The crown city of Sshen was the biggest city he could remember seeing, although he'd known others before. He no longer remembered them as entire entities. He'd been brought to train, and to work alongside his father as he'd grown into Lunavar, its people, its languages, its ways, and mores. His father would be the anchor, and he the assimilated. Unfortunately, the mission had been aborted after only a few years, and his father had gone out to retrieve their homing equipment, and never returned. Rose watched him as he grew and she slept for long periods, as he aged slowly into maturity as well as knowledge. He stepped out of his crystal caverns when necessity demanded, and when he had to learn what he could, so they could return home. What his father had meant, and Rose still warned, Brennan didn't fully understand.

When dark had got as deep as it would, and most tortured souls were either asleep or drugged beyond sensing anything, he stepped out to do what he'd come for.

Inside the inner walls, he tucked the ceramic pass into his sleeve, firmly against the inside of his wrist, in case he might have to return. Then he stepped past the public rooms and vaults open to all the scholars and headed for the Forbidden. Lightbar in hand, he uncoiled a length of rope and gauged the walls as he moved into the velvet black interior of the famous maze of the inner chambers. Up and over, catlike, pausing now and then to look in cases or on pedestals, before traversing the next chamber walls, Brennan made his way inexorably through Sshen's legacy. The allquick set in as he increased his breathing, and he moved rapidly past the obstacles, glimpses of treasure catching his attention here and there.

He lingered, despite misgivings. The vaults were too captivating to pass through without looking at what the emperor and previous dynasties had hidden away. There was a plain stone that sat in a spiked box to prevent its theft. He did not have to read the sign to feel the powerful electromagnetic aura it cast. Then there was the anklet of the slave empress Mahrdin who united the walls of the early Sshen empire. There was the baton of the ArchMage, its gnarled wood etched and inscribed. There was no logical reason for the hairs on the back of his neck to prickle as he passed that one, yet they did.

He paused for more than a moment at a simple wooden bowl large enough to curl a cow in. Resting inside was an opalescent shard of an eggshell. A dragon's shell, the sign said. It needed no further explanation. He pondered the plausibility of it, then moved on, running now. The maze brought him back to the baton, and Brennan smothered a curse, wondering how he had missed a turning.

His skin crawled again. But not in aversion. No. He craved to hold the short staff. It drew him. He broke his cardinal rule. This was not what he had come for, but he took it anyway, sliding it up the left sleeve on the inner side of his arm. It fit neatly along the span from his wrist to his elbow, and immediately warmed his skin though it was made of wood. Continuing on, he swung his hook and rope coil, and went up and over the tall walls, rather than risk misnumbering the maze yet again. His lightbar fluttered slightly as the chemicals began to burn away. Brennan moved as swiftly as he could for he needed enough light to get out.

He did not pause again until he stood at the great case wherein rested three amber jewels known as the Eyes of the Dragon. Like the egg shard outside, they were rumored to be the actual item. He did not know. All his intelligence on Lunavar had not indicated Dragons. Fey peoples of high intuitive ability, perhaps even telepathic abilities, but never Dragons. Quickly, he gathered up the fist-sized shapes and arranged them in a lined, black velvet pouch he had made to carry such things.

He would be out much quicker than he came in, the allquick fiery in his veins like a berserker fury. He needed speed now, not finesse. "I've got everything," he informed Rose. She did not affirm. A faint crackle sounded in his ear. Something in the air interfered with transmission. Of no import. His task was done.

Brennan turned around slowly to spot his position in the maze and reconcile it with the maps he'd drawn earlier and memorized. Something tall, dark, carapace-hard in the shadows, stirred. The Sentinel moved out, into the cold spill of light from Brennan's hand, and it looked like nothing he had ever encountered. The lightbar shivered in his hold, illumination spraying over the thing erratically, making it difficult to know what he was looking at.

Not mortal or mechanical. His heart did a quick jump in his chest. Brennan circled, quickly, fleetly, faster than mere flesh, on an adrenaline high. He would pay for it later, but he had no choice now.

The thing moved with him. Heat seeking? No. Perhaps.

His hand flashed, powder motes drifted on the air with the gesture. If it inhaled, it would be affected by the hallucinatories. He had an immunity to them, but the creature facing him surely did not. Brennan circled again.

It moved on inexorably.

Not breathing. Not animal. Not flesh.

Brennan leaped to pass it. The Sentinel reached out and caught his arm, pulling him down to earth with a crushing grip. Only the ArchMage's staff prevented harm to his flesh, tendon, bones. But he was caught, well and truly, and by something he did not think existed. Something that stank of magic.

It was at this moment that he wondered how he had got there.

ACT I

Brennan took advantage of the slowness of the carriage approach to check himself over carefully one last time. Ear transmitter, in place. Chest camera, good. Clothing . . . just slightly out of style and season as befit the impoverished scion of a scion of a poor holding and without wife . . . of questionable quality as well as faddishness. Good. There would be polite looks, a few jabbing remarks, but all in all, his clothing would be far more remembered than his face. He checked his cuffs again, and made sure his pants were tucked neatly into his boot tops, then ran a hand over his face. The salve, a pleasantly scented unguent, kept his body as hairless as it could, with the only side effect being a tendency to sunburn a little too quickly if he did not take care. His outfit also included a pardskin hat, with the appropriate feather and beaded headband.

His carriage bumped to a halt and the doorman quickly opened the cabin door and let the step down. Brennan got out leisurely, surveying the grounds as he did. He disliked the transmitter as it interfered somewhat with his own preternatural hearing, but it couldn't be helped; he needed recording beyond what he could catch. Something was stirring here, and he needed to know everything he could.

He moved down the carriage step, kicking the edge of his cloak out of the way, and headed toward the front gardens where music and the inevitable milling of people indicated he had arrived fashionably late. The strains of a few strings, a percussion or two and a handful of woodwinds reached him, all more or less in tune and imparting a merry song. These late spring parties always seemed to be aimed at matchmaking and merriment, although a serious amount of diplomacy and negotiation, as well as gambling, took place in the back rooms. That was where he would head after being ingratiatingly social.

He stood in the small line, awaiting his announced arrival, picking up the murmurs about him.

A low-pitched, vibrant voice caught his attention. "Mannoc is back again. I don't like that Jaahtcar one bit. He's too swift in his negotiations."

"He has better information than we do, I suspect."

"Aye. That, and more." A slight cough then, as if noticing that others were a little too quiet, listening. Boots shuffled restlessly as the murmurs trailed off.

Brennan spent a bit of time correcting the epaulets and his cloak, fussing with the line and hang of it, as though quite unaware anyone about him could be saying anything of any interest at all. He stopped only when the herald put a palm across his chest, halting Brennan on the doorway threshold, and called out, "Brennan anj'anj'Risalavan."

Brennan straightened, smiling and bowing slightly as a room full of faces glanced briefly his way, eyed him, dismissed him, and went back to their springtime gossip. He stepped through to let the next pair in and went straight to the sidebar for a libation. The spread of bottles and decanters and jugs was impressive, and he took a moment or two deciding what would please his palate and quench his thirst and interfere least with the potions he had taken this morning. Although already ingested, they were designed to stay relatively inert until he began pumping extra oxygen into his system. Brennan smiled around the room as he poured himself a snifter of S'shen imperial brandy and carried it to a patio corner.

The breeze held the raw edge of winter not quite gone, with the dampness of an impending rain, perhaps shortly after nightfall, although he could not see clouds on the horizon. Clouds built up quickly on the eastern ridge, though, and Brennan was fairly certain most of the afternoon would be under a leaden sky. So he took in a ray of sun now, and enjoyed it, though his newly unguented skin was a bit tender and would soon burn if he wasn't careful. With a subtle gesture, he pulled the brim of his hat down a little to shade his face, and took a sip of the excellent-smelling brandy.

It rolled off his tongue and sent a warming fire down his throat before pooling nicely in his stomach. Brennan smiled at the flavor of it. An excellent vintage, even for the Throne City, pricey and very far from home, where vintages of this kind were usually reserved for weddings or naming days for sons of substantial holdings.

Such a naming day as an anj' of an anj' of Risalavan would not have, Risalavan being impoverished and backwater. Not that the anj' of Risalavan had had an heir; he had not. The sire of Risalavan had had hopes for his son, regardless of the stable accident, an ill-placed kick, which had left his heir with one shriveled testes and the other of dubious abilities, and sent him off to the southern provinces of his holdings in hopes of expanding both his wealth and his issue. After years of waiting, instead, he had received home a box containing the preserved, severed head of his anj' after a fatal hunting accident. In bitter tears, the fortress had been shut up and the sire had retired to meditate and pray for his son's soul.

Brennan had disliked disturbing the vigil of the sire of Risalavan's mourning, hidden in the shadows as the box was set on the altar, and the candles and incense lit, and a veil put over the box's contents. The older man stayed, head down and shoulders bowed, muttering to himself at the altar as everyone else left, not seeing Brennan in the corner shadows. It was of necessity that he waited, then drew his breath in slowly, and stepped out of the shadows.

"Turn if you wish but do not shout. Listen to my offer. Your son had a son, for our purposes. You will receive a handsome stipend from his estates, as long as you accept this. If you do not, I understand, but I will bring no disgrace upon your name." Or at least, he hoped he would not, for it was certainly not his intent. Brennan waited quietly for the man to turn around and look at him, and either deny or confirm him.

Silence reigned for a very long moment. Then the sire of Risalavan said, "You have a young voice."

"I would have to be young, to be an anj' of your anj', would I not?"

"You would have to be a miracle."

"Perhaps. Your son was a whole man once. It is not beyond speculation that he dallied with a village maid or the daughter of a passing merchant, or that there was issue neither he nor you knew about, till recently. You can look at me if you want, if that will help you to make up your mind."

The older man shook his head. "No," he said. His voice was choked. "No." He put his hands on the altar, on either side of the veiled box, and gripped it tightly. The muscles across the back of his shoulders tensed greatly. "Why?"

"Because I must. More than that, I cannot tell you, and it is best if you do not wonder."

"Yet I will wonder."

"I won't blame you for that. A yearly stipend is nothing compared to your grief or your loss, but it will help. We both know it will. All I ask is that you announce when appropriate, in a few weeks, that you have been presented with evidence of your son's anj'. Will you do that?" He watched the man's back, unable to read very much into his stance or musculature.

Then, finally, "As long as you're not Jaahtcar, and I don't hear it in your voice."

"That, I will swear upon my life. I am not Jaahtcar." Nor of any other race of this world, he added silently, and did not let the thought shadow his eyes.

The man turned then, surveyed him with a face etched in grief and regret, then gave a nod. "You," he said quietly, "could hardly bring more shame to the name than I have. I will not dispute your claim to be the anj' of my anj' but neither will I embrace you. You understand that?"

Brennan bowed. "Understand and accept." He took a purse from his belt and laid it on the stone floor of the chapel, near the door. "The first stipend for this year. The others will be sent by messenger, as is appropriate. I will honor your house, and your name, and your daughters and their heirs."

"And if you have an anj'?"

Brennan smiled faintly. "He will be of the line of Risalavan and make you proud." It was not likely, but he needn't disclose more than he already had.

The sire of the house of Risalavan bowed his head, turning back to his altar and grieving. Brennan had paused but a moment longer, whispering words of mourning for his own lost father, and then he'd left.

Brennan slipped through the arched doorway quietly and departed the holding much the same way he'd come in, by shadow and unlocked door, and night. He still found the quiet ways more comfortable than such fanfare as society demanded of him today, but today was another matter altogether. Today he knew being unseen was out of the question, which was why he had purchased a shell of a life to use. The faint stirrings which had led him to Risalavan had grown louder, were now rumbling—the mystery of the nation that called itself the Jaahtcar. They manipulated trading lanes and quarrels, financed wars and uprisings, and prospered. They were like leeches looking for a bloody wound to feed upon, constantly.

And now Mannoc was here. Could his luck be any greater? This was his chance to find out what the Jaahtcar wanted, what they believed their manifest destiny to be. Brennan savored another swallow of brandy, a bare sip lest he disturb the chemistry of the potions he'd ingested earlier, as he surveyed the patio and hoped for a sighting. A low growl of a voice near the outer edge of his hearing range caught his attention, and he pivoted slowly, languidly, to hide his interest.

Mannoc stood head and shoulders above the general population, even though he was bent slightly in conversation with the wealthy merchant standing next to him on the patio, both slightly veiled in blue-gray smoke from the gambling rooms which opened onto the far end of the gardens. As though by unwritten rule, despite the monied and eligible men milling around in that part of the grounds, there were no females nearby except a few servants who did not linger but came and went with quiet efficiency. Although matchmaking seemed to be one of the main intents of this gathering, the gambling room and its gamblers were not to be disturbed. Even more important liaisons of men and money were taking place therein.

Without seeming to, he watched Mannoc. The register of his lower voice made it difficult to catch what he was saying from this distance, although the others were fairly easy to pick up. He would have to go through the recorder later for the nuances and what he flat out could not hear.

"More brandy, sur?" someone said at his elbow, and he looked down smoothly and immediately swapped glasses. She faded off with her tray, and the first sip told him that he'd given up half a glass of good drink for a full glass of a vastly inferior brandy. Brennan frowned in irritation, of half a mind to chase his original drink down to the kitchen and retrieve it.

To hide his annoyance, he turned back into the manor proper and was promptly swept into a dance, glass in hand and all, and his senses reeled in a swirl of color, laughter, perfume, and motion. He bowed out after two dances to stand quietly in the vast doorway which had been thrown open to the afternoon breezes while he brought both his pulse and breathing quickly down to norms before anything could be unleashed. A little sweat peppered his forehead under the hair that had fallen forward, and the breeze felt cool against it, and he could smell the very faint hint of brandy in it as it passed through his pores, carrying with it the even fainter hint of the tonic he called allquick and other herbs.

"Anj' of anj' of Risalavan."

He swung about at the very feminine voice, saying, "Please, call me Brennan," even before he saw her. This was probably a good thing for she had large eyes, a soft bow of a mouth, fair skin, and the most incredible bosom delicately hinted at by a low and lacy necklace, and it momentarily took the words from him. He was grateful for the nonchalant tone in his voice, and managed to hold onto it as he faced her.

"Master Brennan, then. No more dancing?"

"Afraid not at the moment."

She held a bulging coin purse up to him, pouting slightly. "I think this fell from your waistband, then, and I was going to claim a dance as my reward."

He took it from her slender fingers. "I would be very remiss for not rewarding you."

"Perhaps a cold drink and a sandwich in the gardens?" She brought up a fan, waving it slightly, soft tendrils of hair ruffling along her forehead.

"Allow me, then." He put out his hand to escort her, and she took it with barely a touch between them as he tucked his coin purse back into his jacket. He had intended to drop it but chided himself for not catching that it actually had fallen. "I'm afraid I did not catch your name, m'lady."

She blushed slightly, answering, "Please . . . I am syanji' Gryden."

"Terribly formal." He escorted her through a trellis gate into the gardens where a refreshment area had been set up and a canvas canopy rippled in the afternoon breeze, gilt-threaded G neatly embroidered on every scallop. He was escorting his host's daughter, then. "Do all your friends call you that?"

"Oh, no. Please. Call me Lyleen."

"It would be my pleasure." At the stand, he ordered two chilled fruit drinks which looking promisingly clear and not cloyingly sweet with nectar and pulp and two sandwiches of fowl and chutney, and carried them to a small table. Lyleen, to his delight, did not eat like a bird pecking at the bread, but rather ate heartily and with enjoyment.

The drinks were as good as their promise and he enjoyed their mild sweet-tart coolness. They had been watered down, he was certain, but that was not undesirable as far as he was concerned. He let Lyleen chatter away, answering her pleasantries amiably, and he waited.

They had all but finished when someone came up behind Brennan and tapped on his shoulder. Lyleen blinked and looked down, a faint expression running over her face so quickly Brennan could not quite catch it. He made a note to see what the camera recorded, later. He let his shoulder flinch slightly but showed no more surprise than that.

"Anj'anj'Risalavan?" A pleasant, deep voice, rolling out of the man behind him, smelling faintly of green beer and tobacco.

He twisted about in his chair to face the greeter. "Aye, that would be me. And you . . . ?" He looked up into the broad, portly face of a man who really needed no introduction, at least in this part of the world, the very moneyed and important merchant Balatin. Balatin's weathered face showed the years he'd traveled with his caravan, not only as merchant but as guard, his hands gnarled and scarred with the signs of combat, three heavy lines etched deeply into his forehead.

Balatin bowed deeply. "Humble Balatin, trader, at your service. Forgive me for interrupting, Sy'Lyleen, but my partners and I thought anj'Risalavan might enjoy a game or two of chance." He tugged his fashionable waistcoat back into place about his formidable torso as he straightened and stood, smiling, waiting for Brennan's response.

Trap baited and sprung. But he could not have asked for lovelier bait, he thought, standing. "That would be most enjoyable!"

Lyleen's soft lips parted as if to utter a small complaint, but she never got it out as Balatin grunted, saying, "Let me lead the way, it's like a jungle in here," and Brennan fell in dutifully behind, noting that although the trader had grown older and prosperous, it was mostly compact muscle under those fine clothes and he grunted, not because of exertion but more out of exasperation with the fineries that had been forced upon his frame. His supple boots were made for walking and riding rather than dancing, and he moved accordingly. Brennan sized him up, almost as much as they had undoubtedly sized up him and his coin purse earlier. With a smile just at the edges of his mouth, he counted his victory as he headed to the gambling rooms where Mannoc the Jaahtcar and others waited for fresh blood.

Upon entering the room, and suffering a hearty round of introductions, Brennan took stock of the three games going. Qwill was being played at two tables, and the third seemed to be a sophisticated version of bangar dice, the bangar table surrounded by throwers and bettors. He could do well at either, but preferred neither game, particularly, and his purpose here was talk. Mannoc sat playing Qwill, holding the paint-and-gilt cards in one hand, tapping the other on the table idly, seemingly contemplating the mix he held.

As if hearing Brennan's unconscious wish, a balding and spindly player at the Qwill table threw his hand in and stood up, saying, "I think it's time to change my luck."

Trader Balatin pulled the chair out with a gnarled hand, indicating Brennan should sit. "Don't worry, I have new blood."

Mannoc looked up, barely smiling. "Good." He had the darkest eyes Brennan had ever seen, pools of night that made the whites around the pupils look like freshly fallen snow. His skin was uncommonly fair with the purple-and-blue tracings of his veins seen easily at the neck and wrist. The pallor might have looked unhealthy on another, but his entire aura was one of strength and vigor, belying any thought of illness. He was simply a very pale man. From what Brennan had seen of most Jaahtcar, they all were.

He wondered at the lack of tanning pigmentation and if they were originally a snowbound people, perhaps. To hide his examination of Mannoc, Brennan fussed a bit with his waistcoat and trousers as he sat down.

Mannoc smiled thinly. "By all means," he commented, "make sure the family jewels are comfortable. We'll be here a while."

Brennan placed his hands on the table and, while smiling, raised an eyebrow at Mannoc. "My jewels," he said amiably, "are quite in order and well taken care of. My father should have been so lucky."

A muffled snicker ran around the table as the dealer gathered up the cards and began to shuffle them. The lace at his wrists hid the motion as he mixed the cards and quickly dealt them, and then there was a pause. Balatin put his heavy hand on the shoulder of a young man on Brennan's right. "How are we doing, Nedo?"

"I've been keeping your cards warm," said the affable young man. He stood then, and bowed, giving up the seat to the trader. Balatin sat down, throwing his markers into the table's center without even looking at his hand.

The dealer quickly sold Brennan a fair number of markers, tucking the coins away in a common leather purse branded with a stylish G. The first card went out face up to all the players, and the qwill landed in front of Brennan.

"Auspicious," Mannoc murmured. He did not stir his dark gaze from his cards as if he'd known the qwill would land where it did.

Brennan quickly made his choice of draw cards, and the dealer took the qwill, buying it in the discards. There were three more to be had, but no others would show as the remainder of the cards would be dealt facedown. He won quickly, heard no grumbles, and kept winning off and on through most of the afternoon. The anj' of the anj' of Risavalan was not a good winner, in that he gloated a bit, and remarked how the day's work would added to the nest egg he used for his trade of antiquities, the lifework of his heart. The markers piled up steadily in front of him, gamblers dropped out and new ones came in, and Mannoc remained seated across from him, nearly silent, and almost as good at winning.

"Trader, are you?" Mannoc noted as the day wore into dusk, and servants quietly lit lanterns about the room as well as an overhead chandelier, and opened a window for the breeze to clear out the smoke. Balatin sat in the corner, at a table, partaking of a dinner which had been brought in.

"Only in oddities. Antiquities, rare artifacts, remnants of long ago," he answered absently, arranging his hand. The qwill lay in front of Mannoc, and he'd seen the Jaahtcar use it in startling ways several times today already. An interesting opponent. "I am barely a passing scholar in the Fallen, but I find their usage of metal for adornment intriguing. Their creatures, while scarcely fathomable, have a certain charm."

"Charm is about all they had, and little good it did them." Mannoc paused long enough to tap the ash from his smoker, and then inhale another gray-blue flume slowly. "Do you find a market for your oddities?"

"Oh, yes. There is a small but interested group of buyers. A few are scholars, some are merely collectors." Brennan paid a great deal of attention to arranging his cards. "I dabble in it for card money, and my card money keeps me dabbling. It's the pastures that keep my holding going. I came down to the city for a bit to look at the new shearing scissors and place a few orders, see what the winter looks like. My beasts bore well, my staff is carding now, and it looks like there will be a cold winter coming. We'll have the yarn for it. I should do well."

Mannoc tapped the ash off again. "It will be," he said quietly, "very, very cold. I'd hold onto that yarn of yours a while."

Balatin looked up sharply from his bread bowl of stew, a gleam in his eyes.

"Think you so? That might be a wise idea, then. What omens have you read? My herders tell me the caterpillars tell them that."

A slight smile cracked the Jaahtcar's face as he fanned his cards out, closed them into his palm and then placed a few markers in the pool, betting. "I have slightly more reliable methods," he answered slowly.

Brennan nibbled on one lip slightly, eyeing his cards before saying over his shoulder to an anonymous servant in the background, "I think we'll need a new deck, after this," and went back to staring morosely at his cards. He knew just how long he could draw out his response in betting before Mannoc would get restless and demand to see the hand. The Jaahtcar was very good at remaining still, but his right shoulder ticked ever so slightly and Brennan knew he was going to reach for the qwill, in effect demanding a resolution whether Brennan was ready or not, and in answer, Brennan fanned his cards down, putting his bet on top of them.

Mannoc stared but a moment, then rocked back in his chair. "Winner," he said, nodding toward Brennan. "And I could use some fresh air, and some advice from you."

"Of course," he answered smoothly, standing. It had been a long afternoon, but it seemed the wary prey had finally begun to take the bait. He followed Mannoc out of the rear of the card room onto a private patio. The hour had grown late, and the party could be heard somewhere inside, music, laughter, the sound of drinking and eating.

A servant wheeled out a cart heaped with covered plates and backed away quietly, then returned with a second cart of glass decanters and clay jugs, and a capped skin. Brennan reached for the iced juice before Mannoc could pour him a glass of much, much stronger stuff than he wished to take in. The sap he'd drunk in the morning to render his normally deep voice into a pleasant tenor had begun to ease, his larynx returning to its normal size, and he feigned hoarseness from the smoke, roughening his tones. He strode across the flagged terrace, listening to and enjoying the light strains of music reaching them.

A third person joined them, half shadowed, taking a seat on a stretched hide hammock stool. The leather creaked as he sat down in the dusk, all but hidden except for his heavy, striking boots pushed out in front of him. Mannoc poured a thick amber-red drink from the capped skin, and Brennan recognized it for what he thought it was, lyhur, the coppery smell of the added blood in the liqueur reaching him. It was a drink of pure savagery and he could not stomach it, although he'd had to, once or twice. It would play havoc with his senses and his stomach and he was only too glad to avoid it.

He could see from the other's pupils that the true purpose of this break, the card game, indeed, the whole day, was about to unfold.

Mannoc spread open the hedge surrounding the terrace, revealing Lyleen's bloodied, crumpled body. "She hasn't been seen since she stepped into the garden with you earlier. Her blood might be construed as being on your hands." He then proceeded to make Brennan an offer he could not refuse.

ACT III

The Sentinel shook him like a terrier seeking to break a rat's back. Red streaks of pain lightninged across the backs of his eyes and the maze reeled about him, leaving him completely disoriented. Even if he could break free, his senses reeled in vertigo. There was no up, no down . . . no escape. He cried out. Brennan went suddenly limp in the Sentinel's hold as if it had succeeded in breaking him and its jaws relaxed the barest of a fraction. Brennan kicked up, hitting it hard in the throat. His boot cracked . . . something. Hard-ridged shell? Armor? He was not sure as he used his momentum to flip about and somersault back onto his feet. The world righted itself, and he leaped away. He was gone, but it came after him with a grunt.

Brennan sped through the maze, no time for ropes and harness, jumping and catching the wall's top edge if he could, or vaulting onto an exhibit or cabinet if not, and then leaping again. It pursued him, soundless, breathless, heatless. It came over the wall tops or around the corners, anticipating his every move until it was obvious to Brennan. It knew he was fleeing, getting out. It could cut him off at any moment. It was toying with him, exhausting him.

He paused in a corner to catch his breath, pulse roaring in his ears. Certainly he heard the thing lunge past, headed toward the main doors, armored feet rattling on the wooden floors. Brennan threw his head back, staring up. And up. A faint spark of light from the vaulted ceiling caught his eye. A break. An exit.

In moments he had his spikes and rig set to climb. The hardwood held each spike tightly as he ascended, drawing his ropes after him, going as fast as he dared, knowing the thing would sense it had missed him and double back. He climbed, fast but not fast enough, thoughts and pulse pounding in his temples. What was it? He knew he couldn't outrun it. Could he stop it if it caught up with him again?

His weight brought a spike out of splintering wood and it fell away, clattering far below. His harness held, kept him from a similar fate, and he shook another spike loose to anchor it. A handful left. He looked up at the spark of light which had grown to crescent size. Yes. He'd make it. He dared to breathe a moment, feeling the beginning ache and fatigue as the allquick metabolized out of his system. In a few moments he'd be as weak as a newborn.

Brennan drew himself up, set his spikes and ascended as quickly as he could, till one hand reached the cup of the crescent opening, and he pulled himself onto a ventilation hatch and punched out the oxidized grille. Fresh night air roared in as he wiggled through, body now starting to ache in earnest. He straightened on the roof, nimbly crossing tiles, eyes on the streets far below, gauging the time. He was dangerously close to missing the rendezvous. Sprinting across the slanted roof, he paused at the edge for a jump to the next wing. Catlike, he sprang and made it, with ease, and yet his legs felt like lead as he straightened.

A heavy thud sounded behind him.

Brennan whirled, bringing a dagger to hand, knowing it would doubtless be of no use. The thing was on him before his heart could skip a beat, bowling him over, but he let it, rolling with it, bringing his boots up into the center of the thing's gravity and sending it tumbling over him. He scrambled about into a crouch.

It did not look much better in moonlight than it had in the maze. Enameled black, an immense suited being, perhaps even hollow from its quickness. Animated? Yet . . . how? He sensed no transmissions from it, knew of no technology in Sshen that could do it.

It moved with him as he circled.

"You will not leave," it said flatly.

Hearing the voice left a faint, coppery flavor in his mouth. Brennan licked his dry lips, discovered a minute cut, and sucked on it a moment.

He had every contingency covered except for this one.

And it would be the death of him.

He felt sweat under the wax appliance of his fake nose, and it crawled down his skin and into the gluing of his goatee, itching horribly. His breath rattled slightly in his lungs and the back of his neck and his shoulders were beginning to knot up. Perhaps if he dropped the Eyes and moved away . . . but then, no, he would not get what he needed from Mannoc and he might as well be dead if he did not.

Brennan drew the baton of the ArchMage out of his sleeve. The thing's attention riveted to it.

"You sense it, then."

"It burns brightly even on my plane," the Sentinel said.

Its voice vibrated flatly. Without breath, how could it talk . . . transmit? Perhaps he only thought he heard what he heard.

Perhaps.

Brennan circled. "Will you take it and let me go?"

"No. You have done that which is Forbidden, and the penalty is Death."

Brennan felt for a cloth tucked into his waistband. The Sentinel had fixated on the baton with its eyeless, featureless face, and followed every movement of his outstretched right hand. It never saw, if it could see, what Brennan drew clear.

"Let me go, or I will destroy it."

"Blasphemy!"

Brennan snapped the null cloth over the baton. Like whisper-soft silk, it tented over the baton and settled into place. The fine, electronic screen enmeshed within the cloth dampened whatever fields existed and set up its own, decoying.

The Sentinel let out a screech of horror and dismay, leaping at him and his outstretched hand. Brennan sidestepped, snapped a wrist dagger into his palm and aimed for the center of the thing's forehead.

The carapace and the dagger cracked as they hit. The impact drove shocking pain throughout his arm, into the elbow, and even the shoulder. Brennan let go and staggered back. The Sentinel flailed, then fell over onto his back, arms and legs hammering for a moment. The knife vibrated inexorably, eating into its target until its charge evaporated.

By then the Sentinel had stilled, melted dagger sunk into its skull.

Brennan slid the baton back into his sleeve, null cloth still wrapped around it, shuttering its emissions. Whatever they were. He needed the cloth to deal with Mannoc's man, but the thing seemed to be in better use where it was. He had no wish to attract another Sentinel.

Soon, he was hanging off the rain gutter of the roof closest to the street and dropping down lightly. Brennan trotted around the square till he reached the side road he wanted, and took it.

A coach sat motionless in the street. The restive horses tossed their heads as he approached, and got in, the carriage rocking under his added weight.

"You got the items," the Jaahtcar said, and Brennan was faintly disappointed as he noted his contact was not Mannoc. "And more." The envoy frowned slightly. "This was not part of the deal."

"I don't know what you mean."

"You know exactly what I mean."

Brennan grinned in spite of himself, on the edge of his resources. "I was hired to do a job, exchange items, and make a delivery."

"You have a blood debt to fulfill. Hiring is scarcely the word to use."

The envoy leaned over, the plush carriage seat squeaking slightly with his movement, and tugged off Brennan's beard. He tossed the stringy goatee out the window, grimacing. "Filthy thing. Do you think us so simple we could not see through it? You have needs and we have needs. All this . . ." and he waved a winter-gloved hand about lightly, "was to persuade you to work with us."

Brennan made an impatient movement. "Get to it."

Reaching under the seat, Mannoc's envoy drew out a wooden crate. "This is the payment, then."

"Inspection?"

"Take it or leave it. Hand over the pouch. I wish to be through the city gates before the nyrll are loosed." The very pale Jaahtcar watched him. Unlike Mannoc, he had light gray eyes, and they watched Brennan carelessly.

Fingering the pouch tied at his waist, Brennan seized the rope handle on the crate, throwing the lid open. Lying on its side, illu-

minated by the carriage lamps guttering low on oil, was the object
he had nearly died for. Would die without. He dipped a hand inside the crate, confirming. The wreckage of the thing, that is . . .
His heart sank. The weariness that would flood his body had already begun, weakening him, washing like a dark tide over his
senses.

Once it had been a homing beacon, made to withstand weather
and time and the vagaries of the wilderness of an alien world. Not
made to withstand deliberate deconstruction. Lying on the straw
bed next to the metal and glass shards was a stiff, bloodied glove.

"The glove," the Jaahtcar said, with satisfaction, "is a bonus."

The glove had belonged to his father. No doubt the blood did
as well. They knew they handed him his prize, deliberately
wrecked, and they knew they handed him a last remnant of his
father. Brennan looked up, smiling, and the smile disconcerted
the envoy. He realized now, they knew him far better than he
knew them. He would not make that mistake again.

The matching glove, no doubt, could be found with Lyleen's
remains, and the bloodhounds of Lunavar, the nyrll, would ID
him as the killer, absorbing his own DNA markers along with
those of his father. Mannoc had never had any intention of freeing him from that trap. The Jaahtcar would use him as long as
they could, as long as he gave them a leash to do so.

He snapped his left arm and his last remaining dagger slipped
into his palm, and he drove it into the Jaahtcar's chin from below,
and jammed it higher, twisting, when it met resistance, scraping
against bone. Blood spurted.

The man fell over, gurgling.

"No deal."

Brennan gathered up the crate. He might be accused of burning
bridges with that, but satisfaction rolled through him in a warm
wave. The trap had been sprung by the anj' of the anj' of Risalavan, but it had been meant for the mage thief all along, so they
knew just who he was. Perhaps even knew what the beacon had
been.

He took a deep breath. Brennan stepped out of the carriage,
waving up at the driver. "We're finished here. He wants to be
through the gates at dawn's first light."

The driver nodded, as if he had been given his orders earlier.
He gathered up his reins.

Brennan tucked the crate under his elbow, found shadows to slip into, and disappeared into the backways of a world where the word for war was the same in all languages, realizing as he did so that it was the Jaahtcar who'd brought that word to Lunavar. He did not know why. But he would find out, for within that question's answer, he would find a way home.

Cheryl J. Franklin

I can remember being at a sales conference, running from meeting to meeting, and then going back to my room to curl up with a manuscript by an unknown author. Despite the hectic circumstances under which I read this "slush" submission, it was a story which really caught my attention. The author was Cheryl Franklin and the novel was *Fire Get,* the first of a group of novels she has written for DAW, most of which have been linked to the universe in which *Fire Get* is set.

Cheryl is extremely modest about her accomplishments, and when I asked her if she wanted to send us some information about herself, she provided an extremely short paragraph:

"After twenty-four years as a communications systems engineer in the defense industry, Ms. Franklin has reformed. She now dedicates her life to making her cats happy. She enjoys chocolate, good tea, operettas, and video games (adventure and RPG). She is the author of seven novels, all published by DAW Books."

Among the many things she doesn't mention is that she is a descendant of Benjamin Franklin. And obviously she has inherited both a bent for science and for writing from this famous ancestor.

As you will see when you read "Words," Cheryl isn't kidding about devoting her life to making her cats happy.

—SG

WORDS
Cheryl J. Franklin

HOMES of the recently dead all looked alike to Anya Marlow. She was the first to admit the unfairness of her jaded perspective. She had visited too many death sites throughout her long career as a specialist in sensor system forensics. Over the course of thirty years, she had gradually stopped caring about the human element. Her narrow focus made her exceptionally efficient at her job, which meant that her services continued to be valued despite her cultivated lack of social skills.

Virtually every scene of death, natural or unnatural, lay within the range of one of the ubiquitous sensor systems that regulated building environments, provided security, monitored the status of basic home or business supplies, scheduled mandatory types of building maintenance, and supported a variety of other human needs and wants according to personal programming. It was Anya's job both to extract the system data and to ensure that the data were valid. The sensor systems had become much more reliable throughout the years of her career, and tampering had become increasingly rare, but the formality of forensic certification still held considerable legal weight. At times, Anya regretted that her tools had become so sophisticated, her job so routine. These days, her impressive credentials mattered more in the courtroom than in the lab.

The body had been removed before she entered the apartment, and much of the physical forensic work was already complete. At a nod from one of the young detectives—Anya chose not to recall his name, though she had worked with him on several cases—she headed for the sensor panel at the side of a massive oak bookcase. Relieved, she saw that the panel was physically intact, sparing her the need to work together with another specialist for extraction. She connected her analysis station and began to assess the system's data integrity.

She made no effort to extract data content at this point, but some facts forced themselves upon her while she examined the disjointed phrases that ran across her scanner. The dead man, Seth Katani, had lived alone with a single "feline companion." Anya suppressed a moment's shiver, imagining her own dry epitaph if her cat, Dusty, had outlived her. Hurriedly, she forced aside memories that could not be indulged before witnesses. She had excused previous tears with a story of allergies, but that had only elicited a stern recommendation to seek treatment, lest she contaminate a crime scene unnecessarily. She had no intention of sharing her grief. She valued her reputation of cold professionalism.

To regain control, she forced herself to read the words that slipped past her on the display, and she tried to build some sense from the fragments. It was wasted exercise, since a later analysis phase would sort the data into a more readable format, but she needed to occupy her mind. A tax form listed Katani as a retired research consultant, but she saw no reference to the type of research. A peculiar list of five names without identified purpose or order flitted by repeatedly: Rita, Nigel, James, Noreen, Tam. Curiously, Katani's files contained no reference to the word "cat," even in the standing order to maintain food supplies. Dusty's needs had so dominated Anya's home system that she had yet to clean out all "cat" references, even six months after Dusty's death.

Apparently, Katani had deactivated all but the most basic sensor functions. The data files were unusually meager. Other than the odd set of names, which was probably meaningless, the detectives would be disappointed. To her surprise, Anya shared a little of that emotion, though in a twisted form. She wondered if it was her identification with Katani's terse profile that troubled her, or if the data actually justified concern. She experienced a perverse surge of hope for the possible challenge of an interesting case.

She examined the numbers and frowned at the nonzero statistic for tampering. The probability of tampering was low enough to fall within the range of statistical error according to regulations, but the reading was higher than usual—high enough to allow Anya's tiny flare of hope to linger. She chided herself inwardly for allowing even that small emotion to intrude, especially when the hope was so likely to be dashed. Anya had not encountered a case of deliberate data tampering in years, not since the model 3000 introduced sophisticated protective mechanisms and a massive write-once memory core. Physical destruction of the storage unit was a much faster and simpler method of corrupting the data, and it generally sufficed for legal purposes. A decent lawyer could cast doubts on even the best data recovery methods by the favorite tactic of showing a jury the twisted wreckage of a sensor unit. It created a far more persuasive argument than a discussion of the subtleties and probabilistic nature of the electromagnetic data reconstruction process.

The download into Anya's analysis station was complete. She would take her unit back to her home lab for the more detailed assessments. The preliminary data did not seem to warrant physical removal of Katani's system, but Anya applied the obnoxious yellow instruction sticker, nonetheless. She saw the young detective frown at her action, and she girded herself for the inevitable questions.

"Is removal really necessary?" he asked her. "This looks like a simple heart attack. Katani had a known heart condition."

"There are some possible anomalies that need to be checked," answered Anya coolly. She refrained from pointing out the excessive attention already being given to the case if it was a simple heart attack. Katani must have been important to someone.

The detective frowned. He was obviously not pleased by her request, which would require summoning another specialist, delaying case resolution. Of course, he was never pleased to interact with Anya, and she made no effort to counter his blatant dislike of her. She returned the sentiment. He was much too smart, much too conventionally attractive, and much too sure of his own ability to succeed. Anya didn't much care for such cocky young detectives—too young even to comprehend the cynicism that pervaded her.

The detective nodded brusquely, knowing that he could not refute her professional opinion. He had started to turn away, when Anya surprised herself by stopping him. "You have found the man's cat, I assume."

The detective turned slowly back to her. He had donned a peculiar smile, which made Anya regret her momentary impulse of helpfulness. Did he know about her weakness? Did he dislike her enough to use Dusty's death against her? *Stop being paranoid*, she chided herself, stifling panic.

"You mean the 'feline companion'? Yes, we found it, and we need someone to watch it until we complete the investigation. Thanks for volunteering." He waved toward the apartment's bedroom. "In there. You'll find a carrier, as well."

Conflicted emotions threatened to penetrate Anya's stoic surface. She focused on her irritation with the detective. Stunned by his gall, Anya struggled to keep her voice calm. "I am not the animal services department."

"That's why you're the perfect choice," replied the detective smugly, but something about Anya's frozen posture made him relent. His smile faded. While Anya loathed the thought of him actually perceiving her discomfort and taking pity on her, her opinion of his professional abilities did rise marginally. No mockery remained in his voice as he continued, "The animal services department refuses to accept jurisdiction in this case. We really do need a volunteer."

Anya accepted the truce grudgingly. "How can animal services refuse jurisdiction?"

The detective's hesitation gave Anya a moment to wonder what crucial fact she was missing. She was about to rescind her tentative patience with the man, when he answered, "Katani's 'companion' is the result of a genetic research project that Katani led a few years ago. We're not entirely sure what genetic enhancements were done, but the animal services folks don't want to attract controversy."

"Genetic enhancements always inspire controversy," acknowledged Anya. She did not want to give the detective the satisfaction of seeing how deeply he had rattled her, as she realized that his "request" was sincere. She told herself that she should walk away now and leave the detective to deal with his controversial case. She was sure that the detective had asked her to "volunteer" simply to retaliate against her request for the system removal. She doubted that he actually expected her to acquiesce, which made her feel perversely cooperative. "I'll take the 'companion' for now, since I'm headed home anyway. I expect you to make other arrangements for the long term." Anya derived pleasure from the detective's startled reaction, but she did not like the pensive way he stared at her as she headed toward the bedroom.

Gusts from an open window made the bedroom cold. The room was monastic in its simplicity: one twin bed beneath a white coverlet, one small end table, one faded print of vaguely Egyptian artistry, one large wicker basket containing a mass of long gray fur, breathing softly. Other than a head that seemed somewhat larger than usual, the "companion" appeared to be an ordinary cat. The cat was curled in typical feline fashion and appeared to be asleep.

Dusty had been predominantly gray, although Dusty's short fur had been speckled with white. Dusty had also been smaller than this . . . companion. Anya gulped down another threat of tears, regretting her petty impulse to surprise the detective with her cooperative attitude. Dusty's death continued to be a constant source of hurt. Anya did not need any more reminders.

However, she was too proud to tell the detective that she had changed her mind. Assuming that the basket was what the detective meant by a "carrier," Anya decided that she had been given implicit permission to take the basket as well as the cat. She lifted the basket carefully, hoping that the wicker handle was strong enough to support the load. She expected the cat to rouse despite her efforts at gentle motion, but the cat slept as deeply as if drugged. The heavy basket created an awkward imbalance with the lightweight analyzer under her other arm. Anya struggled to make the load seem easy as she walked past the detective, but she could imagine the man's superior smirk.

Anya jarred the basket as she loaded it into the passenger seat of her car. The cat continued to sleep, and Anya wondered if genetic enhancement had reduced normal sensitivities. Surely, the detective would have told her if the cat had actually been drugged. He might enjoy annoying Anya, but he was professional about his work.

At least, the cat gave Anya an acceptable excuse to go directly home. She had always preferred to use her own well-equipped lab, but a nominal appearance at the police facility made certain key officials feel more comfortable. No one wanted to acknowledge that her private setup was far more advanced than the public establishment. When she first compared the pathetic official lab with its published cost, she had concluded immediately that major graft had occurred, but she was experienced enough to keep silent about a matter outside of her control. For once, she could avoid the pretense of needing that expensive display of obsolescence.

Anya lived in a small frame house that had belonged to her family for four generations. The neighborhood had changed from lower middle class to trendy upscale, but Anya refused to sell or rebuild. Inside, she had modernized extensively, converting most of the house into lab space, but the exterior remained virtually untouched. The same lopsided pine tree—victim of a bad pruning long ago—still shaded the corner of the ragged lawn, and the flower beds still held rangy geraniums and old roses that had all seen better days. Anya's neighbors considered her property an eyesore.

Anya sat the basket in the corner of the combined kitchen and dining area. The cat's lethargy troubled her a little, but Anya decided to try a watch-and-wait approach, at least until she had transferred Katani's data from the portable unit to her lab network. She wasn't sure what she would do if she decided the cat *did* have a medical problem, other than haranguing the animal services people who had refused to accept responsibility.

Anya spent a little more than an hour distributing data, initiating various analysis routines, and documenting the details of every step in accordance with the proper legal procedures. Her own home sensor system served as the certified legal witness, which Anya had always considered ironic. If anyone knew how to tamper undetected with a sensor system, it was a specialist such as herself. When she submitted the original application for home certification, she had expected to be denied. Apparently, the legal community valued her expertise enough to humor her. Or perhaps they just considered her too cold and rigid to be untrustworthy.

Returning to the kitchen to start a pot of tea, she sneezed and grabbed a tissue from a box that she seldom used. She realized belatedly that she had aggravated the problem by adding cat fur to her face. Dusty had enjoyed rubbing his chin on the tissue box, and gray fur still clung in spots. How unfair it was that Dusty's fur should remain so long after Dusty was gone. Anya felt the tears start again. She had cried so much in the weeks after Dusty died that she had feared that the allergy story would wear thin.

"You miss him," squeaked a strange voice: strange both in the sense of unfamiliarity and in an oddity of timbre and tone. The source of the voice gazed at Anya placidly from clear green eyes, peering over the edge of Katani's basket.

It's a genetically enhanced feline companion, Anya reminded herself, suppressing her shock. She could not stifle the sense of loss that tightened her throat. What would Dusty have said, if some genetic researcher like Katani had equipped him with vocal cords?

Anya realized that she was returning the cat's unblinking stare, when she should be grasping at an opportunity to question a possible witness. She wished that Katani's cat did not remind her so much of Dusty. The eyes had the same green-blue clarity. "Yes, I miss him." She had not discussed Dusty's death with any-one except the veterinarian who had eased Dusty's pain in the last days. Anya had not expected to voice her own pain to anyone, least of all to another cat, but the sense of a surreal link to Dusty made her speak. "We were together for nearly thirty years. I can hardly remember a time before Dusty." How much could Ka-tani's feline companion understand? Vocal abilities did not neces-sarily require intelligence, as humanity had demonstrated for millennia.

"I miss Seth, too," replied the cat quietly. The name emerged with a purr of strong emotion. "I don't want to believe he's gone."

This is a potential witness, Anya reminded herself, but it was nearly impossible to summon the necessary professional detach-ment. Anya could not set aside the giddy sensation that she was talking to Dusty again, as she had so often, though Dusty's re-plies had never been more than meows, purrs, and body language. "How long were you with him?"

"All my life so far—seven years." The purr of emotion grew louder. Dusty had purred that way as he died. "Thank you for bringing me here. I did not want to stay home without Seth."

"Of course," answered Anya with a twinge of guilt. Apart from the initial protective impulse that had caused her to question the detective, she had not even considered the cat's feelings of loss. She had always dreaded the thought of Dusty being left alone if something had happened to *her.* It was odd, but the phrase "genetic enhanced feline companion" had made Katani's cat seem less real—more of a science experiment than a living being. An ordinary cat would have elicited Anya's sympathy from the start. "Are you comfortable?" The basket had only a thin cushion. Dusty's bed still occupied a corner of the closet, but it looked a little small for Katani's cat.

"Yes."

"Hungry?"

"No." After a pause, the cat hissed softly, "He didn't die here, did he?"

"Who?" Confusion turned to pain, recalling Dusty in the sterile cage with the tubes and IVs piercing skin shaved of its glorious silky fur. "Dusty? No. Not here."

"Good," sighed the cat. "I didn't think so. It doesn't smell of death. Not like my home."

This is a potential witness, Anya reminded herself yet again, a little more successfully this time. As gently as she could manage, Anya asked, "Did you see Katani—Seth—die?"

The cat did not reply, and Anya feared that her social ineptitude extended to genetically enhanced felines. If the detective had realized what the genetic enhancements included, he would surely not have chosen Anya to conduct the interview. "I'm sorry," said Anya, honestly contrite. "I didn't mean to upset you."

"I wasn't there," answered the cat slowly. "I had squeezed out through the bedroom window. Seth always hated it when I did that. He worried about me. I just wanted to stretch in the park for a while. I was bored. Seth hadn't had much time for me lately. He'd been busy traveling, presenting papers, arguing with his detractors. If I hadn't left, everything might have been different." The cat's odd voice trailed into a very feline mewl.

"You couldn't have prevented his death."

"Probably not, but I might have been able to call for help."

Anya could not think of a truthful, comforting reply, and she would not insult anyone with false consolation. She dragged one of the kitchen chairs near the basket and sat, resting her elbows on her knees and her chin on her hands. She restrained an impulse to reach out and stroke the cat's fur, unsure of the appropriateness of such an intimate gesture. "I'm Anya. You didn't tell me your name."

"Teaser. Seth said that my existence teased the prejudices of his colleagues."

Anya smiled. "Seth didn't think much of his colleagues?"

"Some of them were okay. Only a few—the ardent five, as Seth called them—really worked at causing trouble for Seth. Most colleagues found Seth's theories disturbing but worthy of discussion."

"What theories were those?"

"His theories about good and evil. He believed that the balance could be—should be—tilted toward good genetically."

"I can see why his ideas were considered disturbing. A precise definition of 'good' would be difficult to justify, even if the genetic basis of behavior were accepted at such a level."

"He was a wise man," replied Teaser defensively.

"I'm sorry. I did not mean to insult his memory."

Teaser remained miffed. "The ardent five insulted him often enough, and they never apologized." A hiss so enveloped the next words that Anya almost missed the sense of them. "They hated him. That's why they killed him."

"You think someone killed him?" asked Anya in shock. Bereaved relatives sometimes made wild accusations, but Anya did not expect such behavior from a cat, "enhanced" or not. In Anya's experience, cats were far too pragmatic.

"Of course. Seth warned me that this might happen. He recorded the names of his enemies, along with their motives and probable methods. Haven't you found his files yet?"

"I haven't found anything of that sort," answered Anya slowly. "A list of five first names recurs, but the names don't seem to have any additional information attached." True, the analysis was not even close to complete, but Anya could not help thinking of her suspicions about data tampering. The repeated names *were* an oddity.

Teaser sighed. "It was Nigel, then. He was the only one of Seth's enemies who had the skill to delete the sensor system evidence. I can tell you about Nigel. I can tell you about all of them. Seth wanted me to know, in case something like this happened."

"I think I'd better call the detective in charge of the case," murmured Anya, too appalled by this tidal wave of information to remember her pride or her privacy.

"Whatever you think is best," replied Teaser. "Do you have any of those little square cheese crackers?"

"Pardon me?"

"Cheese crackers. I like them."

"I don't think so. Sorry. Is there anything else that you'd like?"

"Not now. I was in the mood for cheese crackers. Too bad," sighed Teaser and seemed to sink back into a defensive torpor. Anya found herself feeling disproportionately guilty for her lack. She scribbled a note on her grocery list, affixed by a cat-shaped magnet to the refrigerator door.

She had to force herself back to the more important issue. Like an automaton, Anya moved toward the phone, then hesitated. She had made such an effort *not* to remember the name of the young detective in charge of Katani's case. It was one of those common names, she thought: Smith or Ng or . . . *Sanchez,* that was it—Nick Sanchez. She lifted the phone and placed the call to police headquarters, which routed her to Detective Sanchez' mobile unit.

"I think you'd better come over here," she said, feeling overly self-conscious, "as soon as possible." She could hear the surprise in Detective Sanchez' grunted affirmative, though he was obviously distracted by other voices in the background. She was glad that he did not have time to question her reasons.

"He'll be here soon," said Anya to Teaser, but Teaser had returned to his semblance of catatonia. Anya hoped that Teaser would rouse to speak to Detective Sanchez. She did not relish the idea of sitcom-style embarrassment. She set aside a momentary suspicion regarding the convenience of Teaser's ability to sleep and awaken spontaneously. Teaser draped one white-tipped paw adorably across his eyes.

If nothing else, she could always present the detective with evidence of data tampering—assuming such evidence existed. There was no denying the presence of the five names, Nigel among them. Surely, those names had meant something to Katani. Anya returned to her lab to check the progress of her analyses: incomplete . . . incomplete . . . incomplete. She seated herself in front of one of her oldest data scanners, a model that relied more extensively on human interaction than later analyzers, and she began to examine the raw statistics visually. She knew that the new analyzers could produce better results than even her expert eye, but the exercise made her feel more productive.

She alternated between certainty that she had spotted something wrong about the data and an equal confidence that she was simply seeing what she wanted to find. By the time the doorbell rang, she was certain only that the preliminary analysis results had uniformly failed to *preclude* data tampering. Noting that Teaser had not moved, Anya answered the door in a mood of frustration.

She did not feel any happier when she noticed one of her less charitable neighbors peering curiously at Detective Sanchez from behind expensive lace curtains. Anya did not even want to contemplate what her neighbors would conclude about the visit of a handsome young man, when visitors of any sort were almost unknown on Anya's doorsteps. She could too easily picture a tabloid-style headline about a middle-aged spinster entertaining young men in an otherwise respectable neighborhood. "Thank you for coming," said Anya coolly, ushering the detective inside as quickly as she could.

Detective Sanchez seemed amused by her obvious nervousness. "I don't think your haste in shooing me inside will allay your neighbors' suspicions."

She decided to ignore his remark. "There's someone here who needs to talk to you about Seth Katani."

"Someone?" he echoed. This was clearly not what he expected from the sensor system expert who avoided human contact whenever possible. Anya gave him extra credit for quickness of wit, however, when he answered his own question almost without pause. "The 'feline companion.'" The products of genetic research no longer seemed miraculous, but few people had the equanimity to anticipate specific results before seeing them. Perhaps Sanchez' cockiness had some justification.

"His name is Teaser. He's in here." Sanchez followed her dutifully to the kitchen. Anya suspected the detective of laughing behind her back, but she could not catch him at it. "Teaser," she coaxed. To her relief, the clear green eyes opened narrowly. She was sure that she heard a suppressed snicker from Sanchez, but she refrained from comment.

"Hello, Teaser. I'm Detective Sanchez." He sounded cool and professional, despite the amused twist of his lips.

"I know."

The equanimity never wavered, at least not visibly. "Dr. Marlow tells me that you have some information for me."

"Nigel killed Seth." The succinct reply erased the humor from Sanchez' expressive face.

"Nigel?"

"The ardent five didn't trust each other enough to have conspired together in murder. It had to be Nigel alone."

Sanchez gave Anya a pensive look, as if suspecting her of perpetrating a hoax. He asked Teaser, "Why didn't you speak to me earlier?"

"I hadn't decided to trust you."

"But you decided to trust Dr. Marlow?"

"Her cat trusted her. I trust her cat's judgment."

Sanchez stifled his laugh quickly, but he earned a glare from Teaser. "I'm sorry," offered Sanchez. "I don't have a lot of experience with cats."

"You're a dog person," growled Teaser.

"My dad lives with me, and he has a dog," admitted Sanchez.

Anya knew that she needed to intervene, before Teaser decided to terminate the interview. Painfully, Anya volunteered, "My cat, Dusty, died a few months ago." Diplomacy was a difficult and ironic exercise for Anya. "Dusty's impact still lingers in the house. Teaser and I started talking about loss. We've both experienced it."

"I'm sorry," repeated Sanchez. His sympathy sounded far more sincere than his earlier apology. He repaired his professional exterior. "We seem to have wandered off the subject. Teaser, I assume that 'Nigel' is Nigel Govorin."

"I'm glad you understand that much, at least," Teaser had not forgiven him for preferring dogs.

"Why do you think that Nigel Govorin killed Dr. Katani?"

"Like all of the five, Nigel threatened Seth repeatedly. Seth was worried that the threats might become real. They all knew about Seth's heart condition. The difference among the five is that Nigel hacks sensor systems as a hobby, so he certainly knows how to bypass the system protections. I heard Nigel say how easy it would be to disable the sensor system monitors and then trigger a heart attack. Anya will be able to tell you how it was done."

"You didn't tell me that you found evidence of system tampering," accused Sanchez with sudden intensity. A serious accusation of murder had eclipsed the grand joke of questioning a cat.

"My analysis is still incomplete," replied Anya, sounding more defensive than she intended. Feeling a perverse need to defend Teaser, she added, "There is a *possibility* of tampering."

Sanchez stared at her as if trying to probe her mind by willpower alone. "We're still trying to reach Dr. Govorin for questioning. He's not at home, and he's not at his office."

"Did anyone else hear him threaten Dr. Katani?" asked Anya. A human witness would make this situation much easier.

"The two men argued frequently, heatedly, and publicly. It appears that Dr. Katani argued with many of his colleagues."

"Seth's ideas were unconventional," said Teaser with a trace of wistfulness.

"So I've gathered," answered Sanchez dryly. "Do you know if Govorin—or anyone else—visited Katani yesterday?"

"I went out yesterday evening, so I didn't see anyone, but I smelled that someone else had been there. Nigel smokes a pipe, and he always reeks of it."

"I didn't notice any particular aroma at Katani's house."

"You wouldn't," sniffed Teaser. "Humans have no sense of smell."

"We have some canine experts available to us," said Sanchez. "I believe their sense of smell exceeds that of felines."

Anya suspected that Sanchez meant it as a taunt, but Teaser accepted the offer and conceded grudgingly, "Dogs are capable enough for that task, I suppose."

"Do you have any other pertinent information to share with me?"

"What more do you need? I've told you who killed my Seth. I've directed you to the evidence. I trust you'll take proper action."

"Yes. Well. Thank you for your help." Anya had rarely seen Detective Sanchez at a loss for words, and his discomfort amused her. He seemed to be struggling for additional questions, but the usual sort of background check hardly applied to Teaser.

"You're not too bad for a dog person," said Teaser.

"Thank you," replied Sanchez. Beneath his dark complexion, he seemed to be blushing. To Anya he added, "Call me when your analysis is complete—or if anything else surfaces."

"Of course." She led him to the door. For the first time, she almost felt sympathy for him. An ambitious young detective could hardly relish the prospect of reporting to his superiors about the interrogation of a cat. She suspected that Sanchez would choose his words with great care.

"Do you think it's possible to polygraph a cat?" he asked her.

"Polygraphs aren't all that reliable, even for humans," she replied, then realized that he was joking. She was not used to the sense of professional camaraderie that suddenly engulfed her. "We'll find evidence that a court can accept," she asserted. "Perhaps we won't need to mention Teaser's vocal talents at all."

"I didn't mean to drag you so deeply into the middle of this investigation. If it's a problem, I can make other arrangements for Teaser . . ."

"Not at all. I rather like having Teaser here."

"Okay. Thanks." Suddenly, Sanchez grinned, and Anya found herself liking him. He waved and strolled to his car. Anya waved back. In a spurt of uncharacteristic friendliness, she also waved at her curious neighbor, who hurriedly closed the lace curtains.

When she reentered the kitchen, she discovered Teaser inspecting the premises. "Do you have any salmon?" he asked her.

"No. I have some tuna."

"I suppose that will do for now."

"I'll buy some salmon."

"Thank you." Teaser rewarded her by rubbing against her legs. Anya could not help but smile.

Anya completed the grocery shopping and fed Teaser before she allowed herself to check on the status of her analysis. She was not sure that she wanted to see the results. She did not know what she would do if the data contradicted Teaser's assertions.

She stared at the results for a long time, wishing to see more than appeared. She remembered how early opponents of the ubiquitous sensor systems had complained about the cold impersonality of the data. She had always considered the impersonality to be a virtue. Humans could be corrupted so much more easily than machines.

Teaser watched her return to the kitchen with a silently demanding stare. Anya said slowly, "Evidence is not always what we want it to be."

"You will do what is just and good," answered Teaser. "You would have liked Seth. You are much like him."

"Am I?"

"You believe in good and evil. You want to do what is good."

"It's been a long time since anyone reminded me of that."

Teaser rubbed against her, and she bent to scratch his ears. He began to purr, and she seated herself on the tile floor to give him better attention. Teaser curled into her lap. For the first time since Dusty's death, she felt complete.

Her feet fell asleep, but she did not want to move and disturb Teaser. The world narrowed to the warm, purring comfort whose head rested on her knee. The sun was setting, and its orange glow treated her kitchen kindly.

The glow of sunset faded into night. Anya's still legs demanded shifting, and Teaser stretched and arose without complaint. She offered him salmon as consolation.

Fed, petted, and contented, Teaser settled down for a nap. Anya returned to her lab and seated herself at the console. She examined the results with great care and deliberation before calling Sanchez.

"Sanchez," he answered.

"This is Anya Marlow." She hesitated. "Have you located Nigel Govorin yet?"

"Yes." He laughed, and Anya considered what a pleasant sound could be created by shared humor. "We had him in custody already. He was arrested this morning for creating a disturbance at a local animal shelter. He tried to steal one of the cats—a cat that looks a great deal like Teaser, as a matter of fact."

Relieved, Anya nearly forgot why she had initiated the call. "So Teaser was right."

"About Govorin's guilt? I think so. The proof is still a little tentative, unless you have some good news for me."

She swallowed twice before answering. She chose her words

with care, "Tell Govorin that he underestimated the model 5000's
self-protection features." Teaser leaped into her lap. Automatically, she scratched his ears. Teaser purred loudly.

Sanchez' hesitation lasted even longer than Anya's. "Thanks.
I'll tell him." After another pause, he added, "With luck, we'll
coax a confession out of him. Frankly, I think he wants to confess.
He seems to have something of a martyr complex."

"A confession would be good," agreed Anya.

"All those taxpayer dollars saved."

Sanchez is smart, and he is observant, she thought, *but he also
wants to do good.* "Yes. Taxpayer dollars. Thanks, Sanchez."

"Nick."

"Thanks, Nick."

Anya entered the police department headquarters in a buoyant
mood, despite her solemn purpose. Anya pondered how much a
week could change the small universe that comprised a human
life. She could not remember when she had last felt so defiantly
happy. Perhaps she had not realized how much it mattered to
have someone waiting for her at home until Dusty was gone. She
would never repeat the mistake of being underappreciative with
Teaser.

Anya greeted the receptionist, "Good morning, Sharon. Is
Nick Sanchez in yet?"

The young woman returned the smile. "He's in, though you
shouldn't expect too much of him until he's had a few more pots
of coffee. He's expecting you."

"Thanks." Anya found him easily. She had visited his desk
often in the past few days.

"You're sure you want to do this?" he asked her.

"I'm sure."

"What does Teaser think?"

"He understands the force of curiosity."

"I suppose he would," answered Sanchez. He gave Anya a
warm smile, acknowledging their conspiracy of silence in regard
to Teaser's abilities.

Anya couldn't help herself. She had to try talking to Govorin
once for herself. She did not doubt his guilt. She had not doubted

it since Teaser told her whose hand had snuffed out Seth Katani's life. Now, of course, Nigel Govorin had confessed. However, her analytical nature longed to understand what could inspire such a drastic act as the murder of someone as nobly-intentioned as Seth Katani.

Sanchez might have tried harder to discourage her, but he recognized her stubbornness. "Just remember," Sanchez told her before she entered the interrogation cell. "He's not sane. You can't expect sane explanations from him."

"I know the diagnosis," replied Anya. "I need to see the reality."

Govorin was such a pale, ineffectual-looking creature. It was still hard to believe that such a pitiful excuse for a man could have taken another man's life. Anyone stronger than Seth Katani would have fought back with ease. The watery eyes peered at Anya blindly. "You're the analyst, aren't you?" He began to laugh like a bad parody of the lunatic that he seemed to be.

"I'm the sensor system analyst, yes."

"There was no evidence of tampering, was there? Was this Katani's way of bluffing me into a confession, or did the creature persuade you to compromise your professional integrity?"

Anya's expression froze. Perhaps this visit *was* a mistake. She asked carefully, "Did *who* persuade me? What are you talking about?"

"It doesn't matter anyway, does it? Not now. Not to me. I'm safe, you see. Safer than you'll ever be. I'll be locked away in a nice, neat little cell far from *them*. Clean, well fed, safe. My mind will remain my own."

Govorin's mind is nothing but a maze of confusion, thought Anya, acknowledging that Sanchez was probably right about the futility of this little interview. "Safe from Katani?"

Govorin tilted his head, and the lank brown hair fell across his forehead. "Safe from Katani's manipulations. Not like you. You're already trapped."

"I don't understand."

"No. You don't understand anything. You sense that you're missing something, and that's why you're here, but it's too late for you. You're already converted. You don't even understand Katani's plan yet, do you?" wailed Govorin. Alarmed by the man's sudden agitation, Anya began to back away, but Govorin flapped his hand at her in appeasement. "I'll try to explain. It won't help, but I'll try. Katani couldn't program his ideas of 'good' and 'evil' into humans directly. All of his experiments with human genetic programming failed miserably. His test results were a travesty."

"Then why did you consider him a threat?"

"You can't see it, can you? You have already become the product of his manipulations, but you can't see it."

"See what?" demanded Anya, stretching her patience out of pity for this sorry, misguided creature.

Govorin's mouth twisted into a weary smile, and he mustered some of the dignity that the past week had stolen from him. "Katani observed that as society becomes more frantic and dehumanized, people have become more obedient to their pets' demands than to any religion or other ethos."

This was not what Anya had expected, but she prompted Govorin to continue, "That's true for some people, I suppose."

"Some people. Enough people. More people when Katani's plan reaches maturity. People think of them as pets, but *they* are the ones that rule."

"They?"

Govorin looked ready to cry in frustration. "You're lost already, aren't you? Don't you understand? It's the cat. Katani created his manipulative, talking animals to 'guide' humans into 'proper' actions. Egyptians worshiped cats openly. Katani believed that such worship could be tapped again with only a little prodding."

"You killed Katani because of Teaser?" demanded Anya, torn between a matter-of-fact acceptance of the premise and a sense of revulsion for the man who presented it.

"The problem is not just Teaser," sighed Govorin, and at last he sounded defeated. "There were others. I don't know how many or how various. Katani traveled all over the world. How many colonies of feral cats exist? How many semi-domestic dogs roam city streets? How many 'wild' animals coexist with humans in the congested suburbs that have replaced true wilderness? None of us will know the effects until a few generations have been born. They're breeding, you see. Breeding and inbreeding.

Katani bred his animals to have the dominant genes. They'll be ruling us all in a few years. That was Katani's warped idea of tilting the balance toward 'good.'"

Anya was silent for a moment, pondering Govorin's words. Given the clear evidence of Teaser's abilities, what Govorin claimed was plausible. Unlike Govorin, however, Anya did not find the idea repellent. In fact, she found Katani's vision—if that's what it was—rather appealing. "So what did you hope to achieve by killing Katani?"

"Did I kill him?" asked Govorin slyly.

"You confessed."

"Yes. So I did. No choice really, once I knew that the cat outlived him. Katani warned me what would happen, and Katani was thorough in such matters. I am too much of a coward to face a lifetime of cringing from every animal and animal-worshiper on the planet." He grunted, "If that abomination of a cat hadn't escaped me, we wouldn't be here now, but I chased the wrong animal. Once I realized that Katani's cat had escaped me, I knew that I had lost. The cat is too persuasive. He was bred that way."

"You wanted to kill Teaser?"

"Of course. He is the abomination of abominations."

Anya could only shake her head at the man's insane folly. Sanchez was right. Govorin was beyond her understanding. "You asserted your humanity by murdering your colleague?"

"You *would* look at it that way. I tried to execute a last gesture of independence. I failed."

"You proved Katani's point about human evil."

Govorin only grumbled, "Fanatics cannot see clearly." Anya did not know whether he referred to himself, to Katani—or to her. "Go away," he said, squeezing his eyes shut. "I put myself here to spare myself from your kind." He reminded her oddly of Teaser, closing out the world.

"I'm going."

She shrugged at Sanchez as she left the building, admitting the accuracy of his prediction. Sanchez acknowledged her with a grin and a nod. She did not stop to talk but hastened toward her car. The supply of cheese crackers was running low, and Teaser would scold her if she served supper without crackers.

eluki bes shahar

eluki bes shahar is a multitalented author who has written novels and short stories in a variety of genres, and under several different names. But *Hellflower,* published by DAW in June of 1991—and the two sequels which followed it, *Darktraders* and *Archangel Blues*—offers a truly unique reading experience for any science fiction devotee. So I was especially delighted when eluki decided to return to this universe in "Read Only Memory."

She also provided us with the following words about this series:

"The *Hellflower* trilogy was my first science fiction novel sale, to Sheila Gilbert at DAW, and all three books are narrated in the first person by one Butterflies-Are-Free Peace Sincere in an artificial dialect drawn from many different sources (rather as if Doc Smith had written the *Lensman* saga in the style of *A Clockwork Orange,* with a little help from Damon Runyon). When I'd finished the *Hellflower* trilogy, I realized I had many other stories set in that universe that I'd like to tell, and I wondered if it would be possible to do without recourse to Butterfly's unique "voice."

'Read Only Memory' is set several years after the end of *Archangel Blues.* The hellflowers have taken Throne, and restored an uneasy peace to the Empire, ruling as advisers to the Princess-Elect. But in the Outfar and the nightworld, the same shadow-war that has been fought between Men and Libraries since the fall of the Old Federation still continues. . . ."

—SG

READ ONLY MEMORY
eluki bes shahar

PANDORA is at the edge of the Empire, so far down Paradise Street that the Core and even alMayne-held Throne are a distant rumor. The Hamati Confederacy is closer, and the Hamat ships with their strange inhuman crews keep the humans on Pandora . . . humble.

"The star-swept Rim," the Court poets call it when they speak of it at all, ignoring both the fact that it is nowhere near the edge of its galaxy and that, nevertheless, the stars in Pandora's neighborhood are dim and few. Anything might fall from those indifferent deeps. Anything at all.

Chodillon was a wanderer, a sometime courier of objects that others did not wish to carry. Her ship—called *Ghost Dance*, by the one who built it, after a ship that had been lost long before she was born—was sleek and efficient and quiet, like its mistress, and Chodillon did not trouble herself to ask whether what she carried had ever belonged to another.

There was someone she had come to meet on Pandora, in a back room of some bar in the dusty, whispering town that was the last footprint on this world of the civilization that had shaped it. A nameless someone—like all the other someones who had sought her out—who would surrender what Chodillon had come to Pandora to carry away. But she had come early to her meeting, and so she had time to spend in the dark dying streets of the port city.

She was a tall woman, and well-armed, and somehow those who met Chodillon's rainbow eyes once hoped never to see them angry. She was not afraid of anything she might meet when she left her ship to walk in Pandora's dusty twilight.

At the edges of Pandora's city the buildings are illusions. All that is left of Man's handiwork are the worthless ceramic shells of structures that have been abandoned as the city slowly dies. Beyond them is nothing but a desert with sand like mouse-colored silk; above them is the dim and empty sky. It is a place to play at savagery, and Chodillon, who did not play, had looked at the desert and was ready to return when a movement from the direction she had come caught her eye.

The red, running figure was barely ahead of the mob that followed it. In its hand it carried something that flashed intermittently in the dim light. The runner fled toward her—not as if it had seen her, but simply as if there were nowhere else to go.

As it approached, the figure resolved itself into a man. In this world of no-color even the faded scarlet he wore shone like blood. The mob that followed him was the usual sort—born or lost on Pandora and unable to leave—but the energy they exhibited was unusual among Pandorans, especially now, when the hour for serious drinking drew near.

Chodillon did not move.

The runner staggered, dodged a flung missile too late, and recovered, having lost only a stride's length to the mob. But it was more than he could afford to lose. Hands clawed at him, and he fell, and the tail of the mob came baying forward, sure of its victim. Incredibly, he rose again, and fought them back, and now they were close enough for Chodillon to hear what they were yelling.

"Librarian! *Librarian!*"

Now she knew what crime had roused Pandora's torpid natives; the crime of which the mere suggestion could raise vengeance as random as the lightning.

A memory, harvested from another's mind, came to the surface of her thoughts. The summery dust of a schoolroom. Outside its windows bright day cloaked the jeweled and artificial glory of the night sky while within the patient pedantry went on: "Librarians caused the Great War by setting monsters to rule Man. Only men may rule Man."

The borrowed memory faded, and now the runner was only a little distance away. Chodillon raised the heavy blaster that she wore, sighted carefully, and burned a neat hole in his chest.

He hung upon the force of the shot for a moment before he fell, lifeless, the living heart charred from his body. Something spilled from his outflung hand and glittered on the paving at Chodillon's feet, but it was not theft that had brought the hunters and the prey so far from the bright lights of Pandora's port.

At the sound of the shot, the mob checked itself as though it had been the victim, and hesitated at the edge of an invisible perimeter barely a stone's toss distant, its violence leached from it by the gratification of its desire. It had what it wanted. The man was dead. The desires of the men who had been its eyes and heart and limbs were of no concern to that many-throated creature.

"That for your Librarian," Chodillon said to the mob.

She stood over the body of the man she had killed until the mob devolved, muttering, into component elements, each keenly aware that it was sober in a time for drinking. As they began to turn away, Chodillon walked forward and picked up the object that had fallen from the dead man's hand.

It seemed to be a necklace of sorts. It was not made to human scale, but the endless loop of ornament suggested no other purpose. The uneven plaques of glass hung awkwardly from their linkages of gold and plastic, and it was still warm from the hand that had last held it.

At last their leader remained.

"Give me the Library," said the man who had been—as much as any other—the leader of the mob. He was Fenshee, and his slanted eyes glinted in a vulpine face that was, nonetheless, recognizably human—more human on many worlds than Chodillon's own.

"There was no Library," she told him, kind enough now, with the necklace in her hand, to explain. She was used to judging men, and saw harmlessness in him. "If you really thought there were, you would have killed me, too."

Killed her, and perhaps himself, rather than wait for the hellflowers to come. That death would have been a mercy, set against what Throne would have done, or the Starbringer, if word reached Mereyon-Peru first. Tech Police or WarDoctors, the end result was the same: death and dust. But he wasn't afraid enough for that, and so, there was no Library.

"He was my brother," the Fenshee said, as if this were an explanation.

Chodillon looped the swirling plaques of glass around her neck

and opened her collar to let them fall against her skin. The Fenshee was still watching her when she turned away and walked
along the path that the others had taken.

The Port remained untouched by the rumors of Libraries in its
exurb. Chodillon did not return to her ship. She rented a room,
though the time she would be here was vanishingly short, lest
unfinished trouble should find her and follow her to her only
means of escape from this world. And when she had sealed the
door behind her, she took out her dead man's prize to inspect it
more closely. Darktrade was not her true business in the Outfar,
only the one that gave her an answer to questions, if any might
presume to ask them.

Under the harsh chemical lights of her cubicle the object looked
more promising than it had on the city's outskirts. Eleven glass
lozenges, a finger's-width thick, a handspan long, bound and
linked by gold and the silvery incorruptible Old Fed plastic.

An artifact, certainly. But of what purpose?

The colors in the glass seemed to blossom beneath her inspection. Sun-gold, blue, and the scattered rose of a nebula's heart.
There were flecks of green like the ghost-lights that sometimes
dance on the hull of a ship; a fugitive violet like night and mourning; and as Chodillon watched, the colors seemed to swirl together, and *change.* . . .

But it was not a Library. It was old, and strange, but it was not
the Machine that had once ruled Man. It was beautiful, but it was
not worth dying for—a Librarian's death, or any other. Chodillon
warmed the plaques in her hands before sliding the necklace beneath her shirt once more. It was time that she went where she
needed to be.

The bar was like all bars. The mob's tale had preceded her, so
that the sullen murmur of the drinkers checked, and hushed, and
started again ragged and loud with exegesis when she descended
the three shallow steps to the serving floor. She walked, with purpose, to one of the private booths at the back, and waited there
for the man she was to meet.

When he came, he would have been forgettable—except for the air of tension that told her: *something is wrong.* Chodillon made herself low on the slippery covering of the padded bench and slid her hand down her leg to touch—no more than that—the smooth and heavy butt of her blaster.

The man she had come to meet spoke of her difficulties—which were not his concern—of the troubles attendant upon reaching here, and finding here, and of the troubles that might have beset a ship alone in the never-never with only a lone woman for crew. Chodillon let him speak, and watched the lazy steam from her flower tea rise to commingle with the smoke from less cleanly pastimes that gathered beneath this roof. And at last the man saw, as she had meant him to, that she was no threat, nor meant to be one: Chodillon, harmless, an employee, a servant, a courier, nothing more. And so, finally, he came to his point.

"We most sincerely regret to have troubled you—and naturally, some compensation must be made—but I am afraid we—I am certain you will understand how these things happen—that is, I regret that we have inconvenienced you, but it has developed that there will be no need for your services after all."

"I see." Chodillon drank her tea and allowed this man to see that perhaps she might not, after all, be so harmless as that.

"It is not a matter of competition. Certainly not. It is only that the . . . item . . . which you were to carry—has gone."

"Gone." Chodillon admired the sound of that—as if the item that she was to have carried had plucked itself up and begun to wander—for which, certainly, no human agency could be responsible. Gone, and with it the reason she had come here, and been placed where it had become necessary to kill a man in order to save him.

"And, naturally, your fee. . . . Some adjustment must be made. But certainly a partial—"

"Is this what you lost?" Impulsively she unsealed the neck of her ship's coverall and drew out the necklace. Colors shone in the rough plaques of molten glass, twisting, *shaping.* . . .

He straightened up and away, as though what she held between her long fingers had the power to harm.

"No," he said sharply, and Chodillon knew that he lied.

"Then there is no more to be said." She dropped the necklace and sealed her coverall back up to her throat again.

She stood, and he stood also, and set a thin wallet with a prerecorded credit on the table. "A partial payment—"

"I don't accept partial payments," Chodillon said mildly. "I
don't accept payment for work I don't do. I thought I'd made that
clear. You have my condolences on your misfortune," she added
in that same neutral tone. "Good night."

The man—whose name she still did not know, nor did she care
to ask him for it—looked as if he felt suddenly that he had done
a worse days' work here than he or his associates could imagine.
He watched her leave, and after that, what he did was no longer
any business of Chodillon's.

So she was free to go. There was no job, and the promise of work
that had led her to Pandora had brought her to no more employ-
ment than chasing ghosts. It as not the first time Chodillon had
come to a place and left it again without what she had come for.

She reached the street. The desert wind—neither chill nor hot,
but born in a place where no things grew—swirled the drug-
smoke and the false perfumes back through the open doors of the
bars and clubs of wondertown. The night was young. The street
was empty. The Pandorans were elsewhere, fortifying themselves
against the dawn that would waken them to the discovery that
they were still here. Chodillon, at least, could leave. *Ghost Dance*
still waited at the Port.

But her steps took her instead back to the room she had rented,
and not to the Port and her ship and her freedom. The necklace
shifted with each stride, drumming gently against her skin.

Riddles.

A mob had chased the scarlet man, calling him a Librarian. Yet
despite invoking the most abhorred crime in all the Calendar,
they had let her take away the necklace that they called his Library, which was not a Library—and for which a man had died.

The necklace which was what she had been summoned to Pandora to remove, yet which its owner refused to claim.

*Memory: Walls of shifting opal porcelain, hiding even the pos-
sibility of summer. Others like her, though they would soon
cease to be in the moment she was Chosen. Voices. "A thousand
years ago Librarians turned with their monster against Man to*

enslave human Man to the unliving Machine. The Libraries were
machines which thought they were alive, and so they set out to
destroy true life. But they were destroyed instead, by the grave
of the Imperial Phoenix, and now only Man decides for Man."

Now Libraries and their Librarians were gone, and there was
only Man. The hellflowers had found the Ghost Capital and destroyed all that survived of the Old Federation.

More than once Chodillon had carried the proscribed wonders
of that vanished civilization to those rich and powerful and mad
enough to buy them. Jewels and toys for the mighty; eldritch art-
works ancient beyond memory. Weapons tinier and more beautiful—and more deadly—than anything that might be bought in
the weapon-shops of today. In the reign of the last Heir, many
such things were permitted. Now that the hellflowers ruled from
the shadow of Throne, every vestige of the Old Federation was
proscribed, yet the artifacts were still traded, conveyed through
the nightworld by those brave or careless enough to do so. And
so of all the people on Pandora who might have come to possess
it, Chodillon was best qualified to say whether this jumble of glass
was a Library or not. And she said it was not.

Still, it was an object the possession of which could be fatal.
And which, though valuable, could be lied about, and feared. She
lay upon her narrow rented bed listening to the gusts of music
which blew up from the street. Footsteps were purposeful and el-
oquent outside her door, but no one came with urgent raps and
hisses to seek her out, and at last Chodillon slept, with the links
of the necklace stacked upon her narrow chest like tablets of ice.

That night she dreamed.

Chodillon saw cities that had long since been worn away to sand
in the flower of their prime, and walked the scented streets of others that were not even remembered in legend. She spoke with
wise and gentle men who were certain that their world would
outlive even the lauded works of their dearest friends, and held in
her hands and mind the cure for a thousand ills. Oxygen from
rock. Food from sterile sand. Such infinite abundance that the
very word for war could once again be lost.

Ancient knowledge, lost and banned. Knowledge that was

wealth and power to any who now possessed it, wealth enough that even the hope of harvesting it was a prize great enough to have summoned Chodillon to Pandora. She knew what the necklace was, now. Not a Library, but the books within it—memory, frozen in crystal, bereft of mind. Memory that spoke and neither thought nor listened.

Treasure enough to die for, but truly irresistible to only one creature in all the universe, and so the artifact's presence here on Pandora must be considered a trap, laid for Chodillon and her distant lover. To take it with her might be to lead the hunters to what she would die to protect. To leave it behind would be to let them know that she had recognized it for what it was and had known the danger.

And so she could do neither.

But there were other ways to spring a trap, and still take the prize.

Thus it began. One day passed, and another, and Chodillon did not leave Pandora. She gave herself to becoming what she had only seemed to be, and let that mask of self guide her actions. She was Chodillon the darktrader, Chodillon the trafficker in strange cargoes, caught in a web of dreaming crystal. That Chodillon slept with the necklace pressed against her skin like a coiled serpent, and like a serpent it whispered to her that all she could want was hers for the summoning of her directed intellect. To leave Pandora was to return to the world where men would come to her and fill her days with their errands, and so she did not. Here was the dream that the necklace brought her, and every night was a thousand years long. Here was the Chodillon who cursed her waking and half-waking hours, and for its weight in jewels bought as much as Pandora could offer of the drug called heartsease, that summons sleep and drives the world away.

But there were days in which neither drugs nor her will could force Chodillon beneath the surface of sleep to read the Library's orphaned books. On those days, cheated, she roamed the streets of the Port, searching the skyline for the echo of vaulting pastel towers that had never been there; gold and coral against a brighter sun. A sky no native of this world had ever seen—that

Chodillon herself had not seen in all her travels—printed itself upon her closed eyelids, waiting to become real beneath a sky through which no sound now echoed save the hydrogen howl of a thousand dying suns. Once, she now knew, there had been music, but the stars, in Chodillon's day, no longer spoke. She would walk until at last exhaustion crept over her and she was able once more to return . . .

Home.

On one such day, the Fenshee who had led the mob found her in the street before the bar where a man had told her there was no reason that she should stay on Pandora. Cold dawn was washing out the sky to a pale daylight yellow. The man held up his hand as if the gesture would stop her.

She was impatient, but he was not the barrier. She stopped and cataloged him with dispassion: a drifter, a luck-rider whose luck had gone. He was as hollow as the buildings at the edge of town and of as little danger.

She drew the ghosts of her old gifts about her, realizing when she called upon them how frail those gifts had grown. But for this man Chodillon once again made herself harmless; someone to be spoken to.

"I'll hire you to take me far away from here," he said when he saw she was listening.

Away. Her ship still waited for her at the Port, siphoning credit from her account and eager to be free, but habit formed her words.

"You can't afford my price, Fenshee."

"Once we had it. Amur Ramun, and Celkirk, and me."

Her eyelids flickered a little at the sound of those names— Chodillon, whose face was as silent and unreadable as space. Amur Ramun, and Celkirk, and Lelchuk. The soft dust of Pandora lipped dun-colored at her boots. She looked at the Fenshee, and her listening grew stronger because now it was real.

"Yes," the Fenshee said bitterly. "We thought we'd be rich— Ramun, my brother, and me."

Amur Ramun had called her to Pandora and then told her there was nothing for her to carry. Celkirk she had killed.

Lelchuk spoke to her now.

"There're places out on the desert, if you know where to look. Shipstrikes; old cities. We found one. A city it had been, maybe. A long time ago. There was this building. Cel didn't want to go in; it looked like it'd already been opened. There was an idol."

"Come inside," Chodillon, said, turning away.

The gaudy night of the barroom was bleached by the wakening daylight to the color of cheap building materials. There were no windows; the light came in through the open door, diffusing as it entered. Chodillon drank liquor, strong enough to burn the skin. Her companion drank cold tea.

"I don't know how to tell you what it was like. Like a woman, but no woman born. There was evil in it, with that thing draped across it like an offering. Old Federation, but it had been dug up before this. Someone put it back there when he was finished."

Chodillon glanced at him, then away. The alcohol set its chemical hands on her perceptions, but it did not bring her any species of oblivion. Each detail of the bar became so sharp that it must hold meaning. The painted idol and the desert city evoked by Lelchuk's words were more real to her than the room in which she sat.

"Cel and me, we took it away. It was the only thing worth taking. The idol was too big, and Cel didn't want anything to do with it. But we brought the necklace back here, and then we came along of Ramun. It was a strike big enough for him to want his cut. Old Federation. But we didn't trust him. Cel kept it with him; Ramun couldn't object; he wanted things kept quiet and clean. And then . . ."

But Chodillon was bored now with the story that told her what she already knew. In her dreams she had seen that city and talked to its designers.

"You've dreamed, too, haven't you?" The question jarred her, and two surprises in one day were too much. Chodillon focused on the Fenshee called Lelchuk and saw danger now.

"Dreamed. Celkirk dreamed. And now you."

"Celkirk died a Librarian," Chodillon reminded him. Celkirk's brother's face twisted with a pain that was close to pleasure.

"Not a Librarian," Lelchuk whispered with awful emphasis. "But he died. You killed him, and then you took it. I told Ramun about you. Scared him off. I wanted you to have it."

It came to her without surprise that the brother of Celkirk was mad, and, maddened, some tiny amount more dangerous than his fellows. The room wheeled in a strange plastic dance, and the liquor in Chodillon's stomach was a separate unwholesomeness. She stood to go, as if she sat with no one and the place itself had wearied her. The necklace stuck and slid against her skin, but the dreams were far away.

"Not a Librarian. They called him that, but it wasn't true. You know. You were there. But he had to die. All those weeks I watched my brother. Now I'm watching you. When it is too late for you . . . I'll be waiting."

"Wait, then," Chodillon said agreeably. Her eyes were fixed on the doorway, but the light that she saw was far brighter.

Riddles.

Where was the Library that Celkirk had died for possessing, if Chodillon did not now have it?

The daylight of Pandora, harsh and soft as smoke, slid like swords through the thousand chinks of the cubicle walls. One sword's point struck the pooled crystal, and the walls daubed and starred with colored light.

Celkirk had not died a Librarian.

But Celkirk had needed to die—so his brother had said, and Lelchuk had led the mob that hunted him.

Not as a Librarian. The distinction was precise and informative. Then . . . as the Library itself?

Chodillon picked up the necklace, and the patterns on the walls flashed to hiding. Yet this was not a Library.

But, somehow, the *cause* of a Library. . . .

The colors in the ancient glass flowed and changed—like living things, or things that thought they lived, but nothing that could answer. Nothing that could think.

Until somewhere, somehow, a human possessed it, and in time was human no longer, possessed in turn by some strange crystal resonance that tuned bone and brain to the music of a vanished civilization. Until the human and the Machine were combined. Until there was a Library that bled.

This, then, was the nature of the trap; a small trap, woven of a brother's pain and guilt, cast without knowledge of who and what she was. If she were an ordinary woman, she would have been poisoned and dazzled as Celkirk had been, enraptured by the necklace until a Library looked out of her eyes.

But she was not.

And now Chodillon knew what she must do to spring Lelchuk's trap safely, and take the prize.

She laid her own trap with care. She set the necklace carefully aside, and turned away from its dreams. She did not need them; another would dream them for her. She went into the streets to buy food, and drugs that she no longer used, and oftener than was safe for him she would turn and find Lelchuk waiting. He waited for the moment when he could raise the city to burn her, when the last of her humanity would be gone and she would be alien for all to see, a monster, a thing that could be killed and, in dying, expiate the death of the brother-not-brother, the monster whose monstrousness was proved. Chodillon waited, regaining the strength she had lost to her mask, letting him think she was losing the battle his brother had lost. Soon enough, she was ready.

The soft twilight made it possible for even Pandorans to dream. Chodillon walked now toward her ship instead of away, and away from a meeting instead of to it.

Dying things expend their last reserves of energy in the brief display that kills them. Lelchuk, waiting with his human hunters, was a dangerous man once again.

And Chodillon was once more a dangerous woman.

She did not stop at the sight of the mob, but met Lelchuk in the street before his bravos and spoke to him as if he were her equal.

"I have what I came for."

He looked at her and did not see what he sought; the hell-thing wearing flesh that he could raise the mob against. And not seeing it, he hated her instead.

"Li—" he began, and made the mistake of drawing while he said it.

There was light in the movement of sunset on her blaster, and then more light as Chodillon fired. Lelchuk fell, and she gazed down at him, her variable eyes hooded.

"But you never asked me, did you?" she asked, as if the dead man could still hear. "What it was?" Then she looked up, and her eyes were mild as they swept the mob.

"He was mad," Chodillon said to those who had followed Lelchuk. "Are you mad, as well?"

The Pandorans let her pass unhindered.

Her ship was where and as she had left it; safe. If there was danger, it must always come to Chodillon alone, and never to her ship and what it held. There were no Port Services on Pandora; she announced her intention to leave to the Port Recorder and received automatic clearance from its computers, and a few moments later the black ship was starborne.

And now *Ghost Dance* was her world again, and Pandora was the dream. She followed the dying light of silent stars until the light itself was blended into the hyper-light the stardancers call angeltown.

When all the world was cool silver, she rose from the Mercy Set and unsealed her coverall, removing the crystal necklace for the last time. She held it in her hands for a long moment, then carried it to a device in the heart of her ship.

To tamper with this device was to doom *Ghost Dance* and the world that held her, but Chodillon opened it with confidence. She laid the necklace on the scanning bed, and waited while the dreams the crystals held were transferred into *Ghost Dance*'s own mind. And then she opened the case and took it out again. The crystals were dark, now. Lifeless.

She walked down into the hold, past the vitreous cradle in which she would soon sleep, carrying the empty books. The Pandorans would forget her. Everyone forgot her, with time, and when she returned in a hundred years to see what new crop their deserts bore, the Pandorans would not know her.

She touched a switch, and her hatches opened onto hyperspace. The fields that were the true body of her ship kept that space at bay, and she stood at the edge of nothingness with the string of memory hanging from her hand.

It had not changed her. There was nothing it could do to make her other than she was.

Librarians had conspired with monsters, so the ancient teachings ran. Chodillon did not. They betrayed their own kind to the suzerainty of machines.

Chodillon did not.

She was as she had always been, as she had been made, and the things that had gone into her making had come from across space and time to be one in her. And sometimes and still she hunted more pieces for her creation, and sought to solve the riddle that had no answer.

"Farewell, kinsman," said Chodillon to memory.

And dropped the glittering chain of glass into space.

Kate Elliott

Long before I met Kate Elliott I began hearing about her from some of my other authors. They told me how talented she was, and that although she had already been published at several other houses under a different name, they were certain that she belonged at DAW. While I don't remember what convention I was at when I was finally introduced to Kate, it was certainly a fortuitous meeting.

We ended up discussing a project that was near and dear to her heart, a very ambitious series, a story so sweeping in scope that it might take eight volumes to tell it. Naturally I asked to see the first manuscript. And from the moment I started reading *Jaran*, I knew that Kate's friends and fellow authors were right. She was indeed a DAW author. And in June, 1992, the science fiction community got the chance to discover just how talented an author Kate Elliott was, when we published *Jaran*. It's hard to believe that ten years have gone by since then, a decade that saw not only the release of three more novels in the *Jaran* series, but the publication of four volumes in Kate's fantasy tour de force, *Crown of Stars*.

When Kate told me that she would like to do a *Jaran* story for our anniversary anthology, I couldn't have been more pleased. And I'm sure you'll agree when you read "Sunseeker."

—SG

SUNSEEKER
Kate Elliott

THEY gave her a berth on the *Ra* because her father was famous, not because he was rich. Wealth was no guarantor of
admittance to the ranks of the fabled Sunseekers; their sponsors
didn't need the money. But there was always a price to be paid,
due at unforeseen intervals decided upon by the caprice of the
self-appointed leaders of their intrepid little band of a dozen or so
sunseeking souls.

Right now, they had started in on Eleanor, an elegant girl of
Bantu ancestry whose great-grands had made their fortune gun-
running along the Horn of Africa (so it was rumored) and par-
layed that wealth into a multisystem exotics import/export
business.

"Sweetkins, I'm not sure I can stand to look at much more of
that vegetable fiber. Cotton!"

"*Algodon!*" Akvir mimicked Zenobia's horrified tone. "I
thought we'd agreed to wear only animal products."

"If we don't hold to standards," continued Zenobia, "it'll be
soybric next. Or, Goddess forbid, nylon."

Eleanor met this sally with her usual dignified silence. She did
not even smooth a hand over her gold and brown robe and trousers, as any of the others would have, self-conscious under scrutiny. Rose suspected her of having designs both on Akvir—self-
styled priest of the Sunseekers—and on the coveted position of
priestess. Of course it went without saying that the priestess and
the priest had their own intimate rites, so after all, if one was
priestess, one got Akvir—at least for as long as his sway over the
group held.

"That a tattoo?" Yah-noo plopped down beside Rose. The seat
cushion exhaled sharply under the pressure of his rump. He was
new on board, and already bored.

"What?" Self-consciously, remembering—how could she ever, ever forget?—she touched the blemish on her cheek.

"Brillianté, mon," he said, although the slang sounded forced. He was too clean-cut to look comfortable in the leather trousers and vest he sported. He looked made up, a rich-kid doll sold in the marketplace for poor kids to play pretend with. "Makes a nice statement, cutting up the facial lines with a big blotch like that. It's not even an image tattoo, like a *tigre* or something, just a—" He paused, searching for words.

She already knew the words.

Blot. Eyesore. Flaw. Birth defect.

She was irrevocably marred. Disfigured. Stained.

These words proclaimed by that famous voice which most every soul on this planet and in most of the other human systems would recognize. Golden-tongued and golden-haired. Chrysostom. Sun-struck. El Sol. There were many epithets for him, almost all of them flattering.

"Ya se ve!" Yah-noo clapped himself on the head with an open hand, a theatrical display of sudden insight. "You're the actor's kid, no? You look like him—"

"If never so handsome," said Akvir, who had bored of his pursuit of Eleanor.

"No one is as handsome as my father," snapped Rose, for that was both her pride and her shame.

"I thought there were operations, lasers, that kind of thing." Yah-noo stared at her with intense curiosity.

To see a blemished person was rare. To see one anywhere outside the ranks of the great lost, the poor who are always with us in their shacks and hovels and rags even in this day of medical clinics in every piss-poor village and education for every forlorn or unwanted child, was unheard of.

"Yeah, there are," she said, standing to walk over to Eleanor's seat. She stared out the tinted window of the ship. The Surbrent-Xia solar array that powered the engines made the stubby wings shimmer as light played across them. Here, above the cloud cover that shrouded the western Caribbean, the sun blazed in all its glory. Ever bright. Up here, following the sunside of the Earth, it was always day.

"You going to see the big head?" asked Eleanor in her lean,

cultured voice. "The archaeological site is called after a saint. San Lorenzo."

"Yah. Sounds very slummy, a little Meshko village and all."

"Quaint," said Eleanor. "The right word is *quaint*. Saint Lorenzo was one of the seven deacons of the Church of Rome, this would be back, oh, way back during the actual Roman Empire when the old Christian—" She said it like a girl's name, Kristie-Anne. "—Church was just getting a toehold in the world. Like all of them, he was made a martyr, but in this case he was roasted over a gridiron."

"Over a football field?"

"No." Eleanor laughed but not in a mocking way. She never used her knowledge to mock people. "No, it's like a thing with bars you grill fish on. But the thing is, that he was burned, roasted, so you see perhaps he was in a prior incarnation related to some form of sun worship. The fire is a metaphor for the sun."

"Oh. I guess it could be."

Eleanor shrugged. Rose could never understand why someone like *her* ran with the Sunseekers. Only except they were, so everyone said, the jettest black of all social sets, the crème de la crème, the egg in the basket, the two unobtainable birds in the bush. That was why her father never came running after her after she ran away to them.

Wasn't it?

She had seen a clip about two months ago as the night-bound told time, for up here in the constant glare of the sun there was only one long long day. He had referred to her in passing, with that charmingly deprecatory smile.

"Ah, yes, my daughter Rosie, she's on a bit of a vacation with that Sunseeker crowd. That's true, most of them are older, finished with their A-levels or gymnasium or high school. But. Well. She's a high-spirited girl. Fifteen-year-olds always know just what they want, don't they? She wanted the Sunseekers." The rest went without saying: The very most exclusive social set, don't you know. Of *course* my child would be admitted into their august ranks.

He had only to quirk his lips and shift his elbow on the settee to reveal these confidences without any additional words passing his lips. His gift consisted, as so many, many, many people had assured her as she grew up and old enough to understand what their praise meant, of the ability to suggest much with very little.

But her elder siblings—long since estranged from the family—called it something else: The ability to blind.

The engines thrummed. Rose set a hand against the pane that separated them from the air and felt the shudder and shift that meant they were descending. In the lounge, Yah-noo flipped through the music files. The mournful cadences of an old Lennon-McCartney aria, "I'll Follow the Sun," filled the cabin. Eleanor uncoiled herself from her seat and walked back, not without a few jerks to keep her balance as the pitch of the *Ra* steepened, to the dressing and shower room, shared indiscriminately by the almost two dozen inhabitants of the ship. She did dress, stubbornly, in fabrics woven from vegetable forebears. Rose admired her intransigence but more than that the drape of the cloth itself, something leather cured in the sun or *spinsil* extruded and spun and woven in the airless vaults of space stations could not duplicate. Style, her father always said, sets apart those who are watchable from those fated only to watch. It puzzled and irritated him that his disfigured daughter had no sense of style, but she had only ever seen him actually lose his temper once in her entire life: that day in the hospital when her mother had backed her up after she stubbornly refused, once again and for all, to undergo the simple laser operation that would at least make her middling pretty.

He wanted to be surrounded by handsome things.

The ship turned as it always did before landing, going down rump first, as some of the Sunseekers liked to say. Her hand on the pane warmed as the rising sun's rays melted into her palm. They cut down through the clouds and the sun vanished. She shivered. Gray boiled up past her, receded into the sky as they came down below the clouds and could see the ground at last.

Rugged mountains rose close beside the shore of the sea, receding behind them. The lowlands were cut by ribbons of muddy water beside which sprawled the dirty brown and white scars of human habitation, a village. The old ruined Zona Arqueológica lay on higher ground, the centerpiece of a significant plateau.

It had been a week since they'd last landed. The texture of the earth, the lush green carpet of vegetation, amazed her anew. She blinked on her computer implant to get an identification of the river. A map of the region came up on the screen, not a real screen, of course, but the simulation of a screen that according to her tekhnē class was necessary for the human eye to register information in this medium. Sim-screens for primates, they would shout when they were younger, but it was only funny when you were young enough to find the parallel between simulation and simian amusing, like being six years old and getting your first pun. But like a bad pun or a particularly obnoxious advert balloon, the phrase had stuck with her.

The lacy mat of tributaries and rivers floated in front of her eyes on the sim-screen, spidery lines that thickened and took on weight and texture, finally moving and melding into the landscape until they seemed to become one. Disoriented, she blinked the screen off and staggered back to find a couch for the final deceleration. The couch snaked a pressure net across her, calibrated to her weight, and she tilted her head back, closed her eyes, and waited for landing. Aria segued into gospel hymn, "Where the Sun Will Never Go Down." Yah-noo hummed along in a tuneless tenor until Zenobia told him to shut up. Finally, they came to rest; the altosphere shades lightened away and everything went quiet. She felt giddy. When she stood up, her feet hummed with the memory of engines and she swayed as she walked, following the others to the 'lock and out onto the plank that led down to the variegated earth of the night-bound, the lost souls—all fourteen billion of them—who must suffer the sad cyclic subjugation to the endless and cruel celestial reminder of our human mortality, night following day following night. Or so Akvir put it. He had not seen night for nine months.

The village itself was so small, so pathetic, and so obviously isolated that at first Rose thought they had inadvertently stumbled across the set for an actie, the kind of thing her father would star in: *Knight in the Jungle,* in which the liberation priest, Father Ignatius Knight, gives his life to bring literacy and the World-WideWeb to a village under the censorious thumb of a Machine Age dictator, or *Dublo Seven, Heritage Hunter,* in which the legendary M. Seven seeks out and recovers artifacts hidden away by greedy capitalists so that he can turn them over to the Human Heritage Foundation whose purpose is to preserve human culture for the all, not the few.

The air was so hot and humid that even her eyelids began to sweat. It stank of mud and cow dung. A pair of skeletally thin reddish dogs slunk along the tree line. Curious villagers emerged from houses and from the outlying fields and trees to converge on the landing spot, a cleared strip beside a broad concrete plaza marked by a flagpole and a school building. There were sure a lot of villagers, more than she had expected. A dilapidated museum stood by the river at one end of the road. The great Olmec head Akvir wanted to see rested in the central courtyard, glimpsed from here as a rounded bulk behind rusting wrought-iron gates. Right now Akvir was head-hunting, as he called it. In the last month they had stopped at Easter Island, Mount Rushmore, Angkor Thom, and the Altai Mountains.

A bird called from the trees. Eleanor stepped out in front of Akvir and raised a hand, shading her eyes against the early morning sunlight. But she was looking west, not east into the rising sun.

Rose felt more than heard the cough of an antiquated pulse gun. Dogs yipped frantically, helping and bolting, but the sound that bit into their hearing was too high for humans to make out.

"Effing hells!" swore Yah-noo behind her. "My transmitter's gone dead."

Who used pulse guns these days? They were part of the lore of her dad's acties, like in *Evil Empire* where he played a heroic West Berliner.

Eleanor shouted a warning as a dozen of the villagers circled in on them. Were the natives carrying rifles? For a second, Rose stared stupidly, thoughts scattering. What was going on?

Akvir started yelling. "Back on board! Back on board! Everyone back on board!"

Voices raised in alarm as the Sunseekers blundered toward the ramp, but their escape was cut short by the unexpected barking stutter of a scatter gun. A swarm of chitters lit on her skin. She dropped to her knees, swatting at her face and bare arms.

The crash of a riot cannon—she knew the sound because her father had just premiered in a serial actie about the Eleven Cities labor riots of fifty years ago—boomed in her ears. A blast of smoke and heat passed right over her. As people yelled and screamed, she lost track of everything except the stink of skunk gas settling onto her shoulders and the prickles of irritant darts in the crooks of her elbows and the whorls of her ears.

Someone grabbed her wrist and yanked her up into the cloud. Her eyes teared madly, melding with sweat; the smoke blinded her. But the grip on her arm was authoritative. She stumbled along behind, gulping air and trying to bite the stinging sour nasty taste of skunk gas from her lips. The rough dead earth of the lander clearing transformed between one step and the next into the soggy mat of jungle; an instant later they were out of the smoke and running along a sheltered path through the trees.

Eleanor held her by the wrist and showed no sign of letting go. She didn't even look back, just tugged Rose along. Rose blinked back tears and ran, hiccuping, half terrified and half ready to laugh because the whole thing was so absurd, something out of one of her father's actics.

Instead of elegant gold-and-brown dappled robe and trousers, the other woman now wore a plain but serviceable ice-green utility suit, the kind of clothes every and any person wore when they did their yearly garbage stint. Woven of soybric, it was the kind of thing fashionable Sunseekers wouldn't be caught dead in.

What had happened to the others?

She tried to speak but could only cough out a few hacking syllables that meant nothing. The skunk gas burned in her lungs, and the awful sodden heat kept trying to melt her into a puddle on the dirt path, but still Eleanor dragged her on at a steady lope while Rose gasped for air—such as it was, so thick you could practically spoon it into a cup—and fought to stop the stitch in her side from growing into a red dagger of pain. Her ears itched wildly.

They hit a steep section, and got about halfway up the slope before her legs started to cramp.

"Got . . . to . . . stop . . ." she gasped finally and went limp, dropping to her knees on the path. Her weight dragged Eleanor to a halt.

"Shit," swore the other woman. "Damn, you *have* been spending too long with the do-nothing rich kids. I thought you weren't like them. Don't you ever get any exercise?"

"Sorry." It was all she could manage with her lungs burning from exertion and skunk gas and her elbows and knees itching as

badly as her ears from the irritant darts, but she knew better than
to scratch at them because that only spread the allergens, and
meanwhile she had to bite her lip hard and dig her nails into her
palms to stop herself from scratching. The skunk gas and the pain
made her eyes tear, and suddenly she wanted nothing more than
for her mother to be there to make it all better.

That made her cry more.

"Aw, fuck," said Eleanor. "I should have left you back with the
others. Now *come on.*"

She jerked Rose upright. Rose had enough wind back that it
was easier to go than to stay and deal with the itching and the
burning lungs and the pain again, the memory of watching her
mother die of a treatable medical condition which she was too
stubborn to get treatment for because it went against the traditional ways she adhered to. She touched her blemished cheek, the
habitual gesture that annoyed her father so much because it drew
attention to the blemish and thereby reminded them both of
those last angry weeks of her mother's dying.

Sometimes stubbornness was the only thing that kept you
going.

Eleanor settled into a trot. Rose gritted her teeth and managed
to shuffle-jog along behind her, up the ghastly steep path until it
finally, mercifully, leveled off onto the plateau. The jungle
smelled rank with life but it was hard enough to keep going without trying to look around her to see. Wiry little dappled pigs,
sleek as missiles, scattered away into the underbrush.

By the time they came out into the clearing—the Zona Arqueológica—Rose's shift was plastered to her body with sweat.
Eleanor, of course, looked cool, her utility suit—wired to adjust
for temperature and other external conditions—uncreased and
without any of the dark splotches that discolored Rose's shift. At
the tuft of hairline, on the back of the woman's neck, Rose detected a thin sheen of sweat, but Eleanor brushed it away with a
swipe of her long fingers.

They stepped out from under the cover of jungle onto a broad,
grassy clearing, and at once an automated nesh-recorded welcome
program materialized and began its preprogrammed run.

"Buenas dias!" it sang as outrageously bedecked Olmec natives danced while recorded prehispanic musicians played clay

flutes, ocarinas, and turtle shells, and shook rain sticks, beating out rhythms on clay water pots. Fat, flat-faced babies sat forward, leaning onto their knuckles like so many leering prize fighters trying to stare down their opponents, and jaguars growled and writhed and morphed into human form in the interstices of the background projections. "Bienvenidos al Parque Arqueológico Olmeca! Aquí es San Lorenzo, la casa de las cabezas colosales y el lugar de la cultura Madre de las civilizaciones Mexicanas! Que idioma prefieren? Español. Nahuatl. Inglés. Japonés. Mandarín. Cantonés. Swahili." The chirpy voice ran down a cornucopia of translation possibilities.

The place looked like a ruin, two reasonably modern whitewashed buildings stuck on the edge of the clearing with doors hanging ajar and windows shattered, three thatched palapas fallen into disrepair. A herd of cattle grazed among the mounds, which were themselves nothing much to look at, nothing like what she expected of the ancient and magnificent home of the mother culture of the Mexican civilizations.

But the technology worked just fine.

Eleanor gave her a tug. They followed a path across the ruins toward the larger of the two whitewashed buildings. Every few meters 3-D nesh projections flashed on and began their fixed lecture-and-display: the old ruins came to life, if nesh could be called life or perhaps more correctly only the simulation of life.

Poles stuck in the ground were the storehouses for the treasure—the knowledge, the reconstruction of the past. Between them, quartered, angled, huge image displays whirled into being: here, a high plaza topped with a palace built of clay with a stone stele set upright in front; there, one of the great stone heads watching out across a reconstructed plaza with the quiet benevolence of a ruler whose authority rests on his unquestioned divinity; suddenly and all of a piece, the entire huge clearing flowering into being to reveal the huge complex, plaza, steps, temples, and courtyards paved with green stone, as it might have looked three thousand years before during the fluorescence of this earliest of the great Mesoamerican civilizations.

Eleanor yanked her inside the building. Rose stumbled over the concrete threshold and found herself in a dilapidated museum, long since gone to seed with the collapse of the tourist trade in nesh reconstructions of ancient sites. All that investment, in vain once the novelty had worn off and people stopped coming. Most tourists took their vacations upstairs, these days. Mere human history couldn't compete with the wonders of the solar system and the adventure promised by the great net, and affordable prices, that opened out into human and Chapelli space.

The museum had been abandoned, maybe even looted. Empty cases sat on granite pedestals; tarantulas crowded along the ceiling; a snake slithered away through a hole in the floor.

"Shit," swore Eleanor again. "Did it have bands? Did you notice?"

"Did what have bands?"

"The snake. Goddess above, you ever taken any eco courses? There are poisonous snakes here. *Real* poisonous snakes." Dropping Rose's wrist, she stuck two fingers in her mouth and blew a piercing whistle. Rose clapped hands over her ears, but Eleanor did not repeat the whistle. Her ears still itched and with her fingers there in such proximity, Rose could not help but scratch them but it only made them sting more. She yanked her hands away and clutched the damp hem of her shift, curling the loose spinsil fabric around her fingers, gripping hard.

A trap in the floor opened, sliding aside, and a ladder unfolded itself upward out of the hole. Moments later a head emerged which resolved itself into a woman dressed in an expensive business suit, solar gold knee-length tunic over plaid trousers; the tunic boasted four narrow capelets along its shoulders. She also wore tricolor hair, shoulder length, all of it in thin braids of alternating red, black, and gold—the team colors of the most recent Solar Cup champions. Rose knew her fashionable styles, since in her father's set fashion was everything, and to wear a style six months out of date was to invite amused pity and lose all one's invitations to the best and most sunny parties. This woman was fashionable.

Two men, dressed in utility suits, followed the woman up from the depths. Both carried tool cases.

"Eleanor," said the businesswoman. They touched palms, flesh to flesh, by which Rose saw—though it already seemed likely given her entrance—that this was the real woman and not her nesh analogue. "All has gone as planned?"

"I'm afraid not. The *Ra* is disabled, but we seem to have run into some competition." She gestured toward the two men. "Go quickly. We'll need to transfer the array to our hover before they can call in reinforcements." They hurried out the door.

"And this one?" asked the businesswoman. "Is this another of your ugly puppies?"

Rose wanted desperately to ask, *What are you going to do with me?* but the phrase stuck in her throat because it sounded so horribly like a line in one of her dad's acties. Maybe she sweated more, because of nerves, but who could tell in this heat?

"When the operation is over, we can let her go." Eleanor spoke almost apologetically. "I just wanted her out of the way in case there are complications. And she's a good rabbit to keep in the hat, in case there *are* complications. She's the daughter of the actor."

"Oh!" the businesswoman crooked one eyebrow in surprised admiration. "Oh! Well, I mean, there was so much publicity about it. She's not nearly as pretty. And that—" She stopped herself, although her hand brushed her own cheek in the place the mark stood on Rose's face. She lowered the hand self-consciously. "Vasil Veselov is your *father?*"

Rose didn't know what to say. She nodded.

The businesswoman waved invitingly toward the trap. "Put her in the basement."

Eleanor took hold of Rose's wrist again and pulled her toward the extruded ladder.

"Go on."

A touch of cool air drifted up from the hole, quickly subsumed in the heat. Rose glanced toward the businesswoman, now making calculations on a slate; she had apparently forgotten about her partner and Rose, much less the great actor.

"Go on." Eleanor snapped her fingers. "Go."

Rose climbed down. Beneath lay a basement consisting of a corridor and six storerooms. Water beads like the sweat of the earth trickled down the concrete walls. Eleanor shoved her along to the end of the row where a door stood ajar. Waving Rose in, she began to push the door shut.

"What are you going to do with me?" Rose demanded, finally succumbing to the cliché.

"Nothing with you. You're a nice kid, Rose, unlike those obnoxious spoiled brats who have nothing better to do with their time than waste it circling the Earth as if that somehow makes them more *especial* than the rest of humanity. Like they're paying for it! What a sick advertising stunt! I didn't want you to get hurt."

"What did you mean about keeping a rabbit in the hat?"

"Planning for contingencies. It doesn't matter. Anyway, I really admire your father. *Sheh.*" She gave a breathy whistle. "I had a holo of him in my room when I was younger. You'll be free to go in an hour or so."

"What's going on?" This request, Rose knew, would be followed by the Bad Guy telling all, because Bad Guys always told all. They could never resist the urge to reveal their diabolical plans.

Eleanor slammed the door shut—not because of anger but because the door wasn't hung true and was besides swollen from moisture and heat and that was the only way to get it to shut. Left alone in the room, Rose tested the door at once, but it didn't budge. She stuck her ear to the keyhole but heard nothing, not even footsteps. At least the itching had begun to subside. Finally, she turned and surveyed her prison.

It was an ugly room with concrete rebar walls, a molding ceiling sheltering two timid tarantulas in one corner, and a floor made up of peeling rectangles of some mottled beige substance. The tarantulas made her leery, but she didn't fear them; she knew quite a bit about their behavior after living on the set of *Curse of the Tarantula*. The rest of the room disquieted her more. The floor wasn't level, and the tiles hadn't been well laid, leaving gaps limned with a powdery white dust. Two old cots made up of splintery wood supports with sun-faded, coarse burlap stretched between stood side by side.

Ugly puppies.

She winced, remembering the businesswoman's casual words. In one corner someone had set up a shrine on an old plastic table, one of whose legs had been repaired with duct tape. Two weedy-looking bouquets of tiny yellow-and-white flowers resting crookedly in tin pots sat one on either side of a plastic baby doll with brown hair, brown eyes, and painted red lips. The doll was dressed in a lacy robe, frayed at the hem and dirty along the right sleeve, as though it had been dragged through dirt. A framed picture of the same doll, or one just like it, lay at its feet, showing the doll sitting on a similar surface but almost smothered by offerings of flowers and faded photographs of real children, some smiling, some obviously ill, one apparently dead. Someone had written at the bottom of the picture, in black marker in crude block letters, *El Niño Doctor*. Doctor Baby Jesus.

Rose knew something about the Kristie-Anne religion. Jesus was the god-person-man they prayed to, although she had never quite understood how you could be both a god and a mortal human being, more or less, at the same time. "The gods are everywhere," her mother used to say. "They are what surrounds us, Mother Sun and Father Wind, Aunt Cloud and Uncle Moon, Sister Tent and Brother Sky, Daughter Earth and Son River, Cousin Grass and Cousin Rain. Gods are not people."

Yet some people thought they could be. Rose sniffled. She wanted to cry, but because crying made her eyes red and puffy, unattractive, she had learned to choke down tears. But she was still frightened and alone.

She tongued the emergency transponder implanted in her jaw, but it was dead, killed by the crude blast of the pulse gun. Everything else she had left on the *Ra*.

"I want my daddy," she whispered.

A flash of light winked in the staring eyes of the baby doll. It began to talk in a creaky, squeaky, distorted voice, stretched, tenuous, and broken with skips and jerks.

"Si habla Español diga, 'si.' Nahuatocatzitziné, amehuantzitzin in anquimocaquilia, in anquimomatilia inin tlatolli, ximotlatolti-can. If you speak English, say 'yes.' "

Startled, she took a step back just as she said, scarcely meaning to, "yes."

"Please wait while I connect you. A medical technician will be with you in a moment. Catholic Medical Services provides sponsored medical advice free of charge to you, at any hour of the day or night. Help will be given whatever your circumstance. Please wait. When the doctor comes on line, state your location and your—"

A fluttering whir scattered the words. After a pause, a barely audible squeal cut at her hearing. The doll spoke again, channeling a real person's voice.

"Please state your location and need. I am M. de Roepstorff, a medical technician. I am here to help you. Are you there?"

She was so stunned she forgot how to speak.

Patiently, the voice repeated itself. "Are you there?"

"I am. I am! I'm a prisoner—"

"Stay calm. Please state your location and we'll send a team out—"

Static broke the connection.

There was silence, stillness; one of the tarantulas shifted, moving a few centimeters before halting, suspended, to crowd beside its fellow.

"Are you still there?" Rose whispered. "Are you there? Yes. Yes, I speak English."

"Please wait while I connect you. The medical technician will be with you in a moment. Catholic Medical Services . . ."

The doll's recorded voice squealed to a bruising pitch, ratcheted like gears stripping, and failed.

A grinding, grating noise startled her just as the kiss of cooler air brushed her face. The table rocked, tilted to the right, teetered, and crashed sideways to the ground, spilling pots, flowers, picture, and doll onto the concrete floor. Nothing broke, except the floor. One of the rectangular tiles wobbled, juddered, and jumped straight up. Rose leaped back, stumbled against a cot, and sat down hard as a man dressed in dark coveralls with a crude burlap mask concealing most of his face emerged from a hole in the floor, climbing as if going up a steep staircase. All she could see was his mouth, undistinguished, and his eyes, the iris dark and the white bloodshot with fatigue or, maybe, some barbaric drug intoxication.

"Quien eres?" he demanded. He carried a scatter gun. With it trained on her, he called down into the hole. "Esperabas un prisionero? Es una muchacha."

Be cool and collected. That's what her father always did in the acties.

"Eleanor put me here," she said aloud as calmly as she could, hoping Eleanor was on their side. She was so scared her knees actually knocked together. "I don't know what's going on. Please don't hurt me. I'm only fifteen. I can't identify you because you're wearing that mask, so I'm no threat to you."

The man climbed out of the hole, crossed to the door, and tested it.

"It's locked," she said helpfully. "I'm a prisoner. I'm not a threat to you."

He cursed, trying the handle a second time. A nasty looking knife was thrust between belt and coveralls, blade gleaming.

A second figure—head and shoulders—popped up in the hole. This one wore an old com-cap, with a brim, the kind of thing people wore before implants and sim-screens rendered such bulky equipment unnecessary. She was also holding an even more ancient rifle, the kind of thing you only saw in museums next to bazookas, halberds, and atlatls under the label *Primitive But Deadly.*

Had the pulse gun killed her implant? She didn't think so; it was technologically far more sophisticated than plain jane location/communication transponders and phones. She blinked to trigger it, caught a sigh of relief as the screen wavered on. Sotto voce, she whispered, "Spanish translator, text only. Cue to voice."

The one with the rifle, dark eyes unwinking as she studied her captive, lifted her chin dismissively.

"Termina ya." A woman's voice, hard and impatient. Words scrolled across the sim-screen as Rose pretended she couldn't understand them. "No podemos dejarla aqui . . .*cannot leave her here. She will go and tell of our hiding place.*"

Adrenaline made her babble, that and her father's maxim: keep them talking. How successfully he'd used that ploy in *Evil Empire*! "Is that an AK-47? I've seen one in nesh but never in the flesh before. Is that a thirty round magazine?"

"No puedo hacerlo . . . *I cannot do it,*" said the first terrorist. *She is too young. She is too innocent.*"

"No [untranslatable] *is innocent.*"

The itch on her ears returned until she thought it would burn the lobes right off, but she clutched the side of the cot hard and the pain of the wood digging into her hands helped keep her mind off the itching and the fear.

Don't give in to it. Once you gave in, the itching—or the fear—would consume you.

"Look at the mark on her face. It is real. It is not a tattoo of a rich child. No one with this type of mark on the face can be our enemy." He took three steps, close enough to hit her or stab her, but his touch—fingers brushing the blemish—was oddly gentle.

"I shoot the street dogs," said his companion. *"Things like this will be the death of you."*

"Then how will the outcome change? I do not like to kill. And I question what this locked door signifies. It should have been left open."

"We've been outmaneuvered. There's another party involved who wants the same thing we want."

He nodded decisively, the kind of man used to being obeyed. She knew that look, that stance, that moment when the choice was made. She had seen her father play this role a hundred times: the charismatic leader, powerful, strong, ruthless but never quite cruel. *"I thought we could use this as a base for storage, but it is compromised. Let us go. They will not take our prize so easily."*

"The girl will make a good hostage."

"You believe so? I do not believe that anyone preoccupies themselves over her." He turned to Rose and, for the first time, spoke in the Standard she knew. "Does any person care for you? Will any person pay a ransom for your rescue?"

Was it fear that made her tremble convulsively? She snorfled and hiccuped as she tried to choke down her sobs. Never let them see you cry. Never let them see how unattractive you are. How scared you are.

Beautiful people were less likely to die.

He gestured with the scatter gun, the universal sign: *get up.* She got up, shakily, followed them down a short wooden ladder into a low tunnel weeping dirt, hewn out of rock and shored up by a brace work of boards nailed together and old rebar tied tightly with wire. Down here they paused, she crouching behind the fearsome woman while above she heard the man moving things before he climbed back down into the tunnel and levered the tile into place. The woman spoke a command to make a hazy beam of light shine from her cap.

Rose blinked down through menus, seeking information on San Lorenzo. It ran across the lower portion of the sim-screen as the man poked her in the back with his gun.

Miocene sedimentary formations . . . salt domes . . the entire San Lorenzo site is a great mound in itself, largely artificial in construction.

"Andale," he said.

The screen read: *Move now. Imperative!*

They crawled until her hands were scraped raw and her knees were scuffed, reddened, and bleeding in spots. Neither of them spoke again, and she dared not speak until spoken to. Not soon enough, gray light filtered in. They pushed out through undergrowth into a ravine where a pair of young people waited, their faces concealed by bandannas tied across nose and mouth, their bodies rendered shapeless by loose tunics worn over baggy trousers. They each carried a rifle, the wood stock pitted and the curved magazine scarred but otherwise a weapon well oiled and clean. The man spoke to them so softly that Rose could not hear him, and as she and her captors hiked away, she glanced back to see the other pair disappear into the tunnel.

They followed the rugged ground of the ravine through dry grass and scrub and past stands of trees on the ridgeline above, Rose stumbling but never getting a hand up from her captors. The sun stood at zenith, so hot and dry beating down on them that she began to think she was going to faint, but they finally stopped under the shade of a ceiba and she was allowed to drink from a jug of water stashed there. The ceramic had kept the water lukewarm, although it stank of chlorine. Probably she would get some awful stomach parasite, and the runs, like the diamond smuggler had in *Desert Storm*, but she knew she had to drink or she would expire of heat exhaustion just like the secondary villain (the stupid, greedy one) had in *Knight in the Jungle*, despite the efforts of Monseigneur Knight to save him from his own shortsighted planning.

The man had brought Doctor Baby Jesus with him, bound against his body in a sling fashioned from several bandannas so that his hands remained free to hold the scatter gun. The bland doll face stared out at her, eyes unblinking, voice silent. As her captors drank, they talked, and Rose followed the conversation on the screen that was, of course, invisible to them.

"We have to fight them," he said wearily.

"I knew others would be after the same thing," she said. "Bandits. Profiteers. Technology pirates."

He chuckled. "And we are not, Esperanza? We are better?"

"Of course we are better. We want justice."

"So it may be, but profit makes justice sweeter. It has been a long fight."

Distant pops, like champagne uncorked in a faraway room heard down a long hall, made the birds fall silent.

"Trouble," Esperanza said.

Rose had hoped they might forget her if she hung back, pretending not to be there, but although Esperanza bolted out at a jog, the man gestured with his gun for Rose to fall in behind his comrade while he took up the rear. The pops sounded intermittently, and as they wound their way back through jungle, she tried to get her bearings but could make no sense of their position. After a while, they hunkered down where the jungle broke away into the grassy clearing she had seen before, the *Zona*, but now a running battle unfolded across it, figures running or crouching, sprinting and rolling. A single small-craft open cargo hover veered from side to side as the person remote-controlling it—was that him in the technician's coveralls?—tried to avoid getting shot. All the cattle were gone, scared away by the firefight, but there were prisoners, a stumbling herd of them looking remarkably like Akvir and the other Sunseekers, shrieking and wailing as they were forced at gunpoint to jog across the Zona. The nesh-reenactments had spun into life; from this angle and distance she caught flashes, a jaguar skin draped over a man's shoulders as a cape, a sneering baby, a gaggle of priests dressed in loincloths and feather headdresses.

The firefight streamed across the meadow so like one of her dad's acties that it was uncanny. Unreal. Shots spat out from the circling jungle, from behind low mounds. A man in technician's coveralls—not the one controlling the cargo hover—toppled, tumbled, and lay twitching on the ground. She couldn't tell who was shooting at whom, only that Yah-noo was limping and Zenobia's shift was torn, revealing her pale, voluptuous body, and Akvir was doubled over as though he had been kicked in the stomach, by force or by fear. She didn't see Eleanor or the woman in business clothes. A riot cannon boomed. Sparks flashed fitfully in the air, showering down over treetops. It boomed again, closer, and she flattened herself on the ground, shielding her face and ears. Esperanza shouted right behind her, but without her eyes open she couldn't see the sim-screen. A roaring blast of heat pulsed across her back as, in the distance, people screamed.

Now the cavalry would ride in.

Wouldn't they?

The screams cut off, leaving a silence that was worse than pain. She could not even hear any birds. The jungle was hushed. A footfall scuffed the ground beside her just before a cold barrel poked her in the back.

"Get up," said the man.

She staggered as she got to her feet. No hand steadied her, so she stumbled along in front of him as he strode out into the Zona. Esperanza had vanished.

The cargo hover was tilted sideways, nose up, stern rammed into the ground so hard that it had carved a gash in the dirt. Bugs swarmed in the upturned soil. The technician still clutched the remote, but he was quite still. A youth wearing trousers, sneakers, and no shirt stood splay-legged over the dead man. The boy's mouth and nose were concealed by a bandanna, black hair mostly caught under a knit cap pushed crookedly up on his head. He had the skinny frame of a teenager who hasn't eaten enough, each rib showing, but his stance was cocky, even arrogant. He stared at Rose as she approached. Her sim-screen had gone down, and his gaze on her was so like the pinprick of a laser sight, targeting its next victim, that she was afraid to blink. He said something to the man, who replied, but she couldn't understand them.

The Sunseekers lay flat on their stomachs on the ground a short ways away, hands behind their heads. Three more bandanna-wearing men waited with their ancient rifles and one shotgun held ready as six newcomers jogged toward them across the clearing, but the newcomers paid no attention to the prisoners. Like the bugs in moist dirt, they swarmed the hover.

"March," said the commander, gesturing with his scatter gun.

No one complained as their captors prodded the Sunseekers upright and started them walking, but not back the way they had come.

Akvir sidled up beside Rose. "Where'd you go? What's going on?"

The boy slammed him upside the head with the butt of the

rifle. Akvir screamed, stumbled, and Rose grabbed his arm before he could fall.

"Keep going," she whispered harshly. "They killed some of those people."

The youth stepped up, ready to hit her as well, but when she turned to stare at him defiantly, he seemed for the first time really to see the blemish that stained her face. She actually saw him take it in, the widening of the eyes, and heard him murmur a curse, or blessing. She had seen so many people react to her face that she could read their expressions instantly now.

He stepped back, let her help up Akvir, and moved on.

"No talking," said the commander. "No talking."

No one talked. Soon enough they passed into such shelter as the jungle afforded, but shade gave little respite. They walked on and on, mostly downhill or into, out of, and along the little ravines, sweating, crying silently, holding hands, those who dared, staggering as the heat drained them dry. After forever, they were shepherded brusquely into a straggle of small houses with sawed plank walls and thatched roofs strung alongside a tributary river brown with silt, banks densely grown with vegetation. An ancient paved road that was losing the battle to cracks and weeds linked the buildings. Someone still drove on it: at least four frogs caught while crossing the road had been flattened by tires and their carcasses desiccated by the blast of the sun into cartoon shapes. Half covered by vines, an antique, rusting alcoline pickup truck listed awkwardly, two tires missing. Three of the houses had sprouted incongruous satellite dishes on their roofs, curved shadows looming over scratching chickens and the ever present dogs. A few little children stared at them from open doorways, but otherwise the hamlet seemed empty.

A single, squat building constructed of cement rebar anchored the line of habitation. It had a single door, through which they were herded to find themselves in a dimly lit and radically old-fashioned Kristie-Anne church.

A row of warped folding chairs faced the altar and a large cross on which hung a statue of a twisted and agonized man, crowned with a twisting halo of plastic thorns. None of the chairs sat true with all four legs equally on the floor, but she couldn't tell if the chairs were warped or if the concrete floor was uneven. It was certainly cracked with age, stained with moisture, but swept scrupulously clean. A bent, elderly woman wearing a black dress and black shawl stood by the cross, dusting the statue's feet, which were, gruesomely, pierced by nails and weeping painted blood.

The old woman hobbled over to them, calling out a hosanna of praise when the commander deposited Doctor Baby Jesus into her arms. As the Sunseekers sank down onto the chairs, dejected, frightened, and exhausted, the caretaker cheerfully placed the baby doll up on the altar and fussed over it, straightening its lacy skirts, positioning the plump arms, dusting each sausagelike finger.

"What kind of place *is* this?" whispered Yah-noo. "I didn't know anyone lived like this anymore. Why don't they go to the cities and get a job?"

"Maybe it's not that easy," muttered Rose, but no one was listening to her.

The commander was pacing out the perimeter of the church, but at Rose's words he circled back to stand before them. "You don't talk. You don't fight. We don't kill you."

Zenobia jumped up from the chair she had commandeered. "Do you know who we are?" Her coiffure had come undone, the careful sculpture of bleached hair all in disarray over her shoulders, strands swinging in front of her pale eyes. "We're important people! They'll be looking for us! You can't just—! You can't just—!"

He hit her across the face, and she shrieked, as much in outrage and fear as in pain, remembered her torn clothing, and sank to the ground moaning and wailing.

"I know who you are. I know what you are. The great lost, who have nothing to want because you have everything. So you circle the world, most brave of you, I think, while the corporation gets free publicity for their new technology. Very expensive, such technology. Research and development takes years, and years longer to earn back the work put into it. Why would I be here if I didn't know who you are and what you have with you?"

"What do you want from us?" asked Akvir bravely, dark chin quivering, although he glanced anxiously at the young toughs waiting by the door. For all that he was their leader, he was scarcely older than these teens. Behind, the old woman grabbed

Doctor Baby Jesus and vanished with the doll into the shadows to the right of the altar.

The commander smiled. "The solar array, of course. That's what that other group wanted as well, but I expect they were only criminals."

"You'll never get away with this!" cried Zenobia as she clutched her ragged shift against her.

Rose winced.

The commander lifted his chin, indicating Rose. He had seen. "You don't think so either, muchacha?"

"No," she whispered, embarrassed. Afraid. But he hadn't killed her because she was blemished. Maybe that meant she had, in his eyes, a kind of immunity. "I mean, yes. You probably won't get away with it. I don't know how you can escape surveillance and a corporate investigation. Even if the Constabulary can't find you, Surbrent-Xia's agents will hunt you down in the end, I guess." She finished passionately. "It's just that I hate that line!"

"That *line?*" He shrugged, not understanding her idiom.

"That line. That phrase. 'You'll never get away with this.' It's such a cliché."

"Oh! Oh! Oh! You—you—you—*defect!*" Zenobia raked at her with those lovely, long tricolor fingernails, but Rose twisted away, catching only the tip of one finger along her shoulder before Akvir grabbed Zenobia by the shoulders and dragged her back, but Zenobia was at least his height and certainly as heavy. Chairs tipped over; the Sunseekers screamed and scattered as the toughs took the opening to charge in and beat indiscriminately. Yah-noo ran for the door but was pulled down before he got there. What envy or frustration fueled the anger of their captors? Poverty? Abandonment? Political grievance? She didn't know, but sliding up against one wall she saw her chance: an open path to the altar.

She sprinted, saw a curtained opening, and tumbled through as shouts rang out behind her, but the ground fell out beneath her feet and she tripped down three weathered, cracked wooden steps and fell hard on her knees in the center of a tiny room whose only light came from a flickering fluorescent fixture so old that it looked positively prehistoric, a relic from the Stone Age.

A cot, a bench, a small table with a single burner gas stove.

A discolored chest with a painted lid depicting faded flowers and butterflies, once bright. The startled caretaker, who was standing at the table tinkering with Doctor Baby Jesus, turned around, holding a screwdriver in one hand. A chipped porcelain sink was shoved up against the wall opposite the curtain, flanked by a shelf—a wood plank set across concrete blocks—laden with bright red-and-blue plastic dishes: a stack of plates, bowls, and three cups. There was no other door. It was a blind alley.

The light alternately buzzed and whined as it flickered. It might snap off at any moment, leaving them in darkness as, behind, the sound of screams, sobs, and broken pleas carried in past the woven curtain.

What if the light went out? Rose bit a hand, stifling a scream. She hadn't been in darkness for months.

This was how the night-bound lived, shrouded in twilight. Or at least that's what Akvir said. That's what they were escaping.

Saying nothing, the old woman closed up the back of Doctor Baby Jesus and dropped the screwdriver into a pocket in her faded skirt. She examined Rose as might a clinician, scrutinizing her faults and blemishes. Rose stared back as tears welled in her eyes and spilled because of the pain in her knees, but she didn't cry out. She kept biting her hand. Maybe, possibly, they hadn't noticed her run in here. Maybe.

In this drawn-out pause, the shadowy depths of the tiny chamber came slowly clear, walls revealed, holding a few treasures: a photo of Doctor Baby Jesus stuck to one wall next to a larger photo showing a small girl lying in a sick bed clutching the doll itself, or a different doll that looked exactly the same. A cross with a man nailed to it, a far smaller version of the one in the church, was affixed to the wall above the cot. Half the wall between shelf and corner was taken up by a huge, gaudy low-tech publicity poster. Its 3-D and sense-sound properties were obviously long since defunct, but the depth-enhanced color images still dazzled, even in such a dim room.

Especially in such a dim room.

Her father's face stared at her, bearing the famous ironic, iconic half smile from the role that had made him famous across ten star systems: the ill-fated romantic lead in *Empire of Grass*. He had ripped a hole in the heart of the universe—handsome, command-ing, sensitive, strong, driven, passionate. Doomed but never de-feated. Glorious. Blazing.

"Daddy," she whimpered, staring up at him. He would save her, if he knew. She blinked hard. The sim-screen wavered and, after a snowy pause, snapped into clear focus.

The curtain swept aside and the commander clattered down the three wooden steps. One creaked at his weight. He slid the barrel up her spine and allowed it to rest against her right shoulder blade.

"Ya lo veo!" cried the old woman, looking from Rose to the poster and back to Rose. She began to talk rapidly, gesticulating. When the commander said nothing, did not even move his gun from against Rose's back, she clucked like a hen shooing feckless chicks out of the way and scurried over to take Rose's hands in hers.

"Su padre? Si, menina?" *Your father? Yes?*

Then she turned on him again with a flood of scolding. The rapid-fire lecture continued as the commander slowly backed up the stairs like a man retreating from a rabid dog.

"*What kind of fool are you, Marcos, not to recognize this girl as the child of El Sol? Have you no kind of intelligence in your grand organization, that it comes to an imprisoned old woman like me—*" She spoke so quickly that the translation program had trouble keeping up. ". . . que ve las telenovelas y los canales de chismes . . . *who watches the soap operas and the channels of gossip [alternate option] entertainment channels to tell you that you should have known that more people would be on that ship than the children of businessmen?*"

The old woman finished with a dignified glare at her compa-triot. "*This girl will not be harmed.*"

"*That one?*" He indicated the actor, then Rose. "*This child? With the marked face? How is it possible? She carries this blot.*" He touched his own cheek, as if in echo of the stain on hers. "*The children of the rich do not have these things.*"

"*God's will is not ours to question,*" she answered.

He shrugged the strap of his scatter gun to settle it more com-fortably on his shoulders. "*Look at her. Even to look past the mark, she is not so handsome as El Sol.*"

"No one is as handsome as my father," retorted Rose fiercely, although it was difficult to focus on the poster since the image blended with the words scrolling across the bottom of her sim-screen.

They both looked at her.

"Ah." Señora Maria waved a hand in front of Rose's face. Her seamed and spotted palm cut back and forth through the sim-screen. Swallowing bile, reeling from the disrupted image, Rose blinked off the screen.

"Imbécil! Que estabas pensando? Esta niña, de semejante familia! Por supuesto que lleva implantada la pantalla de simulacion. Ahora ya ha entendido cada palabra que has dicho, tu y los ostros brutos!"

Without effort, she turned her anger off, as with a switch, and presented a kindly face to Rose, speaking Standard. "Por favor, no use the seem . . . What it is you call this thing?"

"Sim-screen."

"Si. Gracias."

The señora looked up at the commander and let loose such a stream of invective that he shrank back against the curtain momentarily, but only to gather strength before he began arguing with her. Their voices filled the chamber; Rose covered her ears with her hands. Mercifully, the itching had subsided completely. She dared not blink the screen back on, so she cowered between them as they argued fiercely over her head. One of the young toughs stuck his head in but retreated as the señora turned her scolding on him.

Through it all, her father watched, half amused, half ready to take action, but frozen. It was only his image, and his image could not help her.

In the church, the screaming had subsided and now Rose heard whimpering and weeping as orders were given.

"Go! Go!"

"But where—!" The slap of a gun against flesh was followed by a bruised yelp, a gasp, a sob, a curse—four different voices.

"Go!"

Shuffling, sobs, a crack of laughter from one of the guards; these noises receded until they were lost to her ears. The Sunseekers had been taken away.

"Are you going to kill them?" she whispered.

They broke off their argument, the commander frowning at her, the señora sighing.

"We no kill—we do not kill." The señora spoke deliberately, careful over her choice of words. "They bring us better money if the parents buy them from us."

"But kidnappers always get caught in the end."

The commander laughed. "Fatalism is the only rational world-view," he agreed.

"In the stories, it may be so, that these ones are always caught," continued the señora. "We take a lesson, a borrowing, from our own history, but this thing called ransom we use for a different purpose than the ones who stole the children in the old days."

"What purpose?" Rose demanded. She had gone beyond worrying about clichés. "I see the poverty you live in. Are you revolting against the inequality of League economics? Is this a protest? Will you use the array to help poor people?"

The commander's sarcastic laugh humiliated her, but the señora smiled in such a gentle, world-weary way that Rose suddenly felt lower than a worm.

"Hija, I am the inventor of one of the protocols used in this solar array that powers the ship you children voyage on. These protocols were stolen from me and my company by operatives of Surbrent-Xia. In much this same way as we steal it back, but perhaps not with such drama." She gestured toward the poster and the stunningly handsome blond man who stared out at them, promising dreams, justice, excitement, violence, and fulfillment. "No beautiful hero comes to save me. The law listens not to my protests. Surbrent-Xia falsifies their trail. They lay certain traps for me, and so the corporation and patent laws convict me, and I am dropped into the prison. There I sit many years while they profit from what I helped create. All these years I plot my revenge, just like in this story, *The Count of Monte Cristo*, no? Was not your father starring in this role a few years ago? So now we have the array in our hands. I leave—have left—markers in my work. Like this stain upon your cheek, those markers identify what is mine. With these markers, no one can mistake it otherwise. With this proof—"

"And the children to draw attention to us," added Marcos.

"—we will get attention to this matter."

"But you'll be prosecuted for kidnapping!"

"Perhaps. If we get publicity, if a light is shined onto these criminal actions made by Surbrent-Xia ten years ago, then we are protected by exposing them. Do you see? Surbrent-Xia 'got away with it'—they say this in the telenovelas and the acties, do they not?—they got away with it last time because it was hushed."

"They kept it quiet," said Marcos. "No one knew what they had done."

"But why did you have everyone beat up? What did Akvir and Zenobia and Yah-noo and the others have to do with anything or what anyone did ten years ago?"

The old woman nodded, taking the question without defensiveness. She seemed a logical soul, not an emotional revolutionary at all. "We have not harmed them, only bruised them. It is in answer to—it is in—"

"—retaliation—" said Marcos.

"That is right. Excuse my speech. I have been many years in isolation on these false charges. The world, and my enemies, did not play nice with my relatives in the old days. We are not the only ones who play hardball. An eye for an eye."

"But they're innocent!"

"They are all the children of shareholders. That is why they come to ride on the beautiful ship, to be made much of. You do not know this?"

"I just thought—" She faltered, knowing how unbelievably stupid anything she said now would sound.

I didn't know.

Hadn't her father talked and talked and talked about the Sunseekers, how very sunny and fashionable they were? Hadn't she run away to get his attention, so he would be surprised she had gotten into some group so very jet, so very now, even with her disfigurement?

"They are lucky you came to them," continued the señora. "Of what interest are the children of shareholders, except to themselves and their parents and their rivals? But you are the child of El Sol. When you came aboard, everyone is watching."

"Good publicity is good advertising," added Marcos sardonically. "This is what we all want."

Right now, she just wanted her daddy.

"It still doesn't seem right." They hadn't bitten her yet. They hadn't bruised her, not more than incidentally. "To hurt them. They aren't bad, just—" *Just pointless.* "And what about Eleanor? I mean, the other ones."

"The other ones?" asked Señora Maria.

"The competition," said Marcos. "We don't have a positive ID on them yet, but I presume they are working for Horn Enterprises. Horn wants the array, too."

"Horn filed a wrongful use claim against Surbrent-Xia for theft of their cell transduction protocol."

"Which came to nothing. But they had a grievance, too, and plenty of markets out-system who won't ask too many questions about whether they have patent rights. This is so much useless speculation, now. We got the array. They did not."

How could they analyze the day's nasty work so dispassionately, as though it were the script of an actie in development?

"You killed two men! Eleanor was really nice to me!" Another second and she would be blubbering, but she held it in, sniffing hard, choking down the lump in her throat.

"We killed no one," said Marcos angrily. "Just two hurt, in the Zona, but they are only stunned."

"There was blood."

"There is always blood. This other, this Eleanor—no se. There was a hover that flew off once they saw they had lost."

"What about me?"

Señora Maria gestured.

Rose eased up to her feet, wincing with pain as her knees bent. "Ow."

"We should let this *pauvre* go home. She can use the call-up in Anselmo's house."

"The Constabulary will come," said Rose.

"Not soon," said Marcos. "Your flight plan registers a stop at San Lorenzo to visit the museum. They do not know otherwise. They will not be expecting you to leave for some hours. We have time."

"Andale," said Señora Maria.

Marcos shrugged, sighed, and motioned with his gun for Rose to follow him. Perhaps he wasn't the commander after all, or perhaps he was just behaving as men ought—as her mother used to say: respectful toward the etsana, the grandmother, of his tribe.

The house belonging to Anselmo sat riverside, one door facing the road and a second overlooking the bank. A small receiver dish tilted precariously on the roof, fastened to the topmost beam. They had to walk up two steps made of stacked concrete blocks to get onto the elevated wood floor inside. Like the entire village, the little one-room hut was untenanted, except for a burlap cot without bedding, a table, and a bright yellow molded plastic bench pitted with pinprick holes. An old-fashioned all-in-one sat closed up on the table. Looking out through the other door, Rose watched as a loose branch drifted past, snagging on a tree, while Marcos powered up the box and tilted up its view screen.

"Where did you take the others?" she asked. The driftwood tugged loose from its trap and spun away down the river.

He mulled over the controls, not looking up at her, although a hand remained cupped over the scatter gun's readouts. "They will be safe." He spoke to the box in his own language. Lights winked on the console. "Here. You may enter a number. Use the keypad."

She had a priority imavision code, of course, that identified her immediately to her father's secretary since her father never ever took incoming calls personally.

A whir. A beep.

"One moment, Miss Rose. Putting you through."

The secretary did not turn on his own imavision. Although the screen remained blank, Marcos stepped away and turned sideways to give her privacy and to keep an eye out the door. But even so he started when that famous golden voice spoke across the net in a tone richly affectionate and so precisely intimate, using the pet name for her that no other dared speak.

"Mouse?"

"D–d–daddy."

"I didn't expect you to call." He hadn't turned on the imavision. Maybe he was getting dressed or entertaining visitors. Maybe today he just didn't want to see the blemish on her face. "It's been so long since we talked. I've missed your voice so much, here at home. All your little quiet noises in the background. It seems so empty here without you puttering around.

How are you? Are you having fun up there in the eternal sunshine?"

"N–n–no, Daddy. I'm just—" She faltered, glancing toward
Marcos, who still stared out the door at the sluggish river.

"You should be in—" A pause. A voice murmured in the background. "San Lorenzo Tenochtitlan. Some kind of a museum
there, I see. Olmec civilization. Pride of the collection is a large
stone head! What will you children think of next!"

"D–daddy." She wiped away a tear with the back of her hand.

"Are you crying, little mouse?"

"Daddy, I'm in trouble."

A pause.

A silence.

"Rosie, you *have* a contraceptive implant—"

"No, Daddy. No. I'm in *trouble*. Please come get me."

"Come get you?"

The screen flashed, a nova of light that spread, swirled with
color, coalesced, and formed into an image of his face. The most
famous face in the universe, so people said.

He looked put out.

"Come get you?" he repeated, as though she just told him he
had turned purple. "I have three interviews today to support the
opening of *Judge Not*. The ratings aren't as strong as they need
to be. After this a meeting with the Fodera-Euler Consortium to
sign the contract for the Alpha Trek 3-D."

He glanced back over his shoulder, speaking to a person not
within the imavision's range. "What's the time frame?"

"Ten days," said his secretary, off screen.

"And the Consortium wants to begin recording—?"

"Fourteen days."

He turned his brilliant smile on her. He had the most glorious
blue eyes, warming as he stared intently at her through the imavision, as though he were really right by her side, comforting her
infant sobs on a stormy night. He didn't even flinch, seeing her
blemished face in such a close-up. "Listen, Rosie. You hang in
there for ten more days and I'll come get you. We'll make the
most of it, father and daughter reunited, that kind of thing. Let
Joseph know when your first landfall comes once the ten days are
up. I'll be there to meet you. No need to mention you called now
and arranged it in advance. Pretend you're surprised to see me."

"But, Daddy—"

"Are you in danger of being killed/"

Marcos had not shifted position, nor his grip on the scatter gun. "No. I don't think so, but—"

"Rosie. Mouse." His tone softened, lowered. "You know I will never let you down. But as long as your life or health isn't in danger, it can't be done for ten days. I made an arrangement with Surbrent-Xia that you would stick with the Sunseekers for three months. You weren't to know, but I trust you can see how important it is that I fulfill my contracts. You know how tight money is these days—"

"You 'made an arrangement' with Surbrent-Xia! I thought I ran away!"

"You did. You did. Fortunately, you picked the right place to run away to."

"But I want to come home, Daddy. Now. I need to. You don't understand—"

"It can't be done. If I break the contract, we get nothing. Just ten more days."

She hated that tone. "But, Daddy, the—the—" What was Marcos going to do? Shoot her with a nonlethal weapon while her father could see and hear? "I *am* in danger. An awful thing happened. We landed at San Lorenzo and then we were attacked by corporate raiders who wanted the solar array. And then we were caught in the cross fire when another group who had their technology stolen stole it back. I thought they were bandits, first, but it's all some kind of corporate espionage that goes back for years and years, like they're always stealing things, bits or patents from each other and stealing them back and selling them out-system—"

"Joseph! Joseph!" He turned away from her, showing his profile. Always aware of the camera's eye, he never lifted his chin because it distorted the angle of his nose. "Did you get that down? We need more information! This could be a gold mine if we get it into development first. I see it as a serial. A family saga about ruthless technology pirates!" His beautiful face loomed again, grinning at her. "What a good girl, Rosie! I knew I could count on you! Is there someone there I can talk to, who would be interested in a contract? Who has inside information?"

"A contract!" She recoiled from the table, sure she hadn't heard him right.

Marcos was already pushing past her. "What kind of contract? Is there money? Is there publicity? We'll need leverage. . . ." He leaned down in front of the view screen, introduced himself, and began bargaining.

"Daddy!"

"Love you, Rosie! Now, M. Marcos. First we'll need an all-hours contact number—"

"Daddy!"

Marcos ignored her, and her father had forgotten her. Amazingly, Marcos didn't even object, or seem to notice, as Rose left the hut and trudged down the dirt street back to the church, her only companions half a dozen chickens and two mangy dogs who circled warily, darting in to sniff at her heels until she kicked one. Yelping, they raced away.

The church remained empty, abandoned, six chairs overturned and one drying bloodstain, nothing serious.

Only bruised.

Señora Maria had departed from the little back chamber, but she had left Doctor Baby Jesus sitting upright on the shelf, plump arms spread in a welcoming gesture as Rose halted in front of him.

"I speak English," said Rose, her voice choked. Tears spilled, but she fought against them. "I need help."

A whirr. A squeal.

"Please wait while I connect you."

A different voice, this time. A woman. "Please state your location and need. I am M. Maldonado, medical technician. I am here to help you."

A pause.

"Are you there?" The voice deepened with concern.

She found her voice, lost beneath the streaming tears. "I just need your help. Can you connect me to my brother? His name is Anton Mikhailov. He's an advocate at—uh—" She traced down through her sim-screen. "This is his priority number."

"Are you in danger?"

"No. No. Kind of. Nobody's going to kill me. But I'm lost—I'm sorry. I know this isn't what you're here for. I know this isn't important. You must get thousands of life-and-death calls every hour."

The woman made a sound, like a swallowed chuckle. "This system was defunct twenty years ago, but we keep a few personnel on-line because of people who have no other access. It's all right. It's all right. What's your name?"

"Rose."

"Please stay on the line, Rose. I'll get a channel to your brother. If you want to talk, just say something. I'm here listening."

She had nothing to say. She fidgeted anxiously, swallowing compulsively, each time hoping to consume the lump that constricted her throat.

Dull, officious Anton, who worked as an advocate for disabled or troubled children or some other equally worthy and boring vocation. He had left the family fourteen years before, when she was only a baby. He had been raised by someone else, by traitors, thieves, defectives. He had rarely visited his parents and then only on supervised visitations, because the ones who had stolen him had poisoned his mind. Yet he always wrote to her four times a year on the quarter, chatty notes detailing the obscenely tedious details of his life. Each note repeated at the end the same tired cliché: Call me any time, Rosie. Any time.

She didn't really know him. He could as well have been a stranger. Why should he do anything for her if her father didn't even care enough to come when she asked? Wasn't this the only time she had ever asked anything of her father?

All these years she had never asked.

"Patching you through," said helpful M. Maldonado. "M. Mikhailov, I'll remain on stepped-back link if you need me."

"Thank you. Rose?" Anton had a reedy tenor, rising querulously. She didn't know him well enough to know if he was surprised, annoyed, or pleased.

"Anton, it's Rose."

I'm Rose, she thought, half astonished, hearing her own voice speak her own name: a small, isolated voice, lost in the dim room, in the old church, in the forgotten village, in the green jungle, on the common earth beneath clouds that covered the all-seeing eye of the sun. It was amazing anyone could hear her at all. She sobbed, choking on it, so it came out sounding halfway between a cough and a sneeze. She could barely squeeze out words.

"Please, come get me."

"Of course, Rose. Right away. Where are you?"

"I'm all alone."

The buzz of the fluorescent lamp accompanied her other companion: the solitude, not even a mouse or a roach. The world had emptied out around her. For an instant, she thought the connection had failed until Doctor Baby Jesus whirred and Anton spoke again, an odd tone in his suddenly very even, level all-on-the-same-note voice.

"Did you call Dad?"

She sobbed. She could get no word past her throat, no comprehensible sound, only this wrenching, gasping, ugly sound.

The baby doctor sighed with Anton's voice. "He'll never love you, Rosie. Never. He can't love anyone but himself."

Fury made her articulate. "He *does* love me. He says so."

"Love is just another commodity to him. Maybe you get something, but there's always a price to be paid. I'm so sorry. Evdi and Yana and I love you—"

"He does love me."

"I'll come get you. Stay where you are, Rosie. I'll come. Will you stay? Will you be there? Don't go running off anywhere? You're not going to change your mind and follow those damn Sunseekers?"

"But he doesn't want me." She began to sob again, torn in two. She heard Anton reply, faintly, only maybe his voice wasn't any fainter and it was just her own weeping that drowned him.

"I'm coming, Rosie. Just tell me where you are."

She couldn't speak. She could only cry as their voices filtered through the creaky stutter of the baby doll's speaker.

"M. Mikhailov, I'm attempting to triangulate, but the intercessor has been partially disabled so I can't get a lock on your sister's position."

"Do you have a position on the Sunseekers?"

"The Sunseekers?"

"That ship with the new solar array technology. That grotesque advertising ploy—'you need never set foot in darkness again,' something like that. I can't remember their idiot slogan.

Maybe in your line of work you don't have to keep up on the gossip rags—"

"Oh!" said the voice of M. Maldonado. "Isn't that the ship that the actor Vasil Veselov's daughter ran away to—

"That one," interrupted Anton. "Do you have any way to get a fix on it? Here, let me see, they've got a public relations site that tracks— Yes. Here it is. I've got it touched down in a municipio called San Lorenzo Tenochtitlan."

"I'll get all transport information for that region, but if you're in—ah—London, it will take you at least eighteen hours with the most efficient connections, including ground transport or hovercab."

"I have access to a private 'car. Rose. Rose?"

"I'm here." Amazing how tiny and mouselike her voice sounded, barely audible, the merest squeak.

"Rose, now listen. It says here there's a little museum in San Lorenzo Tenochtitlan. Do you know where that is? Can you get there and wait there?"

Of course, maybe it wasn't more than open welts sown with salt, discovering the truth: her father had wanted her with the Sunseekers all along. Had manipulated her to get her there. Surbrent-Xia had paid him to get his daughter onto the ship in the most publicly scandalous way possible. He had set it all up, used her to get the money and the publicity.

"Daddy doesn't want me," she said, voice all liquid as the horrible truth flooded over her, soaking her to the bones.

"I know, Rosie. But I love you. I'm coming. Just tell me where you are. Tell me if you can get to the museum."

"Okay," she said, to say something, because she had forgotten what words meant. A chasm gaped; she knelt on the edge, scrabbling not to tumble into the awful yawning void. What would she do now, if no one wanted her? Why would anyone want her anyway? Blemished, disfigured, stained. Ugly.

"Okay," he repeated, sounding a little annoyed, but maybe he was just worried.

Maybe he was actually worried about her. The notion shocked her into paying attention.

"Okay," he repeated. "I will be there in no less than six hours. You must wait by the museum. Don't go off with the Sunseekers, Rosie. I will meet you there, no matter what. Okay?"

"Okay."

Doctor Baby Jesus fell silent, having done his work. The fluorescent light flickered. A roach scuttled across the shelf, and froze, sensing her shadow. Her tears stained the concrete floor, speckles of moisture evaporating around her feet. She just stood there, stunned, unable to think or act. She couldn't even remember what she had agreed to. The light hummed. The roach vanished under the safety of the baby doll's lacy robe.

"Hola! Hey!"

The young voice, male and bossy, spoke perfectly indigenous Standard.

"Hey! You in here, girl?" The young shirtless tough who had hit Akvir upside the head and cursed at him in Spanish pushed aside the curtain and ducked in. "There you are. I'm taking you back to the village."

"The village?" she echoed stupidly, staring at the rifle he held. Staring at him. He had pulled the bandanna down and the ski mask off, revealing a pleasant face marred only by the half-cocked smirk on his lips. He sounded just like one of her friends from home, except for the Western Hemisphere flatness of his accent.

"The village," he agreed, rolling his eyes. He did not threaten her with the gun. "Those Sunseeker people, they're all there, waiting to get picked up. You're supposed to go with them. We got to go, pronto. You know. Fast."

"That's by the museum, isn't it?"

"Si," he said, eyes squinted as he examined her. "You okay?"

She wiped her cheeks. Maybe the dim light hid the messy cry.

"We got to go," he repeated, shifting his feet, dancing up two steps and pressing the curtain aside with his rifle as he glanced out into the church. "It'll be dark soon. They got some 'cars coming in to get all of you out of here before sunset. You got to get out before sunset, right?"

"The museum," she said. "Okay. Is it far?"

"Four or five kilometers. Not far. But we got to go now."

She nodded like a marionette, moving to the strings pulled by someone else. She got her feet to move, one before the next, and soon enough as they came out of the church she found her legs worked pretty well, just moving along like a normal person's legs would, nothing to it. A group of little boys played soccer along the dirt track of the hamlet, shouting and laughing as the ball rolled toward the river but was captured just in time. They turned off into the ragged forest growth before they passed the house where she had talked to her father; she saw no sign of Marcos except the flash of the ceramic satellite dish wired to the roof.

The boy walked in front of her. He had a good stride, confident and even jaunty, and he glanced back at intervals to make sure she hadn't fallen behind or to warn her about an overhanging branch and, once, a snake that some earlier passerby had crushed with repeated blows. It had bright bands on what she could see of its body, a colorful, beautiful creature. Dead now. She sweated, but he had a canteen that he shared with her—not water but a sticky sweet orange drink. A rain shower passed over them, dense but brief, to leave a cooling haze in its wake. All the time they walked, he kept the big plateau to their left, although they did not ascend its slopes but rather cut around them along a maze of dirt trails.

"Who was that woman?" she asked after a while.

"My great-aunt? She's some kind of crazy inventor, a genius, but she got into trouble with corporate politics. She was in prison for a long time, so I never saw her but I heard all about her. She was a real, uh, *cabrona*. Now maybe she is more nice."

Rose could think of nothing to say to this; in a way, she was surprised at herself for asking anything at all. Just keeping track of her feet striking the dirt path one after the other and all over again amazed her, the steady rhythm, the cushioning earth, the leaf litter.

The forest opened into a milpa, a field of well grown maize interspersed with manioc. A pair of teal ducks flew past. When they cut around the edge of the field they saw a stork feeding at an oxbow of muddy water, the remains of the summer's flooding. Lowlands extended beyond, some of it marshy, birds flocking in the waters.

Another kilometer or so through a mixture of milpas and forest brought them to San Lorenzo Tenochtitlan on the shore of El Rio Chiquito. Here the houses had a more modern look; half a dozen had solar ceramic roofs. There was a fenced-off basketball court and a school with a satellite dish and a plaza with a flagpole where the Sunseekers sat in a distraught huddle on the broad

concrete expanse, staring anxiously westward while a few onlookers, both adults and children, watched them watching the horizon.

It was late afternoon. The sun sank quickly toward the trees.

The *Ra* sat forlornly on the grassy field behind the school,
within sight of the old museum. Its stubby wings looked abraded,
pockmarked, where the solar array had been stripped off.

"Rose!" Akvir jumped to his feet and rushed to her, his hand
a warm fit on her elbow. "We thought we'd lost you!" He was
flushed and sweating and a bruise purpled on his cheek, but he
looked otherwise intact. He dragged her toward the others, who
swarmed like bees around her, enveloping her with cries of excitement and expansive greetings. "You're the hero, Rose! They
said you begged for our lives to your dad and he asked them to
let us go. And they did! All because of your father! They're all
fans of your father! They've all seen his shows. Can you get over
it?"

She stood among them, drowned by them. All she could do was
stare past their chattering faces at the boy who had led her here.
He had fallen back to stand with a pair of village women, his arms
crossed across his bare chest and the rifle, let loose, slung low by
his butt. One of the women handed him a shirt; she seemed to be
scolding him.

"Look!" screamed Zenobia, still clutching her torn clothing.
"There they are! There they are!"

A pair of sleek, glossy hovercars banked around a curve in the
river and leveled off by the boat dock, but after a moment during
which, surely, the navigators had seen the leaping, waving, shouting Sunseekers, they nosed up the road to settle, humming, on
the grassy field beside the disabled *Ra*. Akvir and the others
jumped up and down, clapping and cheering, as the ramp of the
closer 'car opened and three utility suited workers, each carrying
a tool kit, walked down to the ground. They ignored the crying,
laughing young people and went straight for the *Ra*. After about
five breaths, the second 'car's ramp lowered and a woman dressed
in a bright silver utility suit descended to the base where she
raised both hands and beckoned for them to board.

The sun's rim touched the trees. Golden light lanced across the
village, touching the half hidden bulk of the great stone head beyond the museum gates.

With a collective shout rather like the ragged cry of a wounded, trapped beast who sees escape at long last, the Sunseekers bolted for the 'car. Halfway there, Akvir paused, turned, and stared back at Rose, who had not moved.

"Aren't you coming?" he shouted. "Hurry! Hurry! They're fixing the *Ra*, but meanwhile we're going on. You don't want the sun to set on you, do you?"

"I'm not coming."

Everyone scrambled on board, one or two shoving in their haste to get away. Akvir glanced back at them, shifting from foot to foot, as Zenobia paused on the ramp to wave frantically at him. The sun sank below the trees.

He took two steps back, toward the hover, sliding away as they were all sliding away, following the sun. "You don't want to stay here with the night-bound? With the great lost?"

"It's too late," she said.

She had always belonged to the great lost. Maybe everyone does, each in her own way, only they don't want to admit it. Because no matter how diligently, across what distance, you seek the sun, it will never be yours. The sun shines down on each person indifferently. That is why it is the sun.

His fear of being caught by the approaching dark overcame him. He gave up on her and sprinted for the ramp; as soon as he vanished inside, it sealed up and the second hover lifted off with a huff and a wheeze and a high-pitched, earsplitting whine that set all the dogs to barking and whimpering until at last the 'car receded away over the trees, westward. The first hover remained, powering down. The technicians had lamps and instruments out to examine the scarred wings of the *Ra*.

Rose stared at the lines the grass made growing up in the cracks between the sections of concrete pads poured down in rectangles to make the huge plaza. The eruption of grass and weeds created a blemish across the sterility of that otherwise smooth expanse. In the village, music started up over by the museum where someone had set up a board platform in front of the fence. Guitars strummed and one took up a melody, followed by a robust tenor. A couple of older men began dancing, bootheels drumming patterns on the wood while their partners swayed in counterpoint beside them, holding the edges of their skirts.

The boy approached across the plaza, torso now decently covered by a khaki-colored long-sleeved cotton shirt that was, not surprisingly, unbuttoned halfway to the waist. He no longer carried the rifle.

"Hey, chica. No hard feelings, no? You want to dance?"

"I'm waiting for my brother," she said stoutly. "He's coming to get me. He said to wait right here, by the museum."

"Bueno," agreed the boy. "You want a cola? There's a tienda at the museum. You can wait there and drink a cola. I'll buy it for you."

Shadows drowned the village, stretched long and long across houses and grass and the concrete plaza. The transition came rapidly in the tropical zone, day to night with scarcely anything like twilight in between. She had not seen night for almost three months. Was it possible to forget what it looked like, or had she always known even as she tried to outrun it? Had she always known that it was the monster creeping up on her, ready to overtake her? The daylit gleam of the *Ra*'s wings was already lost to theft and now its rounded nose and cylindrical body faded as shadows devoured it.

Laughter carried from the museum as a new tune started up. The smell of cooking chicken drifted on the breeze. Dogs hovered warily just beyond a stone's throw from the women grilling tortillas and shredded chicken on the upturned, heated flat bases of big canister barrels.

"You want a cola?" repeated the youth patiently. "I'll wait with you."

"I'll take a cola," she said, surprised to find that all her tears had dried. She set her back to the west and trudged with him toward the museum, where one by one lamps were lit and hung up to spill their glamour over the encroaching twilight. A woman's white dress flashed as she danced, turning beside her partner.

"Your dad's El Sol?" he asked, a little nervously. "En verdad? I mean, like, we all see all his shows. It's just amazing!"

"Yeah."

Inside she was as hollow as a drum, but down and down as deep as the very bottom of the abyss, there was still a spark, her spark. The spark that made her Rose, no matter who anyone else was. It was something to hold on to when there was no other light. It was the only thing to hold on to.

"Yeah," she said. "That's my dad."

The sun set.

Night came.

SCIENCE
FICTION
DAW

S. Andrew Swann

I first heard of S. Andrew Swann through his agent, Jane Butler. Jane had received a manuscript from Steve and been very impressed. When she sat down and talked with him, she realized that he was not a one-note author. Steve was brimming over with ideas he wanted to write about.

When Jane sent Steve's manuscript to me, I, too, realized this was a young man who could definitely write, whether he was exploring some of the long-established areas of science fiction and giving them a new twist, or charting brand-new territory of his own.

In July, 1993, Steve's first *Moreau* novel, *Forests of the Night* was added to DAW's science fiction list. Since then Steve has gone on to write three more novels set in the *Moreau* universe, as well as works which run the gamut from science fiction to supernatural suspense to fantasy. Recently, his *Moreau* novels have been optioned for the movies.

"The Heavens Fall" is a tale that will send a chill down your spine, and make you think long and hard about crime, punishment, and the price of "justice."

—SG

THE HEAVENS FALL
S. Andrew Swann

"Let justice be done, though the heavens fall!"
—Earl of Mansfield
(1705–1793)

"This is a court of law . . . not a court of justice."
—Oliver Wendell Holmes, Jr.
(1841–1935)

JOHNNY knew him. Mosh Frazier. Mosh of the wild hair. Mosh of the tattoos, skulls, and fire. Mosh of the wide leather belt and the evil temper. Mosh was Johnny's friend. At least that's what Johnny thought.

Johnny had always been a little slow about people.

Johnny's home was a farm shack in the poorest county in up-state New York. All his since Momma died. Johnny let Mosh share Momma's house. In return, Mosh gave Johnny money, gave Johnny beer, brought Johnny women, introduced Johnny to drugs—

Johnny never poked into Mosh's business. Johnny never asked what Mosh did out in the overgrown field in back of the house. Johnny never asked Mosh what he did alone in the shack when Johnny went to town.

Johnny really thought Mosh was a friend. Mosh was good to Johnny. Johnny would never do anything to upset him. Never.

Then Mosh left.

Then the police came.

The police dug up the overgrown field in back of Momma's house.

The police found the bodies of fifteen women.

The police said Mosh didn't exist.

Her head throbs. She's drunk a lot, and downed a lot of pills that she probably shouldn't have. She opens her eyes, fearful of light.

No reason to fear. There's no light except from the moon. She's thankful for that. The bedroom is dark, monochrome and fuzzy. Enough light beams in from the cracked window for her to see that she's alone. Sober now, mostly, she decides that the place is a pit. Smells of beer, old cigarette smoke, and something else—

Mothballs?

Where the hell is he?

(John Schaefer. He is thirty years old and somewhat retarded. He lured me here with the promise of drugs.)

Lured? That isn't a word she'd use. The combination of beer and pills is doing funny things to her head.

Doesn't matter who he is, because the guy's gone. That usually means he's stiffing you, ripping you off. She doesn't worry too much. After all, this is the guy's house. He wouldn't rip her off and leave her here, huh?

She shakes her head and feels a pain that seems more than simple hangover. She—

(Betty Dupree. I am twenty-one years old, and I ran away from home when I was thirteen.)

—Betty steps out of the sagging bed. Her feet sink into gray pile carpet. The carpet's filled with dust, making her feet feel dirty. She's naked, and the cold makes her shiver. The second story of this ancient farmhouse isn't heated.

Wind creaks wood in the walls and rattles windows in their frames. She shivers again.

All Johnny's money came from his disability checks, so they gave Johnny a public defender. The defender's name was Larry. Larry said he was Johnny's friend.

Johnny told Larry about Mosh.

Larry brought in a man with a computer. The man made faces appear on the computer screen. Johnny told the man about Mosh's wild black hair. About Mosh's gray-shot beard. About the earring Mosh wore, the Nazi cross in black, red, and white enamel. About how Mosh's eyes would go cold, and he would sit there for hours staring at Momma's TV, even though it didn't work no more.

He told them about the three scars on Mosh's cheek, and his

broken nose, and the cobra tattoo on his arm that snaked around until you could just see the tail peeking from the collar of a grease-stained T-shirt.

In the end, the image burning on the monitor's screen was Mosh. It was so much Mosh that it frightened Johnny.

Despite the pictures, no one found Mosh Frazier.

They found a lot of bikers in Johnny's county, but none was Mosh. None said they knew Mosh. Most said, like the police, Mosh didn't exist. Larry printed up the computer picture of Mosh and gave it to people, newspeople, mostly.

Once Johnny was scared when the picture showed up on the TV. But then the picture was gone and the news talked about Johnny. Johnny listened because he'd never heard anyone important talk about him before.

The news told him that he was about to have a "competency hearing." Johnny didn't know what that was, but if that hearing said so, then Johnny'd go to court. Johnny didn't want to go to court. If they found him guilty, he'd face a "mandatory life sentence," and a "mandatory empathy treatment," for every dead body they'd found.

Empathy treatments sounded scary.

Eventually Johnny had the competency hearing. They decided that he could stand trial for the murder of the fifteen women found buried on his land.

Betty searches the bedroom for her clothes. She doesn't bother turning on the light. Her eyes are adjusted to the dimness. She moves stacks of yellowing newsprint, freeing clouds of dust to dance in the moonlight.

She sneezes.

She finds her bra and panties hiding by the end table, half-buried in beer cans. Once she does, memory comes like a voice in her ear—

(My clothes were found downstairs.)

—telling her that the rest of her clothes are downstairs. She can't remember much else about last night. Can't remember much of anything.

This is a really bad hangover.

To her disgust, she steps on a used condom from last night. She kicks it away, and it sticks to the wall. She turns away, feeling a burst of self-loathing. This place makes her feel dirty. The money doesn't matter at the moment, and neither does the vial of meth that had been promised to her.

She just wants to feel clean.

The guy—

(John Schaefer. This is his mother's house. His mother died ten years ago.)

—Johnny isn't going to mind if she uses his shower.

That's what she'll do. She makes the decision, and has the odd sensation that someone is deciding things for her.

She shrugs away the thought.

She'll take the shower, get what she's owed if she can get it, and leave. She'll hitch back to Rochester if she has to, but she doesn't want to stay in this house any longer than necessary. If she stays, she feels that the house's rot will eat into her.

Betty walks to the bedroom door. Her feet leave the carpet and are chilled by unheated hardwood. Her left foot, the one that had stepped on the condom, sticks to the floor. She steps over beer cans, food wrappers, and male clothing.

Mason jars of debris fill the top of the bureau next to the door, and she nearly knocks one over.

Her hand catches it before she realizes she'd brushed against it. The move feels as if it was programmed. Betty is frozen by a momentary sense of predestination, a sense she is walking inevitably toward an evil fate.

Betty forces the feeling back. Such an admission might break her, like this mason jar almost broke upon the cold hardwood floor.

She stares involuntarily into the jar. Bolts and washers inside the glass are fused into a solid mass of rust. Within the mass of fused metal crawl cockroaches.

Dozens of cockroaches.

She gasps and her hand lets go of the jar. It falls and she watches, frozen—

(I am frightened. This house frightens me. This house is supposed to frighten me.)

—frozen by fear. She doesn't know why she is scared by the roaches.

The jar hits the ground and explodes into fragments.

Washers and bolts are strewn across the floor. Amid the shrapnel, roaches scurry from the site like an insect cluster bomb. Glass fragments bite her shins, her calves, her feet. The sound echoes through her head as if her skull is exploding, and those are fragments of her brain scurrying to the shadow-cloaked walls.

Johnny isn't going to like that.

(John Schaefer is dangerous.)

"Shit," she whispers to the last visible roach, and she opens the door without moving her feet. Bolts and glass are caught by the bottom edge of the door. They scrape across the floor like fingernails on a coffin lid.

"Forget Johnny," she whispers, "after a shower I am out of here."

(John Schaefer is dangerous.)

Larry told Johnny that the only chance he had was to plead "not guilty by reason of insanity."

"But it was Mosh who did it," Johnny said, on the verge of tears.

"I know, Johnny," Larry said, patting Johnny's hand. "But no one has ever seen this Mosh Frazier. There's no evidence he ever existed."

"I saw him. He was my friend."

Larry nodded. "I know, Johnny. I know that's what you believe."

"Where is everybody?" Betty whispers.

There had been other people at the party. She knows it.

(Tanya Gideon. She's only sixteen but she's gone on so many hard trips that she looks thirty. She was the third one he—)

"Tanya?" she calls.

No one answers.

She inches sideways through a hallway too narrow because of sagging bookcases. The cases hold tattered cardboard boxes and old cracked-plastic radios with missing knobs. There's an old headlight, radio tubes thirty years beyond use, Coke bottles filled with cigarette ash, and children's books dog-eared, water-stained, and smelling of mildew.

She sucks in her tummy and clutches an arm across her boobs to avoid brushing any of the filthy-looking artifacts. She wonders if Johnny might be a little nuts. Before, he seemed a bit dim and helpless. She and Tanya had taken pity on him when—

(John Schaefer picked us up at a highway rest stop outside of Rochester. The same highway where he found the thirteen other—)

—he picked them up.

They picked them up. Not just Johnny.

Betty wonders why she is only thinking of Johnny. Johnny's friend is much more frightening. Johnny's friend is much more dangerous.

At the end of the hall are the stairs, tall, narrow, dark as ink. She looks down and feels the dark reaching for her, sucking her in. Silent whispers urge her on, and she starts down, not wanting to, powerless to stop.

The shower—

(The indoor bathroom was added long after the house was built. When John Schaefer's father lived, there was no indoor water. The shower is downstairs.)

—the shower is down there.

Her clothes are down there.

Tanya is down there.

They are— *(he is)* —down there.

Betty descends the stairs.

During the trial Larry said that Mosh Frazier did exist. Mosh existed as part of Johnny's broken personality. If Johnny had taken part in the deaths of fifteen women, it was because of that other part of himself. The part that was Mosh Frazier. It was Mosh Frazier that was doing it.

They shouldn't punish Johnny. They should help him. Help him get well.

Johnny went along because Larry said it was the best way, the only way, out of this mess.

But it hurt Johnny's mind to think that way. Mosh was a loud fat bull of a man. Mosh was smarter than Johnny. Mosh gave him beers and said, "You ain't bad for a retard." Mosh knew how to find drugs, and money, and women who would do anything for either.

None of that's me, Johnny thought, *and I never did nothing to nobody.*

Johnny couldn't believe that he was Mosh.

Betty descends through the dark.

The stairs creak under her feet. The only other sounds are the winter wind blowing outside and soft dripping from a faucet somewhere.

Drip. Drip. Drip.

She can't see. Dark wipes everything with a black hand. She tries to remember how many steps there are. Her memory is much too fuzzed by drugs and her hangover.

And more than drugs, and more than hangover.

Her mouth tastes like paste. Her head feels like a blood-filled blister throbbing in time to her pulse. Her skin is cold and sticky. And all she can smell is beer, cigarette smoke, and her own rank odor.

"Hello?" she calls again, halfway down the blind stairs.

No answer but the wind and a soft leak from somewhere.

Drip. Drip. Drip.

Betty's heart accelerates. A shadowy sense of déjà vu clouds the aching fog in her skull. This has happened before—

(I am Betty Dupree. I am John Schaefer's fourth victim.)

—happened before. But this is wrong. This is happening wrong.

She shakes the thought from her head. She whispers, "Forget the shower. I find my clothes, and I'm gone."

Her breath burns in her nose and her throat. She feels her pulse in her neck, her temples, her brain. She wishes she'd had the sense to turn on the lights when she'd been at the head of the stairs.

Still, against her will, pushed by something she doesn't understand, she continues downward.

In the end, the jury didn't believe Larry.

Johnny, who could barely read the charges against him, was convicted for all fifteen murders. He was sentenced to fifteen mandatory life sentences. He was also sentenced to fifteen mandatory empathy treatments.

In the short history of the treatments, no one had ever been sentenced to so many.

But New York law demanded one treatment for each of the murdered women.

But none of this meant as much to Johnny as the realization that he was Mosh Frazier. He had to be Mosh Frazier. The police couldn't find Mosh. Everyone said that Johnny was Mosh. Even the newsman on the TV said that Johnny was Mosh, or that Johnny had invented Mosh.

It had to be true.

So Johnny was taken to the state prison, to wait. Johnny waited as correctional officers programmed the first empathy treatment from expert testimony and the forensic record. All Johnny knew was that it was a long wait.

Drip. Drip. Drip.

Betty stumbles at the bottom of the dark stairs. As she pitches forward, she grabs for support and finds none.

Her right hand hits the floor first, lands in something wet, and slides out from under her. She slams into the hardwood floor. The floor beneath her is hot, sticky, and wet. Even though she's dizzy to the point of passing out or throwing up, she pushes herself up immediately.

Her head swims back and forth as her feet slip on the wet floor. Her stomach tries to push its way up through her throat. She realizes what might be here.

(Tanya Gideon.)

Despite her panic, despite the razor of fear ripping at her heart, she fumbles for the lightbulb chain. She knows now that the leak is much closer than she'd thought at first.

Drip.

Closer than the bathroom.

Drip.

Closer than the kitchen.

Drip.

Right next to her.

Her hand finds the chain and pulls it before she is ready.

Betty is naked in the front hall of the house. In the living room, sits Tanya Gideon, sixteen-year-old that looks like thirty.

Half of Tanya's neck is gone.

Tanya's head bobs at an obscene angle as the rocking chair silently tilts back and forth.

Back, drip.

Forth, drip.

Betty gags. She's covered in Tanya's blood. She screams. Backs away. Her feet slip out from under her. She clutches the light's chain on the way down.

For a second, the chain remains taut. The light is extinguished. Betty's weight rips the chain, the entire fixture, from the ceiling in a shower of blue sparks.

She smells burning insulation and, finally, the blood.

Betty rolls over and vomits. Painful spasms fill her mouth with sour bile and the sting of old alcohol.

She's bent over, clutching her stomach.

She hears a footstep.

Larry said that he was still Johnny's friend. Larry said that he would "appeal" the decision. Larry also said that he would do what he could about the "empathy" treatments that Larry said were "cruel and unusual."

Larry said a lot of things that Johnny couldn't understand.

What Johnny understood was the fact that he had to meet Larry in a small gray room that separated them with a giant sheet of glass as thick as Johnny's thumb. What Johnny understood was the fact that Larry could no longer pat his hand. What Johnny understood was the fact that Larry might not be his friend.

While Larry appealed, Johnny would have to endure at least one empathy treatment.

The treatment was supposed to be like one of those video

games, but more. They not only put that funny helmet on you, but they also put wires into your head.

Johnny didn't like that. If Mosh was in his head, they shouldn't put wires there. It might get Mosh angry—

Worse, they might let Mosh out.

Johnny tried to explain this to them, but they shaved his head anyway.

Beyond the door next to her, on the porch, Betty hears him.

(John Schaefer.)

She scrambles to her feet, smearing her own vomit on her hands and her knees. She gasps for breath and her heart wants to tear loose from her rib cage.

Mosh is a maniac.

(John Schaefer is a maniac.)

Betty's thoughts fly in crazy directions. She scrambles through the dark. The windows down here are shuttered and curtained. She's as blind here as she was on the stairs. She stumbles away from the sounds by the door. She can hear it opening, behind her.

In her dash to get away she grabs something soft and wet. She screams again and stumbles off in another direction. Behind her she hears Tanya's body fall.

Drip.

Thud.

The door creaks and a widening sliver of moonlight folds open across the blind TV ahead of her. A shadow crosses the rectangle of light, and Betty runs for the barely visible kitchen doorway.

After the first treatment, Johnny cried for weeks.

The first appeal failed.

Johnny screamed all the way to the second treatment. They had to restrain him. He whipped his head so much that they had to inject a sedative to fit the helmet on him.

After that treatment, Johnny tried to kill himself. They placed him in solitary confinement for six months.

The second appeal also failed.

As the time for the third treatment came, Johnny became violent for the first time he could remember. He clawed, and bit, and the guard sprayed mace in his eyes. They jabbed a needle in his arm before taking him from his cell.

After that treatment, Johnny didn't move for two months. The doctors said he was catatonic. The guards said he was faking.

Five Supreme Court justices said that empathy treatments weren't "cruel and unusual."

The treatments were supposed to make him realize what those women went through at his, Mosh's, hands. Johnny had thought he'd understood that. But he'd been wrong.

The treatments were worse than anything Johnny had ever experienced. The drugs wiped his mind, and voices in his ears convinced him that he wasn't him. It was worse than thinking Mosh actually lived inside his skull. Johnny could believe that Mosh was in his own head and still know that he was Johnny.

But when they had finished whispering in his ear, he was no longer Johnny.

When the voices finished whispering, he was one of the fifteen. He was in their reality, his brain locked behind the mask and the wires, not knowing the world it inhabited was no longer the world Johnny lived in.

First they made him Ginger Harper.

Then they made him Pauline Dickinson.

Then they made him Tanya Gideon.

While he was strapped into a sickbed, wired to New York State's computers, he lived their last moments. Wires triggered their fears in him, ignited their pain in him. And, each time, they took a little more of Johnny away from him, leaving nothing but death to replace what they had taken.

For his fourth treatment, four guards and a doctor came for him. Johnny tried to fight, but he was skinny and weak from years in prison. The needle found his arms before he barely had a chance to struggle.

The worst part of all—

Each time, it took the voices less time to convince him he was someone else.

She's trapped. There's no other way out of the kitchen and the killer is coming toward her. She sees a window over the sink and she dives for it. Outside there's blowing snow and blue moonlit drifts, but she doesn't think of the cold. All she thinks of is escape—

(John Schaefer is after me.)

Mosh is after me.

—but her fingers scrape against a handleless frame, painted shut. Her eyes water as a nail peels back to the quick. She grabs a frying pan from the sink and throws it against the window.

The window shatters.

The wind claws its way in with icicle scalpels.

The blue night outside turns dead black as light floods the kitchen.

Reflexively, she turns around to see—

(John Schaefer.)

NO!

—to see Johnny. He's bundled for the weather, but she sees blood on his jeans. He's holding a shovel, not a snow shovel, but a spade for turning earth. The blade is caked with mud.

Johnny holds it like a weapon.

She knows that Johnny is going to kill her with the shovel. Time slows as Johnny raises the shovel above his head. Betty tries to scream, but her breath is like molasses in her throat. Her body doesn't move. The déjà vu is back, a ghost gripping her heart.

It's Johnny.

Not Mosh.

His face is wrong. His height is wrong. His clothes are wrong.

This isn't the man that killed her.

The shovel reaches its apex. She can't move, rooted by the same force that moved her hand when she dislodged the mason jar. The same force that drove her down the stairs.

The same devil's whisper that's been moving her all along.

She fights it.

She can almost hear the voice, now. It tells her to stand still, wait for the shovel to impact her skull. Tells her to feel the full force of the impact driving bone fragments through her brain. Tells her to feel what it's like to be murdered. Tells her to feel what it's like to die.

The voice is dark, seductive . . .

Her heart shakes her rib cage like a prisoner trying to escape.

The shovel whistles through the air, arcing toward her head.

She forces herself to move.

The scene slows even further as she resists the voice. The shovel's blade screams closer. She feels, *knows*, that she's been here before.

She's died here before.

The devil with the dark, dominating voice drives her through this circle of hell, again, and again, and again.

Betty is no longer even sure of who she is. She could be a nineteen-year-old prostitute named Ginger Harper. She could be a twenty-six-year-old waitress named Pauline Dickinson.

She could even be Tanya Gideon.

That thought, knowing that Tanya's body is only a few yards away, allows her to move. Events snap back to normal speeds as she ducks to the side.

The shovel clangs into the sink.

The gong of impact shatters the devil in her ear. She can direct her own body for the first time.

Johnny—

(The killer. My killer. Tanya's killer.)

Johnny is frozen in shock. He isn't supposed to miss. Betty knows that he is the devil, supposed to kill her over and over, until the end of time.

But she can move, and her devil is gone.

Johnny lifts his shovel, but it is an unwieldy weapon. Betty sweeps a counter full of crusty dishes to shatter in his path. Johnny steps back, raising his shovel.

Betty sees a dirty butcher knife.

Like a machine, Johnny raises his shovel. Betty knows that it is the only attack he can perform, because Betty Dupree's body was found with a shattered skull. She doesn't know how she knows this, but she knows that the muttering devil will only allow Johnny to follow his program. Johnny must kill her. He must kill her with the shovel.

She won't let him.

She grabs the knife and closes on Johnny.

His shovel hasn't reached its apex, and Johnny's eyes widen as she plunges the knife, two-handed, between his collarbones. Even as blood sprays from his mouth, his shovel still travels upward. He is as much the devil's slave as she was.

She yanks the knife and stabs him again.

He backs and tries to bring the shovel to bear, but she closes and stabs him again.

And again.

And again.

She stabs him until the shovel drops.

She stabs him until he drops.

She kneels over him and stabs him repeatedly. She yells at the devil, "I've killed him. I've killed your torturer. No more! No more death!"

Betty Dupree stabs Johnny. *"No more!"*

Ginger Harper stabs Johnny. *"No more!"*

Pauline Dickinson stabs Johnny. *"No more!"*

Tanya Gideon stabs Johnny. *"No more!"*

Finally, as the kitchen fades into darkness, Johnny stabs Johnny. *"No more!"*

Then there's only Johnny.

Then nothing.

It hurts when they yank the helmet off. The doctor leans over with a look of concern. It is the only sympathy the man's shown in four separate treatments.

"Are you okay? Can you understand what I'm saying?"

That's the voice, the devil's voice. It seems a victory, remembering that.

The room is cold, and there are more people here than usual. More than the guards. They must have come from beyond the massive one-way mirror that forms one wall of the empathy room.

"I'm so sorry, Johnny." The doctor says. "You shouldn't have gone through this."

"Wha?" *My voice is slurred. Still drugged.*

"You've been granted clemency by the governor."

"Cold." The word sounds choppy through chattering teeth. "I need my clothes." *All these people.*

The doctor looks puzzled.

Sitting up sends the room spinning. "God, I'm going to throw up again."

"You shouldn't sit up so fast," says the doctor. "This last treatment has been a bad one. No one's gone through four of them in so short a time."

The room keeps swaying. Memory's an unstable black fog. People talk, but the words melt into one another.

"Treatment? Pardon?" Those words should mean something.

The doctor's expression shows concern and, maybe, guilt. "The California Highway Patrol found a biker named Eric Frazier in a trailer park—three bodies were on the property."

"Eric Frazier?"

"They found Mosh, Johnny," says one of the prison guards.

The doctor nods.

"Why are you calling me Johnny?" asks Betty Dupree.

Everyone freezes. In the suddenly silent room, the doctor says, "That's your name, John Schaefer."

Betty knows the devil's voice, and she knows it lies. She looks the doctor in the eyes. "Johnny tried to kill me."

All the color drains from the doctor's face. He reaches for her arm and says, "Please, Johnny—"

"*That's not my name!*" She yanks her arm away from him. John Schaefer, the man who tried to kill her, is dead.

When she pulls away from the doctor, she faces the giant one-way mirror that forms one wall of the empathy room. Betty Dupree sees her reflection in the mirror.

For a moment she doesn't believe what she sees.

Then she screams.

Lisanne Norman

When we say that everyone at DAW is part of our family, it is something we really mean. And Lisanne Norman is certainly an example of exactly how our family continues to extend itself. When my sister Marsha was living in England, she became friends with a young woman who was active in the science fiction community there, and was also a member of a Viking reenactment group. Her name was Lisanne Norman.

At some point, Lisanne told Marsha about a novel she had been working on for some time. As an avid reader, a good friend, and someone with publishing experience, Marsha told Lisanne she'd be happy to look at her manuscript. After Marsha had given Lisanne as much input as she could, she suggested to Lisanne that she submit her novel to me at DAW. And with moral support and an introduction from Marsha, Lisanne finally built up her courage and did exactly that.

Of course, the manuscript was *Turning Point,* and it became the start of her DAW *Sholan Alliance* series, which she is still writing today.

"Passage to Shola" tells the story behind a kidnapping which occurs in one of Lisanne's *Sholan Alliance* novels. In the novel, we are introduced to two of the characters—the Sholan, Taynar, and his Human Leska, Kate—after they have been rescued. Now, readers can discover how they were kidnapped in the first place and learn what happened to them before they were once again reunited with their own people.

—SG

PASSAGE TO SHOLA
Lisanne Norman

DAY 1
"You did *what*?" Jeedah's ears flicked back, then righted themselves as she sat up in bed and looked at Dyaf in horror.

"I put you down to take Taynar Arrazo and his new Human Leska from the Hillfort settlement on Keiss and convey them to Clan Leader Kusac Aldatan's estate on Shola," he sighed. "I assumed you'd leap at the chance of a few days' leave back home."

"The leave, yes," said Jeedah, getting up and pacing around the small room. "But three weeks shut up with that Arrazo brat? That's too high a price, Dyaf! And he's a Telepath—he'll know I don't like him!"

"He has his new Leska to keep him diverted," he said, propping himself up on one elbow. "The trip won't be that bad. Come back to bed, Jeedah, please."

She stopped at the foot of the bed and eyed him steadily. "Just how will having a Leska keep him out of my way?" she demanded, tail swaying rhythmically from side to side in the beginnings of anger.

"Leskas are mind-mates, linked to each other for life. They need to spend every fifth day alone together because of their mental link."

"Great, not only do I get the Keissian system's spoiled brat, but I get him on a testosterone high, too!" she said disgustedly. "In Vartra's name, why choose me?"

"Because you're experienced in dealing with these Humans, and your vehicle is one of the few small long-range couriers on the *Khalossa* that we can spare," he said patiently. "And Commander Raagul wants them out of this quadrant as soon as possible. The new mixed species Leska links are worrisome enough without having to deal with them in a potential war zone should the Valtegans we drove off Keiss decide to return in force."

"So you volunteered me for the job of ferrying them home. Thanks, but no thanks, Dyaf. You can just unvolunteer me." Her voice held the undercurrent of a snarl.

"We all have to do things we don't like, Captain," he said stiffly, his eye ridges meeting in a frown. "That *brat*, as you so aptly call him, with all his airs and graces, has been a thorn in everyone's foot since he arrived. Now that we have a legitimate excuse to get rid of him, we want him out of here as soon as possible."

"You pulling rank on me now, *Lieutenant* Dyaf?" she asked very quietly, stilling her tail.

"Not unless I have to, Jeedah," he said, equally quietly. "I chose you because I know you'll get him home without strangling him on the way."

Jeedah's mouth dropped open in a faint grin as she folded her arms across her chest. There was some truth in that, at least. She sighed, accepting the inevitable. "When do I ship out?"

Dyaf glanced at his wrist comm. "In six hours. Come back to bed, Jeedah, we've plenty of time yet," he pleaded, holding his free hand out to her enticingly.

"No way," she said, bending down to pick her scattered clothing up off his floor. "I've my ship to check over and a psychic damper to be fitted in one of the cabins. You know I insist on doing a full check myself before a mission. Who's crewing with me?"

"Nekaba," sighed Dyaf, letting himself fall back amongst his pillows. "He'll be waiting at Hillfort for you as he was on leave up there. It's not necessary for you to go right this minute, Jeedah. They're fitting the damper on your ship now."

"I *always* check my ship myself. You owe me big time for this, Dyaf," she said, pulling on her tunic and sealing it.

He growled, a low rumble that carried no menace. "Don't push it, Jeedah."

"First you cancel my weekend leave because of this mission, then you let Maintenance go climbing all over the *Mara* when you know I hate anyone working on her unless I'm there! I reckon you owe me."

"All right! So I owe you!" he said, exasperated, as he raised his head to watch her fastening on her weapons utility belt. "What is it this time?"

"Haven't decided yet," she grinned, showing her teeth. "Could be a meal in the Palace Restaurant in Shanagi, or . . ."

"That'll cost me a fortune!" he exclaimed, glowering at her.

"Or it might be a trip to the Storyteller's theater to hear Kaerdhu. . . ."

"Jeedah, have some pity!" he groaned. "You know I can't stand him!"

"I didn't say it would be either of them. What you'll owe me depends on how much the Arrazo brat has annoyed me," she said, putting on her sleeveless jacket and letting it hang open. "I'll collect when I get back," she grinned, blowing him a kiss while flicking her tail provocatively as she turned to leave.

"Take care," she heard him call out as the door shut behind her.

Outside in the corridor, she began to curse softly. Just her luck! She'd been—no, they'd been—looking forward to two whole days off together, which didn't happen very often, and now she had to do a baby-sitting run for Taynar Arrazo—and him with a Leska now! Vartra surely had a sense of humor when He arranged that match! Poor little Human, she'd have her work cut out for her trying to deal with that "precious" young male. She groaned. Three weeks alone with them! Ye Gods! How was *she* going to cope? Dyaf indeed owed her and she meant to collect with interest when she returned!

The weather as she approached Hillfort was squally and thunder-filled, rendering communication garbled at best, so she wasn't too concerned when she couldn't raise the settlement's landing pad. She could just make out the small landing area ahead, its lights on to guide her down. She frowned, her instincts suddenly telling her that something wasn't right but she couldn't quite close her teeth on it. Hillfort was unknown to her, she'd never had the need to land at this site before today.

Below her, the small hut that served as the comm station and waiting area seemed deserted. As the wind gusted around her vehicle, she automatically compensated, realizing on a day like this, no one in their right mind would be waiting out in the open. Slowing the engines, she brought her deep space courier in to land, keeping it idling while she waited for the obligatory good-byes the Human female at least would be saying.

Squinting through the rain-lashed viewport, she saw the hut door open and three figures wrapped against the weather come scurrying over to her. Only three? In this weather, they'd probably said their farewells in the village.

Activating the side door for them, she sealed it as soon as they were on board. Giving them time to pass through the two iris locks and reach the small bridge, she twisted around in her seat to greet them, noticing that Nekaba, his face concealed by a Human hat, was carrying his energy rifle.

"Stow that rifle aft, Nekaba, then show the kits their quarters," she said, looking at the two bedraggled younglings. Taynar stood there motionless, water dripping from his hair and slicker onto the floor of the shuttle, ears flattened to invisibility against his skull, eyes wide and staring with shock. The Human female looked little better. Just as her internal alarm bells went off loudly in her head, a movement from the adult drew her eyes back to him. As she looked down the length of the rifle barrel, she realized he wasn't Nekaba.

"What the hell . . ." she began, then stopped dead, fear clutching her vitals as the armed male removed his hat and threw it aside.

At first sight, he looked Human, but the large, dark green predator's eyes that stared unblinkingly at her from a pallid green complexion were those of a Valtegan. The crest of skin running from the front to the back of his head, lying flat for now, marked him out as no ordinary soldier—he was one of the very few elite Officer Class. Gods, she'd never seen one of them in the flesh before! She thought they'd killed all the Valtegans over a year ago when they'd liberated this first Earth colony. He smelled rank, but then he must have been in hiding for nearly a year.

As he shoved his captives farther onto her small bridge, his stale scent became overpowering.

"Destination changed," he said, his voice a sibilant hiss as he pronounced the Human words with some difficulty. "I tell you where we go."

She pushed her fear aside, there was no time for it now. Slowly, she inched the hand behind her back toward the auto-navigator. She had to lose their route before the damned lizard found it! There was no way he was going to find out where Shola was.

"We can't go far," she said, trying to divert his attention. "This craft is only a shuttle, it isn't capable of deep space travel."

Light flared briefly past her face, scorching her nose before exploding on the console beside her outstretched fingers. With a cry of pain, she flung herself back in her seat, clutching her singed hand.

"Stand." The rifle barrel was touching her temple now, and he had her upper arm in a viselike grip.

Damn, but he'd moved impossibly fast! Holding her hands palms up, she got out of her seat slowly, letting him thrust her toward the two younglings.

Still keeping his rifle trained on them, the Valtegan quickly looked over the controls, hissing with annoyance as he checked out the damage his shot had caused.

Jeedah risked a small sigh of relief. At least she'd managed to wipe the memory bank before he'd realized what she'd been doing.

"There wasn't anything we could do, Captain," said a small voice.

She looked down at the Human female standing beside her.

"He was waiting there when we arrived. He killed Nekaba once he'd found out why we were there."

Jeedah touched her gently on the shoulder. "It's not your fault," she managed to say before she was grasped by the front of her jacket and hauled back to the console.

"This was communications?" the Valtegan demanded, pointing to the sparking section of the control board with the rifle barrel.

"Yes."

He hissed his displeasure, bifurcated tongue flicking out in anger. "You fix later!" He flung her aside as easily as if she weighed nothing. The bulkhead came up to meet her, and everything went black.

Something cold was pressing against her forehead, making the throbbing pain worse. She batted it away and tried to sit up, groaning as a wave of nausea swept through her.

"She's awake!"

Sholan that bad had to belong to a Human. She risked opening her eyes and sure enough, there was the smooth, hairless face of the young female.

"I'm fine, youngling," she mumbled, slowly pushing herself into a sitting position. The movement made her feel nauseous and the pulsing of the ship's engine beneath her only added to her misery. "Any idea where we are?"

"In the lounge, on the floor. He locked us all in here. You were too heavy for me to lift, so I made you as comfortable as I could where he dropped you. I'm called Kate, by the way."

"Jeedah," she said, passing a shaking hand across her forehead to assess the damage. She had a lump the size of an egg just above her right eye. "I didn't mean literally. Are we still on Shola, or in space?"

"In space, but still in Keiss' solar system, I think, because I saw the moon through the window a few minutes ago."

"Porthole," Jeedah corrected automatically. She tried to get up, then wished she hadn't as the room swam alarmingly around her and her stomach heaved.

Kate's hand steadied her as she swallowed convulsively, trying to rid her mouth of the bitter taste. Clamping her teeth together, she tried again, this time getting her feet tangled in the blanket Kate had put over her. Finally she made it and staggered over to the wall seating and collapsed next to the porthole.

"Kate, there's a small first aid kit in my bathing room cabinet," she whispered, leaning her head against the cool transparent surface. "My cabin's the one opposite here—out the door and turn right. Would you fetch it, please?"

Her hands were still shaking as she opened the kit and rummaged through it to find the analgesics.

"Let me," said Kate, taking it from her.

"Blue pack," Jeedah mumbled, praying she didn't have a major concussion. She held out her hand as Kate ripped the packaging open.

"Here," said Kate, putting the pill into her hand. "I brought a glass of water for you."

"Thanks," she said, gratefully. "I should be fine in a few minutes." The pill dissolved instantly on her tongue, but she washed it down with the water anyway, handing the empty glass back to the young female.

Eyes closed again, she waited for the drug to take effect. "He didn't say anything about where he wants to go, did he?"

"No. I expect he wants to go home. Wouldn't you?"

"I suppose. How long was I out?"

"Only about half an hour."

Jeedah felt the seat give as Kate sat down beside her.

"You said this ship wasn't capable of deep space flight, so what happens when we run out of fuel?"

"I lied," said Jeedah, thankful that her stomach seemed to be settling. "What do you know about the Valtegans?"

"Very little. I know they'd taken over the colony on Keiss and that your people came to free us. I wasn't on the first colony ship."

"And Taynar?"

"No more than I do."

Their lack of knowledge was a relief to her. At least they weren't going to panic about their captor's eating habits—yet. She tried to think through what needed to be done next, but her head still ached abominably. Opening her eyes, she glanced slowly round the room, trying to take stock of the situation. They might be locked out of the bridge, but at least the rest of the ship was still open to them.

"What's up with him?" she asked, catching sight of Taynar sitting motionless on the sofa by the aft door.

"I don't know," said Kate, a worried tone creeping into her voice. "He's been like that since Nekaba was killed. It's as if he's running on automatic. He won't speak, and his mind feels as if it's asleep."

"Great. See if you can shake him out of it. We all need to be alert if we're going to . . . get through this." Just in time she stopped herself from saying *survive this*.

"I heard all Valtegans were afraid of Sholans," said Kate. "Why isn't this one? And where did he come from, Jeedah? I thought they'd all been captured or killed a year ago."

"Must have gone to ground somewhere," said Jeedah, massaging her temples gently. The pain was beginning to recede a little. "Be careful of him, Kate. We've only found one other like him. He's one of the command officers who hardly ever set foot on Keiss. Gossip on the *Khalossa* had it that they were a different breed of Valtegan—more intelligent, and not as psychotically afraid of us as the ordinary soldiers were. Stay away from him and let me do all the talking."

Kate nodded, setting the soft brown curls that framed her face bobbing gently.

"You sort Taynar out, I'm going to see if I can find anything useful before he comes back," said Jeedah, getting up slowly.

When Jeedah returned, she had a variety of dubiously useful items culled from her quick search of the kitchen and a brief foray into the cargo areas. If the Valtegan consolidated his hold on the *Mara,* she knew she'd never get the chance to go there again.

There was a large first aid kit, a small electrical tool pack, a signal gun with three flares that she'd gotten from the aircar in the rearmost hold, a small laser-powered spot welder, and a couple of reasonably sized wrenches.

As she put them on the dining room table, Kate left Taynar's side to join her.

"Not much of a haul," Jeedah admitted, picking up the welder. "But I also have my own gun and belt knife concealed in my cabin. Did he search you for weapons?"

"Yes, but we didn't have any. Are you going to use these as weapons?" she asked.

"We are," Jeedah said, heading for the bench seat and lifting off one of the padded cushions. Underneath was a wooden board that she slid to one side. She thrust the spot welder into the cavity there.

"Help me," she said, putting first the cover then the cushion back. "I need to get these hidden before he returns."

Within minutes, they'd hidden everything but the last wrench in the lounge or the small kitchen next door.

"Why does he want us? He could have left us at Hillfort if all he wanted was your ship," said Kate quietly, glancing over her shoulder at the still unresponsive Taynar. "How likely are we to survive this, Jeedah?"

"I was afraid you'd ask that," muttered Jeedah, opening her uniform jacket and shoving the wrench inside out of sight, yet still within easy reach. "Depends on our usefulness to him. You two he needed as cover to get on the *Mara*, me he needs to navigate and run her. We've just got to convince him that since he killed my copilot, you two are now indispensable to me." She leaned back against the table and surveyed the young Human critically.

Kate seemed a practical youngling, one who thought things through carefully from the way the kit had handled herself after the Valtegan had knocked Jeedah out cold. Thankfully she was dressed practically, too—she was wearing the one-piece coveralls favored by the Human military when they were working with the Sholans. There was a saying on Keiss among the Humans—never get a Valtegan to notice you. Given that Valtegans had used some of the Human females in their pleasure cities on Keiss, she was glad one as pretty as Kate was not dressed in attractive off duty clothes.

"What do you know about Sholan craft? Have you ever flown one, even an aircar?" she asked.

Kate shook her head. "Nothing. As I said, I came here on the second Earth colony ship. My father's one of the geologists—and before you ask, I've had no training as a Telepath either. I didn't even know I was one until I met Taynar a couple of weeks ago."

Jeedah shut her eyes briefly in despair, then opened them quickly. "Did you read my question?" she demanded. "How did . . . ?"

"I know what you were going to ask?" finished Kate with a wry smile. "I don't know. Probably because it was the next obvious question."

"Humans have a Talent for reading alien minds. Have you tried reading his? Have you just known anything about him, too?" she asked, trying not to let the hope sound in her voice.

Again Kate shook her head. "No, I haven't."

Inwardly she sighed. Their telepathic Talent was no use to them, then. Taynar, however, should know how to pilot aircars. "How d'you cope?" she asked suddenly. "Living inside each other's thoughts the whole time—and with someone like Taynar?" It was said before she realized it, and when she did, she lowered her ears backward in embarrassment.

Kate grinned. "He's not so bad, and he's very young, really."

He's young? She makes me feel positively ancient! thought Jeedah. Both of them were hardly more than kitlings.

"I suggest we all sleep together for our mutual safety," she said. "We can use my cabin, it's the largest one."

"We can't," said Kate. "Our Link days. That's when we join to let our memories merge."

"Oh, yeah, I'd forgotten about that," muttered Jeedah, tail flicking in discomfort, annoyed with herself for forgetting. She'd made a point of reading all she could on Leska pairs before she left the *Khalossa*. "They installed a psychic damper in one of the cabins for you."

"That's only every fifth day, though. The other nights we can share your room."

She nodded. "I see you got nowhere with rousing Taynar. I think it's time for drastic action," she said, pushing herself away from the table and going over to the young male.

She grabbed his arms and began hauling him to his feet.

Though his body responded to her pushing and pulling him toward the aft door, his mind was definitely a million miles away. She dragged him through the air lock iris and into the first cabin, threading her way past the furniture to the bathing room, then over to the shower cubicle. Kate followed her, her face creased in worry.

"You do realize that what he feels, I feel, too, don't you?" she said.

"In that case," said Jeedah cheerfully, propping the youth against the cubicle wall and stepping back, "brace yourself!" With that, she turned on the cold water.

Seconds later, Taynar was yowling in shock and struggling to get out from under the cold deluge. Beside her, Kate wrapped her arms around herself with a small moan of discomfort.

Like a cork from a bottle, the young male shot out of the cubicle and stood dripping on the tiled floor.

"What the hell do you think you're doing?" he demanded angrily of her as water streamed from his clothing and pelt.

"Waking you up," said Jeedah shortly. "We've been captured by a Valtegan officer and . . ."

"I know what's happened," he interrupted, starting to take his slicker off. "I know everything my Leska knows. What're you going to do about it?"

"Me?" demanded Jeedah, grasping him by the front of his coat. "Us, Taynar. We're all in this together."

"I can sense him coming," said Kate urgently.

Jeedah had barely turned around before their captor was standing in the doorway. He took in the scene at a glance then gestured to Jeedah.

"You. Come. Set course," he said.

"It's not that easy," she began, but his free hand snaked out and grasped her by the arm, his nonretractable claws digging into her flesh. "Hey!"

"I show you where we going. You take us. Now," he said, dragging her into the narrow corridor and hauling her off toward the bridge.

"Look at me! I'm soaking! Get me a towel, Kate." Taynar began to undo his belt and peel off his soaking slicker and tunic.

It was more an order than a request. Kate tried to stop thinking about what was happening to Jeedah and stepped past him into the bathroom to find a towel.

"Stop worrying about her, she'll find a way to get us out of this mess," he said, taking it from her and beginning to rub himself down. "Females always know what to do. That's why she asked you for your help."

"But I can't help, Taynar, and you know I can't," Kate said quietly, picking up his wet clothes and looking for somewhere to put them.

"She'll find something for you to do, don't worry. Females always stick together. See if there're any dry clothes in those cupboards," he ordered as he headed out of the bathing room and into the single bedroom.

Mentally she retreated to the tiny place in her mind where he couldn't reach, the place where she could think her own thoughts, be separate from him. He had a deep conviction that women, including her, not only held the answers to all his problems in life, but were there to smooth it out for him.

"It's not that easy this time, Taynar. Any or all of us could be killed, just as he killed the other pilot."

His ears flicked back and his nose wrinkled in a frown. "Don't remind me. I felt his pain as that . . . animal . . . killed him! We can't do much, Kate, you know that. Telepaths can't fight. We feel the pain we inflict. It just can't be done, Jeedah knows this." He threw the towel on the bed. "Now make yourself useful. Go and look in the cupboard for some dry clothes," he said patronizingly. "Or get my bag from the lounge."

He made Jeedah sit in her pilot's chair and indicated the navigation chart he'd called up on the comp unit. A claw tip touched an area toward what she recognized as Chemerian home space.

"That's too far," she said. "It can't be done in one jump, and that's uncharted space out there."

"Not for me. We do two jumps. Where first?"

She thought quickly, trying to work out what her best options were. They could land outside Shola's system, but that would just create the situation she'd been afraid of in the first place—the Valtegan finding out where their home world was. Still, a courier as small as hers would go unremarked in the time it would take to recalibrate for the second jump. With the comm out, there was no way she could alert anyone to their predicament, but there was also no way incoming messages could be heard. She still didn't want to risk it. Her safest bet was to head for a jump point in Chemerian space and hope that she could overpower him by that time. If she couldn't, then the ever-paranoid Chemerians' satellite warning systems would certainly be alerted as they emerged from jump. With any luck, they'd intervene if all else failed.

She pointed to a bright spot on the map. "There. I can take us as far as there," she said. "Beyond that . . ." She flicked her ears, then shrugged, realizing he wouldn't understand the negative Sholan gesture.

He sat in the copilot's chair, rifle cradled across his lap. "You enter course, I watch," he hissed, leaning forward till he could clearly see her screen. "I understand what you do. Do it right, or I take one of captives and kill it a little at a time."

Hands slick with sweat, Jeedah began to call up the more detailed map of that sector. Star maps there were in plenty in the database, but thank the Gods for Sholan caution, none were labeled. All the standard routes were there, too, but since they'd discovered the Humans and the Valtegans on Keiss, all those maps were security locked and coded. Obviously, he either hadn't realized they were there, or their craft were so different from his that he couldn't find a frame of reference on her nav panel to begin looking for them. That meant she'd have to work out their route the hard way.

Praying that she could still remember her math, she reached for her personal drawer, forgetting for a moment about the Valtegan at her side.

An angry hiss, then a choking pressure around her throat were all the warning she got. As the claws pressed into the flesh over her larynx, she looked into his green slitted eyes, trying desperately to remain calm.

"Comp pad," she gasped. "In drawer. Need it to calculate route."

Just as suddenly the pressure was gone, and she slumped across the console coughing.

"No sudden moves! Next time, you die! I get hatching to pilot!"

"Can't navigate," she croaked, massaging her throat as she pushed herself up. "Kill me and you lose your navigator."

He hissed angrily, forked tongue flicking in and out. "Get pad!"

As she reached for her drawer once more, she noticed how badly her hand was trembling. Dammit! She *must* be careful! Another false move like that and they could all be dead. Despite her best efforts, her ears were flattening and folding sideways against her head. *Let them,* she thought angrily. *Let the son of a tree-rhuddha know how angry I am!*

"We can't jump yet, you know that, don't you?" she said, her voice sounding far calmer than she felt. "We have to get up to speed first, leave this system behind. That'll take several days."

He gave a long drawn out hiss. "How many?"

"Three days till we can jump, then to get where you want to

go, about six weeks, three for each jump." As she said it, her heart sank. There was no way he could survive without food for that long.

This time, the sound he made was an ominous low rumble. "Show me navigation! Plot course, then fix panel!"

After she'd laid in the course for their jump point, he'd marched her to the rearmost cargo bay to fetch the tools necessary to fix the panel he'd blasted. There he'd seen the aircar, and the ceiling hatch above it. Once he'd realized there was a laser turret up there, he'd demanded a tour of the rest of the *Mara*. Back on the bridge, he'd made her reprogram the air locks and irises so he could enter his own combinations. Because it was adjacent to the bridge, he'd also claimed her cabin for his own use.

Since she'd taken the electronic tools already, she'd had to make do with an assortment of what remained in the tool locker.

Once she'd taken the cover plate off, it was obvious even to him that it was beyond repair.

"What this do?" he'd demanded, pointing to the copilot's controls.

"Duplicates some of my controls like maneuver jets, nav, sensors, and gunnery," she'd replied, fixing the panel back together again.

"Communications?"

"No."

"Show me," he'd demanded, hauling her over to take the seat he'd been in. That was when she saw that though he was clawed like her, his claws were nonretractable and too big to use the recessed Sholan controls. He couldn't pilot the ship alone!

When she was finished, he took her to the passenger cabin and locked her in.

"Hey!" she yelled, hammering at the door. "You can't leave me here! Come back!" She didn't want him left alone with the younglings at any cost. Fear for them coursed through her, making her hammer even louder at the door. "I need the younglings! Bring them to me! I need their help to pilot the ship in jump!" she yelled, beating on the door with the sides of her hands till they hurt. "Dammit, can you hear me?"

The door suddenly slid open, almost catapulting her out into the corridor. She grabbed the doorframe barely in time. First

Kate, then a protesting Taynar was thrust into the cabin with her, and the door was sealed again.

"Thank Vartra you're all right. What's he doing?" she asked.

"Treating us like animals," said Taynar disgustedly, straightening his tunic. "What kind of military pilot are you, allowing this to happen to us? He just walked onto this ship without any checks by you. . . ."

Jeedah snarled, her ears lying sideward in anger as she grasped hold of the front of his tunic, pulling him toward her until their noses touched. "Understand this, brat, I am the Captain on this ship. That's one step below the God Vartra to you, and you better remember it!" As he started to object and pluck at her fist, she shook him hard and continued.

"Just what kind of Telepath are *you* that you didn't sense an alien presence at the landing pad, eh? A friend of mine got killed, in all probability protecting your worthless hide! You have no idea what we are dealing with here. This alien is not just a member of another species, he's one of a race of people who destroyed all life on two of our three colonies, who want to wipe us out totally! They're stronger and faster than us, and he's got us trapped here, with him, for the next six weeks. And guess what else you don't know, brat? There's nothing on board he can eat!" With that, she flung him aside. "This is your wake-up call, Taynar," she said as he staggered to the nearest chair and sat down. "You are going to have to pull your weight this time, or none of us will survive!"

"What do you mean there's nothing on board for him to eat? I thought there was plenty of food." Kate's face was ashen.

"He eats freshly killed raw meat," said Jeedah, pronouncing each word carefully. Time to be hard with them. "We have some frozen meat, but it isn't fresh enough for the likes of him. He likes it still bleeding."

"God help us," whispered Kate, ashen-faced as she reached for the bed behind her and sat down. "What can we do?"

"Stop trying to scare us, Captain," said Taynar, ears flat with fear and tail hanging almost to the ground. "You've made your point."

"I'm not trying to frighten you," she said quietly. "I'm in deadly earnest."

"That's why you need him to see us as indispensable to you, isn't it?" said Kate. "So he won't . . ." Her voice trailed off into silence.

"So he won't kill one of us for food," said Jeedah bluntly. "Yes."

"What can we do?" asked Taynar, his voice very subdued.

"For a start, you can work with Kate, teach her how to be a Telepath, and see if you can pick up anything from the Valtegan."

He nodded. "Anything else?"

"Yes," she said, walking over to the food dispenser to the left of the door and programming in a mug of coffee. She hated being that hard even on Taynar, but they had to know what they were up against. "I'm going to have to teach you both how to pilot this ship. Don't, whatever you do, let on to him how much you know in case he decides I'm expendable, you got that?"

"Yes, Jeedah."

"Good. Now get yourselves a drink and maybe something to eat," she said, taking her mug over to the desk. As she sat down, she felt the hardness of the wrench against her side and looked around for a place to conceal it.

"Jeedah, I just remembered something," said Kate hesitantly. "He brought a kind of homemade cage on board with him. It had six of the small, rabbitlike creatures in it."

Jeedah instantly gave the young female her full attention. "He did?"

Kate nodded. "Do you think, perhaps, he captured them as food?" Hope was etched in every line of her face and body.

Jeedah's mouth dropped in a Sholan grin, which she quickly changed to a wide, Human style one that just exposed her teeth. "I'm sure he did. We've got several days' grace then, thank Vartra." Her mind raced as she reassessed their situation. There was cereal in the kitchen—they didn't need it, but the critters she knew could live on it if the Valtegan hadn't brought enough food for them.

"It doesn't change the danger we're in, Kate, but it does mean it isn't as imminent as I'd feared." If only she—no, *they*—could overpower him and take back control of the *Mara* before his food ran out . . . She went back to finding a good hiding place for the wrench.

Half an hour later, the door slid open. The Valtegan, now dressed only in scuffed and dirty green fatigues, filled the doorway. His wide V-shaped mouth was open in anger, displaying rows of tiny, pointed teeth, and his crest was fully raised.

"You hide tools as weapons. You think to kill me!" he hissed, striding toward Taynar, who was nearest. Using only one hand, he plucked him off the bed by the throat, holding him so his feet dangled a few inches from the ground. "For this, I punish you. Next time, one dies!"

"No!" yelled Jeedah, leaping toward him and grabbing at his arm. "Leave him! I'm the Captain, I'm the one to blame!"

With only a glance at her, he shook her off and landed a flat-handed blow on the youth's back. Taynar yowled in pain and shock as he squirmed in the alien's grasp, trying to break free.

"Yours is responsibility for his beating," he hissed, raising his hand again.

Jeedah scrambled to her feet, trying to get between him and Taynar. "He's a Telepath, mind-linked to the female!" she said, ducking as his hand changed direction toward her.

He hesitated.

"You hurt him, she feels it, too." Her words were tumbling out as she tried to think of anything that could help Taynar. "They're only children. Hit me if you must, but not them."

Laughing, he thrust her aside with more force this time so that she went tumbling onto the far bed. "Then the lesson learned well by all," he said, raising half a dozen blows on Taynar while he watched Kate shriek in pain as well. Finally, he let the sobbing youth drop to the ground and watched impassively as Jeedah tried to comfort them both.

"You bastard," she said, her voice low with anger and hate as she looked up at him. "There was no need to do this to them."

"Now you not forget who in charge," he said. "I, General Chokkuh, am. Not you." He left, sealing and locking the door again.

Day 3

Jeedah sat in the corner of the lounge watching the two younglings finish their meal. She felt a wave of sympathy come over her for the young Human. For Kate to suddenly find herself physically and mentally linked to a young Sholan male—and one as selfish and thoughtless as Taynar—then to become a kidnap victim all within the space of two weeks was unfair. Then there had been the beating which both of them had suffered. At least they had emerged from it with only a few bruises.

"It's going to be all right, Kate," she said, widening her mouth in what she hoped was a nonthreatening smile as Kate left the table to join her. "All we have to do is play along with him for now. At least he took the cereal we left out for his rabbits."

"Don't tell me you believe that once we've taken him where he wants, he'll let us go, because you don't believe it any more than I do," the girl said quietly. "He's going to take us with him, isn't he?"

Jeedah hesitated only a moment. "Yes, I'm afraid he is. He'll want to hand over Taynar and me for questioning, and you because of your link to Taynar."

"So what's important here? Stopping him—or escaping?"

The young face in front of her was very pale, her gray eyes enormous, but Kate regarded Jeedah steadily.

"Hey, we're not concerned yet, Kate," she said, patting her hand. "We'll get a chance at him soon, believe me."

"When, and how? He barricades himself on the bridge when you're off duty, and the few times he's taken a break, he does the same in your cabin."

"I know that even Valtegans must need more sleep than he's taking," Jeedah said, lowering her voice. "Then there's the lack of food. Have you ever seen him try our food? I haven't. So every day that passes, he's growing weaker."

"Is there anything we can do?"

Jeedah tried not to look over at Taynar. "Just keep your Leska out of his way. He may not be as afraid of us as the others were, but he still doesn't like it when Taynar and I are in the same room as him. And try to sense his thoughts. How's the training with Taynar going? From what I understand, because your minds merge, everything he knows, you know, which means you've got all his training locked away inside your mind somewhere. It's just a matter of knowing where to look. When we had the language transfers, we could understand what you said, but we had to practice to be able to speak it."

Kate nodded. "That's right. It's going pretty well, but sometimes Taynar isn't quite as patient as he could be."

Jeedah grinned. "Then pull rank on him—remind him you're a female! Shola is a matriarchy, you know, we just don't make a point of reminding the males of it too often. Learning as much as you can about your Talent will help us, believe me!"

Kate smiled, her face losing some of its pallor now that she could see there were still several options open to them. Impulsively, Jeedah put her arm around Kate's shoulder. "You'll see to those things and I'll work out some kind of plan."

Entering Jump was a nightmare. The view ports had been sealed to prevent the visual distortions outside from making them nauseous. And they were flying dumb, without a voice to warn Chemerian space when they did materialize at the other end. The danger of emerging in the same space as another ship was high. If that happened, they would all die. At least that was the best part of three weeks in the future.

"What's it look like out there?" Kate asked.

"I don't know, and believe me, I don't want to!" said Jeedah.

The *Mara* couldn't be left to navigate its way automatically through jump space, it had to be monitored, and for that, she'd told the Valtegan she would need Taynar's help.

"Of course I know nothing about couriers," he said contemptuously. "I'm a Telepath, not a pilot!"

"You've flown aircars."

"Of course!"

Aware of the silent figure of General Chokkuh constantly watching them from the sidelines, Jeedah grasped Taynar firmly by the scruff and pushed him hard into the copilot's seat. "Then sit down and learn!" she snarled. "It's time for you to get your hands dirty, brat!" So far, he'd been behaving himself, but every now and then he reverted to his old self.

Approbation had come from an unexpected quarter, namely Chokkuh, their Valtegan captor. He knew as well as she that the two of them were not enough to cover the ship's safe passage through jump.

"You help," Chokkuh ordered, backing into the lounge area. "Or maybe I amuse myself with your mate!"

Taynar nearly exploded with rage, but Jeedah still had him firmly by the scruff. She leaned forward, her mouth inches from his ear.

"Calm down, Taynar," she growled. "Our Valtegan's not slow. He's seen for himself that you're linked to Kate, and he's not about to do anything too drastic. You're reacting exactly the way he wants you to!"

"If he dares put his filthy aliens hands on her . . ."

"Alien hands, Taynar?" Her voice was purposely mocking. "And just what do you think you are, considering she's a Human?" She watched his ears flatten backward in consternation as he tried to squirm in her grip.

Tightening her hold until her claws began to penetrate his skin, she hissed, "The Valtegans had Human females in their pleasure cities on Keiss, Taynar. They spied on the Valtegans for the guerrillas. She'd survive the experience. It wouldn't be pleasant for her—or you, but then you believe in letting the females do the dirty work, don't you?"

"Not like that, Jeedah! I would never let anything like that happen to her!" he whimpered. "I care about her, honestly I do!"

She released him, sickened with herself for what she was having to become. "Then do what you're told and learn to fly the *Mara*," she snarled, flinging herself into the seat beside him. "Your survival could depend on this!"

He looked over at her, obviously still scared. "Shouldn't we check on Kate first?"

Jeedah gave a snort of amusement. "She's your Leska, Taynar! Are you telling me you wouldn't know if Chokkuh tried to rape her?"

Taynar seemed to shrink into the seat. "What do you want me to do first?" he asked quietly.

"Tell Kate to go to your room and lock herself in."

Day 18

Every day, Jeedah had watched Chokkuh like the predator she was, gauging his weakness, checking the dispenser after his shifts to see if he'd eaten any of their food yet, and making sure she saw his rabbit cage as he left the bridge carrying it when they changed shifts. He hadn't tried their food, and now he was down to the last rabbit. In fact, it had been alone in the cage for the last four days.

She couldn't understand how he kept going. They were running out of time; she'd have to strike soon. In the lining of her jacket, she'd managed to conceal a screwdriver. It would make a good dagger—if she got the opportunity to use it. She'd been waiting for the right moment, when he was weak enough for her to have a chance against his superior speed and strength, but so far, there hadn't been one.

Then toward the end of the week, she'd come on duty to find that the food and drink dispenser on the bridge had been ripped out of the bulkhead, its partly chewed contents strewn across the room.

"Get hatchling female to clean mess," Chokkuh said, pushing himself to his feet and walking toward where his rabbit cage lay.

She grasped him by the arm as he went past.

He turned on her, his teeth bared in a snarl, hand reaching for her throat.

Letting him go, she hastily sidestepped him. "Don't damage the dispenser next door," she said, backing up against the bulkhead. "If you do, we can't eat either; then we all die. You understand that?"

His eyes narrowed as he looked at her. "Your food stinks! Is spoiled . . . dead! Only dirt grubbers like you would eat that . . . that . . . carrion!" He stared at her for a moment, then obviously making up his mind, he grabbed her arm, jerking her toward him and swinging her around so he had her arm locked behind her back and she was in front of him.

Picking up the cage, he forced her through the door into the lounge. Kate and Taynar were huddled by the aft door. Shoving Jeedah into the room, he approached the table and put the cage down in the center.

Immediately Taynar stepped in front of Kate, tail swaying as he glared at Chokkuh.

Jeedah moved slowly toward the younglings, feeling a tiny hot trickle of blood running down her arm. She rubbed at it, trying to stem the blood. It was only a shallow cut, but it wouldn't stop bleeding.

Chokkuh grinned toothily at them, raising his hand to look at his bloodstained claw. His tongue flicked out and he licked it clean with such obvious pleasure that it made even Jeedah shiver.

"Tastes good." He exposed his double rows of needle-sharp teeth in a smile that was far from pleasant. "You are safe—for now," he hissed, turning his attention to the cage. Opening it, he reached for the terrified rabbit. Holding it up, he let it chitter and squeak as it squirmed to get free.

Jeedah watched his eyes narrow and his nostril slits flare briefly, then in one fluid move, he grasped the rabbit's head in his other hand and twisted. The snap of its spine breaking filled the small room.

As Kate gasped, Chokkuh ripped off the head, closing his lips over the neck and beginning to suck noisily as the rabbit's last heartbeats pumped the lifeblood into his mouth.

Taynar's ears flattened into invisibility and with a strangled cry of fear and disgust, he staggered backward into Kate.

Her stomach turning over, Jeedah watched in silence as Chokkuh, the blood now drained from the rabbit, proceeded to dismember it and eat each limb messily, fur, bones and all. His sparse meal over, he licked his claws clean with fastidious care.

The sudden rush of protein into his system had dilated his pupils until his eyes resembled glowing black orbs. He looked at Kate and Taynar, clinging in terror to each other, then at Jeedah.

"Keep your distance. You may be my next meal, a piece at a time," he said, his voice slightly slurred. Turning, he slowly walked back to the bridge.

Chokkuh locked the lounge door behind him, then taking the Captain's position at the controls, slumped back in the seat. His little piece of theater had been necessary: because of hunger and the lack of the calming la'quo plant in his diet over the months he'd been in hiding on that accursed world, he was near to losing his last shreds of self-control. The Sholan Captain didn't realize how close she had come to death when she'd touched him. He needed her alive, not only because she was the only capable pilot—his skills were negligible—but because his people needed her for questioning. As for the hatchlings—he needed them so they could be studied and this strange interspecies mind link understood, and used to the Valtegans' advantage against both the Sholans and Humans if possible.

He sighed, resting his chin on his hand as he leaned on the console. Over three more weeks to go. If only he'd had access to the la'quo plant which suppressed the violence inherent in his warrior genes and allowed him to utilize his intellectual caste heritage—but it had been over a year since he'd had any; if only he'd been able to eat their cooked food—but the meat had been dead too long for the necessary enzymes he needed to be present.

He sighed again. Life since the Sholan starship had arrived had been full of if onlys for him. He'd been completely serious when he'd told them to keep their distance lest his hunger force him to . . . He stopped the thought. Such a barbaric act was beneath his honor and dignity, but in as little as four days, he'd no longer have any choice in the matter.

Day 21

Thoughtfully, Jeedah went over to check the console and their flight path. They were closer than she'd realized to emergence. They'd be there by mid-shift.

Chokkuh had definitely reached his critical point. His skin had been almost devoid of color for the last two days. Through its faint transparency, she could see the network of his veins. His eyes were bloodshot, and he'd definitely slowed down compared to even a couple of days ago when she'd told him not to touch their food dispenser. Now, if ever, was the time to make a bid for freedom—before he reached the same conclusion she had.

A shudder ran through her as she checked the control boards. Everything was green. It was time to go for Kate and Taynar.

Her plan was simple. When they emerged from jump—assuming of course they didn't try to emerge in the same space as some other object—and they'd lost enough speed for her to verify their position, she'd start dumping fuel. The transition from jump to normal space was bound to wake the Valtegan, and when he came to the bridge, she'd be waiting behind the door. Taynar would have to sit in her Captain's seat so Chokkuh would think it was her, but she had to be the one to take the main risk. If either Taynar or Kate got injured, it would disable them both. What one experienced, so did the other: kill one and both died, that was the downside of the Leska link.

Jeedah counted down the seconds to emergence, Taynar sitting in as copilot. As the image that represented them coincided with their marker, she disengaged the jump drive. The craft bucked once and began to vibrate as they hit normal space. The breaking engines cut in, the sound of them deafening in the small craft. The *Mara* seemed to shudder along the whole of her length, then steadied as she began to slow.

Flicking down the view shields, she did a quick visual scan. Ahead of them was the unmistakable primary of the Chemerian home world.

"Kate says he's on his way," said Taynar.

"Damn!" She hit the emergency fuel release once, twice. Nothing happened. No time to worry about it now. "Take over," she said, thumping the release on her safety belt and heading for the door to the lounge.

Taynar fumbled with his belt, finally managing to get himself free.

As she took up her position, Taynar turned around, yelling, "Wait! He's got Kate!"

The door slid open and the Valtegan edged in, holding Kate firmly in front of him. "Return to seat, Captain. I know your plan. Fuel safe, and we near second jump point."

"Let her go, Chokkuh," Jeedah said harshly. "Harm her and you lose the male, too, you know that."

"Maybe worth it. All I need is one Sholan."

Then everything began to happen at once. Kate's mouth closed on the Valtegan's arm and she bit down hard. Chokkuh shrieked in pain, turning his full attention on the source of his injury. Seeing her chance, Jeedah rushed him, screwdriver at the ready.

Kate was plucked free and thrown to one side as he turned to meet the greater threat. All Jeedah felt was a sharp pain across her chest and belly before she hit the wall. She heard a terrible high-pitched scream, then all went silent.

It hurt to breathe . . . Gods, but it *really* hurt! The world swam dizzily in front of her, then Taynar was bending over her, his hand gently touching her face.

"Jeedah . . ." He dropped the rifle. "I finished him. He's dead. I'm sorry . . . if I hadn't called out . . . If I hadn't been slowed by what he did to Kate . . ."

She could see tears coursing through the short pelt that covered his cheeks. Her arm felt like lead as she tried to raise it to touch his hand. He reached down and took hers instead.

"Not your fault, cub. We got him, that's what matters," she murmured, then stopped as coughs racked her, each one a fresh agony lancing through her chest. "Tell Dyaf he owes me a meal. You and Kate, you collect, huh? Gotta pay debts, right? He won't rest easy knowing he owes me." She could hardly hear her own voice now, and she felt cold, so very cold.

"We'll collect, I promise," he said quietly, pressing her hand to his lips, trying to comfort her as he watched her eyes flicker and begin to close.

He waited until her hand relaxed and slipped free of his before he stood up.

"Jeedah?" Kate whispered from the other side of the bridge where she lay.

"She's gone," he said, voice breaking as he bent down to take the ID tags from round his Captain's neck. "Chokkuh's dead, too." He straightened up and taking a deep breath, went over to where his Leska was lying.

"It's nothing. I'm just bruised," she said shakily as he helped her to her feet.

He held her close for a moment, thanking all the Gods of Shola that she was safe, and wishing with all his heart that Jeedah was, too.

Kate began to sob, her horror and distress filling his mind. Pushing his own fears aside, he sent calming thoughts to her and gently stroked her head, making small noises of encouragement. It was up to him now to be strong for both of them.

"Kate, we'll mourn her later," he said quietly. "We need to slow the *Mara* down and get a signal out to the Chemerian space station as soon as possible, just as Jeedah planned."

He felt her nod her head, then she pulled back from him to

scrub at her eyes. "I can manage," she said, her voice still trembling.

He gave her one last hug, then headed over to the console, hesitating a moment before taking the Captain's seat.

Kate limped over and took the copilot's position. "Can you manage it?"

"Jeedah made sure I could," he said, his hands flying over the instruments as he applied the braking engines again and began steering the courier toward the Chemerian system. "Key in the code for the nav maps, please, Kate. I need to know exactly where the satellite station is. Jeedah said there was an approach path logged in the data banks. You send out the signal she prepared for us."

Epilogue.

Dyaf was sitting in the only quiet corner of the passenger lounge at Chagda Station, waiting for the shuttle down to Shola. He'd been nursing the same mug of c'shar for the last half hour now because he didn't feel up to pushing through the crowd at the bar to order another. It was stone cold, but it didn't matter. Nothing much mattered since he'd heard of Jeedah's death.

"Excuse me, Lieutenant Dyaf, may we join you?"

He looked up to see Taynar Arrazo and his Leska, Kate.

He sighed inwardly. If only he hadn't asked her to do that run . . . "I'm afraid I don't really feel like company just now, Taynar. I don't mean to be inhospitable, but . . ."

"We have something for you," said Kate, sliding onto the seat opposite him. She held a small packet out to him. "I know Jeedah would have wanted you to have these."

He took it from her, turning it over before opening it. Jeedah's ID tags and chain spilled into his hand.

"She asked me to tell you that you owed her a meal and we should collect," said Taynar quietly, sitting down beside him. "Said you'd not rest easy until you'd paid her."

Dyaf looked at the tags one by one. "I didn't realize she still wore this one," he said, his voice deepening with emotions he suddenly found hard to control. He rubbed his fingers over the engraved surface. "I got it for her last year, when we decided to stay with each other." He looked up at the two younglings, blinking rapidly to prevent his tears from spilling over. "She told you to collect, did she? Did she tell you why?"

Taynar's mouth opened in a small grin. "She told Kate."

"Because you gave her the job of taking us to Shola," said Kate. "It wasn't your fault she was killed, Lieutenant. If you'd sent Captain Rhokuul as you'd first intended, we'd likely be in the hands of the Valtegans now. Jeedah knew what was at stake. We all did. She wanted you to pay her debt because she knew that then you wouldn't feel responsible for her death."

"We've a private shuttle waiting if you'd honor us with your company," said Taynar.

"A private shuttle?" Dyaf raised an eye ridge. "Didn't know your family went in for such things."

"They don't. In fact, they aren't that impressed with me since I met Kate," said Taynar. "We belong to the En'Shalla Clan now, on the Aldatan estate, along with the other mixed Leska pairs like us."

Dyaf looked at Jeedah's tags again, not sure what he should do. He'd avoided any company that wasn't related to his job on the *Khalossa* since he'd heard of Jeedah's death, but he found himself wanting to go with the younglings. They were the last link to his lost love. When Kate's hand closed on his, he jumped.

"Would you like me to fasten the chain around your neck for you, Lieutenant?" she asked gently. "I am so sorry for your loss. We miss Jeedah, too. She came to mean a lot to us."

He found himself nodding, and handing the chain back to the young Human female. He looked at Taynar as she leaned forward to fasten it about his neck. This was not the petulant cub he'd known on the *Khalossa*. He'd changed.

"So where are we going?" he heard himself say as he felt the comforting warmth of the tags against his pelt. "The Shanagi Palace restaurant?" He got to his feet and waited for them to rise.

"It's overrated," said Taynar, getting up. "We chose a small restaurant in Jeedah's hometown because her family said they'd like to meet you, too."

"I don't think," he began, then stopped as Kate slipped her arm through his.

"They've asked us to bring you," she said quietly. "But first we three will celebrate Jeedah's life."

Julie E. Czerneda

Julie Czerneda is an extremely patient woman. Not only did she herself know where she wanted to be published, but fellow author Josepha Sherman had told her that DAW was the perfect home for her. So Julie sent in a manuscript and waited for it to wend its way through the teetering piles of manuscripts that often make finding my desk a nearly impossible task. Periodically she would call to make sure her manuscript was still there, and I would take a quick look and a quick skim of the beginning, and tell her that it was indeed there, and that what I had read seemed interesting, and I hoped I'd have a chance to read the entire manuscript soon. Finally, because Julie was so nice and so patient, and because the part I had looked at really did seem interesting, I decided to ignore all the pressing things I had to get to Production for a day, and read Julie's manuscript.

Needless to say, Julie's patience was duly rewarded. My memories of the phone call to tell her that I was going to buy *A Thousand Words for Stranger* are very different from Julie's. Someday, if you ask her nicely, she'll tell you her version of the conversation.

A Thousand Words for Stranger proved to be merely the start of a prolific career for Julie as a science fiction writer. Since its publication in October, 1997, Julie has written two other novels in the *Trade Pact Universe* series, two novels in the *Web Shifters* series, and *In the Company of Others.*

"Prism" is a tale about Esen, the main protagonist in the *Web Shifters* novels, which is especially fitting as Julie is currently at work on the third volume in that series.

—SG

PRISM
Julie E. Czerneda

I MAGINE being a student not for ten orbits of a sun, or thirty, but over two hundred such journeys. Granted, I spent the first few decades doing what any newborn Lanivarian would do: eating, metabolizing, differentiating, growing, eating, metabolizing, differentiating, growing . . . I remember it as a time of restlessness, of an awareness I was more, but unable to express this other than to whimper and chew.

The day did arrive when I opened my mouth and something intelligible came out. I distinctly remember this something—web-beings being possessed of perfect memory—as a clear and succinct request for more jamble grapes. My birth-mother, Ansky, remembers it as an adorably incoherent babble that nonetheless signaled I was ready for the next phase of my existence. So she took me to Ersh, the Senior Assimilator and Eldest of our Web, who promptly grabbed me by the scruff of the neck and tossed me off her mountain.

While horrifying to any real Lanivarian mother—and likely to any intelligent species with parental care—this was Ersh being efficient. I was thus encouraged to cycle into my web-self for the first time. It was that, or be shattered on a rock seven hundred and thirteen meters below. Instinct, as Ersh rather blithely assumed, won, and I landed on the surface of Picco's Moon as a small, intensely blue, blob of web-mass. A somewhat flattened blob, but unharmed.

Unharmed, but I recalled being overwhelmed with foreign sensations as my universe widened along every imaginable axis. I floundered to make some sense of it all, until, suddenly, everything became *right*. I knew without being told this was my true self, that there was nothing unusual in losing touch, sound, sight, and smell while feeling the spin of stars and atoms, hearing harmony in the competing gravities of Picco and her Moon, seeing the structure of matter, and being perfectly able to distinguish what was appetizing from what was not.

Appetite. I formed a mouth, small and with only one sharp edge, then began scanning my new universe for something to bite. *There!*

Not knowing what it was, I ripped a mouthful from the edible mass so conveniently close.

Ersh-taste!

Ideas, not just nutrients, flooded my consciousness, new and nauseatingly complex. *Ersh-memory.* Even as I hastily oozed myself into the nearest dark and safe-looking crevice, I gained a word for what was happening to me. *Assimilation.* This was how web-beings exchanged information—by exchanging the memories stored within their flesh. *Our flesh.*

Exchange? I was mulling that over when a sharp, unexpected pain let me know I'd paid my price for the knowledge.

My studies had officially begun.

What followed were times of wonder and the expansion of my horizons . . . Okay, what really followed were centuries of always being the last to assimilate anything and being convinced this was a plot to keep me stuck with one of my Elders at all times. In retrospect, it was probably more difficult for them. The ancient, wise beings who formed the Web of Ersh had made plans for their lives and research stretching over millennia and, as they routinely assured me, I hadn't been so much as imagined in any of them.

Maybe in Ansky's. Ansky's outstanding enthusiasm about interacting with the locals meant I wasn't her first offspring—just the first, and only, to taste of web-mass. The rest grew up clutched to what I fondly imagined were the loving teats, bosoms, or corresponding body parts of their respective species.

I was tossed off a mountain to prove I belonged here, with Ersh and whomever else of my Web happened to be in attendance. While they could have cycled into more nurturing species—the ability to manipulate our mass into that of other intelligent species being a key survival trait of my kind—I'm quite sure it didn't occur to any of them. I was not only Ansky's first, I was a first for the Web as well, having been born rather than split from Ersh's own flesh. This was a distinction that made at least some of my web-kin very uneasy. Mind you, they'd been virtually untouched by change since the Human species discovered feet, so my arrival came as something of a shock. Ansky was firmly reminded to be more careful in the future. Her Web, Ersh pronounced sternly, was large enough.

We were six: Ersh, Ansky, Lesy, Mixs, Skalet, and me, Esenalit-Quar—Esen for short, Es in a hurry. Six who shared flesh and memories. Six given a goal and purpose in life by Ersh: to be a living repository of the biology and culture of all other, tragically short-lived intelligent species. It was an endless, grueling task that took years of living in secret on each world, ingesting and assimilating the biology of each ephemeral form, learning languages, arts, histories, beliefs, and sciences, all while traveling the limits of known space.

Not that I was ever allowed to go.

Ersh had dictated I was to stay on Picco's Moon until I was ready. *Ready?* I understood waiting until my body grew into its full web-size. After all, mass had to be considered when cycling into another form. It was wasteful, if entertaining, to gorge myself simply to cycle into something larger, then have to shed the excess as water anyway upon returning to web-form. Then there was the issue of learning to hold another form. The others presumed my staying Lanivarian from birth till impact meant I'd be able to distort my web-mass into any other I'd assimilated. They were wrong. While I could immediately return to my birth-form for a moment or two, after all this time, I still couldn't hold other forms for any duration. I might have done so faster, had Ersh chosen to teach me what I needed to know—and the others refrained from terrifying hints I might explode if not careful—but Ersh had definite ideas of what and how I was to learn.

Which was the real reason I still wasn't "ready" after two hundred years. Ersh had insisted I be taught—by the others, as well as herself. Since this teaching could not be done by assimilation alone, and she found fault with almost everything I did learn—not surprising, considering I had four teachers who'd never taught before—"ready" seemed unlikely to occur within even a web-being's almost endless lifespan. I was stuck on Ersh's rock, safe and utterly bored.

It would have been nice if it had stayed that way.

*"**E**SEN!"*

My present ears were tall enough to extend past the top of the boulder sheltering the rest of me. I swiveled them slightly to capture more nuance from the echoes ricocheting after that latest bellow from the window. It was important to gauge when Ersh was about to pass exasperation and head for all-out fury, if I wanted to avoid something thoroughly unpleasant in the way of consequences. The Eldest did occasionally give up before losing her temper. *Twice, maybe.*

"Are you going to answer, 'tween, or should I?" a velvet-coated voice from behind inquired, driving my ears flat against my skull.

Skalet? I didn't bother twisting my long snout around to glare at her, too busy quelling this body's instinct to run from threats. I wasn't in any danger, except from heart palpitations at Skalet's bizarre sense of humor. She'd approached from downwind, naturally, having firsthand knowledge of my current form's sense of smell. Providing such unpleasant surprises was simply this web-kin's favorite game at my expense and quite the feat this time, considering she was supposed to be half the quadrant away.

However, Skalet was probably preparing to expose my hiding place to Ersh—her other favorite pastime. "I was just getting up," I told her, attempting to make this more casual than sullen. Skalet had no patience for what she called my "ephemeral moods."

When I finally looked at her, it was to affirm the voice matched the form I'd expected. I may have been the only "born" web-being, but that didn't mean the others were identical. Far from it. Even in web-form, they were distinct individuals, sending tastes as unique as themselves into the air, though this was usually only when they were sharing memories with one another. Revealing web-form to aliens was strictly forbidden, precaution as well as protection.

So normally, they chose another form, picked, my Elders informed me, for its appropriateness as camouflage and its convenience when using non-Web technology. I was reasonably sure their choices had more to do with personal preference, since if it was convenience alone, they'd all be Dodecian and have arms to spare—with a brain able to control all of them at once. Not that I'd been Dodecian any longer than it took to realize successful coordination required a certain level of maturity as well as a room without fragile objects.

Skalet managed to cause me enough grief with her present brain. She stood too close for comfort, straight and tall on two legs, dressed in a chrome-on-black uniform she likely considered subtle but which reflected glints of Picco's orange-stained light with each disapproving breath. *Kraal.* I replayed a portion of memory. Human subspecies. Not biologically distinct, though heading in that direction. Culturally so, definitely, with a closed society built around an elaborate internal hierarchy of family, clan, and tribe allegiance. New from her last trip was a tattoo from throat to behind her left ear marking a particular affiliation; she'd made sure to braid her thick hair to expose every line. I didn't bother reading it.

My obedient rise to my hindlegs produced the expected and ominous silence from the window and lit a triumphant gleam in Skalet's Human eyes. "What did you do this time, Youngest?" she asked as we walked together up the slope to Ersh's cliffside home. As we did, I could see Skalet's personal shuttle sitting on the landing pad. Shuttles to and from the shipcity on the other side of Picco's Moon were the only rapid means of travel across the tortured landscape. The native intelligent species, Tumblers, preferred to migrate slowly along the jagged valley floors, stopping for conversations that could last months. They had a time sense on a par with Ersh's, which I'd long ago decided was why she was usually a Tumbler herself. *Another difference between us.*

"Nothing," I said, quite truthfully. I was supposed to have finished repotting the duras seedlings in Ersh's greenhouse this morning, making that "nothing" undoubtedly the cause of the bellowing. I hated plants. They stank when healthy and reeked when ill. And dirt. I hated dirt, too. Dry sand I quite liked. But no, plants insisted on wet dirt that stuck to my paws and got in my sensitive nose. It hadn't taken more than the thought of coming outside to catch the monthly Eclipse, an event I always missed because of some task or other Ersh invented, to make me abandon the trays.

"Ah," Skalet replied, as if my answer was more than sufficient. "Neither did I," she said more quietly, her steps slowing as if in thought. "Are the others here yet?"

"What others?" I asked. "I didn't know you were coming until now. Are the rest on the way?" My tail gave a treacherous sideways drift before I could stop it, tail-wagging being among those childish things I was supposed to be long past. Lesy tended to bring presents. To be honest, any of the web-kin did, in the form of knowledge to be shared—even Skalet, though hers often tasted more of conflict and politics than wonder. Ersh sorted it all for me first, of course, as Senior Assimilator, but I could always tell the source.

"That's for Ersh to tell us," Skalet said brusquely, our steps having reached the point of our approach everyone knew marked where Ersh's sensitive Tumbler hearing must be taken into account.

*E*rsh *had told us, all right.* I gingerly pushed the seedling into the revoltingly damp dirt with one extended toe. My Lanivarian hands were adept at such fine maneuvers, if a misery to clean afterward. My ears were cocked back, toward the kitchen, straining to catch the mutterings of an argument which had lasted longer than I'd thought possible.

No one countered Ersh's wishes. *Except me.* But that was something my web-kin had come to expect. They all knew I'd give in, come home, do the job, and grovel appropriately. It was unthinkable to imagine otherwise, even for me at my most rebellious. Ersh was the center of our Web. Her word was Law.

Until today, when she'd stated her latest wish and Skalet had tried to refuse.

Another seedling went in, stubbornly crooked until I pressed the dirt to one side firmly with my thumb; I couldn't help humming happily to myself. Although it delayed supper and spoke volumes about my immaturity, the novelty of someone else taking the brunt of Ersh's ire was extraordinarily pleasant—not to mention I was on Skalet's side.

I most definitely didn't want her staying with me while Ersh left home for the first time in my memory.

That this arrangement was designed to punish both of us with Ersh's famed economy of effort was not lost on me, but what Skalet could have done to deserve it I didn't know. Nor wanted to.

Ersh should have told me.

"**I**'ve had enough of you."

My stylo halted its dive at the star chart and I peered up hopefully. "We're done for the day?" I asked.

A violent wave and: "Ssssh."

Skalet was using the com system. Again. As she had most of the morning since Ersh departed—in Skalet's own shuttle, something she'd known better than to protest.

I sighed and reapplied myself to the present lesson. Another three-dimensional strategy calculation, probably containing some unlikely ambush. Ersh must have removed more than usual from Skalet's latest memories of the Kraal before sharing them with me, for this made less sense to me than the last lesson.

Regardless, it would be my fault, I sighed once more, but to myself. Skalet was brilliant and, as a Kraal, had earned considerable acclaim within her chosen species as a strategist. Not an accomplishment she flaunted, given Ersh's obsession with keeping our natures and activities hidden, but there were no secrets in the Web. Well, technically there were any number of secrets held within Ersh's teardrop blue web-mass—most being kept from me—but none of us had that ability. And, when it suited her, or more truthfully, when Ersh was within earshot, Skalet could be a patient and interesting teacher. Otherwise, as now, she was maddeningly obscure yet somehow convinced I deliberately avoided what she saw as the clear, simple path to the right answer in order to waste her time.

Hardly. I was every bit as anxious to have this lesson done and be outside where I could observe the Eclipse. I wrinkled my snout at the problem before me, wondering if accidentally drooling on the plas sheet might somehow ruin it.

Skalet continued talking urgently into the com. "Listen, Uriel. Just bring it down here instead of where we arranged. That's the only change."

Maybe it was the lesson, with its layers of move and counter-move, but I grew suddenly curious about Skalet's conversation with this mysterious "Uriel."

Of course, it's hard to be subtle with ears like mine. "Esen," Skalet said sharply, "if you can't concentrate on your work, go outside for a while."

Perversely, now that she told me to do what I'd wanted to do,

I no longer wanted to do it. I glumly suspected this irrational reversal was another of those indications I wasn't ready to assume an adult's role within the Web. I opened my mouth to protest, then closed it. Skalet had leaned back against the com unit, watching me with the obvious intention of not saying another word in my presence.

So I left.

Picco was a gas giant, her immense curve dominating a quarter of the horizon, reflecting, during her day, a vile combination of orange and purple over the landscape of her hapless Moon. During her night, Picco's silhouette occluded a chunk of the starry sky—the so-called Void. Early Tumbler civilizations had populated the Void with invisible demons. The belief continued to influence their behavior, so that modern Tumblers had a hearty dislike of moving about in the dark. As Ersh pointed out, this was a survival characteristic, given the fragile nature of an adult Tumbler's crystalline structure and the difficulty in finding any level ground on their home sphere. *Beliefs have value,* I could hear her repeating endlessly, *if not always that assumed by the believer.*

Picco's Moon did spin, luckily for those of us interested in a broader array of color, but with aggravating slowness. Once a moon week, Ersh's mountain faced away from Picco to bathe in the light of the system's star. This arrangement was called the Eclipse. Tumbler science persisted in its belief that Picco orbited her Moon and thus the shadow cast on the giant planet's surface mattered more than the arrival of true daylight. Legend said this was the time when the Void tried to drill a hole through Picco herself, only to be foiled by the magical strength of Picco's surface. Festivals and other entertainments were typically timed to climax at the end of the Eclipse as seen from the Picco-facing side of the Moon.

Other things were timed for sunlight. The sort of things I might accuse Ersh of deliberately keeping from me, except that I was afraid she'd chime agreement.

Sex wasn't the mystery. Ersh might presort the others' memories before sharing them with me, but biology didn't seem to be one of the taboos she enforced. On the contrary, we had many discussions, ranging from gruesome to merely nauseating, about the lengths to which species went in order to mix their genes. Oh, I knew all about Tumbler sex. Those individuals interested in procreation wandered about gleaning material from others of presumably attractive growth, incorporating each shard as it was received into their body matrix until they felt sufficiently endowed. There followed a rather orgasmic interlude of fragmentation, resulting in a smaller, presumably satiated adult, and a litter—literally—of tiny pre-Tumbler crystals dropped wherever that Tumbler had been roaming at the time. Somehow, during Eclipse on the sunside of Picco's Moon, those crystals were recovered by their proud parent and given the opportunity to grow.

Somehow. This was where Ersh grew annoyingly vague and, when pressed for details, had begun inconveniently timing my indoor tasks during the sunny side of Eclipse.

Skalet, however, didn't care what I learned, as long as she didn't have to teach me.

I bounded up the last worn stone step to the top of Ersh's mountain and paused to pant a moment. Usually I avoided the place, unless it was one of those times Ersh insisted the sharing of the Web be done here, but there really was no better view. *Just in time.* The orange rim of Picco was disappearing behind the horizon, cut into a fanged grin by the distant range of mountains. Sunlight—real, full spectrum, right from the source light—poured over the surface, losing the struggle where Picco's reflection still ruled, but elsewhere striking the crystalline facets etched on every slope and valley in a display that explained quite clearly why this was a gem dealer's notion of paradise.

Gem dealers. I grinned, walking to the cliff's edge, stopping a comforting number of body lengths short. While Ersh disapproved of irony on general principle, given how often it ended in disaster for the species involved in mutual misconception, I couldn't help but take special pleasure in this particular case. The most prized gems from Picco's Moon? Tumbler excretions. Those legitimate dealers—hired by the Tumblers for waste removal and treatment around their shipcity, the only densely populated area—did their utmost to regulate off-Moon availability and so keep up the price of the beautiful stones, but there was, naturally, a thriving black market fed by those fools willing to try landing where level merely implied nonperpendicular.

To their credit, the Tumblers were dismayed by this risky traffic in defecation and regularly tried to explain, but something kept being lost in the translation of their polite phrase: "ritual leavings."

I sat on my haunches, feeling the warmth of the Sun's rays on my back, and looked for Tumblers engaged in Eclipse activities, feeling deliciously naughty—especially with Skalet to take the blame when, not if, Ersh found out.

But what I saw was a mid-sized cargo shuttle with no markings, banking low in front of Ersh's mountain, heading to our landing pad.

If this wasn't Ersh returning too soon from her mysterious trip, or web-kin with a particularly large present, Skalet was going to be in more trouble than I'd hoped.

The advantage of a shared secret was a mutual desire to keep it. I had no doubt Skalet knew I was nearby, but I also knew this time she wouldn't reveal my hiding place. Not to her guest.

A non-Web guest. Hair persisted in rising along my spine. *Alien.* Human.

And, most intriguing of all, male.

I held the genetic instructions for Human within my web-mass, along with all other species the Web had assimilated, but were I or any of my web-kin to take that form, we would be female. Cycling didn't change who we were—simply what we were. As a result, I'd never been this close to a male Human before.

Shared memory wasn't everything, I realized, aware this was something Ersh had despaired, loudly, I'd ever learn to appreciate.

He was as tall as Skalet, not as whipcord thin, but gracefully built. The wind picked up curly locks of black hair and tossed them in his face—surely distracting, but he didn't appear to notice. No tattoos. Perhaps not Kraal.

Or not wanting to appear Kraal, I thought abruptly, enjoying this live game of strategy far more than any of Skalet's simulations. Kraal didn't mix with other types of Humans, except in formal groupings such as war or diplomacy. He could be—a spy!

Against us? My lips rolled back from my fangs despite common sense. With the exception of Ersh, none of us approached

Skalet's paranoia about protecting our true nature. So, this Human wasn't a threat to Ersh or our home. *Then what was he?* I tilted my ears forward as the male began to speak.

"—nice spot, S'kal-ru. We should have used this from the first—"

His voice might have been pleasant, but Skalet's smooth tenor made it sound like something from a machine. "This is not a secure location, Uriel. We have an access window sufficient to make the exchange, no more. You brought the grav-sled?" At his nod and gesture to the shuttle's side port, she snapped: "Good. Then load it up. I'll bring the plants."

My plants?

This time when my lips curled back in threat, I left them there. What was Skalet planning? She had to mean the duras seedlings and the adult versions in Ersh's greenhouse—these were the only plants on Picco's Moon. While a constant source of drudgery for me, they were also the only source of living mass other than the local wildlife—and Tumblers—available to us.

That source of living mass was crucial. We could fuel and maintain our bodies by eating and metabolizing in another form. But it took a sacrifice of web-mass to energy to distort our molecular structure, to cycle and hold another form. To become anything larger meant assimilating living mass into more web-mass. To replace lost web-mass? The same. It was the fundamental hunger, the appetite we couldn't escape.

Skalet was robbing Ersh's supply? She must have her own source, not to mention plant life was hardly a rare commodity—anywhere but on this world. It didn't make sense.

Being without Ersh no longer seemed a holiday. I was faced with making a decision I shouldn't have had to make—whether to trust one of my own or not. I panted, knowing my emotional turmoil risked my form integrity and trying to dump excess energy as heat before I really did explode. Not as they'd teased me, but the exothermic result of changing back to web-form without control would be more than sufficient to catch the attention of the Human, in his shuttle or out.

I needed somewhere to think this through. Or explode. Either way, it couldn't be here. I crouched as low as possible, cursing the bright Eclipse sunlight, then eased back, paw by paw, ears and nose straining for any sign of Skalet, until it was safe to risk going to all fours.

Then I ran.

What life there is on Picco's Moon prefers to bask deep in the valleys girdling the equator. It's hot down there, for one thing, and the lowermost walls glisten with the steamy outflow of mineral-saturated water so important to the crystalline biology of everything native. Farther up, the walls are etched with pathways, aeons old, marking the migration of species to and from the drier, cooler surface for reasons that varied from escaping predation to a need to find the best conditions for facet cleaning. The annual plunge of the tendren herds over the rim of the Assansi Valley was, Ersh had assured me, one of the most dramatic events she'd ever seen. And she'd seen most.

I couldn't venture an opinion. Long before I joined Ersh on her Moon, the rim of the Assansi Valley had collapsed due to erosion, doubtless hurried along by thousands of impatient, diamond-sharp toes. Life here wasn't easy.

It wasn't easy for visitors either. Had I sought the depths of a valley, my Lanivarian-self wouldn't have survived an hour. As for forms that might, including Tumbler? I couldn't trust my ability to hold them.

So I avoided the Tumbler track leading to the nearest valley, the Edianti, and padded morosely around Ersh's mountain instead.

Not that I planned to go far. I might have Ersh's thorough knowledge of the place, but the Moon's geology was nothing if not active. Today's crevice was likely to become tomorrow's upthrust, making any map based on memory alone unreliable.

I'd begun by scrambling up each rise, and slipping headlong down the inevitable slope, but calmed before doing myself any more harm than running out of breath. I'd grown up here and knew the hazards—evenly divided between those involving Ersh and those involving slicing my footpads open on fresh crystal. As for the utter unlikelihood of a Lanivarian running around on Picco's Moon? The Tumblers who climbed Ersh's mountain for conversation and trade had long ago accepted her proclivity for alien houseguests as a charming eccentricity and, given their inability to tell carbon-based species apart, let alone individuals, paid no attention to what kind they were. Well, as long as they were tidy and didn't eat in public places—Tumblers being thoroughly offended by the concept of body cavities and ingestion providing too much evidence for comfort.

The plants. I had to do something. Skalet and this Uriel were Human—at least one of them likely to remain so—and what did I know about the species which could help? The flood of information on the heels of the inadvertent thought brought me to a gasping standstill. I wasn't very good at assimilating the larger chunks of information Ersh fed me.

A lie. I was very good at assimilating, just better at resisting. New knowledge fascinated me—that wasn't the problem. But each time I bit, chewed, and swallowed Ersh-mass, it seemed there was less of me, of Esen.

The others didn't understand. Their personalities were solid; they were *old.*

So when, as now, I needed information I'd shoved aside in my mind, the assimilation happened suddenly, as if liquid poured into my mouth faster than I could swallow, filling my stomach, rising back up my throat until I couldn't breathe. I endured the sensation, because I had to find a way to deal with this Uriel.

Ah. The turmoil subsided. I *understood* the species as I hadn't dared before. Interesting. Complex as individuals, predictable en masse, amiable yet unusually curious in their interactions with other species.

And many cultures of Humans, including Kraal, valued gems.

I'd snuck back to the landing pad, keeping downwind in case Skalet was looking for me. I doubted it, feeling it more likely she was content to know I'd run and was out of her way. Something in the thought raised the hair between my shoulders.

Watching the two hadn't cleared up any of the mystery. Uriel had finished piling packing crates on a grav-sled, lashing them together as though the cargo was fragile. I could smell wet dirt and bruised leaves, implying they'd been busy—and not particularly careful—putting duras plants into the shuttle. Mind you, Ersh was a little overprotective of the things. I knew from experience they survived being dropped quite nicely.

From what I'd overheard, Skalet was reassuringly adamant that the Human not enter Ersh's abode, insisting she'd move the cargo to a more secure location later. The Human, obviously not knowing Skalet as well as I, then argued he should accompany her. I'd waited for her to dismiss him, but she'd merely smiled and stroked his arm. They'd disappeared inside the shuttle for several minutes. Perhaps, I'd decided with some disgust, Skalet was following in Ansky's footsteps and experimenting with physical liaison. Ersh would not be impressed.

But Ersh must already know, I thought suddenly. Web-kin couldn't hide memory from her. This could be why Skalet had been left in charge of me—to punish this behavior while making it more difficult to accomplish.

As if that *had worked,* I said to myself, feeling wise beyond my years.

Their delay had given me time to put my own plan into action. I patted the bag against my haunch, its hard bulges a combination of luck and the now-helpful sunlight. Judging from the abundance of ritual leavings sparkling around the lower slope of the mountain, Ersh had had more Tumblers visiting than I knew. I'd worried unnecessarily about having to scout closer to Edianti's unstable rim.

"Aren't there any more, S'kal-ru?" Uriel's voice sent me ducking behind my boulder again. "These will barely suffice to start twenty cultures. Mocktap won't accept that as payment for these containers—"

"These are enough. This strain of duras clones amazingly well, my friend, and grows even faster. We'll have plants for a hundred ships within months, providing both oxygen and—"

When her voice trailed away with suggestive triumph, I immediately filled in the gap. *Mass.* Ersh had modified these plants to produce the greatest possible amount of new mass in the shortest time. She'd picked duras over other species because they were hardy, thrived indoors, and, also importantly, were essentially inedible. No point sharing useful mass with other life. And, while the attraction was lost on me, Ersh confessed to finding their compact spirals of green leaves aesthetically pleasing. If Skalet was making sure her Kraal affiliates carried duras plants on their ships, it was for her own convenience as a web-being.

I was lost in admiration.

But what had convinced the Kraal? There were much easier botanicals to use as an oxygen supplement.

"The sap is even deadlier than you promised," the Human answered as if reading my thoughts. "And, thus far, completely undetectable."

Poison. I wrinkled my snout as if at a bad smell. The Web revered life, especially intelligent life, but Ersh hadn't spared me the realities of that life either. Most ephemeral species engaged in self-destructive behavior, including assassination and murder. The Kraal, for instance, granted exceptional status to those who managed to remove their rivals with the utmost finesse and mystery. A game, played with lives. I could see Skalet enjoying the strategy of it, the detached observer watching generations of Kraal worry and pick at their alliances, giving the odd push to a group that caught her interest, then abandoning them in another roll of the dice.

We had less in common than I'd thought.

My plan was simple and should have worked. There hadn't been any flaws I could see. Which had been the problem, really. Failing to see what was right in front of me all the time.

The Human, Uriel, had taken my bait. He'd helped Skalet move the grav-sled a considerable distance around Ersh' mountain, to the side that was more geologically stable, though still riddled with faults and caves. There, the two of them had offloaded the sled, carrying each crate inside.

While they'd been out of sight, I'd slipped up to the sled and quickly pried open the nearest box. Packing material blossomed out at me and I'd fought to get it all back inside before they returned. But I'd had time to see what was so important: Kraal artifacts. Art. Trinkets. My web-kin accumulated and shared memories of such things, not the real objects. What would be the point? There wasn't enough room on Picco's Moon to house a comparably comprehensive collection from any one species, let alone from thousands. Then there was the risk inherent in storing such hard-to-hide treasures.

Treasure? Was that it? Had Skalet somehow become enamored of private wealth? Unlikely, since as a member of the Web she could access more than she could ever spend—Ersh having appreciated the value of economics well before Queebs could count.

There was another possibility. Ersh-memory, Skalet-flavored, floated up. A Kraal dynasty required not only a lineage, with the requisite ruthless progenitor, but the physical trappings of a House—the older and more bloodstained, the better. How long did Skalet plan to use this as her preferred public form? Human life spans were long, but that long? She was capable of such a plan, I knew. And would relish every aspect of it, including the cost.

If this bothered Ersh, something I couldn't predict, she could deal with this errant web-kin. I wanted my plants back in the greenhouse where they belonged. For that, I required the shuttle unloading to take a little longer.

Ears cocked for any sound they were returning, I began setting out my bait. Each crystal blazed in my paws, varied in color and hue, but all flawless, as if the facets had been cut with the skill of a lifetime. Biology was a wonderful thing.

One here. *So.* Two more there. The sunlight reflected so vividly the crystals might have been lit from within. This Uriel couldn't help but see them. Each was worth, conservatively, the price of his shuttle. *There for the taking.*

I backed down the path leading away from the landing pad, looking over my shoulder frequently to be sure I didn't step close to the sheer cliff which made this Ersh's preferred spot for flying lessons. I really wasn't fond of heights. *There.* I rounded an outcropping, intending to leave the last few less obviously in sight before running back to the shuttle, only to find myself surrounded.

Not that the Tumblers were interested in me. I froze, lowering my paw to the ground and letting the crystals fall discretely behind, hopefully out of sight.

They were busy.

It was Eclipse, I remembered, dry mouthed, and, of course, they were busy.

If I'd thought the crystals gorgeous, their makers were beyond description. Their towering bodies took the sunlight and fractured it into streams of color, flashing with their every movement against rock, ground, and one another until I squinted in order to make out what they were doing. They were picking up crystals with their trowel-like hands and holding them up to the sunlight. I could hear a discordant chime, soft, repeated, as though they chanted to themselves.

Then a loud *Crack!*

I cried out as crystal shards peppered my snout and dodged behind the outcrop.

The Tumblers noticed me now. "Guest of Ershia," one chimed, the resonating crystals within its chest picking out a minor key of distress. "Are you harmed?"

Licking blood off my nose, I stepped out again and bowed. "I'm fine," I said, knowing there was no point explaining skin damage and blood loss to mineral beings. It would only upset them. "And you?"

One tilted forward, slowly, and gracefully tumbled closer. "In rapture, Guest of Ershia. Do you see it?" The Tumbler held up a crystal identical to those all around me, then placed it somewhere in the midst of its body. I couldn't make out exactly where in all the reflections. Then the Tumbler began to vibrate, its companions humming along, until my teeth felt loose in their sockets.

There were two possibilities. This was a group of crazed individuals, tumbling around looking for "ritual leavings" as part of a bizarre ceremony, or this was exactly what I'd hoped to find at the start of Eclipse—parental Tumblers hunting their offspring.

Which meant I'd been collecting children, not droppings. My tail slid between my legs.

However, this didn't explain the tiny fragments sticking out of my snout. Or why Ersh hadn't wanted me to see it.

Another Tumbler held up a crystal, identical, as far as my Lanivarian eyes could detect, to any of the others. The light bending through it must have meant something different to the Tumbler, however, for she gave a melancholy tone, deep and grief-stricken, then closed her hand.

I buried my face in my arms quickly enough to save my eyes, if not my shoulders and forearms, from the spray of fragments.

"Ah, you feel our sorrow, Ershia's Guest," this from another Tumbler, who graciously interpreted my yip of pain as sympathy.

I stammered something, hopefully polite, and hurried away. The hardest thing was to resist the urge to fill my bag and arms with all the crystals I could carry, to save them from this deadly sorting by light. No wonder Ersh had tried to keep me away from Eclipse. I struggled with the urge to cycle, focusing on that danger to block the sounds of more shattering from behind. *What if the Web had so judged me? What if I'd failed that day Ersh tossed me from her mountain?*

Different biologies. Different imperatives. Different truths. Different biologies—I ran the liturgy through my mind over and over as I fled home.

"Just a few more minutes, S'kal-ru! I see another one!"

The triumphant announcement brought me skidding to a halt and diving for cover. Uriel! He was running down the path in my direction, pockets bulging, his face flushed with excitement.

I hated it when a plan worked too well.

I was out of options. The thought of going back to join the Tumblers horrified me, however natural their behavior. Cycling into that form was impossible—I needed mass, almost twice what I had, let alone what might happen if sunlight didn't travel through my crystal self in a way that enraptured the adults. I fought to stay calm, to think. Ersh had warned me a truly desperate web-being could instinctively cycle to match her surroundings—the oldest instinct. It would be the death of Esen-alit-Quar. Rock couldn't sustain thought.

"There's no time for this!" Skalet's voice might be melodious, but it had no difficulty expressing fury. I could smell her approaching, but didn't dare look.

"This is the best one so far," I heard her companion protest. "C'mon, S'kal-ru. What's a minute or two more? We'll be rich!"

"Only a minute?" my web-kin repeated, her voice calming deceptively even as it came closer. I shivered, knowing that tone. "Do you know how many moves can be made in a game of chess, in one minute?"

The sun was setting, sending a final wash of clean, white light over the mountainside, signaling the end of Eclipse. And more.

There was a strangled sound, followed by a sequence of gradually quieter thuds, soft, as though the source moved away.

Or fell.

The seedling's tender white roots had been exposed. I took a handful of moist earth and sprinkled tiny flakes of it into the pot until satisfied. Most of the plants were unharmed. All were back where they belonged. It hadn't been me. I'd stayed hidden, afraid of the Tumblers, afraid of the darkness, afraid of letting Skalet know I'd been there.

I hadn't made it back to the shuttle before Skalet, but Ersh had. Apparently, she hadn't left—sending away Skalet's shuttle in some game of her own. Had Ersh set a trap? It paid to remember who had taught Skalet tactics and treachery.

What went on between the two of them, I didn't know or want to know. It was enough that there were lights in the windows and an open door when I'd finally dared return. The Kraal shuttle and Skalet were gone.

The plants, needing my care, were not.

Ersh, as usual, was in Tumbler form, magnificent and terrifying. I shivered when she rolled herself into the greenhouse. It was probably shock. I hadn't cleaned my cuts or fed. Those things didn't seem important.

Secrets. They were important.

"You went out in the Eclipse."

A transgression so mild-seeming now, I nodded and kept working.

"And learned what it means to the Tumblers."

I hadn't thought. To her Tumbler perceptions, I was covered in the glittering remains of children. My paws began to shake.

"Look up, Esen-alit-Quar, and learn what it means to be Web."

I didn't understand, but obeyed. Above me was the rock slab forming the ceiling, imbedded with the lights that permitted the duras plants to grow. It needed frequent dusting, a job my Lanivarian-self found a struggle—then I *saw*.

Between the standard lighting fixtures were others. I'd never paid attention to them before, but now I saw those lights weren't lights at all. Well, they were, but only in the sense that, like a prism, their crystalline structure was being used to gather and funnel light from outside.

They were crystals. Tumbler crystals. *Children.*

"Like us, Tumblers are one from many," Ersh chimed beside me. "To grow into an adult, a Tumbler must accumulate others, each to fulfill a different part of the whole. The very youngest need help to begin formation and are collected for that reason. But Tumblers are wise beings and have learned to use the sun's light to find any young who are—incompatible. It is a fact of Tumbler life that some are born without a stable internal matrix. If they were left, they could mistakenly be accumulated into a new Tumbler only to eventually shatter—crippling or destroying that individual. It is a matter of survival, Youngest."

"You could have told me," I grumbled.

Ersh made a wind-over-sand sound. A sigh. "I was waiting for some sign you were mature enough not to take this personally. You think too much. Was I right?"

There must have been thousands of the small crystals dotting the ceiling. There was room for more. "You were right, Ersh," I admitted. "But . . . this?" I waved a dirty paw upward.

She hesitated. "Let's leave it that it seemed a waste to turn them into dust. Speaking of dust, go and clean yourself. That form takes time to heal."

I nodded and took a step away, when suddenly, I *felt* her cycle behind me and froze.

Ersh knew whatever Skalet knew.

She didn't know—yet—what I knew.

Suddenly, I wanted it to stay that way. I didn't want Ersh to taste that memory of hearing a murder and not lifting a paw to stop it. I didn't want Skalet, through Ersh, to ever learn I'd been there. I wanted it to never have happened. Which was impossible. So I wanted it *private.*

I didn't know if I could, but as I loosened my hold on my Lanivarian-self, cycling into the relief of web-form, I shunted what must stay mine deep within, trying to guard it as I always tried to hold what was Esen alone safe during assimilation.

I formed a pseudopod of what I was willing to share, and offered it to Ersh's teeth.

I'd succeeded in the unimaginable, or Ersh deliberately refused to act on the event. Either satisfied me, considering I couldn't very well ask her. Her sharing was just as incomplete. There was nothing in her taste of Skalet's attempted theft or her plans for the Kraal. Or Uriel's existence. I supposed, from Ersh's point of view, one Human life didn't matter on a scale of millennia. I wondered if I'd ever grow that old.

Our lives returned to normal under Picco's orange glare, normal, that is, until the next Eclipse. Ersh went out in Tumbler form, with me by her side. There weren't many failed offspring this time, but those she found, we brought home to add to the ceiling. More prisms to light the greenhouse. I found a pleasing symmetry in the knowledge, a restoration of balance badly shaken.

Later that night, Ersh surprised me again. "I've had enough of you underfoot," she announced without warning. "Go visit Lesy."

Go? I blinked, waiting for the other side of this too-promising coin to show itself.

"Well, what are you waiting for? The shuttle's on its way. Don't bother to pack—no doubt Lesy went on a shopping spree the moment she knew you were coming. You'll be in a shipping crate, of course, since you can't hold anything but this birthshape of yours long enough to get outsystem, let alone mingle with a crowd. And don't come out on your own. Lesy is expecting you."

Don'ts, Dos, and Details went flying past, none of them important. "But I can come back . . ." I ventured, holding in a whine.

A low reverberation. Not quite a laugh. Not quite a growl. "Do you think you've learned everything you need to know, Youngest?"

My jaw dropped down with relief. "Of course not," I said happily.

Ersh came closer, lifting my jaw almost gently into place with her rock-hard fingers. "You aren't ready, Esen-alit-Quar," she told me in her blunt, no-nonsense voice, the one she used before inspecting anything I'd done. "But you have become— interesting. It's time you broadened your horizons."

I trembled in her hold. Did she know? Could she? Had I been

wrong to believe I could, like Ersh, hide my memories? I drew a breath—to ask or to blurt out a confession, I wasn't sure which—when she released me and turned away, saying only: "Don't worry about your plants, Youngest. Skalet's coming to tend the greenhouse. I think I'll have her dig out an extension while she's here—put some of that military training to use."

This time, I let my tail wag all it wanted.

I wasn't that old yet.